DeLusions

By Ann Marie Graf

DELUSIONS

Book two of the

Love…the Illusion

Trilogy

www.lovetheillusion.com

ISBN-13: 978-1518604263

ISBN-10: 1518604269

Printed on acid-free paper.

2015

First Edition

This book is dedicated to my family.

As the petals congregate to make a single rose, so is the beautiful sight of everyone together....

Chapter 1

AFTER A PLEASANT three months in Italy, Maggie was in the bedroom, packing her suitcase, carefully making a few additions. She and Antonio were due to fly back to New York City the next day. Dana would be arriving in a week to spend time with her, and they could hardly wait to see each other. They hadn't seen each other since the wedding. And Antonio had made arrangements for Dana to stay on their company floor.

Maggie zipped her suitcase, hoping she wasn't forgetting anything. She had enjoyed being in Italy, but was excited to be returning to Manhattan, where she and Antonio had met.

Antonio entered the master suite. "We leave tomorrow morning at seven, my sweetness. You're packed already, I see."

"Yes, I think I have everything." Maggie picked up her list and looked it over. "I hope I didn't forget anything."

"If you did, then you'll have to go shopping." Antonio smiled.

Maggie returned his smile; her face glowed, evidence of her love for him.

"Come here. I can't get enough of you." He reached out, embracing her.

"You are such a distraction," she said, laughing. "It will be your fault if I forget anything, you know."

"Why do you blame me for everything? It's so cruel." Antonio's eyes sparkled as he brought his lips to her ear. "I'm not responsible for *any* of your misfortunes!" he whispered. His face lit up. "Let's go grab a glass of wine. We should celebrate our last night together in Venice before we go back to the States. Soon I'll be busy with work, and what will you be doing?" He paused. "Probably drinking that expensive Italian red wine with Dana and Stanley at Biagio's!"

"I'll be your lady in the ring of fire, remember?"

"Yes, I know. And you will look amazing." He hesitated. "Speaking of amazing, I am so happy that Francis is not along this time…that despicable—" his face turned sour—"piece of mischief."

"Let's not think about him," Maggie said, bringing her lips to Antonio's.

Antonio let out a huff, ignoring her efforts. "Easier said than done! Now his pain-in-the-ass attorney refuses to settle out of court and that's just adding to the trouble! I don't have time to deal with his stupid lawsuit."

"I thought you said McKinley was getting the case settled outside of court."

"Well, that's never going to happen…dealing with Louis is bad enough; that Grant Garrett's even worse, if you can imagine," Antonio grumbled. "They both have *way* too much time on their hands. And McKinley can't stand Louis's attorney. He has a reputation for manipulating the courts in his favor over the most ridiculous cases. He's one dreadful piece of work."

"Well, hopefully it will be over soon." Maggie smiled.

"No, Maggie, it won't! I think Louis is more interested in wasting my time in the courts than getting my money, and I am busy now! In just a couple weeks I start performing! I don't have time for him—

that son of a bitch!"

"Stop! Just stop talking about him." Maggie started unbuttoning his shirt as she leaned in to kiss him. "You need to forget about Francis," she whispered.

Antonio grabbed Maggie and lowered her onto the bed. His dark eyes stared into hers. "I can't believe you're still not pregnant."

"Antonio! We've only been married for three and a half months!"

"I know, but we've been making love nonstop. What does it take?"

Maggie suddenly remembered that she had forgotten to pack her pills.

Good reminder.

She hated keeping such a secret, but she had no choice; Antonio seemed so determined. And as much as she wanted children someday, it was way too soon. They had only been married for a few months, and they'd had a short courtship. Maggie was not ready to add motherhood to her plate just yet. Marriage was proving quite an adjustment…and she had just left London, where she had spent the last six years. Now she was married, living in another foreign country, trying to adapt to everything all at once. But she still loved being with Antonio. He was so good to her. Eventually she would be ready, but timing was of the essence.

Last night, they had cooked a pasta dinner together and then taken the boat. Daphne had come along. Mamma and Papa were visiting friends in Florence for a few weeks, so they had the place to themselves, as was often the case. His parents were gone, traveling a lot. But the estate was so large that even when they were home they had plenty of privacy, and Maggie had really gotten to know and love Mamma. She was so sweet and treated Maggie just like her own daughter. Papa was also very fond of Maggie and she could not help but be fond of him—he was just like his son, always entertaining her with his crazy sense of humor. On one occasion, Antonio had picked a flower from the garden for Maggie, but Papa had insisted that his "bouquet" was way too small and had to gather additional flowers for a "*real* bouquet."

"I've decided to start my own dress line!" Maggie said, with her head against Antonio's chest.

"Really," Antonio sounded amused. "What are you going to call it? 'Better Than Naked'?"

"Stop! I'm serious!" Maggie propped her elbows on his chest and looked down at him. "I was thinking of naming the line after my mother, Katherine White."

"You're going to make granny dresses now?" Antonio smirked.

"No!" Maggie yanked on his chest hair.

"*Ouch!* Why do you always have to torture me?" Antonio laughed.

"You deserved that!" Maggie paused. "Maybe it could be called 'Katie White.' My father used to always call her Katie, but she was Katherine to everyone else."

"If you want to get noticed, use your own name: 'Maggie DeLuca.' It has a nice ring, don't you think?"

"Why would people want to buy dresses affiliated with magic?"

"That's not that crazy. Celebrities are always using their names for designing. Your slogan could be 'For a magical night out.'"

That's interesting...

She imagined the display ad in a magazine.

www.lovetheillusion.com/2246.htm

"I'll think about it." Maggie grinned at him, though she was still leaning toward her first notion.

He kissed her, and kissed her again, until she was no longer able to think about designing dresses.

THE NEXT MORNING...

"This is Gennaro." Antonio introduced Maggie to his pilot as he helped her into his private jet. It was smaller than any plane she had ever been in, leaving her to question its reliability, but when she felt Antonio's hands on her waist she knew she was safe.

"Welcome aboard. Not much luggage," Gennaro said with a quizzical glance.

"My stuff is already there," Antonio told him. "We just have this, belonging to my beautiful wife. But it weighs a lot—at least a couple hundred pounds. Hopefully, it doesn't slow down the plane."

"Would you knock it off!" Maggie glared playfully at Antonio.

She took a seat next to him in the rear of the plane, where there was a pile of blankets. She was about to fasten her seatbelt when Antonio said, "You don't have to buckle up. I promise I will hold on to you if we hit any turbulence."

"Does that include our conversation?" Maggie asked.

"Perhaps." He puckered his lips for a kiss.

"No kiss," Maggie teased.

"It's a perfect day to fly…not a lot of wind," Gennaro told them as he got into the cockpit.

"I'm nervous. It's such a small plane." Maggie cuddled next to Antonio and clutched a blanket in both hands.

"I know. And we are stuck in here for over eight hours," Antonio said, placing his arm around her. "I brought along a bottle of wine. We can chill with that while we watch *Final Destination.*" Antonio picked up a remote that turned on a movie screen that hung from the ceiling.

"*Final Destination?* I hope you're kidding, Romeo."

Antonio chuckled as he stared into her eyes. She frowned.

Soon the jet plane was airborne.

Maggie leaned against Antonio's shoulder, closed her eyes, and recalled the beautiful scenes from their visit to Rome.

www.lovetheillusion.com/2230.htm

"I love you so much," Antonio said in soft voice as he kissed her underneath the blanket.

"Me too," Maggie whispered.

"You're my baby forever." He spoke sweetly as he caressed her arm.

"And you're all mine." Maggie moved her lips on Antonio's. "I'm glad I married you; you're so perfect for me."

"I *had* to marry you," he whispered. "I couldn't stand missing you."

"I can't wait to get back to where we met."

"I know…and I've got a few surprises for you."

"Are you serious? What are they?"

"You know better than to ask. Now stop talking and just kiss."

Maggie placed her lips on Antonio's. Perhaps the eight-hour flight *would* pass quickly.

Then, totally out of the blue, Antonio said, "I hope we have a son. I want to name him after my brother, Matteo."

Maggie was startled by his blunt announcement.

"I want children too, but we're young, and we just got married. We have plenty of time for that." Maggie shuddered at the thought of him finding out that she was on the pill. He had been talking about his desire to be a father ever since they were married, as if it was top priority. She knew he loved children, and of course he wanted his own. She did too, but not just yet. Her decision to go on the pill had been made before they were married, and she did not have the heart to tell him that she was afraid of too much, too soon. So she was waiting for the right time…but the "right time" never came.

Antonio was a carefree, romantic individual, and he spoke his mind as an only child, assuming she was in agreement with whatever he wanted. Money was never an obstacle, and that magnified his ability to live spontaneously, making decisions with little thought. But having a child was not a "spontaneous adventure," to say the least! She already knew that if they had children, it would bring to the table so much responsibility. And it would be hard to juggle his career with family life. Right now, she valued their time together and wanted to get to know him better before they started a family. So far, she liked what she saw. He was a dream come true, and so good that she was fearful of rocking the boat. Things were perfect just as they were, right now. And as she leaned toward his lips, she knew she would never tire of his kiss.

"Maybe you could start a clothing line for babies after we have one." Antonio disrupted her thoughts. "You could call it 'Tiny Matteo's.'"

"You and your marketing ideas! Don't you have enough creativity in your own job? You have to help me with mine now?" Maggie giggled.

"Maybe you should listen to me...." Antonio's dark eyes held her captive. "But I will support you, whatever you want to do."

"What if we have a girl?"

"Then she will get spoiled by me, just like her mother."

"You'll be a great father."

"And you...you are so sweet. You will be a great mamma!" He paused to consider. "How many should we have? Eight? Ten?" He started to laugh.

"That's crazy! Maybe one or two," she said, echoing his laugh, but she felt a sudden chill in the pit of her stomach.

"No," he said. "We need more than that…and I could convince you." He spoke with certainty.

"You and your sweet talk…." Maggie pressed her lips together, lost for words. She leaned against Antonio, overcome by their attraction, but the thought of becoming a mother made her weary.

She closed her eyes, trying to replace the fears of motherhood with the sweet memories of when they first met, unexpectedly, while she was away on business in New York. She had walked into a vacant pub, completely famished, far more interested in finding food than finding love. Love was the last thing on her mind when the plane landed that day, but it had found her when she least expected it.… Soon she was sound asleep to warm memories.

Hours passed, and Maggie suddenly heard someone calling to her. "Mommy, Mommy, quick, come here! I have to show you something!" Maggie sat up quickly, rubbing her eyes, and then realized it was just a dream.

Thank goodness!

She gazed down at Antonio, who had also fallen asleep. She kissed him softly on the cheek and then snuggled next to him, while vestiges of the dream floated across her vision.

…It was a boy. He had dark hair with a bit of wave, just like Antonio. Strange, she felt as if she missed him. She thought about what it would be like to be a mother someday, and soon she was thinking about her own mother, recalling some of her favorite memories.

Her mother was a nurse; she worked in the neonatal unit. But in her spare time, she liked to make quilts. And she would make tiny quilts for all the infants who had extended stays due to illness or complications. But at home, everyone had a large homemade quilt on their bed that her mother had made especially for them. They were each unique, and on several occasions she had even won prizes for her quilts:

www.lovetheillusion.com/2260.htm

www.lovetheillusion.com/2282.htm

She was able to make her own patterns, and all of her quilts had that "vintage" look. One quilt had dresses on it, and as a little girl, Maggie would envision wearing them.

Maggie never wanted to help with the quilts. It took far too much time. Her mother would start a quilt in the fall and often it would not be done until spring. And even though Maggie would always admire the quilts her mother made, she had no interest in making them herself. She wanted to make dresses. Although her mother did not make a lot of clothing, she knew just how to help Maggie with the patterns that she chose. "The trick to sewing is patience," her mother would tell her. "And the more you sew, the easier it gets!"

Now Maggie no longer used patterns. She could sew without them. But just like her mother had said, it had taken a lot of patience to acquire the skill she now had.

Not all the students in her classes at fashion-design school knew how to sew. They would come up with crazy dress designs that were simply impossible to make. Maggie always felt at an advantage, because she knew the construction behind the design. And designing clothing would never tire her imagination.

She thought about the tiny quilt that she was saving; it was one her mother had made. Someday it would fit into a crib. Maggie knew that, whether their first child was a boy or girl, that special, one-of-a-kind quilt would belong to their firstborn. And for a moment, she longed to share with a child the same love that she had shared with her mother.

It was devastating when her mother got sick. She was always such a caring individual, and Maggie missed that. She remembered how carefully her mother would apply the Band-Aids to the scrapes she got when she played outdoors. She could only hope she was as good a mother someday.

Then Maggie remembered Julia. She was anticipating a visit with her in New York and could hardly wait. She had become a close friend, and one she thought of every time she was on a plane. They had been emailing since the wedding, and even though there was an enormous age gap, it seemed they had a lot in common. They both loved fashion and Julia had sent her old photos from when she had dressed in the finest wool suits with matching hats. Maggie had then emailed photos of her latest dress designs, and Julia had been so encouraging.

Julia's husband had been a tailor from Germany and they had owned their own clothing shop. She reminded her so much of her own mother—her mannerisms, her sophistication, and the way she always tried to put the best construction on everything.

Antonio's mother was a sweetheart, but nothing like her own mother. If anything, she reminded her of herself: a creature of habit and always worried about everything. Julia and her mother had that common presence: "Everything is going to be okay."

Maggie snuggled next to Antonio, recalling again the little face in her dream. Motherhood was a great adventure. But timing was a huge consideration. And she would know when the time was right. For now, she could not wait to return to the place that held every precious memory of when she first met Antonio. She closed her eyes, and remembered walking into the vacant pub, where he sat at the bar, drinking a glass of water. And in just a matter of minutes, she wondered who he was, who he dated, how he knew Francis, and then why he had lied about his identity. But more than that, she wondered why, from that day forward, she could not stop thinking about him. Now she had all the answers to all those questions. The only question that remained was how she had gotten so lucky to randomly find true love in the last place she would ever look…a pub in New York City.

There seemed to be no rhyme or reason to love. It just happened. So many times she thought she'd found it, only to see it slip away before she had it in her grasp.

Antonio was different. She had given up on love when she met him. But he had no problem patiently waiting to convince her that he had her heart, long before she was ever ready to admit it.

After several hours, Gennaro let them know: "We are well over halfway!"

"That was a good few hours of sleep." Antonio checked his Audemars Piguet. "I think we stayed up too late last night," he said, looking at Maggie. "Don't tell me, you watched the plane crash without me?" He picked up the remote.

Maggie grabbed it. "Here…I put it on pause."

"Hey! I didn't say you could have that…" Antonio teased.

"Remember, everything that's yours is now mine! And the remote is definitely at the *top* of the list!" She giggled.

"We'll see about that." Antonio took it away from her after a short struggle and then put the movie on. "Now we can watch the plane crash…together…" He made eyes at her.

"You'd better pour the wine first," Maggie told him, setting aside her fears.

"It's just a movie. Planes don't crash anymore…only in movies." He smiled at her and then reached for the wine. "But just in case, we should be happy."

"You're such a troublemaker."

"I promise you are safe with me, my dear."

They arrived in New York City, where it was still midmorning. But despite the new time zone, the memories were not distorted one bit—especially when they made their way down the hall on the fourth floor.

The T-shirt was now on her mind—that "famous" T-shirt of his—that he had left his signature on. She had despised it the day she got it. But soon after that, she had worn it to bed, clinging to the strange possibilities. Eventually, she had come to her senses and tossed it into the bin! Little did she know it was a treasure worth keeping. Luckily, Dana had rescued it. Now she loved that shirt—crazy as it seemed. How had it managed to stay with her, after she tried so hard to get rid of it? It came back to her, just as Antonio did, always sure that they would last.

"Surprise!" Antonio opened the door to his hotel suite.

Maggie stepped inside while Antonio wheeled in her luggage.

The bed was covered with red and white rose petals, and there were red and white roses in vases on the end tables. Everything had been remodeled.

Then she noticed another surprise.

"You put in a fireplace?" Maggie's eyes were big. "It's awesome! I love it. How did you—"

www.lovetheillusion.com/2273.htm

"I had it done while we were in Italy. It is always so cold in New York this time of year, and now we can sit by the fire together. And check out the bathroom!"

www.lovetheillusion.com/2265.htm

"It's so modern…I really like it." Maggie walked in and noticed a new entrance, leading into another room.

"You added space?" she asked.

"Yes! One less room on the floor, but there are plenty of spares, so now you have a place to put all your things.… Just don't fill it up with shoes!"

Maggie smiled at Antonio. She had not been able to resist the Italian-made shoes. Now Antonio would always tease her that they needed to get back to NYC so she would quit buying shoes. There were two pairs she was particularly fond of—she had not left them behind in Italy. They had been quick to grab her attention from the store windows in Milan.

www.lovetheillusion.com/2215.htm

www.lovetheillusion.com/2243.htm

Maggie cast her eyes around the new room. “Wow! This is great!” she said as she admired the closet space and computer desk that sat next to a custom-made vanity with gold trim. “A makeup counter? I love it!”

“Now you’d better always look good!” Antonio teased.

“And you got me a sewing machine?”

“It’s a Juki—top of the line, very industrial.”

“Thanks, Antonio! It’s amazing—I can’t believe you did all this! I *love* my room. It’s so spacious!” She smiled at him as she spun around the space, grabbing his hand to follow her lead. “So, if I get mad at you, I can hide out in here?”

“Not for long! I have the key!” Antonio grinned. “But I assume you need a place to organize your two hundred pounds of luggage.”

"It's so strange being back here." She looked around. "I remember the first time I came into your room. I thought I would find Arianna in here!"

His eyes lit up. "Good thing you never checked that closet over there!" He tried to provoke her. "She's probably still in there! I think you should go check!"

Maggie started laughing again. "You're so lucky she's not!" Maggie paused, suddenly recalling his furry friend. "Should we go visit Cheetos? And Tigger?"

"We can go see Cheetos, but I don't have Tigger anymore."

"Because of the accident?"

"Yeah, they wanted to put him down afterward, but I said no," Antonio explained. "Animals aren't always predictable—and it was my choice to have him. But I found a zoo that offered to take him." He paused. "Tigger always had that wild streak in him. Cheetos I've had since he was small, and it makes a big difference. He has a steady temperament and I have never worried about him."

"Who took care of him while we were away?"

"People from the zoo staff—and they keep updating me on Tigger. I guess he's behaving himself so far. I just got an email the other day. They found him a girlfriend, and now they said she's expecting baby Tiggers! Hopefully they won't take after their father."

"Really? We could visit him at the zoo?"

"If you want to."

"Of course I do! But I think we should go see Cheetos now. He probably missed you while you were away."

"Okay," Antonio agreed. Opening his icebox, he took out a

package of raw meat strips. "He's going to be so happy to see us!"

Antonio grabbed his phone and made a call. "Hey! It's Antonio D…yeah, thanks…it was good…actually great, we had a great time…but we had just a small snack on the plane and now we're famished, so can you send up some veggie paninis…with the works…and add some fresh mozzarella? We can pick off what we don't like.… Half hour… sounds good…just set it in a bag by the door…And some cookies, too."

Antonio looked at Maggie. "Let's go." He grabbed her hand.

They rode the secret elevator to the ground level. Maggie looked at Antonio, feeling suddenly strange that he was now her husband. He raised his eyebrows, grinning at her, as if he could read her mind. "You know, we could have a lot of fun in this elevator." He took her arm and pulled her into a hug.

"Is that all you think about?" Maggie giggled, wrapping her arms around him and leaning back against the wall.

"Pretty much," Antonio said. "I just want to have that baby!" He brought his lips within inches of hers, waiting for her to meet his wishes.

"You'd better quit thinking about that or you're going to be too tired to perform next week."

"Not a chance. I will be wide awake to catch you when you pass out on stage!" His words took her by surprise.

"What? I'm not going to pass out on stage! Once was enough." She recalled the embarrassing moment.

"You might! If you are expecting, you'll be dizzy and lightheaded, so I will have to be ready to catch you! Not to mention that the press is already eagerly expecting our baby, which is taking well over nine months to come out!"

Maggie thought about it, her face covered in a smile, but then she suddenly showed concern. "Do you think there were any tabloids on us while we were in Italy?"

"I don't know—and why do you care?" He gave a very European shrug. "But I am sure if you want an update, Dana will be able to give you the latest scoop!"

They arrived at the steel door.

"Okay! Ready or not, Cheetos here we come!" Antonio placed the key in the hole and leaned on the weighted steel door.

"Cheetos!" Maggie's face lit up. "Did you miss us?"

The cheetah immediately got up from his concrete slab and came over to the steel bars. He held up a paw.

Maggie suddenly wore a big smile.

"He wants a handshake!" Antonio grabbed his paw. "Hey, Cheetos! Daddy is back! You look good! They've been feeding you well, and it looks like you've been behaving yourself, unlike your lost friend, Tigger."

"Let me feed him." Maggie opened the package containing the fresh meat.

"I'll let him out first." Antonio unlocked the padlock that hung on the door to his cage. Cheetos made a proud exit and paced about, happy to be out of his cage.

"He's so awesome!" Maggie's eyes were big. "Here, Cheetos!" She held out the meat.

"Be careful. We forgot Band-Aids," Antonio teased her as

Cheetos approached.

"You said he was tame," she said.

"He is, but you never know…you might be the one to bring out his wild side. Look what you've done to me!"

"Aren't you funny?" Maggie said as she drew her hand across Cheetos' head. "Do you think he's lonely down here? We should bring him back to our room. We have plenty of space now!"

"I would guess there are no pets allowed, even on my floor," Antonio told her.

"They don't have to know. Come on! Let's bring him back with us. He would make a great beanbag chair while we watch a movie," Maggie pleaded.

"You are one crazy lady after being married to me for only three months. You seriously want him in our suite? I hate to think about it—he could be quite messy."

"But you have maid service, right?"

"Ridiculous to imagine they would want to clean up after him. He will leave behind traces of—no, Maggie, we cannot bring him!"

"*Pleeease!* Just for an hour! No one will know."

Antonio gave it some thought. "Okay, fine, but just for one hour. I hope he's not in need of the bathroom anytime soon, though, or it'll be yours to clean up. Lucky we got hardwood and tile." He shook his head at the thought.

"Does he have a leash?" Maggie asked.

"No, he doesn't need one…only on stage. He listens to me and follows me wherever I go." Antonio looked proud.

"Do you think he likes me?"

"Absolutely!" Antonio gave her his sweet look. "Okay, keep quiet, and I hope we don't run into anyone on the way back, or *you* will have a lot of explaining to do!"

Chapter 2

"Oh, my God! Which way did he go?" Antonio paced nervously about while Maggie fidgeted with the treat bag.

"Here, Cheetos! We have treats for you," she called out.

"I can't believe he just took off running like that. He's probably just freaked out and excited I'm back, but now what?" Antonio reached for his phone. "Bradley! It's Antonio. Hey! We just got back, and we…Cheetos is on the loose and—yes, somewhere in this hotel, and—no, don't tell the front desk. We don't need all the guests packing their bags just yet…downstairs, underground, you know…"

"Okay, I'll be right there. Meet me by the elevator," Bradley told him.

"No—just— we don't have time to stand and wait! Just hurry up and do your own search. Call me if you see him anywhere." Antonio put his phone away and ran a hand through his hair.

"Sorry, Antonio. This is all my fault," Maggie said.

"It's okay. He can't go too far. It's just a huge embarrassment, and the last thing I need is the hotel worried about people's safety."

"Well, he would never bite anyone, right?"

"*They* don't know that, but I know one thing: he's in our opening act, so we'd better find him, *pronto*."

THREE DAYS LATER…

"I could barely sleep last night! I'm going to have to cancel my show," Antonio said in disgust, pacing back and forth in their hotel suite. "This is just such a nightmare!"

"No, Antonio. Don't cancel anything yet. We'll find him."

"How the *hell* are we supposed to find him, Maggie? It's been three days!"

Maggie's eyes filled with tears. "This is all my fault. I shouldn't have asked to bring him back to the room."

"Oh, it's just not *like* him to take off running like that! Bradley said that some maintenance guy saw him charge out of an underground entrance that was propped open, and for what? I have no idea! That door is supposed to be closed at all times. Bradley thought the guy was on a cigarette break! Give me a break! I ought to get his butt fired."

Antonio's phone went off. "Bradley!"

"Hey! Check it out, man—on TV! It's now national news that your cheetah's lost, and the latest report from the NYPD is that it's ended up in some national forest somewhere. "

"*What?* That's impossible. How do they even know?"

"They sent out a helicopter on a search, but now they called it off because he's in the wild and they can no longer locate him. The last report was that he was in…I'm pretty sure they said Allegheny—it's some national forest… half a million acres…"

"Half a mill—Allegheny? That's not even—how—that's in the opposite end of the state! I can't believe—I gotta go," Antonio fumed. He typed in a search for "Allegheny" on his phone.

Seconds later, he made a call to Gennaro. "Gennaro! It's Antonio! Cheetos is on the loose—he ended up in some national forest, nearly three hundred miles away! I need to get there, *now!*" He shifted his attention to Maggie. "I have to leave," he told her. "I could be gone for days."

"I could help you find him."

"You can come if you want, but if you do, get ready for the adventure of your life, because we're going 'camping' in Cattaraugus County and we do *not* have time to pack!"

Maggie attempted to swallow away her shock. She quickly grabbed a navy sweatshirt and wished she was not wearing a white sundress. The weather had been exceptionally warm, but the nights were still chilly. And it would be dark soon.

Antonio grabbed a backpack and filled it with a few things out of the refrigerator and then took Maggie's hand and gave it a reassuring squeeze.

Shit. I can't believe this is happening.

Inside the plane, Maggie watched as Antonio stuffed his backpack into a large duffle bag where he had put two sleeping bags, a flashlight, and a compass. She shook her head, paralyzed in fear of their next adventure. "Okay, Antonio, I know you want to find Cheetos, but we cannot sleep in the middle of the forest."

"Trust me. We'll be fine, right after we parachute to our landing."

He must be kidding.

Antonio sat in the cockpit, next to Gennaro. "There's an open spot, right there. We can get out now," Antonio said, pointing.

"Don't you want to try to find him first?"

"No, I've got a tracking device and it's programmed to respond to his computer chip. It'll work like a magnet. It sounds just like a stutter-bark."

Maggie waited for the plane to land, but instead Antonio gave instructions as he started to tuck himself into a parachute harness. "Come here," he said to Maggie, who was sitting on top of a pile of blankets, watching him.

"No way, I am not…no…no. You're crazy. There's *no way* I'm doing that!"

"Come on, we'll be on the ground before you know it. We can ride together."

"Ride together? You mean *die* together! No—I'm not going."

"Maggie, you're coming. You need to help me find him."

"Now you've lost your mind, and I am the only one thinking straight for the two of us. We're gonna *die* trying to find your cheetah!"

"Get over here, and quit being such a worrywart."

"I'm hardly fit for this adventure! Not to mention, I am wearing a white sundress!"

"Believe me, no one will see up your skirt. Now get over here." Antonio gave her a grin as he tightened a strap.

"*That* is the least of my worries!" Maggie gave him a rude look.

"You'll be fine in tandem," Gennaro told Maggie as Antonio suited her up for the adventure of her life. "This is state-of-the-art equipment. And as soon as you two land, I'll circle the area until you capture him."

"I could almost kill you—if I don't die before I get the chance!" Maggie glared at Antonio.

"Don't worry, baby. Till death do us part is a looong way away." Antonio chuckled as he assisted her.

Maggie put her hand over the left pocket of her sweatshirt, where she had placed her pills. *Can't lose these…*

"We'll be on the ground before you know it," Antonio explained. "And then you'll be begging to do it again!"

www.lovetheillusion.com/2250.htm

Maggie finally managed a smile, convinced she was in good hands.

"Okay, hold on tight!" Antonio called out as they parachuted from the small plane. Maggie could barely breathe as she surged down to the open field. The duffle bag had already landed.

I hope I don't hit a tree.

She closed her eyes.

Now, in midair, she wanted to let out a scream, but instead the wind's powerful force sent her into a crazy rush of excitement.

Three minutes later they were both on the ground.

"Are you okay?" Antonio called to Maggie.

Maggie just looked at Antonio, as she absorbed her rough landing. "Yes, Antonio. I lived to tell, with just a banged-up knee."

"Here, let me help you." Antonio reached out his hand.

She gave him a frown. "Let me guess. That was just the beginning of our frightful adventure. We're out in the middle of nowhere. How do you plan to even find Cheetos out here?"

"Trust me, Maggie, we will. We aren't going back without him! He needs to start rehearsing with us this week, or…well, I can't get a replacement! There's only one Cheetos."

"So what next? I go left and you go right?"

"Are you kidding? We need to stick together! I'm not letting you out of my sight. For starters, we need to set up our sleeping bags and make a fire."

Maggie could see the plane fading into the distance. Her heart sank. She did not mind a camping adventure, but this was a little rougher than she was used to. She watched as Antonio gathered brush to make a fire.

Once the fire was burning, he took her hand and said, "Here, you hold the compass while I use the calling device."

"Does that thing even work?"

"We'll find out soon. It's the latest technology. The device not only calls him; it also signals when we are closer or farther from him, like a game of Marco Polo."

"Really?" Maggie thought about it. "So he'll know we're looking for him?"

"I doubt that. I just hope he stays put. Cheetahs move fast…look where he ended up after only three days!"

A half hour later, the sun was setting and Maggie looked at Antonio skeptically.

"Are you cold?" he asked.

"Just a bit."

"We can head back to the fire. Your sleeping bag will be warm. They are pretty well insulated. We can do better in the daylight, tomorrow."

They followed the light of the fire and soon they were back at their campsite.

Maggie unzipped her bag and climbed in.

The smoke from the fire was heating the air and soon she was warm.

"You are brave," Antonio told her with a hint of admiration.

"Like I have a choice." Maggie sulked.

"I promise to keep you safe," Antonio said, as he curled up inside his own sleeping bag and snuggled up next to her. "Bright and early tomorrow, we will start our search again. For now, let's eat some of the food I brought."

"What did you bring?"

"Some fruit…cheese and crackers."

"I hope you brought some booze…something really strong," Maggie said, taking a bite of apple.

"I'm not letting you get drunk out here." Antonio laughed. "No way."

"Come on! I promise I'll be much better company."

"Funny, but we can celebrate *after* we find Cheetos."

You mean IF we find Cheetos...

Maggie stared up at the full moon. The fire was still burning and she was now toasty warm in the sleeping bag, but very tired.

"It's a beautiful night." Antonio's voice was smooth.

Maggie reluctantly peered over at him.

He stared back into her eyes, as the light of the moon revealed that, despite the unfortunate circumstances, they were still fond of each other.

Finally she smiled.

"You did pretty good, parachuting for the first time," he said.

"I assume it wasn't your first time?"

"No, you can tell?"

"You were pretty fearless." Maggie grinned.

"But I knew we'd survive," Antonio said playfully.

"We still have to make it through the night," she said.

"If I was worried, we would have to make the most of it, tonight.... It could be our last." Antonio sounded amused.

"I'll trust your intuition," she said sarcastically.

"So then there's no chance for our last kiss?" He sounded disappointed.

Maggie started laughing. "Our last kiss?"

"Yeah, if we don't survive the elements out here, then we'll regret not having our last kiss."

"Maybe we should...just in case," Maggie decided.

"I agree wholeheartedly." Antonio brought his lips to hers.

www.lovetheillusion.com/2229.htm

THE NEXT MORNING…

“The compass says we’re going north,” Maggie told Antonio, as he blew into the caller. “What is that supposed to sound like, anyway?”

“A female cheetah that wants to mate. Am I pretty convincing?”

“This is unbelievable. We could be out here for days…. Weeks!”

“Maggie! We just got here! You need to chill out and stay focused. According to the radar detector, we are getting closer.”

“That’s great, Antonio, but I can’t see the fire anymore, and I have no idea where we are,” she said, exhausted.

“That’s why we have a compass!” he explained. “We are four miles out… northwest of our campsite, give or take a mile or two.”

“What!”

“Just kidding! Don’t worry, we aren’t lost…yet.” He grinned.

“I really want to strangle you, but I had too much fun last night.”

“Parachuting?”

“No, Antonio…” Maggie’s eyes glazed over. “Our last kiss…which obviously wasn’t our last, but it was fun pretending.”

“We can pretend again tonight,” he murmured.

Maggie’s eyes widened. She suddenly remembered the small case inside her pocket. "I have to make a pit stop quick—again—sorry…" she announced as she stopped in her tracks.

"Pick a tree, any tree," Antonio teased.

Maggie took a sip from her water bottle, then held it up. "We only have a few more water bottles, Antonio. What are we going to do when they are gone?"

"Then I call Gennaro, and he can drop another bag of supplies." He appeared to have no worries.

Maggie gave him a doubtful look as she headed for a tree with a wide trunk. "Don't watch!" she called out.

"Don't worry, can't see a thing!" Antonio called back.

She quickly swallowed her pill, waited for a minute, and then popped out from behind the tree.

"All done!" she announced, taking a few more drinks of water.

"I would lay off that if I were you. That's the third bathroom trip you've made in the last hour." Antonio grinned at her.

She grinned back.

At noon, Antonio's phone went off.

"There was a cheetah spotted just west of where you are," Gennaro let him know. "I'm circling around in the plane right now, but I haven't seen him yet."

"How do you know?"

"Some park ranger saw him. It's on the news and now they sent out a squad team to track him down. They're worried about people's safety in the park."

"Well, they'd better not even think of shooting him," Antonio said. "We've got to keep moving. My radar device says we are within a few miles of him. Thankfully, he's got that chip." Antonio put his phone away and turned to Maggie. "Run! We have to hurry."

"Oh no, Antonio! Are they going to shoot him?"

"He's a wild animal in a state park, and not the kind that people want to run into."

"If anything happens to him, it will be my fault," Maggie said in concern as she trailed behind him.

"No, Maggie, I'm pretty sure the guy on his cigarette break was the culprit, and wait until I get my hands on him! The entire hotel staff knows that my cheetah is gated down there and that door is to be closed and locked at all times…not only for Cheetos, but for security reasons…Wait…shhh…Did you hear that?"

Suddenly a gunshot went off.

"Oh *no*!" Maggie's face turned pale. "We must be close."

"Don't worry! Cheetos is way too fast for those idiots! Listen, that rustling…there it is again." Antonio held the caller to his lips and blew into it. "Look! There's a ranger with a gun…and there's another guy."

Maggie saw the two men, but also spotted something moving in the brush to their right. It looked dark, but then she saw a few spots. "Antonio!" Maggie screamed. "It's Cheetos! He found us!"

Cheetos was covered in mud.

Antonio's face lit up and they both started running to the great cat. Cheetos sprinted up to them, his lithe body eating up the ground.

"Bad kitty!" Antonio reached out to him. "Now you sit! And don't move!"

As soon as Antonio gave his command, Cheetos dropped to the ground, resting his head on his paws as if he knew he was disobedient.

Antonio reached inside his backpack and pulled out a thin rope with a clip at one end. He fed the rope through the clip and then secured it around Cheetos' neck.

Maggie reached out to pet Cheetos. "I'm so glad you're okay." She looked up and saw the two rangers making their way out of the woods.

Maggie, Antonio, and Cheetos stood together and faced the rangers.

"That cheetah belong to you?" the taller ranger asked.

"Obviously," the stocky shorter one proclaimed. "You must be Antonio?"

"That's right." Antonio stared at the two of them.

"You know his escape made national news?"

"Not surprising," Antonio grunted. "I hope that gunshot wasn't for him. You know cheetahs are endangered. He was rescued from the wild; I've had him since he was just a baby."

"Is that right? So he's tame?" the taller one wanted to know.

"Yeah, like the tiger," the stocky one said, jokingly.

"Are you going to help us or not?" Antonio asked.

"We've got a squad team arriving soon, with a cage."

"That works." Antonio looked at Maggie, who still wore a smile.

"I just phoned them. They're bringing a tranquilizer," the taller one informed them.

"He doesn't need a tranquilizer," Antonio insisted.

"Well, I doubt if he's willing to ride back in a trailer attached to a four-wheeler." The rangers approached Cheetos.

"We can sit with him," Antonio insisted.

"That's your call." The stocky one laughed.

"Oh *no*, Antonio—LOOK!" Maggie stared at the crowd of reporters gathered for the return of Cheetos. She turned to look at Antonio, whose hair was matted in various directions and decorated with twigs and leaves. His chin was bristly, and he had mud on his clothing. She looked down at her white sundress and noticed blood had dried on the scrape on her knee. *We must look ridiculous!* She quickly ran her hand through her hair, while Antonio burst out laughing.

"Maggie, it's not going to be your favorite picture, okay?"

"Hopefully, they have a dark lens!" Maggie huffed, while they sat next to Cheetos in the trailer pulled by the four-wheeler. "It was actually sorta peaceful in Italy. Now we're back living with the paparazzi."

"It could be worse. This will be a good story for the public. At least it will hit the papers, not the tabloids…less vicious, more respectable."

"Maybe Cheetos will scare them away." She laughed, leaning against Antonio and holding on to his arm.

The four-wheeler came to a rest, and Antonio hopped out after Cheetos, lending his hand to Maggie to help her out as well.

He kept her hand in his while Cheetos stood next to them on a leash.

"Antonio! Antonio DeLuca! Tell us how your cheetah escaped!"

the first reporter called.

"Isn't there a fine for camping in undesignated areas?" A woman reporter asked in a nasal tone.

"How did you find the cheetah on a half a million acres?"

"Is it true that you both parachuted from your private plane?"

Antonio handed the leash to Maggie and approached the press. Maggie held the rope in a tight grip, guarding Cheetos while the cameras focused in on Antonio.

He spoke into a microphone held by the woman reporter.

"I'd like to thank Chuck and Randy for helping us out of the forest. We spent less than a day tracking him, thanks to the latest technology. He is trained to come to a call that works in conjunction with this electronic device. The device can detect the location of his microchip."

"How did he escape?" one of the reporters interrupted.

"We were visiting him underground, and he got away from us. We had just returned from Italy, and he must have been cooped up too long. But he's safe now, and that's what matters. And now he will be in my opening act!" Antonio grinned. "Just for the record, he is harmless, and nothing like Tigger."

The reporters laughed in unison, while Antonio went on to explain: "If you want to see *him*, you will have to make a visit to the zoo!"

Maggie reached into her sweatshirt pocket.

Where did they go? My pills are…gone!

She saw Antonio approaching her.

"I'm so glad Cheetos has been found," Antonio said. "Now we can drink that wine and celebrate!"

www.lovetheillusion.com/2228.htm

Chapter 3

Antonio came out of the shower stall with a towel wrapped around his waist.

"Where are you going, my dear?" he asked.

"To pick up some Tylenol. I…I have a headache."

"A headache? From what? Your bad hair day?"

"No, Antonio, I just need to—"

"I can call the front desk. We can get that delivered ASAP, whatever you want."

"That's okay, I really don't mind. I can go get it myself."

"Okay, but they can send it up here faster than you can go get it, guaranteed."

He smiled at her.

"Really, Antonio, I'll be right back…I just maybe need some fresh air…"

"You want to go camping again?" Antonio laughed.

"I'll be back soon," she said, giving him a sweet smile and grabbing her purse.

"You'd better hurry. When you get back, I'll have the fire burning and a glass of wine waiting for you."

"Okay, I'll be back soon," she promised, her eyes locked in his.

Sorry, Antonio. We are NOT having a baby now...

Maggie headed to the practice room.

She punched in the combination pass on the keypad and made her entry. She walked into the dressing room, where costumes and wigs were laid neatly against the wall. She dropped her bag, and started to sift through the fabulous costumes. *So delightful, but all I really need is a wig!* On a top shelf the wigs were in cubbies, arranged according to color! *This ought to work*, she thought, pulling a blonde one out of its protective plastic. She placed it on her head, and then knelt next to her bag, digging to find a compact mirror.

"I love it," she whispered to her reflection.

She reached into her bag for a clip, quickly gathering the wig into a ponytail.

Then she finished the look with a dark shade of lipstick.

She tucked the mirror back into her purse and stood, feeling like a brand new woman.

www.lovetheillusion.com/2198.htm

She strutted through the hotel lobby, where she grabbed a cab.

"To the pharmacy, please, on Baker," she ordered the driver.

The cab pulled up to the curbside. "Wait here," Maggie said, and handed the driver a fifty-dollar bill.

"Yes ma'am!" he replied.

She walked quickly over to the pharmaceutical counter and made her announcement: "Here to pick up a prescription for Ms. White."

She watched as the technician located a small white bag with her pills.

"Will that be all?"

"Yep." She handed him cash.

"Nice ring," he said, nodding at her ruby.

Maggie quickly put her glove back on.

Mission accomplished!

www.lovetheillusion.com/2284.htm

She got back into the cab, enjoying her perfect view of New York City, all lit up at night. But she was anxious to get back to Antonio. And, now that he no longer had his mind on finding Cheetos, she was absolutely certain she could not be without her prescription. Fortunately, big cities were so accommodating, with a pharmacy on every block.

How can we have a child? We can't even keep track of a cheetah! Maggie stared out the window of the cab. She wanted to be a good mother, the best, not stuck in halfhearted mode. There was no doubt that Antonio was going to be a great father, but there were still things outside of his control. The paparazzi would be an exceptionally nosey adversity, prying their way in where they did not belong. That would be a terrible thing for any child to grow up with. Their first child would have his or her face on some magazine before it was even old enough to look in the mirror. Maggie's heart sank as she contemplated her own mother's protective ways, wondering how she would ever be able to protect her child in Antonio's crazy world.

"I missed you." Antonio gave her his sweet look when she stepped through the door.

Don't look at me like that.

She could smell his cologne, and immediately felt guilty. She set her purse down.

"Is your headache gone now?" he asked, with a hint of suspicion.

"Pretty much…" Maggie looked at Antonio, feeling a bit anxious from his prying. He was so good to her; she did not have the heart to tell him that she was scared to have his child. She would know when the right time came, and it was certainly *not* now. But, she did not mind the efforts he was making and, as she looked at him, she suddenly glowed.

He's so cute.

"Come here, pretty lady. Come and drink this wine with me. Tomorrow night I will be getting things ready for rehearsal already, so we have to enjoy tonight."

Maggie sat down next to him, and he placed his arm around her.

"I love you," he told her.

"Me too." She looked sweetly at him.

He's too good to be true.

They watched the fire in the fireplace. Finally they could relax together. She put her head on his shoulder as he threaded his fingers through hers. The DeLuca ring was back on her right hand, enclosed in his left, where he wore the band she had chosen from the jewelry store next to the pharmacy.

She looked into Antonio's eyes, wondering how she could love him any more than she did.

"Did you remember to pack that costume you made, for the ring of fire?" he asked.

"I did!" Maggie recalled the dress she had made while they were in Italy. It was white, angelic, with layers of chiffon that would waft up from the sides of the dress at the slightest breeze. And she recalled when Papa had to take a picture after she came down the steps, wearing it for the first time.

www.lovetheillusion.com/2220.htm

"That will be a stunning image on stage," Antonio said, "with those layers of fabric, rippling in the breeze of the fan. You did a great job with that. Imagine all that in the ring of fire."

"I'm glad you like it." Maggie smiled at him.

"So…have you forgiven me for making you jump from a plane?"

"I'm still thinking about it."

"It was a perfect adventure with a perfect ending!"

"It was a bit lucky," Maggie admitted. "I still can't believe we found him. And so soon. Do you think he was scared out there by himself?"

"Who knows, but I can't believe those idiots tried to shoot him."

Maggie noticed her glass was nearly empty. "Good wine." She smiled at him, redirecting his attention.

"I suppose you want more of that." Antonio grinned. "You can get drunk with me now and I promise to take advantage of you."

"Or maybe *I'll* take advantage of *you!*" Maggie returned his smile.

"Not a chance. My glass is half full."

"You mean it's half empty!"

He gave her a strange look. "Whichever, but either way, I can still keep track of you."

"Like I'm going to disappear."

"Where did you go before? To get your headache medicine…?" he questioned her. "The Upper Peninsula?" He furrowed his brow. She gave him a strange look. "Well, you were gone for over an hour!" he let her know. "How long does it take to get to the gift shop from here? Not *that* long."

"Really? It didn't seem that long…" She shifted her eyes off of him and stared at her purse. It was sitting on a table next to his fan mail.

Smile and look happy, or he's going to lose his mind. She contemplated his temper.

Maggie studied his lips, outlined in his dark, after-five shadow.

She brought her lips to his.

"That's better," he murmured. "I don't like you running around New York City without me."

He knows I left the hotel?

She offered an explanation. "Okay, Antonio! The headache meds that I take are prescription; they're stronger than what you purchase over the counter. I had to go the pharmacy to pick them up! You don't want me to have a headache, do you?" Her tone was aggravated by his persistence.

He let out a huff. "Guess not." He still looked suspicious, though.

He'd better not have Bradley spying on me...

She quickly placed her lips on his again, until he kissed her passionately.

And they made love for hours.

SEVERAL DAYS LATER...

"Maggie!"

"Dana!" Maggie wrapped her arms around her best friend. "I'm so excited you're here!"

"I know! Me too! We're going to have so much fun in New York City! And I love my hotel suite! Perfect view, so amazing!"

"Hey, we should grab a bite to eat. Antonio's at rehearsal right now and busy getting ready for the show...and I thought after we eat we could work out in the fitness room. Wait till you see it! We have our own, for the crew. It's private. You'll love it; it overlooks the city!"

"Okay, sounds like a plan!" Dana's face glowed.

"So, is Shane upset that he stayed behind?"

"No, he's busy working on the house. You should really see it. It is looking so amazing now! I brought pictures."

"That's great!"

"And guess what! You will never believe it, and I really can't wait to tell you..." She turned to the side, and patted her stomach.

"You're still so skinny…" Maggie admired her so-called baby bump. "I would never know. Unbelievable…when did you find out?"

"Actually, a couple weeks ago. We both want children right away. Why not, right?"

"Why didn't you tell me until now?" Maggie wondered why she kept secrets. "I mean, I tell you everything, right?"

"I just did, silly. I had to tell you in person."

"So, is it a boy or girl?"

"Well, we're waiting…it will be a surprise, but did I tell you, we already have the names picked out?"

"And?"

"Patrina for a girl, and Calvin for a boy," Dana said. "Patrina Slavoski or Calvin Slavoski. Sound good, don't you think?"

"I just can't believe that you're…I'm shocked! You're going to be a mom, already! I'm so excited for you!" Maggie shook her head.

"I know. It's a bit crazy, but Shane and I have been together for over three years, and he's almost thirty, so we decided to start our family right away!"

Maggie realized Antonio was turning twenty-nine next week.

"Antonio wants children," Maggie let her know as they sat down at a table at an Italian pub.

"Sooo…don't tell me…we can experience the journey of

motherhood together?" Dana's face lit up.

"I highly doubt that! I'm not ready to have a baby. But it's all Antonio talks about."

"But you're waiting? Nothing wrong with that—children are a big responsibility. You don't want to rush into it…right?"

"Antonio has no idea I'm on the pill!" Maggie whispered.

"Seriously? Maggie, that is crazy! He has no idea?"

"No, and he's already wondering why we're not pregnant. I'm just waiting for the nightmare to explode! But we *can't* have a child! Do you know how we spent the first two days of our arrival? Tracking his cheetah. It got lost—don't ask—ended up in the forest three hundred miles from here and I had to parachute from a plane and then sleep in a sleeping bag with no tent; the only bathrooms in sight were wherever you wanted to go and I would have to be freaking *nuts* to have a baby with him right now! Antonio's this wild and crazy adventure-seeking lunatic who doesn't even organize a single thought before doing half the stuff he does. I think he married me to keep himself alive!"

Dana just shook her head. "But eventually you have to tell him…right?"

"How do I do that? He speaks for the two of us! And right now, I really just want to develop a dress line in memory of my mother. I was even going to use her name—Katherine White or Katie White…which do you like better?"

"Whatever you think," Dana told her.

"Antonio thinks I should use 'Maggie DeLuca'! And he even came up with a slogan: 'For a magical night out!' Oh, and he thinks I should design baby clothing for our first child who, by the way, he has already deemed will be a boy—and be named Matteo after his brother. He says 'Tiny Matteo's' could be the name of *that* clothing line! So cute of him to enter my world of designing." Maggie paused, and then recalled her latest fear. "Might as well keep him focused on my career, because I am scared to death to have his son—a spitting image of *him*...wild and crazy!"

"Um...my advice? Those are some incredible marketing ideas!" Dana wore a look of confidence. "Tiny Matteo's? That is so *sweet!* And I think the slogan 'For a magical night out' would be perfect for that teen dress line that you started with Francis. Katie White or Katherine White, either one, sounds like, maybe...I don't know...*maternity* clothes!" Dana said.

"Seriously?" Maggie frowned. "No offense, but I'd rather not use his name to gain recognition. That is such a crutch. I want to prove I can do it on my own. And why would you think my mother's name sounds like a maternity line...because you are expecting and need a wardrobe?" Maggie laughed.

"It just does, Maggie. Antonio is so right! You should listen to him. He knows what he's talking about. I mean, look at his show and how he is successful with that—of course he knows how to get attention, how to stand out. He's a marketing genius—he's huge, and he knows what he's doing. I would listen to him if I were you. And...using the DeLuca name? It's a guaranteed success, so why not use it?"

"Maybe," Maggie reconsidered, feeling emotionally let down. "I just feel driven to do something in memory of my mother. I mean, it has been my dream for so long, and she was my inspiration long before I met Antonio. I need to do this on my own."

The waitress came and they ordered.

"So," Dana said with a grin. "How's married life?"

"Good..." Maggie grinned back at her. "But I'm happy to get back to the States where everyone speaks English. Antonio's such a sweetheart, though. He would always translate for me....everything past *per favore*, *grazie grazie*, and *oh amore...Amo Antonio*! Yes, he taught me how to say that. Of course he wants to hear me say I love him in Italian with my American accent."

"I'm glad you finally can say it."

"I know. I really do love him. It was strange living in Italy but I'm so glad just to be wherever he is. But regardless, we are not ready to be parents."

"I understand, absolutely...you don't have to explain to me. But I think you should tell him that you want to wait to have that baby. It's not a big deal, Maggie. I'm sure he would understand."

"Uh...I'm not so sure about that.... He keeps talking about how much he loves children, and when Matteo died it was really hard on him. I think he thinks if he has his own child, it will ease the pain, and he says now that he's almost thirty it's time to have a baby. I don't have the heart to tell him that I don't want to just yet!"

"That is complicated..."

"Yes, it is. And listen to this: Last night I had to run out to the pharmacy to refill my birth-control prescription. It fell out of my pocket as we were chasing through the woods to find Cheetos! He got suspicious, wondering where I went. Don't worry! I went incognito—

just a precautionary measure—you know the press just can't get enough of us. That's another reason why I hesitate to have a child. Poor thing. It would be hounded: 'Oh, look! Antonio's baby!' on the cover of every stupid magazine! I don't want that for any child, much less mine!"

"It's hard to maintain privacy, I'm sure," Dana said sympathetically.

"Italy was not so bad. Here? A nightmare. New York is not the worst…sometimes people just stare, and seem to mind their own business, but the paparazzi are always wanting those embarrassing photos, and wait until you see my bad hair day after two days in the forest! They never take a 'graceful' photo—one you can be proud of! They are always these 'what a nightmare' moments that you would rather not share. And I know better than to *ever* wear a bikini!"

Dana laughed, and then suddenly looked as if she was having an epiphany.

"What is it?" Maggie asked.

"Okay! I can't keep a secret any longer. We're going to have so much fun tomorrow night!"

"Of course we'll have fun; what do you mean? Just like old times, right?" Maggie said.

"Yes, Maggie! But—this is going to be so incredibly brill! Surprise! I have two tickets to see Kin Marsh at Pars Loco! I bought the tickets right after Christmas, the day they went on sale!"

"No way!"

"Yes way! And now we just have to go shopping so that we look amazing because…you know what will happen!"

"What?"

"I reckon we could be in the papers! And it will be a grand photo! Picture this! We are dressed to the nines, fur shrugs, diamond sling-back shoes, purses from Dolly's of Hollywood, *and* we can hire a Bugatti Veyron!" Dana paused while Maggie shook her head. "Can't you see us, Maggie, riding around New York City? It would be simply amazing and for only just fifteen hundred dollars for the whole night! I already checked the price! It's much cheaper here than back home! Come on, Maggie! Please! You must have a purse lined in plastic and I bought the tickets—believe me they weren't cheap. So what do you think? Can't you splurge for the Bugatti? Antonio wouldn't mind, would he?"

"I can't drive in New York City! Are you out of your mind?" Maggie started laughing.

"I can drive us!"

"Yes, on the wrong side of the road."

"After a few drinks, it's all the same!" Dana teased.

"No Dana, I can't let you!"

"I say we work out… Then we go to the shops, hire a Bugatti, and then…get ready for the night of your life at Pars Loco! No worries, I am certain I can get us there because it will come fully loaded with a GPS!"

"I think you've gone completely mad!"

"You can't say no, Maggie, please!" Dana insisted with puppy-dog eyes.

"Okay, Dana, but I do not want to be in any papers and…where is Pars Loco?"

"Upstate. It will be a *huge* bash. It's the largest dance floor in New York! I'm quite sure there will be reporters everywhere because Kin Marsh is enormous and has quite the following!"

"Right…and…" Maggie paused, suddenly delighted. "We should definitely be there!" she finally agreed, wearing a bashful grin.

"Yes!" Dana explained, "Channel Seven's doing a full coverage of the event already. And I'm certain that the paparazzi will be there! A black tie event—how can they stay away— right up the alley of the rich and famous, and I'm thrilled to hang out with you. Best friends, right?"

Great…

"Yes, we are, but just remember I can't *stand* the paparazzi so we need to lie low…sunglasses and a bit of a disguise, and don't forget you're pregnant, Dana! You can't get too obnoxious in your condition."

"Hey! Did I tell you I have to have fun now, because six months from now I'll be waiting to hear the word 'mummy' every time I hide out in the loo!" She started to laugh.

THE NEXT DAY…

Dana came out of the fitting room, "So what do you think?" She stood in her chosen nightclub attire.

"It's interesting," Maggie decided. "What do you think of this?" Maggie asked, showing off her own choices.

"You look great! We both do!" Dana chuckled. "This will be *so* much fun!" She burst out laughing. "I can see the headline now: 'Two British Divas Party in NYC and Speed Around in Their Bugatti!' My idea is a good one, now, don't you think?

www.lovetheillusion.com/2202.htm

"This is seriously insane, Dana. I never thought of *trying* to be in a tabloid…and it's actually funny. Come to think of it, I *do* deserve a good photo for a change, you're right about that…" Maggie paused. "But will the paparazzi even notice us?"

"They will! I have a plan," Dana told her.

Maggie suddenly looked concerned. "And what is that?"

Dana smiled back at her, her hands wrapped around her waistline.

Antonio is going to kill me.

Chapter 4

The crowded bar had become "standing room only" as people gathered to see Kin perform. He was several minutes into his second song, and Maggie was enjoying his music.

"Do you think now's a good time?" Dana asked Maggie, and took a sip from her virgin daiquiri. When Maggie looked doubtful, Dana quickly said, "Don't forget, you can be the hero."

"I think we should maybe wait a bit," Maggie let her know. She thought Dana's plan was a bit strange. But she watched as Dana got up anyway and went to stand outside the ladies' room. She passed Maggie a quick nod. Maggie turned around on her barstool and watched the bartender, while pondering the awkward event Dana had conjured up. He had no idea. He was scurrying about in a frantic attempt trying to distribute everyone's drinks in a timely manner. She turned around to look at Dana, who gave her a quick wave.

I am so stupid. Why did I let her talk me into this?

Maggie sat uncomfortably in the foreign environment, thinking her time with Dana was about to go sour. She peeked over her shoulder to get an update on Dana's whereabouts, but she had disappeared.

Here it goes...

Maggie spun around to locate Dana. She bounced off her chair to proceed as planned, but she was too late.

"Quick! Help!" a woman shouted frantically as she ran out of the ladies' room. "Someone's passed out in the ladies' room—she's on the floor! Hurry, someone, help her!"

"Anyone know CPR?" the bartender yelled in a panic.

Maggie shifted her eyes around the room to gather the various reactions. The music was blaring, but several patrons had heard the commotion.

"Dr. Sullerwurt here…" a voice spoke up in the distance, and a man flashed his badge. "Call the paramedics, now!" he ordered the bartender as he headed to the ladies' room. Maggie watched him disappear behind closed doors.

"This is so ridiculous," Maggie muttered under her breath as she drank down the rest of her vodka and tonic.

Moments later, the paramedics arrived and hastily made their way through the crowded bar.

Dana soon made an exit, supported by a pack of three ER technicians who looked relieved that things were under control. "Thanks so much!" Dana gasped. "I think I'll be fine—just a bit lightheaded from the pregnancy." She gave a smile.

"Are you with her?" a buff tech asked Maggie.

"Isn't…isn't that DeLuca's wife?" Another one suddenly recognized her.

Maggie gave a fake smile and nodded. "Yes, that's me."

"Could we all get a photo together?" the other technician asked. As he approached them and put an arm around Dana, a camera crew from Channel 7 news team appeared on the scene.

"Can I get statements from all of you?" a crewman asked, assuming everyone was thrilled to oblige.

"Most definitely!" the ER techs said in excited agreement.

Maggie froze in amazement as she realized Dana's plan was complete. She stood up straight, thinking that perhaps this photo could redeem her image to the public; that yes, she did, on occasion, have "good hair days."

"Smile, everyone," the cameraman said. And just seconds later, he said, "It's a good one!"

I doubt it.

"What happened?" a reporter intervened after the photo was snapped. "Did this woman pass out from too much alcohol?"

"No! I was drinking a virgin daiquiri," Dana was quick to inform him. "I am expecting, and a bit famished…must have gone too long without a bite to eat." Dana gathered sympathy.

"Order the lady a steak sandwich. It's on me!" the slim ER gentleman made a request as he smiled at Dana.

"Make that five! We'll all have one!" another man said. The bartender wrote down the order and then filled everyone's drinks. Maggie had to admit that at least Dana's stunt had provided additional entertainment.

Kin was soon on break and standing among their group! "Wow! I think there was more excitement out here than there was on stage!" He managed a laugh.

"Yes, thanks to my pregnant pal Dana!" Maggie slapped her on the back.

"Careful with the pregnant lady!" the slim ER man exclaimed. "I'm Calvin, by the way."

"No way! *Calvin?* That's the name I'm using if I have a boy!

Now there's a story to go with it!" Dana started to laugh.

Maggie rolled her eyes at the slim possibilities while noticing that someone from the camera crew was still taking photos of their group, now that Kin had joined them. It was definitely turning into a memorable night, thanks to Dana.... *Right...?*

"Hey, we should all go dancing after this!" someone said.

"Sounds like a plan!" Dana agreed.

THE NEXT MORNING...

"Hey, Sleeping Beauty...did you have fun last night?" Maggie heard Antonio's voice cutting into her deep sleep. She rolled over, slowly opening her eyes. "Since when do you sleep in stilettos?"

"Um...I guess I was really tired. Too tired to take off my shoes...and my dress..." Maggie sat up slowly.

"Yes, I can see that! And I think I'm suffering from a bad case of déjà vu recalling the last time you were out with Dana!" Antonio said, agitated. "What did you do at Pars Loco?"

"It was quite memorable. Dana passed out in the bathroom, and soon afterward we were visited by the paramedics, camera crew, and even Kin came over and talked to us. The next thing I knew, we were at a different dance club and..." Maggie paused and put a hand to her head. "I guess I don't remember much after that..."

"Isn't Dana expecting? What's she doing out at a bar?"

"It wasn't really like that. She was drinking virgin daiquiris all night and...that's about it..."

"Yeah, well, there must be better opportunities than to subject yourself to her ideas of entertainment." Antonio let out a huff.

"She had tickets bought already, Antonio. What was I supposed to do? She already thinks I'm a prude! And I haven't seen her since the wedding."

Antonio shot her a rude look and was about to say something when they heard a knock on the door.

"Maggie! I brought crumpets! Do you have a toaster?" Dana looked wide awake. "And I really need to borrow your straightener; mine doesn't fit into the outlet."

"Dana… You're here so bright and early!" Maggie smiled.

"I reckon we can start the day with some crumpets! And I brought you Jaffa Cakes and Pimm's! You miss them, right?" Dana organized everything neatly on a table.

www.lovetheillusion.com/2285.htm

"We don't have a toaster…" Maggie told her. "We usually just order room service."

"Don't you like to cook?" Dana smiled at Antonio.

"Making toast is hardly cooking, but if you want to toast the crumpets, the kitchen staff at the Atrium will be happy to oblige."

"Perhaps we should just open the Pimm's and play some cards. I brought those along also," Dana informed them.

"You brought Pimm's! That's amazing!" Maggie finally focused.

"I knew you'd be delighted." Dana looked pleased.

"Isn't it too early for that?" Antonio asked.

"Never!" Dana started to laugh. "Don't worry, we'll behave ourselves today…unlike last night. But it *was* absolutely unforgettable, and I can't wait to see us in the papers! I'm quite certain we looked amazing! Maggie looked particularly astonishing and…it will be one of her better ones!"

"I'll see you later," Antonio interrupted her. "I have a meeting with Stanley." He slammed the door on his way out.

"What now? He's not happy?" Dana questioned.

"Why did you have to mention the papers? That should stay our secret. Antonio never reads them, but I don't want to set off his temper either, okay?" Maggie grew concerned. "I'm sure he does *not* approve!"

"He's in them all the time, and now that you're married, he should know that you will be also. Anyway, why would he care?"

"Antonio's overprotective and keeps track of me like I'm his child instead of his wife. I don't care for it one bit, but I know he means well."

"Speaking of children, it can't be true what I read now, can it?" Dana looked curiously at Maggie. "I mean, it was so strange that…" She paused, suddenly bridling her tongue. "So sorry, I should know better than to assume…"

"What now?" Maggie eyed her cautiously.

"Never mind…it would be inappropriate for me to even mention it."

"Right…but now that you have…you have my curiosity! So…what? Just say it, why don't you?"

"It's the most ridiculous thing ever and I'm quite certain it's not true, so it doesn't bear repeating, but obviously it's on the minds of the public now after—I'll just shut up now before I regret—forget I said anything at all." Dana shut her mouth and bent to the Jaffa Cakes.

"Just spill out the crap, Dana—whatever it is, I want to know now!"

"Well…" Dana's eyes were big. "After we all saw a wedding photo of the two of you…and that came out the week of the wedding…shortly after that was a photo of Antonio and Nicolette! She claims that she had his son and it's in the courts and everything. The headline went something like: 'Will the courts prove that Antonio's already a father?' The child is two—almost three—with dark hair and eyes, and Nicolette is fair—and blonder than you can ever imagine. So it's quite strange—and she's after his money to get support for—his name's Mickey—but it really doesn't matter now, does it?" Dana stopped and just stared at Maggie.

Maggie sat frozen, her mind churning.

"It can't be true," she said finally. "There's no way…. Why would someone even try to pull that off! It's such a waste of time! Unless it is true…but that's impossible."

"Surely Antonio mentioned it."

"Of course he did not mention it! He has no idea! He never reads those stupid magazines! And he yells at me if *I* do!"

"Well, he's definitely aware of this one!" Dana told her. "He has a solicitor on the case, so he has to know!"

"He's got an attorney? How would you know?" Maggie asked. "Antonio hates the press coverage and never reads—"

"Maggie, the lawsuit's for over a million dollars! He has to know about it!"

"Over a million dollars? That's not good, it can't be..." Maggie said. "He never told me, and what does that mean...It *is* true?"

"It's on the news and everything, Maggie.... Don't you watch, ever?"

"We have been in Italy, and I—no! I haven't heard a *thing* about it!"

"I wouldn't worry about it...it can only be a rumor, right? But for sure, he's got a solicitor on the case and the whole ordeal's quite obviously public information."

"This is just so...disturbing!" Maggie sighed. "He had *better* not have any child out there with someone else. I would kill him!" Maggie shook her head. "You know what I can't stand? It's all the people out there wondering! It's so appalling to think of how naive I look and like a fool to be married to him if he's lying to me. Now the public doesn't know for sure and..." Maggie let out a groan. "This is just awful." She paused. "I want to see this stupid magazine *and* the crazy lady who thinks she had his baby!"

"No, Maggie, you don't. And sorry, but it's not confined to just one paper or magazine. There are several, and...just let it go..." Dana put a hand on her arm. "Antonio's a good man, so you've nothing to worry about. I'm sure of it."

"I think I prefer Pimm's to the tea right now." Maggie picked up her phone to call the Atrium. “Yes, this is Maggie D.... Could you please send up a fruit platter with oranges, strawberries, and also a cucumber…thanks…yep…to the room.” Maggie put the phone down. “We can start drinking Pimm’s in a half hour.”

Dana stood up. “I’ll be right back; I forgot my phone,” she said. “And Shane said he’ll be ringing in the afternoon. It’s already afternoon, London time…”

Maggie watched the door close, and as soon as Dana made an exit she grabbed her computer and looked for the latest “scoop.”

www.lovetheillusion.com/2261.htm

www.lovetheillusion.com/2262.htm

www.lovetheillusion.com/2289.htm

Maggie closed her computer.

It can't be true...why didn't he tell me? I have the right to know...

SEVERAL HOURS LATER...

Maggie looked at the bottle of Pimm's, which was now half empty.

"Everything will work out, Maggie," Dana said. "I don't think you should drink any more Pimm's. And one's enough for me in my condition. I have a splendid idea! I think we should do a bit of shopping and get your mind off of everything."

"I don't feel like shopping right now." Maggie sighed. "I hate that stupid woman. Antonio's already busy with Francis's lawsuit and now this, too? Why can't people just leave us alone?"

"Just pretend none of it's happening. After the Pimm's, everything's a bit brighter...right?" Dana chuckled. "And it'll be even better after we go shopping. I need a new handbag and a few pairs of shorts for summer. And I think you'll feel much better after you buy a couple pairs of shoes, don't you think?"

"I would need at least *ten* pairs to forget such a crisis. All I can think is who is this woman? Did they go out? Once? Twice? Were they dating? Did they sleep together? How often? I can't even stand the thought of it. And he must know her, somehow, or why would she even be able to accuse him?"

"Maggie! This sort of thing happens all the time in Antonio's world. He probably has a topnotch solicitor and soon it'll be all over; so why even spend time thinking about it? He probably doesn't want you to worry about it, and that's sweet of him, don't you think?"

"Of course he doesn't want me to worry about it because he's happy thinking I don't know anything about it!" Maggie stared into space. "I *despise* his secret, Dana! And I hate that he's not told me!"

"Maybe you're even?" Dana let go of a laugh.

"Even?" Maggie frowned. "What can you possibly mean?"

"You're on the pill, which is quite the secret," Dana said. "And Antonio's hiding the latest scandal from you! You both have secrets, see?"

"My secret's nothing compared to his! I have every right to be concerned over having a child with him and now this is just making matters worse!"

"Talk to him about it," Dana suggested. "You'll feel better then."

"We already had a discussion when we were on our honeymoon—while we were making love! He said he wanted children. I agreed, and so he assumed that meant right away! I was already on the pill and didn't have the heart to tell him. I thought perhaps in a few months I would change my mind about waiting, but the next thing I knew he was missing for days and I had no idea where he was. Turns out, Francis is suing us and it hardly seems a good time to have a child. Now, there's another lawsuit pending.

When will it be over? This is no time to have a baby!"

"Lawsuits can take years to settle. Surely Antonio will become suspicious soon if you don't get pregnant. Shane and I got pregnant the first month we tried!"

"It's not always that easy, though, right? Maybe for us it's different. He'll never know. You can only conceive several days out of the month, and perhaps…"

"Maggie, listen to yourself…trying to justify. As time drags on, it will only get worse, don't you see? You need to tell him, all right?"

"After I finish this bottle of Pimm's." Maggie started laughing.

"No more Pimm's for you. Let's go shopping. Come on."

Chapter 5

"Hey, Sleeping Beauty…looks like you had quite the eventful day." Maggie heard Antonio speaking to her, as she lay crashed out on the couch. "I thought you were going to keep all your shoes in your new room." He chuckled. Maggie slowly opened her eyes, realizing that Antonio was opening up the boxes of shoes to take a look. "These are nice. You should wear them when we celebrate my birthday. I made reservations at Schwister's. It's a German restaurant overlooking a garden and a river with ducks. I can't wait to celebrate that I'm still not thirty."

Maggie sat up, rubbing her eyes, and then peered at Antonio, who was holding up a strappy silver wedge—the one with a feather and hot-pink accents.

"I can't imagine what you wear with these. Lingerie?" Antonio looked amused.

www.lovetheillusion.com/2252.htm

"Give me those, Antonio." Maggie grabbed the shoe from him. "Don't you know that's the *last* thing a woman thinks about when she buys a pair of shoes? I can design something—anything—to go with them, and believe me, it won't be lingerie!"

"It's my birthday, so what if I like the idea? You could wear them when we go out." He winked at her, but then eyed the stack of shoeboxes. "It looks like you will be very busy now…designing something for all of these…How many pairs of shoes can one woman need when she only has two feet?" He still held the strappy sandal in his hand.

"Do you see the four-inch wedge on those, Antonio?" She sat up, still feeling the effects of the Pimm's. "I bought them so that I can clobber you!"

"Why, what have I done now? I promise I like them all. And you can buy more if you want." Antonio grinned.

"Just stop talking, Antonio, unless you want to tell me about Nicolette! You knew Dana was coming and you thought she wouldn't say anything? I think you know better and so what—you think it's amusing? Why don't you tell me how she's managing to sue you for some ridiculous amount of—"

"Maggie! That's enough! Trust me; you don't need to worry about it." Antonio set the shoe down, then reached for her arms, peering down at her.

"Why wouldn't you at least tell me?" She squirmed beneath him. "Did you go out with her? Did you have sex?" Maggie tried pulling away from him.

"I said you don't have to worry about it." Antonio won the struggle and hovered over her.

"Yeah? Well, I *am* worried about it." Maggie stared up at him.

"Were you together or not?"

"We went out a few times, but Mickey's not mine, believe me." Antonio spoke sweetly. "We were together, but we never, you know…" He playfully leaned in to kiss her.

"No, don't kiss me!"

"We never had sex, Maggie." Antonio sat up. "We made out, but never that… She's crazy to think I'm the father, believe me." He paused. "Stanley's taking care of it; I'm way too busy to deal with any of it, and the lab results should be in shortly."

"What? You had to get tested?" Maggie sat up straight on the couch next to him.

"Yes, there are photos of us together and she has even more than the press, if you can imagine. It's *quite* the nightmare, but it will be over soon…right after the DNA tests come back. While I was at it, by the way, I had them do another test." He raised his eyebrows.

Maggie lowered hers. "What test?" she asked.

"I got tested to make sure I can even be a father. I wonder why we still aren't pregnant when, in fact, we are together every minute."

"You did what?"

"It's not me." Antonio paused, and then glanced over her, somewhat suspiciously. "I think *you* should get tested. It's been almost four months. Something's not right." He wore a look of confusion, seeming to question her.

Maggie felt her jaw drop. She quickly closed it and shifted her eyes, contemplating his latest announcement. She struggled to get a deep breath and then let out a huff.

"That's silly, Antonio. We can have that baby soon enough. But for now, we have two pending lawsuits, and you should be worried about those before having a child. That poor child will hit the spotlight, landing in some crazy circus ring, and it'll be much better if everyone's aware that it does not already have a sibling!"

"Are you afraid to have my baby?" Antonio looked concerned. "Trust me; everything's under control."

"Under control?" Maggie started laughing. "That's a joke!"

"Come here." Antonio pulled her into a hug as they lay on the couch. "You're always worried, for nothing. What am I going to do with you? I can't help that my life is crazy; I told you it would be, and you should know better than to worry. Believe me, the only child I want is the one we will have, hopefully soon. You know I love you."

He attempted to kiss her again. She closed her eyes and kissed him back, realizing there was nothing that would kill their passion.

"So, tomorrow night, you need to meet me at the restaurant," he said. "It's a mile south of here; you can have Salvador drive you, and I'll be waiting for you."

"Why can't we go together?"

"I have to get something first; then I can meet you." He looked at her mysteriously.

"What's *that?*"

He grinned. "It's a surprise."

Maggie rolled her eyes, explaining, "There have been enough of those lately." She gave him a sour look while wondering what to get him for his birthday.

"This one's a nice one…promise."

THE NEXT EVENING…

A photo, taken in Rome…that's what I'll give him. She placed it in a photo frame.

They were celebrating his birthday tonight.

And she already had a dress to go with the pink shoes. It was one of her new designs.

Hope it's not too fancy…probably…

www.lovetheillusion.com/2251.htm

As soon as she stepped out of the cab she saw Antonio standing next to the entrance to the restaurant.

www.lovetheillusion.com/2234.htm

"For you." He handed her the rose.

"My surprise…that's sweet. Thanks…I'll trade you." She took the rose and handed him his gift.

The hostess seated them in a reserved spot, away from the crowd, right above the ducks. “Hopefully they stay put.” Antonio took a seat, looking down on them as they swam in the water.

“Maybe they’ll gather to sing happy birthday to you.” Maggie giggled softly.

“They’re probably more interested in us feeding them,” he teased.

She opened her menu. “I could order a salad with croutons.”

“Right there…don’t feed the ducks.” He pointed.

“Aww…no fun.” She peeked at him over the top of her menu.

“So, what’s Dana doing with herself this evening?” Antonio looked amused. “One of her last nights here…”

“I think watching the pay-per-view movies.”

“A night in for her… That must be painful…”

“I know…and I told her not to wait up.”

He smiled, able to read her mind. “She’ll have to watch *every* movie there is.”

“Probably.”

“So what could this be?” He picked up the gift and started ripping the paper. “A picture of us…nice…” He looked out over the water, recalling their honeymoon in Rome.

www.lovetheillusion.com/2269.htm

"We had a lot of fun that day," he said.

"I know; that's why I framed it." She smiled in recollection.

"We could have even more fun tonight…" He winked at her.

"Perhaps—" Maggie noticed a few people staring in their direction—"if we can stay under the radar."

"It's a good table we have. Not a lot of people in here." He seemed proud of the arrangements. "But with you wearing that dress, it's hard to go unnoticed." He grinned. She suddenly felt his foot under the table, stroking her leg. "We could go for more attention." He tried to embarrass her.

"Stop! Not funny." She kicked back.

"Come on, it's my birthday." He wore a childlike grin as the waiter set down a flight of German wine.

"This is how you want to spend your birthday, just with me?" Maggie asked.

"Of course." He set his menu down, "I don't want a big party. We can party, just the two of us. Maybe go out dancing…keep the paparazzi busy…" He chuckled. "It will be good: from the dance floor to the bedroom floor…" He stared at her until she blushed.

Maggie suddenly caught a glimpse of a baby bottle floating next to the ducks, and at the same time heard a commotion. "Theo, why did you do that?" the mother shouted while her youngest was screaming from a double stroller. Theo reached over to play with the water. "That's it; we're leaving." The mother grabbed him, placing him into the stroller.

"I think it's good we aren't parents yet," Maggie said, watching the fiasco.

"Why would you say that?" Antonio let go of a quick laugh. "I thought maybe that could be my birthday present: you know, you could tell me that I'm going to be a father."

"You already got your present. And you think this looks like a maternity dress?" She looked down at her pink dress. "Now that is *seriously* funny." She watched his face change in disappointment. "Sorry, Antonio, not yet. But look on the bright side: you get to keep trying."

"Then soon, my dear, we'll have that baby. I'm absolutely sure of it…maybe tonight. We should go for twins!" he said, then paused. "How long would that take?"

"That's not how it works!" Maggie sipped her wine, feeling a few steps ahead of him where that was concerned. She smiled at him, suddenly feeling guilty for holding on to her own agenda.

Time to change the subject!

"It's strange to think we met a year ago, here in New York," she said.

"Yeah, I will never forget the first time I saw you. You walked into Biagio's, wondering where everyone was, and then shortly after I invited you to sit by me you got ketchup on your blouse. It was so funny—it made my day—and that's when I decided I had to get to know the pretty lady. But it was such a disappointment when she thought I was a creep and kept giving me the cold shoulder."

"You want to know what I was really thinking?" Maggie's mouth curled in a grin.

"Yeah, I know…who is that waiter…?" Antonio laughed.

"No, after that." She looked at him mysteriously. "Do you

remember when we ate at Bouley? And I disappeared in the ladies' room, and when I came back to the table I said I had to leave?"

"I do…"

"Well…I was pretty sure at that moment that if you had raped me, I wouldn't have pressed charges." She grinned.

"Really?" He grinned back. "So I didn't have to marry you? You had me pretty well convinced."

"My attraction to you could have been the death of me."

"Then have a baby with me…"

"We can't…"

"We can… We just have to try harder."

Maggie reached for her wine.

"Tonight…" He sipped from his glass, his eyes glued to hers.

She stared back at him, wondering how long she could stay on the pill.

"So, what should we order?" Antonio looked over the menu. "So many things I never tried before."

She suddenly felt his foot on her leg, again. She looked under the table. "How am I supposed to choose an entrée with you distracting me?"

"It's my birthday and I want a baby."

"Did you not just see that bottle floating in the water?"

"I did, sweetheart."

"Good, then think about that for a while."

"I am…and you'd be a perfect mamma."

"Antonio! Your foot is caught in the tooling of my dress. You're gonna rip it."

"I'm being careful."

"You need to put your shoe back on, now!"

"Who says?"

"Restaurants have rules about that."

"See, you sound like a mamma already…talking about the rules…."

"Someone has to keep you in line."

"But it's my birthday; you're taking away all the fun."

"Yeah, and you got your present…so behave yourself."

"But I wanted something else."

"I know…a baby. Well, that is maybe next year. It'll take at *least* nine months from now."

"Then I want you right now, under the table. Let's go."

Maggie burst out laughing. "You're so crazy."

"Come on," he teased, enjoying his ability to get to her.

Maggie closed her menu and set it down on the table. "This is ridiculous. I can barely think about food anymore."

"Really?" He sounded amused. "There must be something you like."

"I'm not a huge fan of German food…it's hard to decide." She studied the menu.

"You want to leave and go somewhere else?"

"Where…?"

"Like back to the room?" He tilted his head, his foot still sliding along her leg. "We'll get room service later….much later."

"Okay, birthday boy…we can try to have a baby."

The waiter approached their table, but Antonio still had his eyes on Maggie as he said, "We'll just have… the check…please."

If only he knew.

No sooner did they step inside the private elevator than Maggie had her hands in his hair. Antonio took her in his arms and started kissing her. She leaned into him until he stood against the wall in the elevator, where he hit another button on the panel, sending them to the top floor. "Tell me there are no hidden cameras in here," Maggie whispered as Antonio started unzipping her dress.

"Not a one," Antonio said as she unbuttoned his shirt. The next thing she knew, her purse had fallen onto the floor, the contents spilling out. She looked down out of the corner of her eye to where her pills lay, under her shoe, as Antonio held her partially in the air. She kept her eye on the package as they enjoyed a kiss. That's when the lights in the elevator went out.

"What just happened? I can't see a thing," Maggie said as she felt Antonio's arms around her in a tight grip.

"Just a second," she heard him say as he moved to the panel of elevator buttons to fix the lights. She quickly bent down to rescue her pills as the elevator hit the top floor, coming to an abrupt halt. She shoved them into a zipped compartment, and when the lights came back on, she looked at Antonio. It was obvious that he'd been too distracted to notice.

So lucky.

"Let's get out here." Antonio grabbed her hand.

"We're at the top of the building! We need to go to the fourth floor, Antonio! Have you forgotten where you live?" Maggie started laughing.

"Me? You're the one who's been drinking Pimm's..." He let go of a laugh. "There's a great view...I want to show you...thirty-six stories high, and no one's up here..."

They stepped onto the roof, which was protected by a guardrail.

"Wow! It's awesome at night. Everything's lit up and the stars are out..." Maggie's face glowed.

"I thought you'd like it." Antonio grinned. "So, are you glad you married me? Tell me you are..."

"Of course. Why would you even ask?" Maggie smiled, looking up at him.

"Because I love you and...I just want to make sure you're happy and that you aren't mad at me because of Nicolette."

"Why would you bring her up?" Maggie cast him a sidelong glance. "It's in the past, unless she has your child and you forgot to tell me. Then I *would* be upset."

"She doesn't, Maggie, I already told you. You trust me, right?"

"I do." She spoke softly.

"That's good," he answered. "You know I'd never lie to you." He started with soft kisses.

Maggie froze in his arms, kissing him back, while pondering her cover-up.

I should tell him.

"Antonio?" She leaned back in his arms, staring up at him.

"Yes?"

"What if it takes a while for us to have a child? There's nothing wrong with waiting, right?"

He paused to think. "We can't wait too long, Maggie, especially if we want a big family," he said softly. "I'm almost thirty. Family is everything…and they will have everything! And they can be an asset to the show, you'll see." He smiled into her face, revealing his agenda.

Maggie contemplated his excitement, not wishing to burst his bubble. "I just worry that they'll grow up too fast in the spotlight. How will we keep them safe from that?"

"Why do you even ask me that? I keep *you* safe, don't I?"

He started kissing her again and soon she realized their discussion had once again come to an end…

THE NEXT DAY…

"We made love on the rooftop last night; it was amazing," Maggie told Dana as they sat in the Atrium Café, sipping their morning tea. "*And* he told me that he and Nicolette never even had sex…That was a relief!"

"See, I told you! Now you drank a bottle of Pimm's for nothing! And I only brought you that one bottle. But at least you got some amazing shoes!" Dana laughed.

"I shouldn't be so stressed out, but I just spent the last three months of my life where no one speaks any English!"

"You're always stressed out. You need to relax."

"Easy for you to say…but I'm so glad to be back in the States where everyone understands English…well, almost everyone. Eventually I will have to learn Italian, but it will take a while…" She paused. "*Grazi*, *grazi*, *amore*, *Italiano ristorante*, and *prego* weren't all that helpful! Some days I felt like I was living in a cage. I have everything I need, Antonio makes sure of it, but it's all those things that money can't buy that keep a person sane!"

"Must be nice to be filthy rich, though…"

"I don't know…there are other things to worry about: We can never control what ends up in the press. That's an endless struggle, and so I fear for our children. How will I keep them out of the spotlight? He wants them on stage, part of the show. Is that a good life for a child? Someone has to worry for them. It may as well be me, and I worry before they're even born because he doesn't have a care in the world!"

Dana listened intently, trying to imagine what it was like living in Maggie's world.

"He just lives life as if every day will be better than the last, regardless, and he's being sued for millions of dollars! Who doesn't know that we live in a constant state of disaster! Francis… Nicolette…and the media…"

"Yeah, I can't believe how the papers keep track of him, almost daily."

"Antonio says it doesn't really matter what they print…but it bothers me!"

"So did you finally tell him that you are waiting to start a family with him?" Dana asked.

"I tried, but it ended in another lovemaking session. I should be so pregnant by now, it's funny. I ought to be carrying twins…maybe even quadruplets. I feel bad, but what should I do?"

"It's simple: just have a baby! It's not that bad! I only puked four times from morning sickness, and now the hard part is over. Now I just eat more and wait to grow a baby bump." Dana patted her stomach.

Maggie frowned. "The hard part's over? Did you forget labor? I heard it's a nightmare! I'm so terrified of pregnancy, giving birth, and after it's finally born it will change everything; children are a lot of work." She recalled the bottle floating in the water. "I'm not ready for that. I haven't even had a chance to get my career off the ground. Antonio keeps me so busy. Not to mention…where would our child even go to school? Three months in Italy and six in the US? There are serious complications for us, aside from the media. Antonio hasn't even given a thought to any of it! He lives day by day; he's lucky *someone's* thinking for the two of us…"

"You do spend a lot of time thinking," Dana told her.

"So, enough about me…did you have fun in New York? I can't believe you leave tomorrow. I wish you could stay for our opening show."

Dana's smiled. "I know, me too. But I had fun. New York is amazing. And I love shopping here; I've found some really cute maternity clothes!"

"You won't need those for a while."

"In the second trimester. That's when the clothes get tight."

Maggie's phone went off.

"Is Antonio checking up on you?" Dana chuckled.

"No… It's Julia!" she said, recognizing the number. "We've been emailing ever since the wedding. She lives just outside Brooklyn and she needs a place to stay while she's remodeling her house, so I invited her to stay on our company floor."

That night, Maggie lay in her bed pondering the responsibilities that having a family would entail. She felt as if a time bomb was about to explode. She did *not* want to have a child yet. He did; and he was already sharing his concern. There were no easy answers, and she wished for a moment that she could start over; that she had told him before so much time had passed. She never meant to keep secrets, but he had never given her the chance to explain how she felt. Rather, he had just assumed, now that they were married, they would have a family. Perhaps it was the Catholic way…but it did not seem fair. She could not leave such a big decision to fate.

A FEW DAYS LATER…

"So good to see you!" Maggie said as she gave Julia a hug.

"Thank you for having me. This will be such a nice getaway."

"I love it here. It's strange that a hotel can feel so much like home," Maggie said.

"I was so excited to come. They're sanding the wood floors now, and the new kitchen cabinets go in next," Julia told her.

"Well, we have plenty of room," Maggie said as she led Julia to her suite on the fourth floor. "You have a great view of the city, so make sure you draw the drapes. Here are your keys." Maggie handed her two plastic cards. "This one's for your room, and this blue one is for our private elevator…don't lose that one!"

"Don't worry," Julia said. "Now give me another hug." She reached out to Maggie. "I can't wait to see the show tonight. That was so nice of Antonio—to send me a ticket in the mail, postmarked from Italy."

"I can't wait for you to see the show. Antonio said everything's ready to go; he's been so busy since we got here. He's there now. Dana just left…she was keeping me company. Wait until you see me in the show. I'm the lady in the ring of fire." She smiled proudly. "It's an easy job… I don't even have to rehearse for it. But I do get to make my own outfits."

"I bet it's beautiful. It's so nice that you help Antonio out with everything." She wore a soft smile. "I have never had front-row tickets before in my entire life, so even at my age I get to do something new and exciting." Julia opened the door to her suite, enjoying the first glimpse.

"Hope the smoke doesn't bother you! Antonio has smoke coming out from under the curtain, and when it does, you won't be able to see or breathe until it clears!" Maggie told her.

"That won't bother me, I promise!" Julia still smiled, setting her things on the bed. "So, how was Italy?"

"It was great. But I was a bit frustrated trying to learn Italian!" Maggie started to laugh. "I think it will take years!"

"Isn't Antonio teaching you?"

"He tries…but he usually just speaks for me because when I speak no one understands me and he thinks it's so funny! I have spent the last three months feeling pretty helpless, but his family is amazing and I love his mamma. She went with me if I had to shop and she speaks Italian pretty well, but with a British accent. She gets around pretty good."

"I spoke with her a little at the wedding. She did a great job planning that. I was surprised how she put that together in such a short time."

"She is so sweet and Antonio has a great family. Now, unfortunately, he can't wait to add to that."

"Having children is a lot of work. You're already so busy trying to start your business designing, and Antonio's also busy performing."

"Exactly. We need to wait to have a family. One thing at a time, right?"

"It's nice when it works out like that." Julia looked around her room. "This is so nice. I really love it. Thank you for letting me stay here."

"It's really no problem. I will love having you here."

"Maybe I can help with your dress designs."

"I'd love that. You know, I designed several dresses in memory of my mother. I want to have a label with her name: Katie White. I brought a few along. Maybe I can sell them in some of the shops here."

"That would be wonderful. What does Antonio think of the idea?"

"Well, he just wants to have a baby! That's all. Don't say anything, but I'm on the pill, thinking straight for the both of us."

"He doesn't know?"

"No…he doesn't know, and I know that's bad…but we have plenty to think about—it's just too much too soon."

"That's quite the secret you are keeping, dear."

"I know, but I want to get my career off the ground, and after severing ties with Francis it's not so easy. I can't have a baby and career all at once! Yes, I feel guilty, but then I think of the alternative, which is—I can't, I just can't!" Maggie sighed. "I just want my own dress line."

"Motherhood is the greatest journey there is! But I understand wanting to wait."

"Dana's already having a child."

"Now she can tell you everything you're missing!" Julia told her with a smile.

"I suppose," Maggie said.

Maybe after the lawsuits are settled...then I'll think about it.

AFTER THE FIRST MAGIC SHOW PERFORMANCE…

"It was great! And you looked amazing in my ring of fire," Antonio told Maggie as they sat down next to the fireplace. "Are you warm now?" He placed his arm around her as they sat down on a blanket.

"Yes, thanks." Maggie smiled at him. "Julia said she loved your show."

"It's *our* show now, Maggie. And you will always be my lady in the ring of fire."

They snuggled together, watching the fire.

"What did you do before you met me?" Maggie murmured.

"You know: Nicolette, Adrianna…" he teased.

"Sorry I asked." Maggie elbowed him.

"I'm only kidding." Antonio winked at her.

"You are such a troublemaker," she told him. "I imagine our son will be worse than you...*if* we have one."

"One? We'll have at least two," he said.

"Maybe I'll have only girls." Maggie teased him.

"No!" Antonio said in alarm. "Not so fast...all those female hormones...we need at least one son to pass on the DeLuca name. And he can be a magician, just like his father."

Maggie rolled her eyes at him. "I can hardly wait."

"Do you have gum?" Antonio asked suddenly, out of the blue. "I think they put onions on that panini I ordered before the show! I said 'fresh mozzarella, tomatoes, and avocado,' but I did not ask for onions. And now I really want to kiss you..."

"I have some in my purse." She nodded to the leather couch.

Antonio got up and went over to it. He picked the purse up, but as soon as he did, she realized her pills were still in there.

NO!

"Here, let me get it." She leapt to her feet. "I can get it for you."

"Don't be silly. I'm sure I can find a pack of gum."

Maggie watched impatiently as he rummaged through her purse.

Hurry up and find the gum! She stood next to him.

"What's this?" Antonio pulled out her pills.

Maggie felt her stomach drop.

He shook his head as his discovery registered.

"I...uh...give me those." She tried to grab them out of his hand, but with little success.

"What are these? It better not be...don't tell me, Maggie, what are you doing with these? Is it what I think it is?"

"Give me those, Antonio! And give me my purse."

"Forget the gum. What else do you have in here?" He looked at her in a state of shock.

She remained silent.

"These are yours?" he finally asked, holding up the container. "Don't tell me you are taking these!"

"Don't be mad, Antonio. I wanted to tell you, but you never gave me the chance! So there! Now you know: I'm not ready to have a child just yet—and I am sorry. I love you— but I want to wait."

"You lied to me?" His voice was firm.

"I didn't mean to," Maggie said softly as Antonio turned the bottle of pills in his hand. His face was dark and his eyes glinted.

"How could you?" he asked, trying to control his voice. He went over to the fireplace and gazed into the fire.

"No, Antonio!" Maggie reached for the pills, trying to grab them out of his hand. But he held them out of reach, and then tossed them into the fire.

"I can't believe you just threw them in there!" Maggie exclaimed. "Don't you care about me, about what I want?"

"You *lied* to me," he said. "You think I'm a fool?" Antonio's dark eyes stared into hers. "I told you I got tested and what…you think it's a joke that I want children?"

She stood silent while taking a deep breath, hoping he would understand, but he said, "Next time we make love, it will be without the pills. You decide when…"

Maggie sat in shock as she pondered his new terms.

"You can't be serious! Antonio, that's ridiculous."

"All this time, I wonder why—why would you lie to me?"

Maggie stood silent.

Finally she spoke: "I wanted to tell you but I didn't think you would understand. You never gave me the chance! I tried, more than once, and you! You just think about what *you* want!"

"Is that what you think of me? You think I would make you have a baby, against your will? Who do you think I am? Meanwhile, you question me about Nicolette! You should know me by now, Maggie, but you don't! Why? Tell me! Instead, you're making me crazy!"

"I'm sorry!"

"Sorry?" Antonio looked absolutely furious.

Maggie held her breath, wishing she could die. She watched as he left the room, slamming the door on his way out. Maggie lay down on the bed, her eyes filling with tears.

"I love you, Antonio, really I do," she sobbed into her pillow.

Chapter 6

Maggie sat up in bed, still wondering where Antonio was. She stared into the fireplace, which was full of ashes, realizing her pills were completely disintegrated.

Where are you, Antonio?

She felt sick without him.

She finally took a shower and then sat impatiently on the couch, waiting for him. He must have spent the night somewhere else. She reached for her phone.

"Where are you, Antonio? Call me!" Maggie left a message on his phone.

Hours passed, and she finally left the room. She ran into Amber in the hotel hallway.

"Amber! Have you seen Antonio?"

"We have a rehearsal at one o'clock today," Amber told her, "but I have no idea where he is now."

Maggie managed a smile. "If you see him, tell him I am looking for him, please!"

"Sure. I will," Amber told her, looking somewhat confused.

Several days later, Maggie lay on their bed gazing up at the ceiling. *Where IS he?* She had never seen him so angry before, and now she was starting to get scared. She was desperate to patch things up. How had things become such a mess? She meant well; so did he. She had every right to want to wait. He, being a few years older than she, had every reason to want a child right away. *Who got to make that final decision? Someone had to give in, right? Who deserved the greater happiness? Would they take turns?* She was pretty sure she wanted to win this battle. Antonio could win the next one…whatever it was. What could be worse than having a child before you are ready? But they were married now, and she did want a family someday. What was standing in the way? Her career? Maybe, but she had barely gotten things off the ground. Now that she no longer worked for Francis, she had lost those connections. It would be a lot of work. How could she have a family and a career? After she got her career off the ground, *then* she could have a child or two…but not ten…hopefully he was joking about *that.*

Maggie checked her phone.

He still has not called? He's so stubborn!

Guess I'll be big enough for both of us; I'll have to be the mature one.

Suddenly the door to the hotel suite opened. It was Antonio. His hair was messy and he had not shaved.

"Where have you been, Antonio?" Maggie asked.

"A few doors down. Why do you care?" He sounded crabby.

"I know you're mad at me, but I've been worried sick for the past three days. Why are you staying away? We need to talk this out."

"What's there to talk about?" He glared at her. "You think I'm so selfish, but now I'm doing *you* a favor."

"A favor?" Maggie just stared at him. "And what favor's that?"

"Just making sure we don't have that baby you don't want." He opened the door to his armoire and grabbed a few shirts off the hangers. “See you later.” He spoke in a hostile tone.

“Antonio!” Maggie shouted at him. “What are you doing? What room are you in and why are you avoiding me? I hate sleeping in here without you.”

“Sorry, but that’s not my problem.”

She watched the door slam.

He’s so immature! This is just ridiculous. He wants a child so badly, but he can’t quit acting like one!

She opened the door a crack and peeked out, watching what room he went into.

THREE HOURS LATER…

Maggie banged on the door to room 445.

“I did not order room service… What do you want?” Antonio stood at the door with his hair wet from the shower and a white towel wrapped around his waist.

“You…you are…you have the immaturity of a child, Antonio! Come back to our room, now, so we can talk this out! It has been three days already and we perform tonight! How can we look friendly when we hold hands on stage and you lead me to the ring of fire?”

“I promise to look friendly.” He shrugged and then offered a small smile.

“When are you coming back? Don’t you miss me?” Maggie looked downcast.

“Maybe, but I’m still mad at you.” Antonio broke their eye contact.

Maggie grabbed his arm and pulled him close. “This is killing me, being away from you. Are you going to be mad at me forever?"

"Probably not."

"We're married and now we have separate housing…" Maggie complained.

"We can't both have what we want—that's obvious," Antonio told her.

"I know, Antonio! You win! I haven't taken the pill for three days! Are you happy now?"

"No, Maggie…that is *not* what this is about, in case you don't know!"

"Yes, Antonio, it is! You want to have a baby and I don't! And now that you have destroyed my means of eliminating our chances, I can probably get pregnant! Except that you are in a room by yourself, so the possibilities are quite slim!" She grabbed his towel flirtatiously.

"Excuse me, if you don't mind." He looked sternly at her and then left her standing at the door as he went into the bathroom. Maggie wandered in and sat down at the edge of the bed. She looked around the room that had little in it other than a bed, TV, and shower. Soon he made an exit, dressed in a pair of jeans.

She watched as he put on a shirt and started to button it.

"Antonio!" Maggie stared at him. "I hate it when you're mad at me! How long will this last? I think we should go get a glass of wine and talk this out!"

"There's nothing to talk about, Maggie." Antonio gave her a cold stare.

Maggie sat silent.

"You think I would *make* you have a child before you're ready?

Why would you think that? What have I *ever* done to you that would make you think that? I waited to be together until *after* we were married. What else do I have to do to prove my love for you? You said you wanted children too; so sorry I made the rash assumption—and now…I'm sorry I threw your pills into the fire…I will wait until you are ready, but I am sad that you can't tell me, your own husband, how you really feel!"

"Well that would be obvious…look at the joys I was putting off!"

"No, Maggie! I am mad that you lied to me. How are we supposed to have a family together when you lie to me?"

"I wanted to tell you, but you never gave me a chance!"

"You can tell me anything! Why not that? I always care about what you want! Tell me when I haven't!"

"This is just a huge misunderstanding." Maggie stared at Antonio. "I am sorry! And now you hate me."

"Why wouldn't you tell me that you were on the pill? Don't you think that's my business?"

"I was just waiting until the lawsuits were over—but I still wonder about everything having a child would entail. Even the simple things are not simple. For instance, how would our child go to school when we are traveling everywhere?"

"Seriously, Maggie? That is at least five years away and you're thinking about it already? That is the least of our worries! I can hire private tutors! Oh, and by the way, I have a present for you!" He threw a magazine at her at feet. "There you are! It's what you want to know, right? Before you have my baby…"

Maggie looked down to the floor and read the headline:

www.lovetheillusion.com/2266.htm

Maggie spoke quietly: "Sorry. I am so sorry, Antonio. I just…I love you and I can't stand to think of you with anyone else and…"

"Well, I hope you aren't surprised."

"No, it's just that…" Maggie paused, choosing her words carefully. "When I met you, I entered a whole new world. And it's a scary one for me, Antonio. You are used to it now. I am still not. I'm trying to proceed with caution because I'm afraid. Sometimes I wonder: Will we last? Can we survive the media? I want to trust you, and I think I do, but it is all so overwhelming. And I spent the last three months in Italy with you! I left my friends behind to be with you, so don't think for a minute I don't love you. I can't stand the thought of being without you but I fear that a child will complicate things for us. Things are already complicated."

"I know, Maggie." Antonio looked upset. "There are some things that money can't buy. And plenty of things I can't control. But I promise that, no matter what, I love you and that should be enough. It has to be, because I can't promise anything else."

"You don't have to promise anything else." She looked at him sweetly.

"That's good." He returned her look.

A few moments passed, and then he asked, "Should I come back tonight?"

"Yes, please." Maggie felt his arms around her. "Kiss me," she said, "so that I know you're no longer mad at me."

"Fine, we'll have a kiss, but only one. We can't risk any more than that," Antonio said, smiling.

Maggie felt his lips on hers. "Great! So, now you're going to torture me?"

"No, Maggie. You are going to torture *me!* But I promise to behave myself until you get the refill."

"I did not order a refill." She looked up at him.

"What…? No…" Antonio spoke under his breath, as she stood wrapped in his arms. "You need to order a refill, and soon," he whispered.

Maggie saw that her phone was going off. She picked it up, and read the text: Meet me at Gratsi's on Claiborne @ 7.

Francis is here? For the spring fashion show…and he wants to see me?

Maggie looked up at Antonio, hoping not to give alarm, but he read straight through her futile attempts.

"Who is that?" he snapped suspiciously. Maggie handed her phone to Antonio. "You must be kidding," he said when he saw it was Francis. "What does he want?" Antonio read the text. "No *way* are you meeting him. Over my dead body." Antonio handed her phone back and shook his head. "Don't respond to that," he ordered.

THE NEXT MORNING…

Maggie was in the shower when her cell phone went off.

Bradley? What could he possibly want? She saw that he had not left a message.

Maggie sent a text: What's up?

He sent one back: Stop by the lobby ASAP.

"What could possibly be happening in the lobby?" Maggie muttered. With a cup of hotel mocha in her hand, she went down to the lobby to meet Bradley.

"There you are," Bradley said as she walked up.

"Am I first in line for a parade, or what?" Maggie asked, but he didn't smile.

"Uh…I think you might want to check out the latest in that gift shop over there. They've got a magazine displayed and you can see it from the entrance. I would hate for Antonio to see it. Perhaps you could ask them to move it or, I don't know—I'd hate for him to see-"

"I already *saw* Nicolette and her illegitimate child, and Antonio could care less about the latest media frenzy. You seriously called me for—"

"That is not—Antonio will care about *this* one, believe me, girl, because you're on the cover with that Kin dude and Dana and… You'd better see it for yourself."

Maggie shrugged. "Okay, I'll go look, for whatever it's worth, but…" She headed for the shop.

Dana, you and your brilliancy! This is my worst photo yet, and the caption—even WORSE! Antonio is going to kill me. She stared at the cover:

www.lovethellusion.com/2275.htm

Maggie quickly gathered all of the magazines out of the newsstand and put them on the marble countertop. A male clerk stood behind the counter, eyeing her up and down. "Yes, this is me," Maggie admitted. "The latest abomination, and I will just… purchase…all of these! Charge it to my room!"

"How many do you have?"

Maggie thumbed through them. "Fifteen! Fifteen effing magazines!" She glared at him as he grabbed one and held the scanner over the barcode.

"Sorry," she muttered under her breath. A minute later, she left the shop with the magazines in a tight clutch.

"Dana!" Maggie held her phone between her shoulder and ear.

"Maggie, is that you?"

"Yes, are you there?"

"I'm in Harrods of London now picking up a few items for the baby room. I can't hear—the connection is awfully bad…Can I call you back?"

"No! Dana, I—fine, whatever—hurry up! Call me back—I can barely hear you."

Maggie stepped into the hotel suite, glad that Antonio was busy with rehearsal. She lit a match and tossed it into the fireplace. "Light!

Fire! Flames! Go on, now! *Burn* all of this rubbish!" But the match went out, so she lit the entire book of matches and threw it in. "There! That oughta do it!" she said with her teeth clenched, staring at the pages quickly taking to the flame. Her phone went off. She immediately held it to her ear.

"Dana! Thanks for calling ba—"

"It's not Dana! It's Francis!"

Maggie's eyes widened at the sound of his voice.

"Uh…Francis?" Maggie felt that non-removable lump in her throat. She watched the magazines disintegrating. "Where are you—you're in New York?"

"It's that time of year again! Don't you know, New York's PL fashion show's just several days away once again, and it'll be huge this year! My latest collection has the longest time slot and I was thinking I could fit in a few extras…just wondering if perhaps you would have a few designs to show off? Also, Angel Anna's is looking for a variety of teen evening dresses and I don't have time for such a narrow margin, so I thought it'd be a great opportunity for you—if you're even still designing. Kensal could model for you, if needed, and I have three spare mannequins you can use for displays. And they have an awards show afterward for 'Most Original,' a grand prize of fifteen hundred euros! It's a great opportunity to gain recognition and stand out in the world of fashion design. Kenneth Cole will be there, Ralph Lauren, and BCBG, to name a few."

"Well, it's so nice of you to think of me, but I didn't pay the fees in time and we just got here a few days ago."

"No worries, Maggie! You can sit at my table, just like old times.

And the fees? I paid plenty; you can sign in under my name, and you must have business cards, right? Just bring them along and people can contact you if interested."

"That sounds great…can I get back to you?"

"You may, but I'll just assume you'll be here, Maggie, and so will buyers from all over Europe and everywhere imaginable. It's a great opportunity to get your foot in the door."

"When is it?"

"In a miraculous three days! Five in the evening…same place as last year!"

"Okay…" Maggie stared into the fireplace.

"When you arrive, simply go first to the information desk and just tell them you're meeting with me. I'll have a name tag and an entry pass waiting for you. Don't be late!"

"How many dresses should I bring?"

"Well, at least two to dress the mannequins," Francis said, "and a couple for the runway. And remember, there's a cocktail party on a boat afterward—black-tie event—so make sure you're dressed accordingly."

"Thanks, Francis! I owe you!"

"No problem, Maggie! I look forward to seeing you!"

Question remaining: How drunk does Antonio need to be to let me go to this? Maggie wondered.

She lay down on the zebra-print bedspread and stared up at the ceiling. Her phone rang again.

"Dana?"

"Yes! I'm sorry that I took so long to call you back. But there is a huge sale and the lines are exceptionally long and I couldn't hear you over the noise…and there's something I have to tell you."

"Uh…yeah, well, I'm sure I already know!" Maggie let out a groan. "I am standing in our hotel suite burning a stack of magazines with the latest…our night out with Kin! Antonio will kill me if he sees it!"

"Relax! You said he never reads them, and even if he does, he knows it's all a bunch of hoopla, right? Please don't hate me, Maggie, but I am more worried about…well, I was approached by a woman reporter while I was at the airport, going through customs. She said she needed to talk to me and I thought it was about my flight. Instead, she asked if I had visited you and was asking strange questions like: did I know if you were aware that Antonio already had a child? I didn't even know what to say, and then I said that you wanted to have children but that you were waiting, and then I realized that Antonio has no idea that you're on the pill and he could find out now if that hits the press. I am so sorry! The lady gave me money afterward. I said I didn't want it, but she said that she always pays the people she interviews! Now once she had given me several thousand pounds, I thought bloody hell! I hope I didn't make trouble for you!"

"What? Are you kidding? You talked to a *reporter* about me and Antonio? Why would you even do that, Dana? This is the *last* thing I need. We just got in a huge fight when he found my pills in my purse while he was looking for gum!"

"So he already knows! That's good," Dana sounded relieved.

"No, it's *not* good. He was sleeping five rooms away from me for three nights! Finally things are okay and now they are about to get bad again. He'll be furious if that ends up in the press."

"Okay, Maggie… Well, before I even knew what was happening, I realized I had opened my big mouth and sooo sorry. But you should know that I got the entire baby's room furnished with the money and I am so glad to have that done, you know. I can tell everyone it's from you and Antonio!"

"That's no gift from us, Dana. Listen to you; you're irrational! How can you think that would make me happy? I would rather pick out my own gift than have you announce that you spoke to the media on my behalf and gave out information that's nobody's damn business!"

"I'm so sorry!"

"Just forget it. I have to go!" Maggie hung up and put her face in her hands. *"Ugh!"*

She sat up, staring into the fireplace, where a heap of ashes was all that was left of the magazines. "Why do I bother?" she said under her breath. "They're probably so busy now just printing more! More crap! That is what I just can't take any more of…" Maggie lay back down on the bed. "Uhh," she moaned.

"Is everything all right?" Antonio entered the hotel suite.

"No, I've had the morning from hell. How has your day been so far?"

"It's been good. What are you doing in here, having a fire all by yourself?"

"That fire is not for me. I had to rescue my own reputation from the newsstand that claims I was out with Kin! We were in a group, so technically, yes, we were out together, but we were not 'together,'"

Maggie explained. "I just bought them all from the newsstand in the main lobby gift shop and tossed them into the fire! That stupid media has everyone probably thinking I am a ho!"

"Now you know how I feel. Did you tell Dana that her wonderful idea backfired?" he asked nonchalantly.

Maggie just stared at him, so he went on: "Surely you have better things to do with your time than burn magazines. Why don't you see how that new sewing machine works?"

He seriously does not care?

"Antonio! Don't you care that it looks as if after only a few months of marriage I am out with a new guy?" Maggie said.

"Well, I saw you afterward, crashed out on my bed, so I already know the truth. The photo they took must be the highlight of your night. Quite frankly, it looks to me like a long night in a pair of shoes that fits way too tight!" He smiled.

"Aren't you funny," Maggie grinned at him.

He grinned back. "Do you want to go up on the roof?"

"Now? Why, are the helicopters circling around in the broad daylight?"

"No, but we could sit up there and have a talk."

"A talk? That's all you want to do—talk?"

"Umm…yeah…maybe more. But we can't, you know, unless you changed your mind about having that baby."

"Right. Well there is something I need to talk to you about, but it's not that."

"Okay, let's go." Antonio took her hand. "First we need to grab a blanket, though. It could be a little chilly up there."

On the rooftop, Maggie lay next to Antonio on the blanket. "It's so strange you can hear traffic; there's a lot of noise, but you can't see anything other than the sky," Maggie said.

"I know. Pretty amazing. And it's peaceful, don't you think?"

"Yes, it is." She looked into his eyes.

I really want to kiss him.

Bad idea.

"Antonio?"

"What is it, dear?"

"I have to tell you something, and don't be mad."

"What, you bought me a box of condoms?"

Maggie started laughing. "No, but Francis called again today. He says I can attend the fashion show and bring my dress designs along. I was thinking about the ones I brought and I should maybe make a few extras, since…well, it would be such an amazing opportunity." She paused. "It was quite thoughtful of him to invite me, don't you think?"

Antonio sat up straight. "Are you kidding me, Maggie? Trust me; he's up to no good."

"Maybe I could try to talk to him about the lawsuit and everything…and get him off your back."

"No, Maggie. Leave that to my attorney. You have a very narrow-minded view of Francis."

"What's that supposed to mean?"

"Exactly what I said! And you need to stay away from him."

"You don't understand, Antonio! I would *love* to go to this fashion show! I could start making dresses tonight! He has spare mannequins and Kensal can wear my designs. And I could see Cassandra! You should be happy for me—"

"Happy for you?" Antonio burst out laughing. "What a joke, Maggie! I have no idea what he's up to, but he's a filthy piece of trash and there's not a bin large enough to fit all of his baggage. Please, don't think I'm going to sit up on this rooftop, talking about him and… No, Maggie, you're not going to that!"

"Quit treating me like your child, Antonio. Perhaps we *should* have a child so that you can quit hovering over me and start worrying about someone else for a change! If I want to go, I'll go!"

"No, Maggie! You will *not* go! I will not have you keeping company with him—have you forgotten he tried to kiss you? Not to mention his ridiculous lawsuit is still pending. And now what? I'm just supposed to send you into his open arms?"

"It's not like that, Antonio! I want to start my own dress line! This is a starting point for me, don't you see? It's my dream! And all you can do is take the wind out of my sails!"

"Wind out of your—I bought you a sewing machine, Maggie! Didn't you see it? Enough of this! I'm going back now." Antonio got up. Maggie sat on the blanket, staring up at him.

"You are going back now? Why? You can't get your way, so we're done talking?"

"If that's how you see it," Antonio said stubbornly. He reached for her hand to pull her up.

"That is so not fair, Antonio! Why can't you understand?" she asked, as he lifted her to her feet.

Antonio brought her into his arms and held her tight, whispering with his lips inches from hers, "Why do you always want to fight with me, Maggie? I'd much rather make love than war."

Maggie stared into his dark eyes that held her captive as he kissed her on the lips.

"How's that for starters?" Antonio murmured.

Maggie looked at his lips, then closed her eyes.

I am going to the fashion show, whether he likes it or not!

Chapter 7

"I tried out my new sewing machine," Maggie said to Antonio. "What do you think of the dress I made?" She stood and did a pirouette. "It took me all day!"

She turned to look at him.

www.lovetheillusion.com/2208.htm

www.lovetheillusion.com/2210.htm

"I love it! That looks great on you." He nodded. She smiled back at him.

www.lovetheillusion.com/2209.htm

"Do you think it's edgy enough…unique enough?" she asked. "Does it make you look twice?

Antonio stared back at her. "I love it on you! So much that I want to take you out in it, right now!"

"You're not serious."

Please no.

"Yes, right now." He came and stood behind her, slowly running his hands up and down her hourglass figure. She leaned back against his chest as she heard him whisper in her ear: "Pick out the shoes to match and let's go!"

He can't be serious.

www.lovetheillusion.com/2211.htm

She turned around in his arms, facing him, suddenly realizing he *was* serious.

"Don't you have rehearsal tonight?" she asked. "I thought the dance team had practice."

"That's tomorrow night. Do you want to go or not?" Antonio caressed her as she stood in his arms, wearing the dress.

Maggie frowned, realizing the dress was for the fashion show, not dinner with Antonio. But as she stood in his arms, she realized she was more than happy to oblige. She quickly smiled at him, ignoring his efforts to drive her crazy, and soon she heard him say, "I just have to take a shower, then we can go…I will reserve a private room for us at the Carriage House. You have never been there and they have amazing food. Afterward we can stay overnight in one of the honeymoon suites with the giant Jacuzzi. You can bring your bathing suit."

Maggie bit her lip, unable to refuse. "Okay," she agreed.

I will have to be careful in this dress, not to spill… she came to a quick conclusion, while gazing up at Antonio.

AN HOUR LATER AT DINNER…

"Cheers!" Maggie held up her glass of wine and Antonio clinked his against hers.

"Here's to us. It's been a year since we met, and I'm still crazy about you."

"Me too." Maggie smiled at him, but then realized they had never finished discussing the birth control issue. She stared at Antonio, contemplating the dilemma.

Problem number one: He looks really hot in Armani Exchange. Problem number two: It's been over a week since we slept together.

Problem number three: I really want to kiss him. Problem number four: He will kiss me back. Problem number five: I just remembered I forgot my bathing suit!

Not good.

Hey girl! Everything will be fine, she told herself. *Just don't drink more than one glass of wine! And DON'T do anything to jeopardize the dress!*

She shifted her eyes away from Antonio, realizing she could not let him get to her. She turned her thoughts to the three dresses she had made in the last two days, trying to decide which one she liked the most:

www.lovetheillusion.com/2267.htm

Antonio had only seen the first. She could not risk the others.

"Maggie, what's on your mind…you seem distracted. Are you happy to be back in New York, or do you miss Italy?" Antonio asked.

"I miss your mamma and papa! But it's nice to be back here…where we met." She took a sip of wine. "Actually, I miss London, just a little."

"We could visit there on our way back to Italy, in the fall."

"That would be great—then I could see Dana. She will have the baby by then." Maggie's face suddenly grew sour.

"What's wrong? Are you jealous?" Antonio smirked.

"I don't even know if I want to see Dana right now," Maggie admitted.

"Really, why's that?"

"She sold information to the press!" Maggie waited for his reaction, but he just gave a quick look of surprise and then waited for her to continue. "I don't think she meant to, but either way, someone gave her several thousand pounds after they questioned her on her way through customs—about our plans to have a baby! Now it will be the next scandal, I'm sure…based on whatever she said or didn't say, leaving them to draw the worst conclusions." Maggie let out a sigh. "They'll be wondering whether I'm pregnant or not, and if I'm not, why."

"There you go! Now you can wait to see if your prediction is right! It can be so enlightening, the possibilities…" Antonio grinned at her.

"I hate thinking about it! I want them to know that we are happily married, but they will not do an article on that ever, right?"

"They could, but seriously, Maggie, you really have to keep your head out of the tabloids! You worry about what people think, but all you need to worry about is what *I* think, and I think I totally love you." He gave her his sweet look.

"You don't care about my reputation at all?"

"According to them, we deserve each other, right?" He laughed under his breath. "I seduced Nicolette until she finally had a child…and you are pursuing Kin—who's much younger than you, by the way— behind my back! I'm sure it's an amazing read. If they wrote the truth about us, the whole nation would fall asleep from absolute boredom!" He grinned at her. "Like I told you when we first met, I would be in my grave by now if I spent time worrying about it!"

Maggie nodded slowly.

"I promise, Maggie, it will get easier. You just need to grow thick skin around that delicate heart of yours. Toughen up, okay? And drink this wine with me!" Antonio eyes held hers.

"Don't look at me like that," Maggie said in alarm.

"Like what?" He suppressed a smile.

"You know, like you can't say what you are thinking and it better not be *that*... because I am still thinking about our discussion and have not reached a decision yet. But believe me, when I do, you will be the first to know!"

"So we are waiting to be together till then?" Antonio sighed. "You need to drink more wine."

"Forget it, Antonio. Your plan is not working. My dress stays on tonight and you can forget your wild ambitions!" She grinned at him.

"We'll see." He grinned back.

"You are such a troublemaker." She held her breath, trying not to breath in his cologne.

"I'm not trying to take advantage of you, I promise." He tried to keep from smiling.

"Yeah, right…if you didn't burn my pills, I would be trying to take advantage of you right now. But since you can't behave yourself, now I have to punish you."

"Such a harsh sentence!" He poured her more wine.

"I don't want any more of that. You can drink the rest," she said, taking the bottle from him and pouring the remainder into his glass.

"Another bottle?" the waitress asked after taking their order.

"Sure." Antonio tried not to laugh.

"No!" Maggie exclaimed as the waitress turned around at her command.

"Yes? No?" The waitress waited for their decision.

"One more…you can bring it now," Antonio said.

Maggie watched the waitress walk away. She then kicked Antonio's shin under the table. "Antonio! I am not having more than one glass. And you have drunk three glasses and now just ordered another bottle! You're going to be sleeping in the bathtub!"

"I am not going to be sleeping in the bathtub. I'll be sleeping naked, next to you!"

"Funny, real funny," she told him, realizing she had never seen him drunk before. Suddenly she felt flushed. *What am I going to do with him? I am in so much trouble. I hate this dress.*

AN HOUR LATER…

Maggie looked at the second empty bottle of wine, as she took a few more bites of her food.

"Good steak," Maggie said, staring at Antonio, wondering how drunk he was.

"And the wine is even better," he said, holding up his glass.

"You should know!" Maggie looked him over. "I can't believe you drank nearly two bottles of wine, Antonio."

"Time to get out your purse! You'll have to pay the bill because I think I am too drunk to find my wallet."

Maggie started laughing. "Oh, I can find it for you!"

"That won't be necessary. I was only kidding. Did you know the finer the wine, the less drunk you get. I'm better off than you think."

"Is that so?" Maggie said, amused.

"Are you disappointed?" He made eyes at her. "Because if you were getting ready to take advantage of me, I can pretend."

Maggie stared at him, trying to dodge his playful efforts.

"Should we go?" she finally asked.

"Yes! I can't wait to get in the hot tub." He reached for her hand.

So much for having only one glass of wine...

TEN MINUTES LATER...

"I can't go in. I forgot my suit," Maggie told him regretfully, as Antonio unlocked the room to their private getaway.

"You are going in, my dear, either with that dress and those shoes or naked!" Antonio teased as he picked her up, holding her in a cradle. "You decide!" He laughed as he walked over to the Jacuzzi and held her over it.

"No, Antonio, put me down! You are so drunk!" she told him.

"I am not. I'm completely alert, wanting to kiss you right now!" he told her as he walked them over to the bed. He dropped her onto the bed, landing on top of her.

"There! I threw you onto the bed instead of in the Jacuzzi! Are you happy now?" He trapped her beneath him.

"I am always happy with you," she said, succumbing to their

mutual attraction as his lips were within inches of hers.

"Don't worry; I'm not going to kiss you." He smiled at her. "I know better. It would be downhill from there."

He rolled off of her.

She looked over at him.

"So...you're...going to sleep now?"

"No... I am waiting patiently for you to take advantage of me! Then I don't have to feel guilty! The question is... Do you like rejection?"

"You can't reject me!" She met his challenge, moving on top of him. "Because I am going to drive you completely crazy!" Maggie looked at him, and then placed her lips on his.

"Making love is so hot if it comes with a risk, don't you think?" Antonio whispered as she kissed his neck.

This is so frightening. Why did I show him this dress? Dana is right; I might as well design maternity clothes for the both of us, name it after my mother, and then everyone is happy...

"Think about it. If you take that risk of getting pregnant, but deep down you aren't ready, it just goes to show that the passion is so hot that you can't resist it," Antonio explained, breaking her away from her thoughts as his fingers playfully ran along the seams of her dress while his other hand played with her hair.

"Did you forget the zipper?" he finally asked.

"What?"

"The zipper...in your dress! Where is it?"

"It's invisible," she told him. "See! I am at such an advantage because you drank so much that you can't find it!" She giggled.

"Believe me…you are at such an advantage *if* I find it! Where is it? You have to tell me." He continued his search.

"You're too drunk to find it…that's hilarious! Good thing you could at least find your wallet."

"You can have my wallet if you help me find the zipper. And why is there such a thing as an invisible zipper? For torture?"

"A dress looks better when you can't see the zipper!"

"But now you are like a present that I can't open." He let out a huff. "I'll have to rip it off." Antonio grabbed onto the spaghetti strap with his teeth after he ran his tongue across her chest.

"Don't you dare rip this dress, you and your two bottles of wine…" Maggie pushed him away.

"Fine…I will just…go to sleep now." He rolled off of her and stared up at the ceiling.

"Is that right? I feel…*so* bad for you!"

"I know…I am still a gentleman, even when drunk."

"I wish you weren't." She grabbed his hand and placed it on the zipper slider.

"Drunk?"

"No, silly, a gentleman." Maggie laughed.

"So are you inviting me *not* to respect your wishes?"

"I am." She grabbed hold of his shirt, pulling it out of his pants. She ran her hand across his chest and then…

"This is dangerous, Maggie. You will hate me tomorrow. I can't risk it."

"Risk it, Antonio. I totally want you," Maggie whispered with her lips on his.

“Okay, but don’t say I didn’t warn you,” he whispered back as he unzipped her dress.

THE NEXT MORNING…

“I don’t think it’s fair,” Maggie told Antonio while they sat in the hot tub together.

“What’s that?”

“Last night? Your method of seducing me to get what you want!”

“What are you talking about?” He smiled at her. “You were the sober one and I was just following your lead! Case closed!”

“Case opened, Antonio. I am going to the fashion show!” Maggie grinned at him.

“What does that have to do with anything?” He frowned.

“You always get what you want! That is what I want!”

“Does that mean you’re pregnant already?”

“I don’t know, but I’m not on the pill anymore!”

“Sorry I threw them into the fire.” He poured on the sweetness.

“Yeah, well they said I had to wait for my refill…not so easy the second time! The pharmacy tech said they needed the okay from my doctor, who was conveniently out of the office for two days! I just told them to forget it!”

“The second time?” he questioned her.

“I lost the first package when we were running through the forest trying to find Cheetos!”

“Really…” He quickly drew the connection. “Headache medicine…aren’t you clever.”

“Sorry...” She smiled at him.

"You look really good naked in the hot tub right now."

Maggie's jaw dropped. "That's not even funny, Antonio!"

"Sorry." He winked at her.

"You are *not* sorry!" Maggie shifted her eyes to the floor, where her dress lay in a crumpled heap. "And *that* was supposed to be displayed on a mannequin!"

"Yeah, I figured. That's why I took you to dinner in it instead! You make it very difficult to stay a step ahead of you, but I try, you know."

"Sorry." She winked back at him.

"You are not sorry either! You need to quit lying to me. You are a walking web of deception!"

"Fine! Then for starters, I am going to that fashion show and there is nothing you can do about it. And there are already four dresses hanging in my closet that look way better than the one you threw on the floor over there!"

"Then I'm coming with you," he said promptly.

Bad idea.

"Francis doesn't have a ticket for you."

"I can get in for free. I promise!" He sounded amused.

"Antonio! Why can't you just let me do this one thing! After that, I will have several leads and everything will take off from there!"

"I said you can go, but I am coming. See, we can compromise!"

"Compromise?" *Antonio and Francis together again? That is a horrendous compromise…*

"I promise to behave," he reassured her.

"Like that is even possible for you." Maggie still looked

concerned.

"That is my final offer, sweetheart!"

Great…

I may as well just issue my own "press release!"

The next day, Maggie sat diligently at her sewing machine, sewing the rest of the dresses she would bring along to the fashion show. She was now working on the last: a yellow satin dress with brown glitter tulle.

She was so excited, not only to be attending the fashion show, but also to have her designs on the runway. Last year, only two of her designs had been presented on mannequins, and that left her wishing for more. Now, for some strange reason, Francis seemed to want to reconnect with her and offer her a greater opportunity. His intentions were never clear; however, she could not refuse such a monumental spotlight.

She wondered what Francis had been up to in the past year. Being in New York brought back a few memories of them working together. They got along well, simply because Maggie was able to take on all of the gofer duties that he aimlessly tossed her way. She gracefully accepted the demeaning position, hoping it was a stepping stone on the route to eventual success. She could not help but wonder how her replacement had fared. And she looked forward to seeing Cassandra and the other models. *Were they still putting up with him?* Francis was exceptionally pompous, extremely demanding, and such a perfectionist that she was certain whoever took over her job was exhausted by now, mentally and physically. *Perhaps I'll meet her.*

The one saving grace, working for him, was that you could gather sympathy from the rest of the staff members. Francis was usually at the center of everyone's complaints.

Chapter 8

THE NIGHT OF THE FASHION SHOW…

"This could not be better!" Antonio exclaimed. "I just got word from Stanley that everything was settled out of court. Finally! And I only had to pay out twenty thousand dollars for stealing you away from Francis. I can't wait to see his ugly face!" Antonio stood in front of the mirror, adjusting his bowtie. "Do I look okay?"

www.lovetheillusion.com/2203.htm

"Yes, Antonio, you always look okay…" Maggie's voice was cautious.

"Just okay?" He sounded disappointed.

www.lovetheillusion.com/2217.htm

"As you always say: 'Trust me, you look amazing.'" She let go of a grin.

"That's better! Hopefully I have the best bowtie there. He suddenly got silly. "I have to look good when I see Francis!"

www.lovetheillusion.com/2214.htm

"I hope I don't regret this." Maggie made eyes at him.

"No worries!" He lightened the mood. "I promise to lie low…except for the limo and the bodyguards."

www.lovetheillusion.com/2236.htm

"Right, Antonio. I'm sure everyone will see you arriving…"

This is such a mistake.

TWO HOURS LATER…

“There they are, lined up with the cameras!” Maggie sat stiffly, peering through the dark glass of the limo. The street was closed off for security reasons, but people were lined up behind the tape.

“Antonio!” someone shouted as soon as he stepped out.

www.lovetheillusion.com/2240.htm

“Look! Antonio Deluca’s here!” Maggie heard the commotion as they made their way to the entrance.

“Over there!”

“It’s him!”

“Mr. Deluca!” someone called out from the press. “Can I get a photo of the two of you?”

“Don’t fight it, honey, just…smile pretty,” Antonio spoke under his breath.

“Right, I always forget,” Maggie responded with her teeth clenched into a smile.

www.lovetheillusion.com/2241.htm

"Uh, I can't believe I brought you," Maggie said, grabbing hold of his arm as the limo drove off behind them.

"Why would you say that, Maggie? You are part of my magic show, but I can't come to the fashion show? That's mean." Antonio frowned.

"Antonio! Look at the commotion you're causing, and we haven't even made it through the doors. You're nothing but a distraction. And wait til Francis sees you."

"I'm going to upset Francis?" Antonio faked a frown. "What a shame." He smiled.

www.lovetheillusion.com/2253.htm

Antonio held the door open for her. "After you, my dear."

Maggie rushed over to the front desk, as several security personnel stood in a group with Antonio. "I'm meeting Francis Louis. He said there'd be a pass waiting for me."

"Antonio! What a pleasure! Welcome! I assume you came along with Maggie. That is such an excellent surprise! You can have a seat next to her, in the front row."

"Passes for both of you," the gentleman at the welcome center informed them. "And here are a couple complimentary drink coupons."

"I'll take those," Maggie said, grabbing them out of his hand.

"Antonio! Oh my luck, it *is* you!" It was woman in a red suit, with blonde, permed, shoulder-length hair. "Someone said you were coming and—oh, so sorry if I was rude—my name is Chelsea Edwards. I am with Vera Hughes and we were wondering if you would be so kind as to walk our models down the aisle. It's all formalwear and you are obviously dressed for the occasion. I would just really love it if you could…*pleeease?*"

"I don't see why not." Antonio looked at Maggie, waiting for her approval.

"Go ahead!" *You might as well make yourself useful.* Maggie let out a sigh.

"All right, then come with me!" Chelsea took his arm and led the way.

"I'll meet up with you later," Maggie told Antonio as she watched them walk away.

"At the punch bowl?" Chelsea called out to her as she hung on Antonio's arm.

"Perfect!" Maggie smiled.

Easy to remember, because I would love to punch him right about now.

Maggie was making her way over to the fondue fountain when she spotted Francis. It was definitely strange to see him again. She crossed her fingers, hoping it would be a profitable night.

"Maggie, is that you? I barely recognize you now that you're living among the rich and famous." Francis stood, welcoming her.

"Well, I made my own dress, so I'm not sure what you could possibly mean."

"It looks great. I put in a few good words for you. Tessa Banks is here, and so is Gia Tellies. Did you bring your business cards?"

"I did! Thanks."

"Go ahead and set them on that table over there, and I'll show you where your three dresses are displayed."

"Uh…okay." Maggie looked over at the food table, where a group of models was hovering around Antonio. "It will be a long night," she told herself, hoping the excitement of his arrival would soon reach a plateau.

She followed Francis until she stood in front of her designs.

"There they are!" Maggie's eyes lit up.

www.lovetheillusion.com/2206.htm

www.lovetheillusion.com/2207.htm

www.lovetheillusion.com/2231.htm

"I used the 'Mine by Design' label," Francis explained. "I own the rights, but you can design under that label if you wish."

"Okay. Thanks, Francis."

Maggie got some food and then took a seat next to Francis.

"Now Maggie," Francis said, "you must know that Antonio got quite a steal on dragging you away from me, and I hope you take that as a compliment. I can't see how he thinks he can just marry you and off you go, leaving me hanging."

"Oh, I'm sure you're doing quite fine without me, Francis, but I do appreciate the compliment," Maggie said. "So did Cami come along? I was hoping to meet her."

"That replacement of yours is nothing but trouble. And no, I did not bring her! She shows up late every day for work, saying the bus either broke down or was running late, and she leaves early too, saying that her daughter left school with a flu when in fact there is no one on this planet who can be ill that often."

"That must be rough."

"*And* she takes lunch breaks that extend into the afternoon hours…and when she returns her hair's a completely different color! I need her to take over the teen dress designs, but she's so lazy she has yet to make even one!"

"Really?"

"But she constantly gives me advice on designing—as if I am even interested in her opinion. Now I've simply lost patience with her and was hoping that perhaps you could help me out."

"How's that?"

"You could ship me some of your teen designs, because I certainly don't have time for those. Several of my buyers still insist that they'd like to order those as well. Usually the margin's quite small and that's where you come in."

"You want me to work for small returns?"

"Let's face it, Maggie, you don't do your job for the money. Being married to Antonio, you must be in it for the fun, so that's how this works so beautifully! You'll earn a reputation for your designs, which eventually will grow into larger opportunities."

"I don't know…"

"I can send you fabrics…from Paris, Madrid, Dubai, Milan—wherever you want! And *you* can send *me* finished product. The ones they select, I'll send to layout and design so that we can make patterns and then they can get mass produced. What do you think?"

"It sounds okay, but I'd rather work with the buyers directly myself."

"That would be a disappointment. They're all so demanding: 'We want that dress, but in a different color'; 'Can you rush that order as soon as possible?' They always strive to give me that malicious headache and believe me, you're way better off not even dealing with them."

"Really?"

"Absolutely. My latest encounter was a buyer from France! She wanted a rainbow assortment of long, flowing gowns that I insisted only looked dazzling in peach! She wanted gowns in black and red and possibly teal. I should have said 'No!—it would be a horrible sight in those colors!' But instead I followed her suggestion. After I had made them all she realized my added attempts were simply in vain because I had already created that dress in the best possible hue—a perfect blushing peach, soft, romantic, and breathtaking."

Maggie sat annoyed, as Francis continued. "Now, had she requested the original, shipped in a large quantity to begin with, we would have been at the end result right away! So what do you think?"

"Well, maybe I could send one or two, but I had hoped to have my own label and perhaps start a dress line in memory of my mother."

"Nonsense! Such a waste of time. Who will ever recognize your mother when they purchase your dresses? And as for labels, how would you choose?"

"I thought—"

"I have five labels now, all of which my wonderful R&D team

took months to come up with. Everything sounded too this or too that…finding that perfect-sounding label takes a lot of thought and patience. Now I have the 'Louis Dress' label—which was my first and favorite—'Magnetic Threads,' which is my latest, and the 'Party Dress' line, which I put you in charge of and that Cami has done absolutely nothing with…'Melodic Evenings,' inspired by the earlier fashion eras, and 'Enchanted Knights'—that has a British flavor—but you know that I started out with just one: the 'Louis Label'" He paused as Maggie discreetly rolled her eyes. "I believe it is *that* label—with *my* name alone—that started my string of successes! I can't tell you how rewarding that is! And who would have ever known? It is hard to even think back to the time when 'Louis' was insignificant!"

"Antonio thinks I should use the slogan 'For a Magical Night Out.' What do you think?"

"Slogans? That's a whole new concern. My biggest is 'Imagine Yourself in a Dress by Louis'—probably my favorite. I also have 'A Knight Enchanted…' with the beautiful lady wearing my dress, sitting on a white horse next to her knight. And I have 'Let Music Play for You' for my 'Melodic Evenings' label…"

"I remember seeing that in a fashion magazine…where the lady is on the piano. Very memorable."

"'A Magical Night Out,' though…that's nonsense. Too simple, and I am quite shocked that Antonio has now taken an interest in fashion. I was even more surprised to see him here tonight. But what a pleasure it is; now I'll have to speak with him, later," Francis said.

"Is that a good idea?" Maggie pictured the two of them together.

"Oh, everything's fine. Speaking of Antonio, where is he?"

"He got hauled off to walk models down the runway for Vera Hughes." Maggie let out a huff. "Figures…I'm sure he's in good company."

"Vera Hughes? Is that right? They have some of the top models on the runway. But I try to cut corners on that because I would rather have people looking at the stunning dress rather than at all the faces of the top models out there who love to charge ridiculous fees! Ha! Now, imagine that! They have yet another outlandish choice, which is definitely in my favor! They are putting that charming husband of yours on the runway! Foolish marketing plan if you ask me—no one will ever even have a chance to notice their designs—but you have to admire them for trying something new."

"I suppose," Maggie said.

"Ladies and gentlemen!" came the announcer's voice. "Please find your seats as this year's spring fashion show takes place right before your very eyes. Get ready to drop your jaw at the latest designs from top designers all…over…the…world!"

Music followed the announcement and Maggie sat still next to Francis, wondering where Antonio was. *He is such a brat.*

"First up, we have designs from Francis Louis, top European designer, located in the UK…"

Maggie sat up straight, waiting anxiously for her designs to appear.

"I paid top dollar for the first-time slot," Francis let Maggie know, "and I have the most time as well. And Miranda is wearing your designs, not Kensal. They fit her better."

"Thanks so much for letting me present, Francis. It's so generous of you."

"Well, I miss our time together. Believe it or not, all the models quit except for Kensal. She really is a dear, but off the rest of them go to make more money with a different designer, never stopping to realize that if it weren't for my name on their resume, they would be waiting tables somewhere."

"Why did they leave?" Maggie asked, even though she knew the answer.

"Latasha had an offer from Shark Daze—some swimsuit company—wanting her to shoot in the Caribbean—who wouldn't want that life? And Cassandra moved to Germany to be with her family. Loyalty is pretty much dead these days, but wait until you see Milly and Miranda—my newbies. Such a sight on the runway. They are young, but very fine."

"So you're down to three models now instead of four?"

"That's right. They have to change so quickly! But my opinion? They are quite fortunate. Several designers here tonight have only brought two! Of course that means we will have seen plenty of the dress by the time they are ready to exit.... Apparently they are unaware that it's best to give the viewer a quick glance as opposed to 'Okay, I'm getting bored already.'"

"And now, presenting...Francis Louis..."

www.lovetheillusion.com/2256.htm

"This next designer is a joke! Nothing but outrageous disasters." Francis spoke over the music. "They come every year, and why, I have no idea. Who would step out of the house in their eyesores? I patiently wait for the music to switch to the sound of…a death march, perhaps." Francis laughed under his breath. "They are worlds away from competing with me! Although they manage to find gorgeous models…so nice we have *something* to look at."

Maggie watched the presentations, thinking they were actually somewhat interesting. She decided she liked them all!

www.lovetheillusion.com/2255.htm

After all, designing was an art form. What one person liked another did not, and so that was always the challenge: to make something that everyone agreed was simply amazing! Perhaps that was why Francis was at the top; he liked to design the classics—designs that were of an older style, yet modernized.

Maggie suddenly felt small. It was hard to stand out in such a demanding world. And although Francis was right, she did not need the money, Maggie was motivated for other reasons. She needed something to do in NYC while Antonio was busy with his performances. Even though she participated as his lady in the ring of fire, she did not need to be at the rehearsals. Occasionally she would come just for fun, but she needed to divert her attention to something that she personally enjoyed. And designing was her outlet. Now she would also spend her days learning Italian, so that when they returned in the fall, she would be able to get around better. Antonio had tried to help her, but it was obvious he just assumed he would be taking care of her in her helpless state. The next time she would surprise him and not be so helpless.

"Hey!" Francis whispered to her as the fashion show continued. "Our Manhattan boat cruise will be just fabulous, don't you think? A cocktail party on the river, while we watch the awards…I can hardly wait! There are three awards for 'Most Original.'"

"That is exciting…" Maggie was certain he would get one.

"Awards are such a wonderful addition to the show. I have plenty of them, but you never tire of adding to your collection! As you know, my office space is full of them, and soon I will need an additional wall."

"Really…"

"Speaking of space, I could use Cami's office if I can replace her with you, because you would work from home. See how this is so beneficial to the both of us? You need that flexibility, with Antonio's lifestyle, and I need more room! But for now, I need to talk to Gia Tellies. She is here tonight and is a *huge* international buyer for the celebrities. She can get your designs anywhere! And in the top-notch boutiques of the rich and famous in Hollywood! That is exactly where you want to be! You can set your own prices, which can be completely outlandish, because those famous people have a ton of money!"

"Well, you obviously don't need Gia's help to get your designs on the celebrities."

"I know, but I am interested in her for other reasons."

"Francis, I think she's half your age! Be realistic! She could probably get any guy she wanted."

"Maggie, age is nothing! It's all about power. Look at all the women who would chase your husband if he wasn't already married to you." Francis' "whisper" became a bit louder. "Now I have the envy of all the designers here, and she is well aware of who I am! I will speak with her tonight." He laughed under his breath. "But Maggie, you always amaze me with your innocent mind."

Maggie gave a half smile and shook her head.

Just like old times. He hasn't changed a bit.

Her eyes suddenly lit up as she saw Antonio coming out on stage for the first time "in her world." A dark-haired model with baby-blue eyes was the first to accompany him. Maggie watched impatiently as the model held on to his arm and strutted down the runway. She wore a colorful dress made of thick poly knit and a variety of bold bright shades.

www.lovetheillusion.com/2279.htm

So lovely...to share him. Maggie slumped in her chair as the crowd went crazy, calling out his name. She was certain that one of Francis' predictions had become a reality: no one was paying any attention to the dress designs. They were all focused on Antonio.

So annoying...

She watched ten minutes of fabulous displays, all worn by gorgeous models who hung on Antonio's arm as they made their way down the aisle.

He should have stayed home, she finally decided as she watched impatiently for it to be over. The show concluded with two models on Antonio's arm, each kissing his cheek as they stood at the end of the runway. She bit her lip, wondering how long she could remain a "good sport."

Antonio soon nodded at Maggie, making his way over to sit in a chair next to her. She forced a smile to camouflage what she was really thinking—realizing none of it was really his fault.

After all, he had come along to protect her from Francis, which she was pretty certain was a waste of time. Outside of his ridiculous lawsuit, she was still uncertain as to why Antonio despised Francis so much. Yes, Francis had tried to kiss her, but surely Antonio was well aware that Francis was no threat to their marriage.

Now the fashion show had come to an end, and soon everyone would be headed to the cruise ship where they would enjoy cocktails and wait for the announcement of the awards.

Maggie was sure that Francis would be receiving one of the awards—as was he. Though his ego could be tiresome, she could not help but admire his determination and wondered if it was the key to his success. *What specifically brought success? Was it hard work and determination, self-confidence, passion, or a combination of them all?* For a moment, she felt privileged that he insisted on taking her under his wing. If only she could convince Antonio to let her walk in his shadow until she made it big on her own. But Antonio had a mind of his own, and he assumed he was right about everything. Francis was not part of his equation that he felt would lead her to success. Maggie had always carried a weight of pessimism with her—she was eager, yet overwhelmed by everything—but Francis seemed to be that guiding light to keep her positive and focused. Since she had quit working for him, she had been so busy spending time with Antonio that she had no time to even think about her career. And since they had been married, Antonio thought about having a family. But now that Antonio was busy with work again, it only seemed right for her to resume her own ambitions.

"Ladies and gentlemen, we hope you like what you saw tonight! And now…the cruise ship waits! Get ready for an amazing tour of the city, all lit up at night, as we serve you cocktails and hors d'oeuvres while you anticipate this evening's results! Get ready for an unforgettable night."

Maggie got up, bracing herself in her high heels while holding on to Antonio's arm. Finally, he was hers again. They followed the crowd of people who all seemed to know which direction to head for the next event. And on their way out, she admired a fashion display ad belonging to Francis.

www.lovetheillusion.com/2270.htm

Aboard the ship it was colder, and Maggie slipped on a white sweater. Antonio noticed she still shivered, even with the sweater, and he took off his suit coat, placing it around her shoulders. She smiled at him as he held her hand in his.

"Look at you," Antonio said, admiring Maggie. "My lady in red. What do you want to drink before you accept your award?"

"Oh, I don't know—just a rum and Coke," she laughed, as she considered. "I highly doubt there is any award waiting for me—other than that you are no longer flocking with the beautiful models," she said stiffly.

"No worries. Trust me, Maggie. You will get one. Wait and see. Your dresses on the runway were amazing and those beaded dresses on the mannequin…I am sure that everyone noticed those dresses!"

"You're sweet, but I am guessing that Francis will get one

instead! He has been around for years. No one even knows who I am, other than your wife."

"We'll see."

"I'm just celebrating that right now I'm the only woman on your arm."

"There's no competition for you; you should know that by now."

"You're sweet."

"I mean it." He squeezed her hand.

She followed on his arm as he ordered their drinks, and soon she couldn't help but be glad that he was along.

"If I could have everyone's attention please!" a gentleman in a Barbour trench coat spoke into the microphone beside the bar. "It is now time for the awards! And it is wonderful to see such a successful turnout for this event. This year marks our tenth anniversary, and to celebrate that we have extended the evening with champagne and awards on a cruise. You can visit the bar now for a glass of champagne, compliments of 'the House of Blues.' And now! First up, we have Enrique Fajardo from Barcelona, an international buyer known for selecting garments made with unique texture and from the finest fabrics."

Enrique came to the microphone. "It was an amazing night. I have never been so impressed by all the fashion designs as I was tonight. I am thrilled to have been able to see everything first hand and am also so honored to have been selected to offer my choice for award for 'Most Original Design.' It was a tough decision, but I am pleased to announce that I have chosen Francis Louis as my top pick! I love all of his fashions, and I believe that they are so unique and timeless; a perfect blend of the old and the new."

The crowd cheered loudly and Francis waved his hand in the air. He was enjoying every minute.

The MC took over again. "Next up, we have Kellie Landers, who is a native of the Bronx and an expert in what the customer loves to buy…Kellie?" He handed her the mic.

"Good evening, everyone! I am so honored to be selected, and like Enrique said, it is so tough to make a decision, but I am going to ask you to give it up for 'Prenella,' for not only having the most amazing models, but for having such a hot guy walk them down the runway! I loved all of their fashion designs…they were definitely original! Cheers to that effort, and have a blast everyone!" She handed him the microphone as if her comments were unnecessary, while Maggie glanced up at Antonio.

"And last but not least, we have, from LA, Gia Tellies, who has been in the fashion industry for over ten years now, gracing us with her lovely presence since the first event here in New York City. She is now a buyer for many of the stores in Hollywood, California, and she has left the warm sunshine to be with us here. She is well known for selecting the preferences of the rich and famous, so hats off to someone who knows the business well and owns the respect of buyers and designers everywhere!"

Gia took over the microphone. "Hey, everyone! I am thrilled to be a part of such a fabulous evening and I know you don't want to listen to me rant and rave about what you all witnessed with your own eyes so, short and to the point, I would love to nominate Francis Louis' partner in crime—" she laughed—"Maggie White! You may have made a hit in Vegas, but you also made a hit in the fashion world today with that plum metallic that you designed. It was a breathtaking sight! I would love to wear that dress myself before it makes its way into any of the specialty shops! I have a vision to find someone to design one-of-a-kind dresses that would never be duplicated, and I think Maggie would be my top pick!"

Maggie's jaw dropped and she looked up at Antonio. "I can't believe she noticed my dress!"

"And now…Cheers to those who won, and to the rest of us who just want to celebrate a beautiful night on the river. We still have an hour left to party, so don't let any time go to waste. In just a half hour, we will hear from the three winners. After a few cocktails, I decided it would be only fair to give the three of you a few minutes to gather your thoughts on what inspires your designs that we have chosen tonight!"

"See! I told you." Antonio smiled at her while embracing her in a hug. "Looks like you got recognized—and by Gia Tellies of all people! She's at the top, Maggie! You can do whatever you want now!"

"It's amazing," Maggie said slowly, in disbelief. "I still just can't believe it. I wonder if I really deserve her recognition—I mean, there were so many dresses on display. I am so flattered that she noticed mine!" Maggie's face suddenly shone even brighter. "You know what this means? I don't have to work for Francis! I can do fine without him, don't you think?"

"Absolutely! I have a ton of faith in you. You just need to have a little in yourself," Antonio told her. "You never listen to me. But trust me, soon your fashion designs will be all over the world."

"This is so exciting! I feel like someone needs to pinch me, so that I realize this is not some crazy dream." She looked up at Antonio, who smiled sweetly at her. She remembered meeting him, just a year ago, and thought about how much her life had changed since then, for the better. "I'm so lucky," Maggie finally admitted. "But I am even luckier to have you."

"It's a good feeling," he admitted.

"Cheers!" Francis interrupted, handing Maggie a glass of champagne. "And congrats!"

"Oh, thanks Francis!" Maggie took the glass from him. "Congratulations to you too… It's a perfect night for both of us!"

"That could not be further from the truth!" Francis said, "I wanted recognition from Gia, not Enrique… She's so spicy hot. Now I will have to use your connection to get to her!"

Maggie noticed Antonio was giving Francis the evil eye. She elbowed him, hoping they could be on friendly terms. "I owe it all to you, Francis, really I do." Maggie took a sip of her champagne. "And I would be happy to introduce you to her."

"Just remember, Maggie, you are young. You still can use my suggestions on occasion, and I think it would be beneficial to both of us to keep in touch."

"Forget it, Louis," Antonio said. "Maggie's bright enough to design on her own, without you, and tonight's the proof. So, you can say your goodbyes after tonight!"

"The lawsuit is over, I think we should call a truce," Francis held his head high. "Let's not burn bridges."

"But it's so tempting when *you* are standing on the bridge!" Antonio still gave him an evil eye.

"Stop, you two! This is a fabulous evening. Why ruin it? Let's bury the hatchet and move on." She held up her glass to make a toast. Their three glasses met, but Antonio refused to smile while Francis still wore a grin.

Maggie finished her champagne quickly, hoping it would take effect and relax her enough so that she could speak in front of everyone in just a few minutes. Then her eyes widened. "I have no idea what to say!" she told them. "I hate being in front of big groups of people, and now I have to do a speech."

"Just smile and... You look beautiful." Antonio smiled at her, attempting to bolster her confidence.

"Maggie!" Francis cut in. "It's all about knowing your audience. The people out there watching you already know you're superior to them. You won, they didn't! Hold your head high and look 'em in the eyes, knowing they wish they were you!"

"Listen to you, Louis!" Antonio said. "You prideful son-of-a-bitch! No one has anything in life, whether it's money, fame, or acknowledgement, without the support of others! It's those people who are the true heroes! My fans are my heroes! If they didn't love to watch magic, I'd be playing hockey."

"Stop! Antonio…just don't…" She brought her hand to his lips, hoping to silence him. "Just…let's have a peaceful moment between the two of you. Can you just do that for me, *pleeease?*"

"Maggie, you have so much faith in that husband of yours, but I'll tell ya, he's the last one to tell me how to behave."

"Ladies and gentlemen, it is now time! Grab your cocktail and circle round our winners as they enlighten us with what makes them passionate about what they do."

"I'm going to talk about my mother," Maggie told Antonio. "She's my inspiration." Maggie handed her empty glass to him.

"First up, recognized by Enrique for 'Most Original Design,' is Francis Louis!"

Maggie watched as Francis walked quickly to the front and took hold of the mic. "This is another award I will treasure," he said. "And I must tell you that for me, my drive to design comes from within. It is always a delight to surpass what I have created in the past. Occasionally I will even wake in the middle of the night with an idea that has to come out! And that's when I realize that I have been inspired to create and share with the world an entirely new design. I crawl out of bed and start sketching! And perfection—that is the key. A design is never finished, as long as it can be improved. Perfection takes time, careful consideration, until finally you feel confident to let go, knowing that it is indeed unsurpassable! I design with immense attention to detail, and I believe it is that attention that has brought me success." He paused briefly. "Thank you. Oh! And one more word of advice. You always must remember, as you are striving to be at the top: It is a tall mountain that you must climb very rigorously, never looking back, and remove any obstacles that lie in the path of your success. It can be very trying at times. Friends become enemies and enemies become friends, but in the end…you have what you have been waiting for!" Francis handed the microphone back to the MC.

"He's somethin' else," Antonio said, shaking his head.

"And next, we'll hear from Prenella…"

Maggie watched as a man and woman made their way to the front. Cassidy, a redheaded woman wearing a royal-blue lace cocktail dress, took hold of the mic, while the man—who looked sharp in a lemon sweater, pinstriped dress shirt, and thin black tie—stood next to her and smiled at the audience.

"Thank you for this award! We are thrilled to receive an award for the first time ever! It is always a challenge to design something that looks original without landing in the category as simply weird! So, we are pleased to accept this award, and my personal inspiration comes from all those people out there who love fashion and dare to be different! You all rock!" She handed the microphone back to the MC.

"I don't feel well," Maggie told Antonio.

"And next up, right out of the nest of Francis Louis, we have Maggie White!"

"It's just stage fright," Antonio told her. "Ignore the audience, look at me, and you'll be fine."

"No, Antonio, I won't. I hate being in front of people and now I am seriously sick. I don't think I can do this."

"Trust me." Antonio held her arms and looked into her face. "I will be wearing a huge smile and it will melt all your fears away, I promise."

Maggie looked at Antonio as he let go of her arms, motioning for her to go up.

"Where…is…Maggie?" The MC called, scanning the audience.

"Go on, you'll be fine." Antonio nodded to reassure her as he stood next to Francis, who seemed amused by her stage fright.

Maggie held the microphone with both hands. She stared into the sea of faces, thinking that everyone appeared blurry. *I think I am dizzy.* She quickly wore a smile. "I…think….thank Mom…eh…my moooomma…sh…uh…inspired me…and…ah…my mom…thanks to…" Maggie paused, realizing her words were slurring. "Just ma…ma…my…mooooom…" Maggie suddenly dropped the microphone onto the floor.

"Quick! Someone help her. She's had too much to drink!" someone called out.

Antonio rushed up to grab to her, while she hobbled off of the platform.

"What's wrong?" Antonio looked worried as he held on to her.

Help me.

"I can't…I don't know…I feel…ah… sick…" Maggie slurred. Antonio suddenly realized she was hallucinating.

"Oh, no, honey!" he said in a panic. "You look delirious…Are you okay?

"How much did she have, Antonio?" Francis wore a grin. "She can't even handle her liquor?"

Antonio suddenly looked alarmed. "Only two, Louis…" He noticed Francis still wore a grin. Antonio's face grew angry, as he quickly drew his conclusion: "You worthless piece of—what did you put in her drink? I'm gonna kick your ass—you good for nothing—piece of shit!" Antonio grabbed hold of him by the shirt and forced him through the crowded boat. "You're gonna pay for this!" Antonio spoke with his teeth clenched, while slamming him into the guard rail of the boat.

For the first time, Francis appeared shocked by Antonio, as he watched his temper unleashed before his eyes. "What are you talking about?" Francis said.

"You drugged her, and you know it!" Antonio shouted at him.

Maggie watched in a dizzy fog, slowly shaking her head but frozen to her surroundings. The next thing she knew, Francis was struggling to get away from Antonio, but Antonio punched him in the face. Francis' glasses flew off, and now the crowd was gasping at the commotion. Francis started wrestling with Antonio, but Antonio leaned into him, and hurled him across the rail.

Where did he go?

"Man overboard!" she heard someone scream. She made her way over to the rail, next to Antonio. Below them, Francis was treading water next to the boat.

"Francis!" Maggie shouted as she stared down into the water, her vision still misty. "Antonio!" She turned to him. "What did you do?"

"He tainted your drink!" Antonio held onto her. "Are you okay?"

"I feel dizzing and sick…eh, really sick…nooowooooah…" she mumbled, losing her balance and grabbing Antonio's arm for support.

"Dizzing?" Antonio echoed, looking at Maggie in concern. "Look at you. You are messed up."

Antonio then looked into the water at Francis, shouting at him, "I hope you drown, you bastard!"

Now the sound of sirens was getting louder. Antonio cradled Maggie in his arms while Francis paddled viciously to make his way to the pier, where a couple of guys were lending their hands to assist him out of the cold, mucky water. They braced him as he pulled himself onto the dock, until he was finally kneeling on all fours, drenched, dripping wet in his custom tailored suit from Pendleton.

Two officers approached the scene, along with a paramedic team that ushered Francis into their care. He was shivering uncontrollably.

"I need a statement from you." One of the officers approached Antonio. "Follow me," he said.

Outside the franchise that offered the boat tours, the officer questioned Antonio.

"You want to tell me what happened?"

"I punched his stupid ass off the boat," Antonio admitted.

"Do you want to tell me why you would do such a thing?"

"He deserved it!"

The officer managed a laugh, but then turned serious. "Look, I know *exactly* who you are, and just because you are a celebrity doesn't give you any right to push a man off a boat, for any reason."

"He drugged my wife!" Antonio finally blurted out.

Another officer approached the scene. "You, miss, come with me…"

"She's not going anywhere without me." Antonio spoke for her. "Believe me, this whole scene is not what it appears, and I can tell you the truth: Francis Louis got what he deserved. And I am proud to bring him to justice!"

"Sir, uh…Mr. DeLuca," the officer said condescendingly, "you might want to change your story into at least an accident, following a brawl, unless you want to face charges for attempted manslaughter."

"That's exactly right! I wanna kill 'em!" Antonio spoke above the law.

"You will have to come back to the station with me, so I can formalize your statement."

Maggie watched as the officer put Antonio in handcuffs, removed his wallet, and then led the two of them to his parked car.

Great…from the limo to the back of a squad car.

Chapter 9

Maggie sat quietly in the back of the squad car, staring at the bars that separated them from the officer. Her head still in a fog, she suddenly realized that Antonio had a show the following evening and now it looked as though he would have to cancel it.

After a few minutes the squad car stopped in front of the police station.

"Get out!" The officer stood at the door, waiting for the two of them to exit the squad car. *We are in so much trouble,* Maggie thought as she crawled out, stepping carefully in her heels. She wanted to grab Antonio's hand, but his hands were cuffed together behind his back.

The officer led the two of them into the police station, where they followed him down a cold dark hall until they arrived at an empty room where they would proceed with the questioning.

"Have a seat." The officer's voice was void of sympathy.

Maggie looked at Antonio, thinking perhaps her vision was becoming less misty, but she was still sick to her stomach. She placed her hand on it, hoping to gather some sympathy.

"Give me your names, beginning with your last name, and spell them please." The officer held a pen over a paper.

Maggie stared at the clock on the wall that seemed to represent a moment of tragedy for them as they endured a whole new adventure—one that would undoubtedly be unpleasant.

"DeLuca, D-E- capital L-U-C-A," Antonio began. "Antonio, A-N—"

"That's good. Now who is this?" He nodded at Maggie.

"That's my wife, Maggie. M-A…"

"Okay." The officer set his pen down, recognizing them. "She has the same last name…?" He placed his chin in his hand, somewhat amused. "So, you want to tell me what happened?" The officer sat across from them, trying to look professional. It was the first time he had ever arrested a celebrity. "You first," he said, looking at Maggie.

Maggie swallowed a lump in her throat that would not dissolve. She looked at Antonio, wishing he would talk for both of them, but the officer was staring at her. She cleared her throat.

"After the fashion show, we were on a cruise boat," Maggie started to explain, "and Francis gave me a glass of champagne. The next thing I knew, my head was spinning and everything looked blurry. When I got up to do my speech…I was having trouble speaking…my words were blurry." Maggie spoke clearly, thinking it was strange that she felt better aside from her stomach ache.

"You mean your words were slurred?"

"Yes," Maggie said timidly.

"You feel okay now?" The officer looked confused.

"Better, but I still have a huge stomach ache and a headache, and I think I might be sick."

The officer suddenly looked concerned and picked up his pager, "Yes, it's Officer Pangolin…I need some assistance. We need a blood draw, urine sample, and complete physical done on a woman who claims she was a victim of drug abuse."

"No!" Maggie objected. "I don't want all that. I feel fine," she let him know.

"Trust me, Maggie, you need to do what they say." Antonio spoke in a whisper, his teeth clenched.

The next thing she knew, an officer was speaking to her from the doorway: "You, ma'am, come with me."

Maggie stood up slowly, wishing she could curl into a ball and die.

I can't believe this is happening.

She heard the officer continue to question Antonio on her way out. "So, she drank a glass of champagne that you believe had a toxic substance in it, and then what?"

Antonio squirmed with his hands still cuffed behind his back. "I know Louis did it! She was fine before he gave her that glass of champagne and she only had two drinks so she wasn't drunk. That bastard tried suing me after I married her and now he's just out for some sick twisted revenge."

"I see…" the officer said.

Antonio went on: "Maggie looked ridiculous up there, trying to give her acceptance speech, all according to *his* plan to make her look *completely* incapable of making any decisions on her own, much less designing a dress for someone to wear!"

"And why would he want to do this?" The officer said, confused.

"He wants her trapped, working for him! But she is talented, able to succeed without him! I think he's afraid of the competition!" Antonio defended her.

The officer sat silent for a minute after writing down notes. Then he said, "I'm going to have to write you up for..." He paused to consider, and then shook his head as if he was letting him off easy—"for...disorderly conduct for now," he finally concluded. "And hopefully the results from the lab will verify what you have told me...otherwise it could be ugly: attempted manslaughter. Francis Louis, is that his name?"

"Yes."

"If he is guilty, then he will face his own charges. For now, I have to detain you overnight; bond is set at a hundred thousand dollars, and you can make one phone call tomorrow afternoon, when our staff is back in."

"What!" Antonio said in outrage. "I am not the criminal here! I was defending my wife! You should have been there! It was ridiculous! I don't even think she could see straight, much less speak!" Antonio wrestled with his handcuffs until they unsnapped. He stood and held them up in front of the officer.

The officer dropped his jaw while opening his eyes wide. "You...how did you..."

"You forgot about my profession." Antonio scowled at him as the officer stood. "But don't worry, I won't charge you for watching." Antonio tried to conceal a smirk. The officer looked dumbfounded; obviously he had never seen a trick like that before. "Like I said," Antonio explained, glaring at him, "*I* am not the criminal here. You can put those on Louis!" Antonio dropped the handcuffs on the table in front of the officer and started to walk away.

"And like *I* said—" the officer grabbed hold of Antonio, wedging his arms behind his back again and forcing him to walk towards his cell—"we will make a final decision on your terms and condition, *after* the results are back. As for now, you can add 'attempting to resist arrest' to the list." The officer grew curt, as if he had his hands full.

Several hours later, Maggie was finally done with the tests after spending several hours at a medical facility. "I will drive you back," the officer told her. "Where do you stay?"

"At the hotel on…" Maggie paused, before announcing, "I am not going back without Antonio."

"Ma'am, you need to tell me where you are staying. Where do you live? At a hotel?"

"I am not telling you where!" Maggie spoke sternly. "I'm *not* going back without Antonio," she repeated.

The officer made a call on his phone while she stood next to the squad car that was now parked outside the medical facility.

She fearfully listened as he announced: "I got directions. I know exactly where you live. Follow me."

She trudged behind him, longing to be with Antonio.

"What is happening to Antonio?" Maggie asked. "Why can't he come back with me?"

"He is being detained for attempted manslaughter. If what he says is true—we will know when the test results are back—then perhaps just disorderly conduct."

"Oh, no…" Maggie said softly, hoping Antonio was right, and that Francis had drugged her.

She sat quietly in the back of the police car as a tear rolled down her cheek. She did not know how she would spend the night without him, much less months and years should they determine he was guilty. Maggie's heart sank at the possibilities as she wiped her tears off her cheeks.

Then she heard the officer say: "Here you are. We will let you know when the results are back. For now, try to get some rest."

Maggie reached for the door handle, realizing it was three in the morning.

"I can't believe the guy lives in a hotel." She heard him mumble under his breath as she got out of his vehicle.

She walked quickly into the private rear entrance, relieved that there were no reporters swarming the premises yet. She ran to the elevator, and soon was on the fourth floor.

"Maggie! Maggie! What happened? We saw the breaking news on TV…is it true that Antonio went to jail?" Maggie saw Amber and Angie running toward her as soon as she stepped off the elevator.

"It's a nightmare…the whole event. He should have never come…"

"Oh, no…then it's true?"

"Yes. Francis drugged my glass of champagne and when I got up to do my acceptance speech, I could barely speak. That's when Antonio lost it! He slammed him into the guardrail on the boat, and the next thing I knew, Francis was 'man overboard!' Now Antonio's in jail."

"That's not what they're saying on the news…" Angie let her know.

"Yeah," Amber explained, "they said that 'After a night of too much champagne, Antonio settled the lawsuit out of court.'"

"What? Antonio could care less about the settlement. He was happy it was over with. And for only twenty thousand dollars," Maggie told them.

"So now what?" Amber asked.

"I don't know… This is just so humiliating," Maggie said. "Antonio looks like the bad guy when in fact Francis should have 'douche' tattooed on his forehead!"

"This is terrible! Is he even going to be back for our performance? It would be our first cancellation, ever…" Amber contemplated the possibilities.

"Hopefully the results will be back soon," Maggie said. "I had to go through a complete physical and it was mortifying. A male doctor checking me over for any signs of abuse, and it was just ridiculous. I felt like I was double-victimized! And Antonio told me I had to get tested, obviously to save him, or there was no proof. At least that is over with, but now Antonio is in jail and it's killing me to think of him in there."

"I hope everything works out," Amber said, overwhelmed. "When will the results be back?"

"Who knows? I could just scream right now, and I hate Francis. He is such a jerk! And everything Antonio says about him is so true! Why can't he just leave us alone?"

"I hope Antonio is right about him tainting your drink. How will they ever prove he did it?"

"I don't know…" Maggie shook her head. "I have to go," she told them. "It's been a long night."

Hours passed. Maggie lay in bed, wide awake. She thought of Antonio in his jail cell. He did not belong there, she was certain. But when would the truth be told? Now she wondered how long she would have to be without him and she broke out into a sweat. She thought she was running a fever, and it felt as if the room was spinning while she shook from her chills. Her nerves were frazzled, she hadn't slept, and now it was noon the next day. The shades were drawn; the room was dark as she lay on the bed, wishing it would all go away. She longed to be back in Italy. She closed her eyes, desperate to recall those perfect moments…

The flowers that Antonio would always leave around the house for her to discover….

www.lovetheillusion.com/2249.htm

www.lovetheillusion.com/2242.htm

www.lovetheillusion.com/2276.htm

The grocery store where she went when she wanted to make him a special dinner…

www.lovetheillusion.com/2213.htm

The bench where they would sit to have their morning coffee…

www.lovetheillusion.com/2223.htm

And the fabric store she fell in love with, where Antonio had set up an account so that she could get anything she wanted. The tapestries there were so incredible and she would spend hours picking and choosing fabrics to sew dresses for the dolls that she had collected over the years.

www.lovetheillusion.com/2205.htm

Maggie felt bad for denying Antonio the opportunity of being a father, and now she wondered if he would ever have that chance. If the test came back clear, that there were no drugs in her system, it would appear as a huge lie on Antonio's part and he would have to go to trial. Life would never be the same. Maggie tried to still her trembling body. She picked up the photo of them dancing at the benefit, recalling their perfect moment of dancing together, wishing she was in his arms.

www.lovetheillusion.com/2283.htm

He wanted a family so badly, and since they had returned to New York City, it seemed ridiculous at best to add that to the plate of existing complications. Antonio had said being married to him would be crazy—"a crazy adventure," he had told her, to be exact—and now she was feeling the effects of that precisely. It left her even more doubtful of how they could ever have a family. Would things ever be normal? No, they would not, and it seemed each day brought a new bout of disaster. Maggie's fears had resurfaced, leaving her to wonder when she could ever be ready to have a child with him. She loved children too, but she did not want a child to be at such a disadvantage, living such a chaotic lifestyle. If she had been pregnant and endured the tainted cocktail, what would have happened to their child? It was a scary thought in itself. And yet, there was so much to worry about in such a short time. In the past month, she had jumped from a plane, slept in a forest while pursuing a cheetah, and drunk a drugged cocktail delivered by Francis! She had made the right decision not to have a child just yet!

Now she knew she had to refill her prescription, and soon. At least for now, Antonio was away and her problems of conceiving were at an all-time low since he was behind bars. And they had only been together that one night since he threw the birth-control package into the flames of the fire.

Maggie let out a groan, and turned to lie on her stomach. She stared at the clock on the wall. Closing her eyes, she reminisced about being in Italy.

A knock on the door pulled her out of her daydream.

Maggie refused to answer, but the knock grew louder.

Maggie shouted at the door: "Just...go away!"

It was now four in the afternoon and she did not know who could be bothering her. She did not wish to talk to anyone, or see anyone, other than Antonio, and she knew it wasn't him. He had a key. Maggie rolled over, burying her face in the pillow, wishing to drown out the noise when she heard a voice accompanied by a knock.

"Maggie! It's Julia! Open up this door, now!"

Julia? What is she doing here? Does she know?

How embarrassing.

Maggie kept silent.

"Maggie! I know you are in there, now open up!"

Maggie sat up slowly, got out of bed, and walked over to the door.

"Thank goodness you're all right!" Julia marched in with a tote bag of supplies. "I have orders from Antonio to pay you a visit and make sure you are okay."

"He called you?" Maggie sat back down on the bed, looking frail.

"He used his one phone call to call me and said that I should contact Stanley to post his bail after he gave me a key to the fourth floor of the hotel so that I can check up on you and make sure that you are okay."

"Oh…" Maggie collapsed on the bed, staring up at the ceiling. "That's Antonio…always concerned for me." She let out a sigh. "So you know about the latest disaster."

"Not really. Antonio only had one minute to tell me what was on his mind—that he was being detained and that I needed to get over to the hotel and take care of you ASAP!" Julia looked at Maggie. "I am flattered he would ask me. And he must be a smart young man; he knows I will see to it that you are okay." She reached for Maggie's forehead. "You look flushed, and you feel warm. You're running a fever." Julia reached into her bag. "I have something here to reduce your fever—you're probably dehydrated."

"I don't want anything. I just want Antonio back." Maggie's eyes filled with tears. "What if he stays there for life?"

"That won't happen, dear, I am sure of it," Julia told her. "You need to worry about yourself now, and get that toxin out of your system; it looks like you are having withdrawal symptoms."

"I threw up twice last night, and I'm just exhausted from everything."

"Here." Julia handed her a cup. "Sip this; you'll feel better."

Maggie thought it was strange that Antonio called Julia instead of one of his staff members, but she now knew that Antonio counted Julia as a family member, and that he must trust her. She had been a good friend ever since they met on the plane. And although she was older, it seemed insignificant to their friendship, and the fact that Antonio trusted her made Maggie trust her all the more.

"I just want to die," Maggie moaned under the sheets. "I hate everything. I just want Antonio back and I want to go back to Italy. It has been one problem after the next, ever since we returned to the States."

"You have to be strong for both of you. Once you are better, we can visit him. Then you'll feel much better."

"Feel better? No, I won't! Antonio's behind bars, Julia, all because of me! Francis drugged my champagne and I was never sicker in my entire life, but I am even sicker thinking about Antonio locked up…wearing orange…"

www.lovetheillusion.com/2216.htm

Maggie's thoughts flooded with her last vision until she felt her eyelids slowly drooping. Soon she was asleep at last.

THE NEXT DAY…

Maggie sat up slowly. Her nerves still felt stretched.

"You're still here?" Maggie saw Julia resting on the couch.

"Yes. I'm not going anywhere, dear."

Maggie shook her head as she recalled the events of the fateful night.

"Francis got an award," she told Julia. "He was recognized, but it wasn't good enough. He wanted to be recognized by Gia, and instead, she recognized *my* dress! So he slipped something—we still don't know what—into my champagne, and then when I got up to do my acceptance speech and tell the world what inspired me, all I could do was mumble about my mom…it was so terrible…so embarrassing. Everyone thought I had too much to drink—again! According to the press, I'm a drunken idiot already and this is just going to make it even worse…but that is the least of my worries! Antonio is in jail!" Maggie felt her heart breaking. "I just want him back!"

"He will be. Right now, you just need to think: One day at a time.

You know you love Antonio and he loves you; you will get through this, too."

"He must feel so helpless in there," Maggie said.

"If it makes you feel any better, I think Stanley is on top of that. He went over to post bail today, so we will see. Possibly, Antonio could return tomorrow, for good, provided that the tests indicate that Francis tried to harm you. That would mean that Antonio acted in self-defense, although it is difficult to determine how the courts will settle that one."

"It's simple! Francis can take Antonio's place behind bars!" Maggie decided.

Julia smiled. "He's a celebrity. He has that in his favor…people usually like to defend them, regardless."

"Everything is my fault," Maggie reflected. "If I hadn't insisted on going to the fashion show, Antonio and I could have stayed home, away from Francis. Why didn't I listen to him?"

"You are a strong woman, Maggie. We always have a mind of our own. I'm sure it's one of the things Antonio loves about you, but now you have to be strong for him. He would not want you sitting around feeling sorry for yourself."

"I want to go see him."

"Does that mean you are better?"

"Still feeling just a little strange, but I really need to see him."

"I can call us a cab," Julia suggested.

"No, I'll call Salvador. He can take us."

"Go to the jail in a limo?" Julia started laughing. "I've never been in a limo before, *and* I have never visited a jail either! Two new adventures in one day; I’m quite excited now.”

Maggie managed a smile. “I will call him!” She picked up her phone. “He’ll be happy to help us out.”

Maggie stood in the shower, but her thoughts only left her frustrated. The water seemed to be drowning her in her own misery as she contemplated the latest catastrophe. Hopefully, everything would resolve quickly.

TWO HOURS LATER…

Maggie entered the lounge of the jail, feeling like a stranger. The concrete walls were cold and heartless as she took in her surroundings.

“I can just wait here,” Julia told Maggie.

“Are you sure?”

“Yes.” Julia sat down in the lounge area.

Maggie went over to the window, where a clerk was stationed behind a glass barrier.

“I am here to see Antonio,” Maggie said with a twinge of trepidation. “Antonio DeLuca.”

“You are his wife?” The woman recognized her.

“Yes.”

“Okay. You need to sign in here.” She handed her a clipboard. “We can only allow a ten-minute visit.”

“Ten minutes?” Maggie cried. “Why—”

“Do you want to see him or not?”

“Well, yes, but…Isn’t he going to be released soon, anyway?”

“I have no information on that.” She spoke apologetically. She got up from her desk and met up with Maggie. “Follow me.”

Maggie followed her down a hall until they arrived at a private visiting room with a glass partition.

“Wait here,” the woman told her. “I’ll go get him.”

Maggie sat down, horrified by the reality of Antonio’s detainment. *This is…so awful.* She thought perhaps her symptoms were subsiding, but the anxiety she was now feeling was making it difficult to determine whether or not she really felt any better at all.

“Maggie!” Antonio came into the room across from hers that was partitioned with a glass barrier. “How are you?”

“How am I? How do you think? Terrible! But the real question is how are *you*? You must be miserable in here, and I hate being at the hotel without you! How long are you going to be in here?”

“I don’t know. The results were supposed to be back within twenty-four hours, but there’s supposedly a delay.”

“A delay?” Maggie said. “Why? Why would there be a delay?”

“I don’t know, but I’ve missed one show already, and will soon miss another if they don’t speed things up around here.”

“Isn’t Stanley coming to post bail?”

“Yes, but they’re stalling on that as well.”

“This is so awful! I can’t believe this is happening. And Francis belongs in here, not you.”

“Yeah, well, my thoughts exactly. And I think I may regret having said that I wanted to kill him, but seriously, Maggie, I just lost my cool when I realized he drugged you. What if I hadn’t been along? Then what? There is no way you can work for the guy.”

“I know. I wish I would have listened to you.”

"Maggie, I know you want to design, but why can't you be happy just designing costumes for my show?"

"I am, but I love to design dresses! It's way more fun and I…I didn't think things would have ever ended up like this. I feel so terrible, about everything."

"It's okay. It will pass."

"I hope so." Maggie looked doubtful, checking out his orange attire. "You are such a cute criminal." She finally let go of a laugh.

He let out a huff. "Yeah… Not exactly my choice of wardrobe."

"Actually, it's a *terrible* fashion statement," Maggie agreed, shaking her head. "But I wish I could crawl through this hole and give you a big hug and a kiss!"

"Me too, Maggie, I really miss you. It's so boring in here! I wish I had at least a magic marker so I could draw on the walls!"

"Yeah, then they would probably write you up for disorderly conduct, *again*!"

Maggie laughed as Antonio smiled at her.

"It's good they locked you up!" She made eyes at him. "You are such a threat to society, trying to add a child to the population…" She teased him, trying to lighten the mood.

"I know…" Antonio smiled at her, but then his face grew serious. "I hope they discover the truth soon…very soon." He looked downcast. "This is so bad for my career, Maggie. Parents do not want some criminal entertaining their children."

"But you're not a criminal!"

"Well, we know that, but I hate to see what they print in the press! Usually I could care less, but this could ruin ticket sales. People will think I'm some wacked-out freak if the media does not present the story correctly."

"Can't we offer an interview to clear things up? I promise I would gladly go!" Maggie told him.

"Maybe, but sometimes the damage has been done so that no one believes you anyway. Perhaps, I can search out some charity, beyond my brother's, to make amends."

"Just let me know what I can do—I will do anything to help you."

"I wish I could kiss you right now." He smiled at her.

"Me too. I love you."

"I love you too." Antonio stared at her. "I can't wait to get out of here!"

"Hopefully soon…hopefully…"

"Time's up!" She heard the guard announce.

Maggie slowly stood, forlorn at the thought of leaving without him.

Outside the jail, several reporters were lined up, trying to get a word in as they made their way back to the limo.

"Maggie! Maggie White! How long will Antonio be behind bars?"

I'm Maggie DeLuca now, don't you know?

"Is it true that Antonio threw your boss overboard?"

He's not my boss anymore.

"Could you tell us the story behind their animosity?"

Francis drugged me, I wish you knew!

"Walk fast," Maggie whispered to Julia, "and don't say anything."

They crawled into the limo and Julia turned to Maggie. "So, how is Antonio? Is he surviving?"

"I guess. It kills me to see him in that stupid orange shirt and…"

"I know. I hope he's out soon. What's taking so long?"

"I have no idea. The tests were supposed to be back in twenty-four hours."

Maggie's phone went off.

"Stanley?"

"Yes. I'm calling because—did you visit Antonio yet?"

"Yeah, I just left the jail," Maggie told him. "This is killing me, Stanley."

"Then you know…"

"Know what?"

"Huh? He didn't tell you?"

"Tell me what?"

"Oh…it's not good news," Stanley said.

"Was Antonio supposed to tell me something?"

"Never mind."

"What? I want to know, Stanley…what is it?"

"He must not want you to know."

"Come on! What? You *have* to tell me. Where are you? I'm coming there now!"

"Fine…you can meet me at Biagio's—they're closed now, we can talk."

Maggie put her phone away. "I can't believe it," she told Julia. "Stanley has something to tell me and he sounds upset."

"I wonder what that's about." Julia eyes narrowed.

"I know." Maggie turned the possibilities over in her mind.

"Francis is involved, remember?"

"Meet with Stanley, and then give me a call. I'm in room 492, remember?"

"Okay," Maggie agreed as they exited the limo.

"Hey…Stanley…" Maggie sat down at the bar at Biagio's as old memories came rushing back. Stanley had been waiting on her when she first met Antonio.

"A glass of wine?" he asked, setting out a glass.

"No, I'm still recovering from my tainted champagne," Maggie reminded him. "So, you wanted to see me?" She wished he would just get to the point.

"The test came up clean."

"What?" Maggie felt the words sharply entering her brain. "That's impossible! How do you know?"

"I went to post bail and now I can't because they said Antonio lied about the drugs to excuse his behavior. He didn't tell you?"

"No."

"He probably didn't want to upset you. And there has to be some mistake, right?"

"Yes! Do you know how sick I've been for the past two days?" Maggie said. "I was totally fine before that glass of champagne!"

"Yeah, I'm pretty sure that Francis has pulled his slimy strings to keep Antonio in jail. Who knows what will come of this…"

"That's not a big surprise. Question is: Where do we go from here? Antonio has another show in two days!" Maggie closed her eyes, exhausted.

"That's the problem. I don't want to keep cancelling his show, but at this point it does not look good at all," Stanley said, nodding. "Did you see the latest news report, front cover of the *New York Times*: 'Magician Antonio, Trapped in Jail'?"

"No—I didn't…Isn't it nice of them to keep track of his whereabouts? I wish they could do an article on Francis for a change. And what a creep he is!"

"That will never happen. He doesn't have the interest of the public like Antonio does." Stanley poured himself a whiskey on the rocks. "My hands are tied. I have no idea how to bail him out of this one."

"So, you can't even post bail?"

"Everything's on hold," Stanley explained, "and for what I have no idea!"

"This is so miserable." Maggie looked around Biagio's, recalling their pizza dinner. "I really miss him."

"We all do," Stanley told her. "Did you know that everyone has moved out of the hotel temporarily? The only ones left are you and Julia."

"Really?"

"Yeah, no one knows when the next performance will be, so they are just waiting for a call back. I have no idea when that will be. None of this is good for his career. I'm so busy with refunding ticket sales, and every time we cancel, it just adds to the catastrophe."

What next? Maggie envisioned the current disaster on the cover of a magazine:

www.lovetheillusion.com/2278.htm

"I have to go, Stanley. Julia's waiting for me and…I'll talk to you later."

Maggie got up to leave.

What's his problem? He has no idea how to help Antonio?

"Julia, it's Maggie. I'm headed back to the floor now," Maggie spoke into her cell phone. "Things are a mess…the test came up clean."

"No… How can that be?"

"If I knew, we wouldn't be having this conversation."

"Do you think Francis has tampered with the evidence somehow?" Julia asked.

"He's probably paid someone…question is who?"

"Are you thinking what I am thinking?" Julia sounded amused.

"What's that?"

"We need to beat Francis at his own game…" Julia said.

"Yeah, you're right, but I bet that's easier said than done…Just need to think a little… We are smart; we can figure out a plan. And I think I have an idea already." Maggie's voice was bright. "I'm calling in room service for us; we need some nutrition as we conjure up our plan."

“I’m in…just let me know what I can do to help,” Julia told her.

“This will be good, Julia. And when I’m done with Francis, it will be the last time he messes with me. Or Antonio!”

Chapter 10

"Why...why...*why*...did I go to that fashion show?" Maggie blurted, as she paced around Julia's hotel suite. "Obviously, Francis will send me to the grave long before I *ever* get my dress label in a boutique! Why did I work for him in the first place? What was I *thinking*? He was friends with Mr. Sixty—I should have known better! But I believed it was miracle from the heavens—come my way. What planet of stupidity was I on?"

Julia smiled. "You would have never met Antonio if it weren't for Francis."

"I know, that's true. But it's so hard to have any gratitude where Francis is concerned. And now look at us! I have to do whatever it takes to get Antonio out of jail!"

"What's the game plan?" Julia asked.

"I hate my plan, but it's the only way possible. And it means spending more time with Francis. He's here for the month taking care of business—whatever that means—and perhaps—I know it's a stretch, but maybe, just maybe, he'll let me into his circle of friends. And for the right amount of money—Antonio's money, that is—I can get someone to confess! What do you think?" Maggie asked Julia.

Julia shook her head. "My head is spinning."

Maggie exhaled, and then said, "Well, don't think for a minute I'm going to let him sit in jail!"

"Relax! Try anyway," Julia said. "I'm sure that Antonio's staff will see to it that things are resolved quickly."

"If only that were true! Stanley's resolution is scotch—on the rocks! What a joke...So it's up to me. I am now accepting Francis' offer to work for him! Much better intentions this time around—don't you think?"

"Sounds...ugly," Julia said.

"I'm sure it will be, but it's time to get started...with a short and sweet phone call to Francis." Maggie picked up her phone. "Enjoy!" She waited till she heard his voice.

"Francis? It's Maggie..."

"Maggie...what a surprise."

"Yes, well, I just wanted to check and see how you're doing? If you are okay? And I wanted to thank you for inviting me to the fashion show. I've been thinking that I really should accept your offer and help you out with those dress designs. Hopefully, we can move past the latest disaster."

"That would be great!" Francis sounded surprised. "Is everything okay with Antonio? I heard he's still in jail."

"He is...it's a shame...but he really needs to mind his temper. After three months of being married to him, I'm appalled at how he behaves!"

"It's fine, Maggie, you don't have to apologize for him."

"But I should, Francis. I mean, you have done *so* much for me and I owe *everything* to you. Antonio wants me to design his costumes, and that is just no fun at all! I miss designing dresses, and I told him so. Now he does not want me to work for you, but we both know better—that we can both benefit from such an arrangement—immensely!"

"My thoughts exactly…I'm so delighted. How 'bout we meet for lunch tomorrow, at noon, say…at Blue Hill. You can bring your designs with you and we can discuss everything then."

"Sounds great, Francis. And thanks so much! I really owe you!" Maggie grinned at Julia. "See you then!"

AT BLUE HILL (THE NEXT DAY)

"Hey! Maggie, I'm over here!" Francis waved to her from across the room.

He's such a creep!

"There you are!" Maggie approached his table. "This just feels like old times, doesn't it?"

"It does." Francis handed her a menu. "I just ordered champagne for us to celebrate," he explained as he opened up the menu to have a look. "Feels good to have you back. You can't imagine how awful the past year with Cami has been! She never did a thing right!" He paused, and then professed, "This calls for celebration!"

"I agree…" *Not!* Maggie picked up her menu. "You look great since I saw you last year, Francis. Have you been working out?" She buried her face in the menu so he could not see her contempt. *Champagne again…seriously? I must be nuts.*

"Every morning, first on my list is the gym," Francis told her proudly. "I lift weights, then I move to the treadmill, and then back to the weights. I make it top priority. It gets the blood pumping. And it helps to have a clear head when you start the day—eyes wide open after a vigorous workout. That's what the experts advise! The earlier the better—get it out of the way, otherwise you make excuses and never end up in the gym. The busy schedule gets in the way, and pretty soon you don't know where the day went! I remember a week in LA; I was meeting a client there. He was so tired in the mornings and I thought he looked hung over, but hadn't even had a drink the night before! Turns out, he'd never exercised a day in his life, and he is quite a bit younger than me. I look incredible compared to him!" *I hope his head does not explode...* "Staying fit is top priority, and then you must reward yourself with a little champagne here and there just to keep things in check…I did great again today, and so I get rewarded." *The pressure's building...it has to explode...* "Such a simple thing, and yet people don't take the time to reward themselves for their efforts. Hard work always deserves a payout."

"I agree!" Maggie watched him pour her a glass of champagne. "Cheers to that 'payout'!" She made a toast. *And I am so ready to work hard to put you away!*

"Cheers." Francis raised his glass.

"Cheers," Maggie said, motivated by "business." She passed an envelope of photos, with her dress designs, to Francis. "Here…"

"Now, just so you know," Francis was quick to explain, "I only need a few. A couple to start, and then we will see where to go from there. Did you talk to Gia after the boat ride and tell her that I would like to meet with her?"

"Uh…no, Francis. We were in the…uh, police car, remember?"

"Oh, that's right. And now Antonio's gone…for a while. That's too bad. You know, he never seemed to like me and I could never figure out why…" Francis seemed amused.

"It's baffling why you two don't get along…I think it's a shame."

Maggie stared at her glass of champagne, thinking Francis was the last person she wanted to share a toast with. "But time will tell…maybe we can all be friends someday."

"Mixing business with friendship? You have a lot to learn. See, usually it's a mistake…friends do not make good business partners, and so once they share in business, rarely are they still friends. Jealously…greed…or simply the inability to realize that someone's idea may surpass your own! Friendly business partners is all one can hope for, and now you know! But Antonio and I could never be friendly business partners…it would be a lost pursuit. You and I…we might just be a different story…"

Maggie just stared at him, wondering if he thought he made any sense or if he was just trying to mess with her head.

"So do you want to see my designs?"

"Absolutely."

"Okay. Well, here are just a few…"

www.lovetheillusion.com/2126.htm

www.lovetheillusion.com/2127.htm

www.lovetheillusion.com/2128.htm

www.lovetheillusion.com/2233.htm

www.lovetheillusion.com/2232.htm

"Interesting," Francis said. "The white one is nice. I can picture it on Kensal."

www.lovetheillusion.com/2237.htm

"So you like them?"

"Possibly…they're not bad." Francis paused, setting the photos aside. "So, Antonio has given his approval for us to work together?"

"Yes." Maggie bit her tongue as she stared at her photos. "My life with him is a disaster. I never imagined how difficult it would be to be married to a celebrity. What was I thinking?"

"You should have listened to me," Francis told her. "But young love…it always has a mind of its own!"

"It's just too much…the tabloids, the paparazzi, the bodyguards… The whole lifestyle is just overwhelming. I miss the simplicity of life…"

"Simplicity has its own complexity." Francis took a sip of champagne.

Please don't get philosophical with me. I might barf.

As Maggie tried with all her might to look interested in his latest revelation, he continued: "Life is all about finding out what keeps you happy. And you will find that too much simplicity is always a problem, but too much complexity is also a problem…which is where you have landed being married to Antonio. People strive for simplicity, only to find that if there's not a little bit of complexity, they're unhappy! So, you see, it comes down to balance…a little of both!" He held up his glass to make another toast.

I just loathe him…

"So, Francis, I hope you can forgive Antonio. He just acted irrationally, and… It's a bit outrageous that he would accuse you of tainting my drink, don't you think?"

"I do!" Francis gave her a strange look—one she was unable to interpret. "I will have to find it in my heart to forgive him."

"Yes, I guess you will… So, you must feel a bit sorry for him, sitting in jail now, don't you? I mean, he just probably overreacted after a few cocktails, and now that we are going to work together I think it is so important that you two get along. And for starters, when I dropped in to visit him, he told me to let you know that he was really sorry for what he did." Maggie bit her tongue—*again*—as she revised her plan. "Maybe you could pull strings to get him out of there? And then…I could introduce you to Gia!"

"He's the magician!" Francis laughed. "Let him free himself! It's funny how people harbor that animosity, and it's just never a good thing. Antonio is proof! If only he could let go of his misperceptions of me, none of this would have happened. And even if I had done what he accused me of…he could never prove it, right? One must think! *Before* taking action! Haste makes waste! And the wrong decisions leave you with regret."

Plan one…failed. Plan two…random assumption…

"So…the jail guard. I spoke with him, and he seems to know you quite well, Francis."

Francis' face twitched. "We go way back, to when I was—" Francis suddenly stopped, his face full of regret. He shook his head. "So…let's take a look at your designs again…" He was opening the envelope when his phone went off. Maggie watched suspiciously as he took the call.

"Yep, pretty soon…say maybe an hour or so…I'll see you then," Francis spoke quickly.

So enlightening...I wonder what piece of slime he is meeting with...

Maggie picked up her phone to send a text to Bradley, while Francis firmed up the plans for his next business meeting. "Can't wait…" he said, closing out the conversation.

Neither can I... Maggie watched as the waitress approached.

Not even hungry.

AN HOUR LATER…

"They just took a left!" Maggie told Bradley, who was following the taxi ahead of them.

"I got eyeballs, Maggie," Bradley said as he yanked on the steering wheel. "You'd better duck down in that back seat there so he don't see you. I'm sure he's got no idea who I am, but you just had lunch with the guy—"

"I can't believe he knows the jail guard…I randomly made that assumption—and guess what! He does!" Maggie held on to the driver's seat as she knelt behind it. "That means that they are in cahoots to keep Antonio locked up, which means I will have to pay off his 'friend' to spill the scoop!"

"That sounds pretty crazy to me," Bradley said. "And what's the price for that one?"

"Mmm…I don't know…maybe a million!" Maggie peeked out of the window. "Has to be more than Francis paid him…hopefully it will be enough!" She paused to consider. "Surely Francis' friends are not loyal beyond the dollar, right? What do you think?"

"I think I'm about to be the next guy floatin' in the river if Antonio finds out I'm helpin' you."

"We won't tell him. I need to do this for him and I am grateful for your help! We cannot let him sit in jail! Stanley—the smart one—has no idea what to do to help Antonio, so it's up to me…and you."

"Yeah, well, Antonio may have called Julia to keep an eye on you, but he's completely unaware that you need a bodyguard now, not a nurse!"

"I promise to wrap this up quickly!" Maggie stared out the window where Francis' taxi was waiting.

Bradley gave her a doubtful look. "Good luck with that…" He pulled up to the curbside, where they watched as Francis got out of his car and approached an apartment building. "Now what?"

"I get out and follow him?" Maggie suggested.

"Are you crazy, lady? No!" Bradley said. "*I'll* do that. You wait here!"

She watched as Bradley got out and attempted to follow him. Soon, she could no longer see Francis or Bradley.

Maggie sat curled up in the back seat, organizing her plan.

Someone had to know the truth. She was sure that Francis was covering up the truth with a huge lie. Perhaps they could never prove that he had tainted her drink unless someone had actually seen him do it! What were the odds? But, if Francis was masterminding a cover-up, then he was indeed suspicious! Things could get ugly, but she knew one thing: she would stop at nothing to free Antonio.

Ten minutes later, she saw Bradley making his way back to the car.

"Hey!" Bradley said as he got in. "I know a few people at the jail—guards, that is—and I know the deputy! Perhaps they could help us…"

"So there might be a leak somewhere?"

"Maybe…I could ask around, see what I can find out. The guy that Francis went to see is in apartment five. I would say we have not accomplished a whole lot, yet. But now that we have an address, we can find out who he is. Unfortunately, Francis probably has more than one friend!"

"That's hard to imagine," Maggie said under her breath. Then, louder: "So you think you can find out who lives there?"

"I can try."

"How?"

"The station has records. I know people there…I can work on that. Meanwhile, you need to stay put, and don't get too cozy with Francis! From what Antonio says, he's worse than you would imagine."

"So far, he has tried kissing me and tainting my drink…only small misdemeanors, right?"

“It’s always a challenge to get proof, Maggie. That is what you really need. And according to Antonio, Francis is an expert at covering his tracks!” Bradley explained.

“That’s not good.” Maggie sighed.

“Nope.”

“Poor Antonio!” Maggie’s heart sank. “He’s been victimized simply because he was trying to protect me from Francis.”

“I have known Antonio for quite a while now and he will do anything for the people he loves.”

“That’s why I need to fight for him now,” Maggie told Bradley. “You’ll see! I’ll get him out of jail if it’s the last thing I do!”

“I’ll see what I can find out for you,” Bradley offered. “I admire your determination. But you have to promise me one thing.”

“What?”

“Never meet with Francis alone. I don’t need you disappearing. And keep me posted if you need assistance. I know karate and carry a gun! You have fingernails and stilettos…not much of a weapon…” He laughed into the rearview mirror.

“Sure, Bradley, whatever you say.” She smiled.

Maggie was walking through the hotel lobby, her sunglasses and baseball cap added for disguise, when she noticed a magazine exposing the latest trauma that she was experiencing firsthand:

www.lovetheillusion.com/2277.htm

I have to put an end to this, now…

Maggie's phone rang and she reached for it impatiently.

"Maggie, it's Dana! Is it true? I saw in the *Report News* that Antonio's in jail!"

"Yes, Dana, shortly after you left everything took a turn for the worse…but I am working on getting him out!"

"You are…what?"

"Stanley tried to post bond, and for some reason they denied it. And the test results are inconclusive, so that is not helping matters any."

"What test results? So…it's true? Antonio pushed Francis off a cruise boat? The article says, 'Antonio's feud with Maggie's ex-boss turns ugly as he settles things out of court.' Then it goes on to say how Antonio has a temper and did not want you working for him and that Francis sued him for ending the contract and—"

"I think the article forgot to mention that Francis put something in my drink! Or so Antonio believes. After that, I can't remember much of anything…other than riding in a squad car for the first time ever…"

"Wow…you sure know how to keep under the spotlight of

trauma. But at least you don't have to worry about having a baby!"

"Ha! Isn't that the truth! That would have been a minor complication compared to this!" Maggie stepped off the elevator and headed to Julia's room. "So, is everything the same in London?"

"Just the usual: cold, damp, rainy…but I am so excited! The baby's room is finally done!"

"That's great… So, how are you feeling?"

"I feel great! Just a little thicker around the middle, and I think I can feel it kicking me now!"

"That's so cool! I am so excited for you! Is Shane excited too?"

"Yeah, he says that my cheeks are always rosy now!"

"Mine too, but not from pregnancy. Francis has been giving my face a whole new color for the past week now."

"Sounds like you have your hands full. I hope everything works out…and then try to stay out of the papers, will you?"

"That's a joke. I think Antonio makes the news every month!"

"It seems he does! And I loved our photo!" Dana sounded overjoyed.

"Are you kidding? You looked great—I looked like I was sleepwalking."

Dana laughed. "LOL! I miss you! I wish you were still in London!"

"Antonio said maybe we could visit on our way back to Italy this fall."

"Please do! I'll have the baby by then! Have you ever held a newborn?"

"No, can't say I have…"

"Let's plan on it!" Dana sounded excited.

"Okay, I'll talk to you soon." Maggie stood in front of Julia's door.

"Yeah, keep me posted. And did I tell you that I said a prayer that Antonio gets out of jail soon?"

Must be fun to live in Utopia...

Julia opened the door. "Maggie, you're back! How's Francis?"

"How do you think? Just as miserable as always, but Bradley and I followed him and he has a friend—or acquaintance—who lives in an apartment about a mile from Blue Hill. Bradley is going to find out who he visited and go from there. And Bradley also knows some of the staff at the jail where Antonio is, so he's helping me with everything!"

"Well, dear, while you were gone, I came up with my own plan and it just might save Antonio a little money."

"What do you mean?"

"My daughter Christine knows a woman here in the New York area. They went to school together. I probably never mentioned that before she had five girls, before she met her husband and moved to London, she was an officer..."

"Okay..." Maggie gave her a strange look. "Let me guess: she wants to fund our efforts?"

"No, silly, her friend works for the FBI...undercover...she helps with all the drug busts and Francis would find her very attractive!" Julia explained.

"No way!"

"Yes way!" Julia wore a malicious grin. "She could sabotage his efforts and she is quite the looker! One night with Francis and I guarantee she would own a wealth of information that we could use against him. She is an expert!"

"This is great, but how is she going to meet Francis?"

"Simple! He's staying at the hotel here, right? And there is a band playing on the weekend—Friday night. And so…it will be a big night in the Big Apple! You need to invite him to come and meet you, and then she will show up 'randomly' and pretend to know you, and the rest will be history!"

Maggie considered the plan, and then grinned. "I absolutely *love* it!"

Chapter 11

"Francis, it's Maggie."

"Yes, I recognize your voice."

"Well, I was calling because... Did you know that there's a band playing Friday in the pub lounge—first floor—at Club B? I was going to go check it out. Do you want to come?"

"Don't tell me you want to mix business with friendship already, Maggie?"

"You shouldn't think of it that way...I just thought when we met for lunch that you seemed a bit stressed out. Perhaps you could use a night out...and I need to keep my mind off of Antonio..."

"Maybe I could..."

"You know Antonio usually keeps me so busy, but now that he's gone I'm so restless, and even feeling a bit lonely."

"When does it start?"

"Seven."

"I'll see you then," Francis agreed. "And this evening will be a toast in a whole new direction! We will not mention work at all."

"Like that's even possible for you, Francis."

"You are too clever and you know me all too well." He chuckled. "Then...perhaps, we should check out the women's fashion statements and gather some ideas on how to modify the 'bar scene attire' into something more classical...trampy yet elegant."

"Ha ha... Sounds like a plan! I'll see you then!" Maggie grinned at Julia.

"Hook, line, and sinker!" Julia grabbed her laptop. "Now I'll show you a photo so you'll know who will be approaching you as your long-lost friend! Her real name—Felicia Jensen. Her undercover name—you pick! And I hate to tell you this, but she already knows what you look like…you have been in the news quite a bit, and finally… That's a good thing!"

"I can hardly wait," Maggie said sarcastically as she looked at her watch. "But I scheduled a visit with Antonio this afternoon and I am excited to tell him!"

"No! You must be careful. There are cameras, ears listening in on conversations. You must keep everything between you and me, and don't mention any of this to Bradley. If word gets out, it will ruin everything!"

"Okay," Maggie promised. "It's our secret!"

That afternoon, Maggie sat in the limo, waiting to arrive at the jail, where she would see Antonio again. It almost seemed inappropriate to be making a visit to the jail in a limo, but Antonio had given instructions to Salvador that he was in charge of driving her anywhere she needed to go. She thought perhaps it was his way of protecting her while he was away.

She could not wait to see him. It had been over a week, and he'd already had to cancel three shows. The whole situation was devastating. She wondered how he was managing, all alone, living behind bars. Perhaps, by now, he had regrets.

She recalled her promise to Julia, not to mention their plans to Antonio. She knew he would blow a fuse if he knew she was spending Friday night with Francis, who was still in New York for another few weeks. But that was her last concern. Who knew what Bradley would come up with? Maybe nothing. It was best to have a back-up plan, and Julia seemed to be quite resourceful. It was sweet that she cared so much, and it was obvious she did not have anything standing in the way of her devotion. And she seemed to be one smart woman. Maggie could only hope that her plan would work. Little by little, they would uncover the truth.

"I can wait here," Salvador told her, breaking her out of her daydream.

They had arrived.

As she reached for the door, the wind caught her hair as if to signal that 'last felt freedom'—a bridge from reality—and seconds later she felt the gloom and despair clinging to her as she absorbed the atmosphere.

"I'm here to see Antonio DeLuca." The woman at the desk gave her a quick smile.

"Yes, Maggie. Follow me." They took a walk down a long hall, and a moments later the woman said, "Have a seat. I'm Patty, by the way, and I'll have one of the guards let Antonio know you're here."

Maggie took a deep breath, trying to pull herself together.

Five minutes passed, and then he finally appeared. She was surprised by the smile on his face….

www.lovetheillusion.com/2227.htm

"Antonio!" Maggie saw him approaching in the same orange shirt and pants.

"Hi Maggie." Antonio took a seat behind the window.

She tried not to betray her shock. His face was thick with whiskers and it appeared that he had lost weight.

"Are you okay?" Maggie studied him. "You look…thin."

"I'm okay." Antonio broke eye contact.

"No you're not, Antonio, you must be miserable."

"Over a week of boredom…what can I say…I'm going nearly insane in here… And they have me doing janitorial services—I hate it, every minute."

Maggie tried not to laugh. "You're cleaning the toilets?"

"Urinals…" He did not smile back at her. "And there are fights that break out. The other day some guy punched another guy and there was blood everywhere. Then security came and we were all ordered back to our cells. We were outside—first time I had seen daylight in three days— in the courtyard, playing Frisbee golf, and then five minutes later…back in the cell. Life in here sucks! I've gone from doing what I want, when I want, to doing nothing at all. It's so miserable. Last night I couldn't even sleep. I wish I could…then at least maybe I could dream about you." He looked sweetly at her.

"I know…I think about you all the time." She stared back at him.

"I've hired an attorney to get me out of here!" Antonio told her. "I met with him today. A quarter million I gave him—up front—and said, 'Get me the hell out!'"

"And?"

"It could take months! I already lost three shows! It's just bad for business, and I only work this time of year, until fall!"

Maggie kept staring at him, wide-eyed, wishing she could offer hope. But she kept her lips sealed. Who knew for sure if her plans would even succeed? Imagining the worst, her eyes filled with tears.

"No, Maggie, don't cry." Antonio spoke sweetly.

"I really miss you!" Maggie brought her face up to the glass, where the mouthpiece was. "I just want to kiss you." She stared at his lips, outlined in thick whiskers.

"Me too, Maggie; I lie on my cot at night and think about our honeymoon and I just want to hold you in my arms again. It's the only thing I live for every day…Just that hope that soon we will be together again." He paused. "I wrote you a note." He slid it through the grid.

"Should I read it now?"

"No, later, when you get back—read it tonight at ten, before bed. I'll be watching the clock, knowing that you are reading it then."

"Okay." Maggie put it in her pocket. "This is killing me, you know."

"Just be strong. We have to be strong. I will get out of here, I promise." His dark eyes stared into hers. "Question is, when?"

Antonio spoke softly, and his voice carried a trace of doubt.

"I just hate that you are in here!" Maggie sobbed. "I hate being without you."

"Me too, Maggie, me too," Antonio gazed back at her. "Just promise me, whatever you do, stay safe. Make sure if you go anywhere, Salvador is driving, and do not under *any* circumstances speak with Francis!" Maggie stared back at him, silent now.

"Maggie!" Antonio suddenly looked alarmed. "I mean it!"

"Yes, Antonio; you have nothing to worry about. Julia is taking good care of me. Thanks for sending her, by the way. She's a great friend." Maggie wiped her tears away.

"Yes, she's a gem," Antonio agreed.

As Maggie left Antonio, she thought over his warning about Francis. Obviously, she understood his concern, but she could not let that get in the way; her desire to return to a normal life with Antonio far outweighed her concern for her own safety.

Friday night arrived, and it was time to meet with Francis.

"You look great!" Julia looked Maggie up and down. "Now, you didn't forget to call Bradley, did you?"

"He's already at the bar with Rainelle, keeping an eye out, making sure that nothing else lands in my beverage." Maggie took one last look in the mirror. "But I highly doubt Francis would be dumb enough to pull the same stunt twice!"

"I'll wait up for you," Julia told her with a grin.

"Okay…but are you sure? It might get late…"

"I won't be able to sleep until you return safely and fill me in on the night's events!"

"All right, then. I hope to be back before midnight."

Maggie took the private elevator to the first floor. As soon as she stepped out she heard the music playing, leading her to the pub.

And there's Francis... already here. He's so punctual!

...his only redeeming quality.

Oh my... wow! Maggie suddenly saw Felicia approaching. There was not a second to lose.

"Maggie! Is that you?"

"Ah..." Maggie realized she had not yet chosen a name. "Madeline! What a surprise!"

"I can't believe it! When was the last time I saw you? Must have been years."

"Yeah..." Maggie gave a laugh she hoped was natural. "You look great!"

"So do *you*!" Felicia seemed to own a few stars for acting. "You know, I'm only in town for three short days, and what are the chances that I run into you? Small world!"

Three short days... is that enough time?

"I am so glad you did! You'll have to sit next to me," Maggie said. "Now, what can I get for you?" Maggie leaned over to motion for the bartender.

"I can get the first round," Francis said, acknowledging her acquaintance. "What would you ladies like to drink? It's on me..."

Such a terrible... déjà vu.

"Just some tonic water for me!" Maggie said quickly, with her eyebrows raised at Felicia.

"I would love a glass of chardonnay!" Felicia said, landing on a barstool between the two of them. She batted her eyes at Francis. "And who is this charmer?"

Maggie swallowed, trying to keep her face straight as she introduced him. "This is my boss, Francis. We worked together in London, and now I am reconnecting with him here in New York. You know, after three months in Italy, it's time to get back to work."

"I heard about the incident on the boat!" Felicia told Francis. "Some men just can't mind their temper, can they? Good thing that Maggie can assume the role of the breadwinner now, right?" She played along, casually turning to Francis: "I never thought Maggie would fall for the old 'marriage card.' It's just one of those wrong turns in life! But in all fairness to Cupid, no one ever sees trouble headed their way…love can be so blinding. I was married three times! Now…no more! I just swing from one handsome man to the next and never look back! Much happier now, I must say! Not to mention, it's *so* much easier to be on your own…no one else to look after, or to look after you!" She giggled as she sipped her chardonnay.

Maggie noticed that Francis seemed to have taken an immediate liking to her.

She is so good…unbelievable…single and gorgeous…I love that. And way too tiny to be a police officer!

Maggie stared down at her red stilettos.

Should be a fun night, she thought. But the next thing she knew, her mind was on Antonio.

"Excuse me! I'll be right back!" Maggie left for the ladies' room. "Watch my drink!" Maggie teased Francis, letting him know that she "trusted" him.

Maggie stood in the bathroom stall, recalling a year ago at Night Owls, when she tried to gather her sanity while trying to determine Antonio's intentions. The bathroom seemed to be the only place in a crowded city to gather one's thoughts. Leaning against the stall door, she reached into her purse and took out the note Antonio had given her. As she read it, she soon felt immersed in the battlefield of finding Antonio's freedom.

Maggie,

As I sit for hours and days, with only my own thoughts, I remember last year when we met in New York City. You came into Biagio's, and after that things were never the same. You walked into my life and have been in my every thought ever since. Now it is those thoughts of you that keep me sane while again we are apart. And every time I think of you, I also think about how much I love you. When I am finally out of here, I can't wait to be with you and reveal that my love for you has only grown stronger, every day.

Antonio

Maggie closed her eyes, wishing to feel his embrace and the sweet taste of his kiss. She imagined their reunion: they would sit together by the fire, relaxing after the chain of exhausting events. Antonio would open a bottle of wine and soon they would forget the misery of being apart. He would resume his efforts to be a father and this time she would gladly give in. Hopefully, he would be freed soon.

I need to stay focused. She wondered how Felicia was faring with Francis—surely she would arrive in a stall soon herself—ill from her call of duty to be intimate with him.

"Maggie!" She felt a blunt hammering at her back from the other side of the door that she leaned against.

"Yeah?" Maggie opened up the door. "How did you know I was in—"

"A woman always pays attention to a good pair of shoes—nice sandals by the way—but I stopped in to let you know that it is time for you to leave!"

"What do you mean, *leave*? I just got here!"

"Yes, but I can take it from here. When you return, say that you suddenly feel sick and that you have had a pounding headache all day…"

"You left your drink!" Maggie alarmed. "What if—"

"I finished it and said I would get the next round, so no worries."

"Okay, I'll be right out, and—you are *sure* you want me to leave?"

"Yes, Francis has been all over me and I'm sending him mixed signals, just to keep him on his toes. But don't worry—he's the persistent type, and very soon I will get way more from him than he ever will get from me."

"You sound like an expert! I hope it all goes well. When will I hear?"

"I'll contact Julia tomorrow. It's better if nothing ends up on you."

"What do you mean, ends up on me?"

"Traces of evidence—phone calls, text messages…no one even knows that Julia and I know each other. I mean, what would *I* have in common with an eighty-year-old woman?"

You might be surprised.

Maggie waited a few minutes, and then made her way through the crowded bar. The music was so loud; she had to wonder how Francis and Felicia were even managing to carry on a conversation.

"Maggie, you were gone so long, I thought you fell in!" Francis said as he sipped a glass of whiskey on the rocks.

"He's so funny!" Maggie gave Felicia a wink. "I could use a laugh right about now because I'm not feeling so great. I have had a headache all day—almost to the point of feeling nauseous. I think I need to head back."

"So soon, Maggie?" Francis was surprised. "That's what happens when you drink a tonic at a bar with no alcohol. You probably need a good stiff drink to relax you after a stressful day. See what marriage does to a person? I can still remember my ex-wife! She always used to give me a headache," Francis recalled. "Now, I hardly ever get 'em."

"It was great seeing you," Felicia said to Maggie. "I hope you feel better…" She turned her attention to Francis. "Now, I hope at least *you* are staying to keep me company?"

"You bet." Francis gave her a sloppy wink.

She is way too hot for him.

Maggie scurried out of the bar, acknowledging Bradley, who gave her a quick nod on her way out. She was absolutely certain he was on edge, owning the information he did, worried that Antonio would have a fit if he found out he was assisting her endeavors. But now she was all too anxious to let Julia in on the news: The campaign to destroy Francis was well underway.

"What are you doing back so soon?" Julia opened the door, wearing a printed flannel nightgown, as Maggie marched right in.

"Felicia said I could leave."

"That was quick." Julia motioned for her to have a seat on the bed next to her.

"I know. But believe me, she has *everything* under control, so what does she need me for, right?" The evening's events flashed through her mind's eye.

"I can only assume she will work wonders," Julia said.

"Well, not much happened so far…" Maggie told Julia. "I drank a tonic and then headed to the bathroom, where I spent a moment away from everything, just thinking about Antonio, and—I really miss him. I don't know how much longer I can handle this. Our whole relationship has been one long separation after the next and we got married so that we could be together…so ironic, right?"

"I know. It's been rough, but now things can only get better."

"I hope so." Maggie imagined the possibilities. "It better not be *downhill* from here. And just so you know, Felicia said she would call you and fill you in on the details. I thought I would return with a grand scheme of events, but I have nothing. Now, you have to let me know as soon as she calls you. I want to know everything!"

"Of course. I'll tell you everything, once I know." Julia gave her a warm smile.

"Then I'll see you soon. And call me!" Maggie headed for the door.

"Okay, dear. Try to get some sleep!"

Soon she stood in front of the door to her hotel suite, contemplating another lonely night without Antonio. It was unbearable. She really missed him. She fidgeted with her key as she unlocked the door, and walked into the dark room groping for the light switch.

Suddenly, she felt someone grab her around her waist from behind, and instantly she let out a scream. She wrestled to free herself from the stranger's tight hold, but she was trapped.

"How's it going, sweetheart?" She heard Antonio's voice.

Maggie immediately realized she was standing in Antonio's arms. She turned to face him, pressed tightly against him while releasing the breath that was trapped in her lungs.

"I missed you," he whispered.

"*Antonio?* What—How did you...?" Maggie breathed in the familiar trace of his cologne. "You scared me, Antonio!" She let go of all her fright, as she stood wrapped in his arms, melting into his warm embrace.

"What's wrong? Afraid of the dark?" Antonio asked. It seemed his playful side had returned.

"Not anymore—" She felt his lips on her neck. "I wasn't expecting you—how did you get out?" she asked, still in shock.

"Francis can't keep me locked up forever," Antonio explained. "Money talks, but fortunately…I have *way* more than him. I think I'm out for good."

"I'm so relieved," Maggie said, melting into his arms. She looked into his eyes and started unbuttoning his shirt.

"Where were *you?*" Antonio asked in a whisper as he let his hands fall to her waist. She quickly fell against his bare chest, letting go of all her restless energy, feeling safe at last.

"With Julia," she mumbled.

"A night with Julia? In those shoes?"

She realized her shoes were resting against his bare feet.

"Yes." Maggie froze.

"I just love kissing you…" Antonio told her, as he reached his hands into her hair. "I really missed you." He placed his lips on hers, kissing her passionately.

I missed you too…so much. She closed her eyes, drenched in his kiss.

With her eyes closed and her arms around him, she soon felt her heart racing again, as he pressed her up against himself while guiding her to the bed.

"Make love to me, Antonio, and don't ever stop," Maggie whispered as Antonio lay on top of her.

"It seems like it's been forever," he admitted, his dark eyes staring into hers.

"Forever…" Maggie stared up at him as the city lights cast a spotlight on him through a crack in the curtains.

"I promise," Antonio said, gazing back at her, "that this will be our best night ever."

Chapter 12

It was three a.m. when Maggie's cell phone roused her as she snuggled under the sheets with Antonio.

"You wanna get that?" Antonio whispered.

"No," Maggie decided as she lay with her head against his chest.

Seconds later, the phone went off again.

"I wonder who that is," Antonio said. "Who could be calling this late at night?"

Maggie was imagining the possibilities when her phone went off for the third time. *What the... Who is that?*

"Maybe I should get it." She got out of bed and slipped Antonio's T-shirt over her head. "It could be a family emergency, or perhaps Julia needs something." Antonio's eyes followed her as she reached for her phone. She quickly scanned three text messages, all sent by Francis:

www.lovetheillusion.com/2212.htm

I'm dead!

"So who's the night owl?" Antonio checked his watch. "It's three o'clock in the morning!"

"Uh…it's Julia. She needs some…uh…Tylenol for her…arthritis. I'll be right back." Maggie grabbed her bathrobe and covered herself.

"Hurry back."

"I will…" She blew him a kiss.

She grabbed her purse after locating some Motrin and then headed out the door.

Seconds later, she pounded on Julia's door, but there was no response. She reached for her phone and waited until she finally heard Julia's voice.

"Yeah, I'm outside your door," Maggie said, quietly. "I know it's really late, but I need to talk to you."

"Okay dear, I'll be right there." Julia's voice was sleepy.

Soon the door opened and Julia stood in front of her, puzzled by Maggie's return. "What's wrong? Are you having trouble sleeping too?"

"*That* is an understatement! And no, I haven't slept yet. You'll never believe this—Antonio is back! He's in our room. He surprised me and—"

"He got out! That's great! But then what are you doing here?"

"We have a *huge* problem," Maggie said as she stepped inside, her anxiety mounting. "Francis just contacted me! He sent three messages asking who Felicia is and how long I have known her, and now he wants me to call him. I'm so freaked out. Now Antonio's back, and he obviously has no clue that I'm even still talking to Francis, much less working for the guy, and now—sorry!" Maggie flew her hands up in the air in a panic. "I just told Antonio that you needed some Tylenol for your arthritis!"

"Well, then, you'd better give me some!" Julia laughed.

"No, Julia, Antonio's gonna go ballistic if he realizes what we're up to. I just figured that he was stuck in jail and he would eventually appreciate my efforts. But now he's out and this is a *huge* mess because Francis knows I tried to set him up!"

Julia frowned. "You don't know that for sure. Maybe he just likes her and wants to know about her."

"Of course he likes her! He likes anything with two legs!" Maggie let out a huff. "The question is, why would he be calling *me* at three a.m.? This is a disaster! Don't you see?"

"Don't worry. We can outsmart Francis, if we haven't already!" Julia smiled at Maggie. "Relax. You have nothing to worry about! Felicia's an expert!"

"Okay, well, Antonio's an expert at finding out my business…and hopefully Bradley doesn't say anything."

"His loyalties will perhaps follow his paycheck."

"Exactly! He said he wouldn't tell Antonio, but that was when he was in jail! I need to call him and make him promise—again—not to say anything. But then, if I tell him, he'll probably start following me everywhere to keep me safe! And that's when Antonio will definitely suspect something. *Help!*" Maggie shook her head. "I've created a *huge* mess!"

"Okay, one thing at a time." Julia reached for her laptop. "Perhaps Felicia sent an email already."

Maggie watched as she typed in her password.

"Sorry, Julia, I know you're probably tired and now I'm keeping you up…" Maggie said suddenly. "And I can't stay too long! Antonio is probably already wondering where I am."

"Wait! She did send me one. Here it is." Julia opened up the email to read: "'Just got back to my place after several hours in Francis' hotel with a soaring view of the city!' How's this for excitement." Julia chuckled. "'No sooner did we take a look at the view than he started kissing me. *Yuck*…ha ha. I told him I would love to join him for a hot shower, so he jumped at the opportunity. I said he should go ahead of me as I needed to make a few calls. That's when I bugged his phone after I gathered a list of all his contacts! It's a long one. Needless to say, I left him in the shower, but I doubt he's still in there! I'll let you know when I gather my leads."

"Oh *nooo*!" Maggie sank her head into her hands. "This is such a disaster—she has no idea that Francis is on to her—how can she not know any better? Francis is far from clueless!"

"Hey! He doesn't know anything for sure…Perhaps she just 'changed her mind.' Women have a right to do that, don't they?"

"Well yes, but…he's definitely suspicious! Why would he call me in the middle of the night?"

"Just relax…I'm sure Felicia has things under control…I mean, you should know she wasn't about to sleep with him!" Julia laughed.

Maggie laughed back.

"Well, of course not, but…" Maggie sighed. "Why me, *again*?"

"Just get some sleep, and in the morning call Francis and act like you haven't a clue. He can't prove a thing! There are plenty of coincidences in this small world…even in New York City!" Julia grinned. "Felicia just got cold feet! And you'll need to convince him."

"I will?" Maggie paused to consider. *Just great…* "Okay." She grabbed her purse. "Francis gives everyone cold feet, right? So no surprise there." She rolled her eyes. "Let me know as soon as you know anything at all. Text me. You do know how to do that, right?"

"Actually, I do!" Julia gave her a wise look.

"See you later."

"Get some sleep!"

"Yeah, right, you too," Maggie mumbled as she closed the door behind her.

Maggie lay in bed, her eyes wide open. Her cell phone was turned off. Hopefully, Francis was not still trying to call her. Did he know that Antonio was out of jail? He soon would. Regardless of the potential outcome, she could not call Francis back in the middle of the night. Tomorrow, she would return his call and indicate surprise that his one-night stand was a failed effort. And if he had any suspicions that he was being investigated, she would have no clue in that department.

She snuggled next to Antonio, who was now sound asleep. Surely he was happy to be sleeping in his own bed again. It was such a relief to have him back, and now she considered her haste in taking things into her own hands. But every day that they spent apart had seemed an eternity. Neither of them had known if and when he would be released. She had no choice but to do what she had done. Now, surely, this too would pass, and eventually things would return to normal.

While Antonio was sound asleep, Maggie started to wonder: *How evil was Francis?* Would she be in danger if he suspected she was involved in bringing him to justice? Francis had a way about him that almost made him appear harmless. But Antonio always claimed to know better. Francis never spoke of his personal life. He only talked about business. And Maggie realized now that she knew him on a very superficial level. However, when he discussed his ideas, she felt as if he was opening up and sharing his very soul. It was who he was—a fashion designer.

Many people have a dark side. How dark was Francis? Was Antonio's perception of him exaggerated? Had he really put something in her drink? Or was it a coincidence that she was ill? Maybe she had simply been seasick.

Maggie recalled being in a boat once as a child. Her father had made plans of taking her brothers on a charter fishing trip, and she had been heartbroken that she had not been invited. That's when her father decided that she could come, after all. She could still remember having that orange lifejacket around her neck, and only an hour into the trip she had gotten sick, losing her breakfast all over the lifejacket. Her brothers had been appalled and offered no sympathy. Since then, she tried to steer clear of any boat outings.

What had happened to the test results? *Were they accurate?* Or was the evidence tampered with? *Who would ever know for sure?* Maggie realized she was living in a strange world—one where money could move mountains, and logic and common sense did not matter. What did Antonio mean when he said that Francis had money, but he had more? Had Antonio falsely accused him? Had he bought his way out of jail? Was he just as guilty as Francis in using money to attain power? Something did not make sense. If Antonio was innocent and simply acting on Maggie's behalf in self-defense, then why was he being detained? Obviously, Francis had survived, but the charges—attempted manslaughter—were serious enough…and if that was the case…Maggie recalled Antonio's harsh words to the officer: "I want to kill him!" That undoubtedly went on file as…something…*not good.* How had he suddenly gotten out? Would the newspaper offer clarity? Maggie knew better. Surely, they would have a field day. Whatever they did finally print on the subject matter, she was quite sure, would be disconnected fragments of the truth. She would never know the real truth. Now, as she lay next to him, she wondered, *what just went down?* There were too many strange pieces that did not fit together. If Francis had paid someone off to conceal evidence, then who had Antonio paid off? The whole situation was disturbing. Of course, it was a relief that Antonio was out of jail, but it left her with a strange feeling. Should she just "let it go?" Her curiosity was killing her. Did Bradley know anything? He was part of the security crew. Would he give up information, or was he sworn to secrecy?

Maggie felt frustrated as she contemplated the possibilities. Even after three months of marriage to Antonio, she still felt as though he carried that layer of mystery. There was something—some part of him—that she felt was held in reserve. And when he did not want to discuss matters, he would let her know. Maggie excused his behavior, assuming that he was acting in his protective mode, wishing to shelter her from things that were beyond control, and it was always apparent that he cared very deeply for her, so she tried to dismiss her curiosity. But this whole situation had left her beyond curious. Would Antonio explain what happened if she asked, or was he done explaining? And what had he possibly meant by "I have more money than Francis?"

Maggie was lost in her thoughts for hours, until she realized dawn was breaking. Hopefully, a new day would shed light on her many questions.

"I just got a shipment of props in," Antonio told Maggie as they sat at a small round table in his hotel suite, eating their room-service breakfast overlooking the streets of Manhattan. Maggie drank her coffee, trying to reenergize from the sleepless nights. It was all starting to take a toll. "Do you want to come with me and check them out?" Antonio tried to redirect her thoughts. Maggie just stared at him, feeling a combination of bliss and exhaustion.

"Sure," Maggie agreed, wondering when she should call Francis. It was only nine a.m. Was he still sleeping, or had he been up all night? She pictured him, completely irate, waiting impatiently for her to respond to his three text messages. It seemed a deep breath of stagnant air did nothing to calm her nerves as she anticipated his voice, yelling into the phone.

"Is something wrong?" Antonio asked.

"No, just tired." Maggie told him. "So, what are your plans for the day, besides playing with the new toys?"

"I have to meet with Stanley this morning, catch up on business as usual. We are going to reschedule the shows we lost…hopefully that will make up for refunded ticket sales."

"Are you out for good?" Maggie asked hesitantly. "I mean, are the charges dropped?"

"Trust me. Everything's good."

"That's great. I am so glad this nightmare is over." Maggie studied him, wondering what else he could be thinking about.

Let me in, Antonio!

"What happened?" Maggie finally asked. "How did you get out so…suddenly?"

"There are some things that you are just better off not knowing." Antonio sipped his coffee, his dark, mysterious eyes peering into hers.

"Knock it off, Antonio! Don't treat me like a child! Why can't you tell me? How do you think I feel, sitting here for over a week, by myself, while you are locked up and doing time for threatening Francis, and now suddenly you are free! What happened to the test results? How did they show nothing? I'm still wondering if I was just seasick. I just don't know what to think! Did Francis pay to cover up evidence? Did you? Why can't you just put a stop to all these crazy thoughts racing about in my head?" Maggie stared at him, while he gave her a blank stare. "Antonio!" she shouted. "Tell me! I'm your wife! I have a right to know."

"No, Maggie. The less you know the better off you are. Trust me." Antonio got up and tossed his dishes into a small bus pan and waited for her to do the same. She let out a huff, and flung her dishes on top of his.

"Imagine that!" Maggie announced. "We are done eating and talking—right at the same time! Great timing!" She sat down on the bed. "Go ahead! Go about your day and have a good one! I will just spend the day sewing—something complicated, and mysterious, and completely irrational!"

"Maggie!" Antonio grabbed her hands in his. "Things get complicated in my world, but if you know I love you, then that should be enough. I have to go." His tone was cold and she knew she had gotten all the information he was willing to share: nothing!

So frustrating.

Maggie watched Antonio leave their hotel suite! *How could he?* Maggie felt lost…lost in a crazy world. Now they were back in New York, where they had met. Would life with him ever be normal? She stared at her sewing room from the edge of the bed. She soon thought of the past night, their hours of lovemaking that sugarcoated every catastrophe. Maybe it was time to go jogging…she couldn't remember the last time she had gone. She could jog through Central Park. It would bring back memories of when Dana had first announced her engagement, just a year ago. Who would have ever thought she would be back, one year later, married herself!

Maggie opened the door of her suite, dressed in her workout attire, with a cap and sunglasses in hand, ready for disguise as soon as she made her way through the back entrance of the hotel lobby.

But no sooner had she opened the door to her hotel suite than she saw a woman standing outside. She was dressed in a navy blazer and black pants—casual, yet classy, with her beautiful long, wavy blonde hair. Maggie studied her—*gorgeous*, behind the dark sunglasses that she wore.

www.lovetheillusion.com/2257.htm

Maggie took a step back. Before she knew what was happening, the woman had marched into the suite.

"Is Antonio in here?" she asked.

Who is she? Maggie wondered, staring her up and down.

"Don't play sweet and innocent with me. I know he's in here somewhere... Question is how many women are in here with him?" The woman headed for the bathroom, seeming to be familiar with the layout of the suite. Maggie felt her stomach hosting an entirely new lump of discomfort.

"He left," Maggie told her, wondering if she should cooperate with the woman.

"How convenient." The woman glared at her. "Let me guess..." She gave her a snotty look. "You're Maggie?"

Maggie's mouth dropped open as she kept her eye on her when she suddenly realized who she was. *Oh...yikes! It's Nicolette!* Maggie stood, silently frozen, wondering what to say or do next as Nicolette stared back at her.

"Please, just leave!" Maggie told her, grabbing her arm and attempting to guide her out of the room. "Antonio is not the father of your baby! So just leave us alone!"

"Don't be so sure about that, you poor excuse for—are you having fun playing his precious wifey? So pathetic!" she muttered.

"What do you want from us?"

"The truth! Mickey is his and he won't admit it, and now I am going to deal with this on my own!" She spoke harshly. "He's been dragging me through the courts for justice…and I'm taking matters into my own hands now! Where is his lame ass, anyway?"

Maggie tried to calm her. "I'll tell him you stopped by. I assume he has your number."

"That he does, but does he call me? No! I'll just sit here and wait until he returns!"

Maggie's eyes grew wide as she watched Nicolette, who picked up the photo of them dancing at the benefit—the one that sat next to the bed. "Look at this! How sweet!" she said sarcastically.

Then she dropped the photo on the floor.

"No!" Maggie cried.

"Oh, did that disturb you?" Nicolette asked, cocking her head at Maggie.

My favorite picture…

Maggie's heart was throbbing at the sight of the broken glass.

"I'll call him," Maggie finally decided. She picked up her phone.

"Can't wait!" Nicolette said.

Maggie spoke nervously into her phone. "Antonio! Nicolette is here…in our suite. You need to get here, *now*!"

"What?" She heard the shock in Antonio's voice. "I'll be right there." Maggie felt her hands shaking as she held onto her phone. "He's on his way." Maggie stood, staring at Nicolette.

More insanity...

More mystery...

More craziness…

A couple minutes later, Antonio arrived. "Nicki! How did you get in here?"

"Still have the key, lover boy!" She held up a magnetic card key.

"Maggie, you need to leave," Antonio told her.

"What? Why should I leave?" Maggie frowned at him.

"Trust me. I'll explain later. Just go…visit Julia."

"You must be kidding…*Antonio*… Why would you…" Maggie gave him a strange look. Shaking her head, she left the room. "Uh, never mind…" She closed the door, realizing arguing with him was pointless.

Who's the biggest idiot here? I have no idea, but like hell I'm going to Julia's.

She placed her ear on the door.

"How much, Nicki?" Antonio questioned her. "You have to promise me this is the last time!"

"You know I can't promise that! Do you know how expensive it is to raise a child, all on my own? You and your millions…you're not even going to miss it, Antonio!"

They said something too low to hear, and then Antonio laughed. "That's crazy! And way too much…Stanley will never agree to that."

"Quit acting like he's in charge of your money!"

What the...I can't even believe this…Maggie felt her pulse racing as she held her breath, gathering bits and pieces of their conversation.

"Thanks, Antonio!" She heard Nicolette's voice again.

"Do me a favor," Antonio said.

"What's that?"

"Give me your hall pass."

"I will not!"

"Then you can forget it," Antonio said sternly.

Whispering followed and Maggie was no longer able to hear what they were talking about.

This is such a joke! Maggie strained her ears in a failed effort.

Suddenly the door opened, and Nicolette flew past Maggie and vanished from her sight.

Maggie went into their suite, where Antonio stood, his hands in his hair.

"Spill it, Antonio!" Maggie stood facing him, with her hands on her hips. "What is the deal with her? Why don't you start with *how* and *why* she has a hall pass to our floor." Maggie gave him the evil eye.

"I gotta go." Antonio walked past Maggie.

"Where?" Maggie pursued him.

"I have to meet with Stanley," he explained as he hastily stepped into the elevator.

Maggie grabbed him. "I'm getting stressed out, okay? Did you see our photo? It's broken! What is up with the two of you? You'd better start talking to me, now!"

Antonio watched her. "I'm sorry about everything that just happened. Just try…not to let it upset you."

"Are you out of your mind? How can that not upset me? I hate your damn secrets! If you don't start talking, I'm going to…check into a different hotel!"

"That's not necessary."

"So that's it? You're not going to tell me anything?" Maggie grabbed his arm and dug her nails into his skin.

"Stop that! You're hurting me," Antonio whimpered.

"Let me guess….you had a child with her…and now you are paying alimony to shut her up and keep it out of the press."

"Maggie! How can you even suggest that? You should know better. The whole situation is just complicated. And believe me, it's not what it looks like."

"But you can't say?" Maggie said, aggravated.

"Just give me some time. I have to take care of a couple things—then I can tell you. Please, just be patient."

"Be *patient*?" Maggie asked. "You must be kidding! What are you hiding from me? Please don't tell me Mickey is yours."

"He's not, Maggie. Just let it go. I would just rather not have you involved in this whole mess. Trust me."

Trust me. His favorite words.

"Okay, but I don't see what the big secret is! I heard you two talking and I know more than you think."

"What's that?" He grabbed hold of her and placed his lips on hers while they stood in their private elevator.

"Stop! Quit kissing me!" Maggie wiped her lips on her sleeve. "I can't stand the thought of you kissing that…that bitchy Nicolette. And don't tell me you didn't at least kiss her."

"Maggie, this is just one of those corpses that lie in the maze of being a celebrity. I brought you into my world, and I told you it was crazy. Money and fame are not all they're cracked up to be."

Maggie looked at him skeptically.

"She and I had a past," Antonio explained, "but I was never in love with her like she was with me. And Mickey's not mine."

"How do you know that for sure?"

"Because we never slept together. That night was a disaster, but... Can we just drop this! I really don't want to talk about it, okay?"

"Why not? Do you have a clue how I feel? Like maybe I can't trust you..."

"That's ridiculous! Do you know how much I love you? You have no idea! This whole situation is just...complicated."

"Try me, Antonio." Maggie followed him as he stepped off the elevator.

"Look, I have to meet with Stanley. We have a day's worth of problems to take care of." He took a deep breath. "Meet me for dinner...at Bouley. It's been a year!" He gave her a sudden grin.

Maggie gasped. "Why should I want to have dinner with you?"

"We will talk then, okay? I promise."

"Fine. But if you don't have the story I want to hear, I am checking into a different hotel!" Maggie warned.

"Don't be foolish. I'll see you at ten, after close." Antonio still wore a grin. Despising his hold over her, she watched as he turned and walked away.

Maybe I have lost my appetite.

And now...time to call Francis!

I almost forgot.

Chapter 13

With her phone pressed to her ear, Maggie waited nervously for Francis to pick up.

"Maggie? What took you so long to get back to me? If we are going to work together, you'll have to be more prompt in returning my messages."

"I'm still wondering why you have to call in the middle of the night! Don't I own the right to a good night's sleep?"

"Where have you been all your life, Maggie? Don't you know that business always interferes with a good night of sleep?"

"Okay, well, I am not getting enough of that since Antonio went to jail."

"Good thing he's out now."

Francis knows?

"Yes…that's good news, don't you think?" Maggie choked out.

"I'm trying to be happy for him. But we need to talk about why I called." Maggie felt her stomach curl into a ball. "Don't expect for a minute that I will dismiss the sudden disappearance of Madeline. I had her in my grasp and then—suddenly—like the waves on an ocean's shore, she rushed out on me."

"Sorry to hear, Francis. Perhaps you need some tips on capturing women." Maggie felt that lump in her throat. "But if you want, I could give her a call and find out what you did to chase her away."

"That won't be necessary. There can only be one reason she left, and I'm sure we both know exactly what I am talking about. Your loyalties to Antonio are so admirable, but you should know that you are in way over your head if you think you can bring me down."

Maggie forced a laugh. "Francis, don't be silly. I have no clue what you are talking about."

"She is the first woman to ever walk out on me, and I am quite certain she has an agenda. What that is I can only imagine. But I took the bug out of my phone, by the way."

Maggie felt alarm pouring into her veins. "Why would she do that, Francis?" She kept her composure, even as she felt her heart skip a beat.

"You tell *me*, Maggie! There is no reason for this, you see? Antonio is out of jail. And let me tell you that *I* dropped the charges. I pulled many strings behind the scenes to get him out!"

"You…what?" Maggie asked in disbelief.

"Why don't you sleep on that tonight, Maggie…And just for the record, we work together now, so you had better report at noon tomorrow at Blue Hill. Lunch is on me, and we will not be discussing matters of business nature. Soon you will know way more about that husband of yours than you ever wanted to know!"

Maggie started to reply, and then realized Francis had hung up.

So awful…

I think I should pass on that opportunity…but it is SO tempting!

"Maggie! There you are!" Amber approached her as she headed back to her suite.

"Hey, how's it going?"

"Not good!" Amber let her know. "Rainelle just quit, and now we have no makeup artist!"

"What? Why would she do that?" Maggie asked, feeling temporarily distracted from her own personal dilemma.

"Probably because Antonio fired Bradley!"

"He what? When? How do you know?"

"Don't tell me…" Amber's voice took on a note of surprise. "You had no idea? The news is all over…everyone on the dance teams knows and… How can you not know? Didn't Antonio tell you?"

"Are you kidding? He tells me nothing! I'm still wondering how he got out of jail! I visited him that same day…he acted as though he would be in there forever! I didn't know what to do, so, I…" Maggie shut her mouth abruptly, and then asked: "When did Bradley get fired?"

"Just two hours ago! And shortly after that, Rainelle quit!"

"This is all my fault." Maggie quivered, recalling her adventures with Bradley. "I need to talk to him—where is he?"

"How is it your fault?" Amber asked, confused.

"Believe me, it is…" Maggie felt drowned in remorse.

"Bradley is an awesome guy… Why would Antonio just fire him?"

"I can't believe he fired him."

"He's gone, completely gone—from the hotel and everything! It's so terrible! I tried calling him, but he doesn't pick up. And now Rainelle is gone! Who is going to do our makeup for the show tomorrow night?"

"Makeup?" Maggie shook her head. "I have no idea, but that's the least of my concerns. Ever since we got back to New York, it has been one disaster after the next. And Antonio leaves me in the dark! Every day a new surprise! Why can't he surprise me with a dozen roses…or a box of chocolates? No, that would be way too ordinary for him! He goes for the shock and mystery tied up with some wretched bow!"

"Being married to him must be difficult." Amber looked around. "Hey, I heard Nicolette was here."

"From who?"

"Angie saw her parading down the hallway. She is such a blinding sight in her Brooks Brothers attire. She's spoiled rotten, and her father is so filthy rich!"

"That can't be…she was in our suite begging Antonio for money! She thinks she has his child…who knows what's going on with that!"

"I remember when they dated," Amber said. "Sorry, I shouldn't bring that up…and don't worry. None of us liked her."

"How long did they date?"

"A long time…maybe a year," Amber said.

"A year?" Maggie found it hard to believe. "What happened?"

"They just stopped seeing each other—all of a sudden. No one knew."

"That's so strange." Maggie pondered the possibilities. "How did they meet?"

"She is Shagan's daughter."

"Shagan? Who's that?"

"You don't know who Shagan is? He's owner of this hotel! He owns the whole chain throughout the US."

"Is that…significant?"

"The story was that he did not trust anyone dating his daughter because they all wanted a piece of the money she came from. Antonio is so wealthy, he has no interest in her for that, you know. He said she was beautiful, and the next thing we know she started coming to his shows. She used to sit in the front row, and I don't think she missed one."

"So she was his first lady in the ring of fire..." Maggie wore a look of pity.

"No, Antonio never had her on stage. It was always a secret that they were dating, until it hit the press several years ago that she was carrying his child. It was all so strange, because that is when the relationship just completely dissolved. We never heard a thing about her after that, and Antonio would never talk about it when we would ask. He is a very private person, if you have not already figured that out."

"Yes, I am well aware of his privacy battles. But I am his wife! And you know what? He never mentioned her to me once! He said he never loved her! Yeah, right..." Maggie let out a sigh.

"I wouldn't worry about it. Antonio is a good guy, Maggie. What happened with them is in the past, and no one likes to talk about their ex, right?"

"I guess." Maggie suddenly had flashbacks of Jasmine and Phillip. "So, you think Mickey is...his?"

"I...why, I...don't know." Amber suddenly got a strange look on her face. "Just because the press says so doesn't make it true. I really don't know anything else. And what I told you is just the rumor, if you know what I mean."

"Yeah, I get it." Maggie managed a smile. "Thanks for sharing what you…ah…think you know?"

"I'm pretty sure what I told you is true, but I haven't a clue about his sex life, if you know what I mean." Amber giggled. "He always had a lot of women around before he met you, but I never thought he was serious with any of them. Only Nicolette, and that ended suddenly."

"Right…" Maggie frowned, realizing she was more confused than she had ever been. "I need to get back to the room."

"Okay, see you later!"

Yep...

Maggie pounded on Julia's door.

"My head is just spinning!" Maggie told Julia as she entered the room. "I'm supposed to meet Antonio for dinner tonight, and I just…don't even want to go! My whole day has been one obnoxious surprise after the other, and guess what! Nicolette came to visit today… Do you know who she is? Let me tell you! She thinks Antonio is the father of her child… No big deal, right? Just a small wire in my feather cap today! Isn't that just great news? His name is Mickey, by the way…and the only saving grace is that he is cute. He's three years old and she is still insisting that Antonio is his father! What is that about? Supposedly they dated before we met!"

"Sounds like quite the racket." Julia's face twitched as if she was searching for advice.

"Antonio said I have nothing to worry about, but I *am* worried."

"I can understand…but if Antonio said—"

"That woman is nuts…and why would he even be acquainted with her?"

"Who knows…but it's in the past, right? And probably for good reason."

"No, it's not in the past! Not if she shows up in our suite *today!* That means it is very much in the present! I could hear them talking through the door! She wants Antonio to give her money…but I just found out from Amber that Nicolette's father is filthy rich! What is the deal with that? It doesn't even make sense!"

"Does Antonio know who the father is?"

"I don't know! And what he does know, he won't tell me! I'm going crazy! No sooner does he get out of jail than I want to send him back! Then there's Francis—I called his hairy butt back today and he claimed he dropped the charges and pulled strings to get Antonio out of jail. But that's not what Antonio says! He says that Francis has money, but that he has more…that can only mean one thing. Is it the same guy that Francis paid? If so, the guy must be—what—crazy rich all in a day? None of it makes any sense at all."

"Well, maybe this will make you feel better," Julia said. "I heard back from Felicia. Hopefully, it will make your day to know that she is getting a large piece of the puzzle solved. The guy that you and Bradley followed works at the jail. She knows his name, which is a good start. She will be contacting his superiors to check into things."

"That's good, but it hardly even matters now." Maggie paced back and forth. "Did you know Bradley was fired for helping me? And Rainelle, his wife, has now quit the makeup crew, so everyone will be ugly on stage…as if that matters. And, one more thing to give me a heart attack… Francis found the bug in his phone! He knows he's been set up! Now I miss the good old days when I was stressed about having a child!"

"Just try to relax, dear." Julia spoke softly, trying to calm her.

"*Relax?* I am coming completely unglued! Do you realize what has happened all within a day? And now Antonio wants to meet for dinner at Biagio's—late tonight. That's where we met a year ago, remember? Him and his obnoxious humor! He says we can talk about everything tonight. And I told him that if I don't like what I hear, I will be checking into a different hotel! I have his credit card with no limit! I could be gone for years! See how he keeps track of money? He doesn't! And who knows what he's passing over to Nicolette!"

"Wow…that *is* a lot in a day, but just for starters, you need to sit. Pacing around nervously does not do you any good."

"I can't sit right now! I'm trying to organize everything in my head—which piece of the fallout is the most disturbing— but what can I do about any of it anyway, right? Bradley, Francis, and lovely Nicolette… Actually, she bothers me the most." Maggie sighed. "I *hate* to think of them together. But then, I hate that Bradley is fired. I really like him! And that's so not fair. Why would Antonio do that?" Maggie paused. "Do you realize that Francis probably wants to kill me? Perhaps *that's* the solution to all of this! I could be…dead!" Maggie's eyes popped open. "Oh NO*!*" She panicked. "No wonder he has agreed to work with me…so he can keep track of his target. I'm gonna die!"

"Antonio will keep you safe."

"I can protect myself. I'll buy a gun."

"That's definitely crazy."

"Yes, Julia, that's my life—everything crazy."

"So, what are you wearing to dinner tonight?"

"So that's it?" Maggie stared at Julia. "You can't deal with any of this either, can you?"

"Nope. But who could? You got Sherlock Holmes, *Fatal Attraction*, and James Bond, all in one day."

A closet full of clothes...but what to wear for this "special" occasion... Maggie choked on her thoughts as she stood pondering the upcoming event: dinner with Antonio. Was it worth dressing up for? She was pretty sure it wasn't. But she had to take the bit of advice Julia had given her.

A turtleneck will be perfect. I hope he hates it...

www.lovetheillusion.com/2204.htm

At Biagio's, where they had first met, Maggie sat across from Antonio and placed her napkin in her lap. "This is nice," Maggie said stiffly, admiring the candle and tulip bouquet that sat in the center of the table. "You hired a wait staff?" She suddenly saw a gentleman approaching with a bottle of wine and an appetizer served on a brochette.

"I'm keeping a few people on past close… Don't worry, they are being well compensated." He gave her a wink.

"That's *so* thoughtful of you, but for starters, I am less interested in the appetizer and wine and more interested in why you would fire Bradley." Maggie tried to keep her voice calm.

"He's a traitor." Antonio placed his napkin on his lap and leaned forward to explain, "I know about your little outing, Maggie. And I'm *not* impressed!"

Maggie swallowed her shock, wondering how he knew from behind bars that she and Bradley were following Francis.

"Who told you?"

"I told *you* to stay *away* from him, not follow him! Why don't you ever listen to me? And then Bradley gets wise and follows your suggestion! Both of you…complete idiots!" Antonio gave her a stern look.

"Well, isn't that noble of you, Antonio…trying to protect me from the jail cell. But you can't fault me for trying to help get you out! I was miserable without you! And Bradley? He was just trying to help. I want him rehired immediately, or I'm *not* sitting here, eating dinner with you…"

"Not going to happen—he's done! He was supposed to be looking out for you while I was gone, and for your information, following Francis was not on the list!"

"So that's it? You can't just…find it in your heart to forgive him? You are such an insensitive jerk! How can you do this?"

"Don't question my objectives, Maggie. You need to let it go. Trust me!"

"*Trust* you? What a line of crap, especially after my visit from Nicolette...She broke our picture! And you give her money? How much did you give her, Antonio? Did Stanley cut her a check? Or should I just ask him instead of you?"

"She needs my help," Antonio said. "But Mickey's not mine."

"So you claim. But then why do you care so much? What tracks are you trying to cover, Antonio?"

"It's not like that...I feel responsible for everything that happened with her."

"What do you mean 'everything that happened with her'?"

"She got into drugs and...it's just not really dinner conversation...*please!*"

"She's on drugs?"

"Not when I first met her; it's just a long story, and a sad one. She had everything, and I don't think she ever worked a day in her life. I think it led to a lack of ambition. She just lived to party."

"That's sad."

"It is."

"So you are absolutely sure that Mickey's not yours?"

"Yes! Why would you keep asking me that? We were together that night, but I left and when I came back, she was high as a kite and with—she probably doesn't even remember. I don't have the heart to tell her."

"Tell her what?"

"The same person who got her hooked on drugs got her pregnant. I stuck by her...paying for her rehab and...we spent a lot of time together after that, but not romantically. I was trying to help her, you know." He sat back and looked up at the ceiling. "At first, everything was great. We would go out together and have so much fun, and then one day…I remember the first time she showed up stoned, and I was like 'Whoa…what's up with you?' She was all crazy, acting like a wild woman, and the next thing I knew, I felt I had no choice but to act as her guardian angel, always watching over her to make sure she was okay. Just about the time I thought I had found someone I could fall in love with, who wasn't out for my money—because she came from enormous wealth—I found out she was into drugs over her head. It was devastating."

"Sorry…" Maggie finally said, feeling the anger and fear drain out of her. "So is she still addicted?"

"No, I got her to clean up, get off the drugs when she was pregnant, for the sake of her child, Mickey. She stayed with me for weeks, but it was only so that I could help her."

"Sounds…difficult…"

"That is what I love about you, Maggie…your innocence. You have no idea what it's like, trying to find someone in my world. People who don't have money want it, and they will do anything to get it. Those who have it misuse it and often spend it on drugs and…now you know why I felt so lucky when I met you. When you came in here a year ago, I could not believe you didn't recognize me, but that was a good thing! For the first time in my life, I felt as though someone could just like me for me."

"I do, *Chad!*" Maggie smiled, recalling the day she met him. "I thought you were pretty cute and funny…and seductively sweet…" She made eyes at him.

He managed a grin.

"I hope you still do?" His eyes were fastened on hers.

"I definitely do…" She grinned back at him.

"Did you make your dress?"

"I did."

"Figures…"

"Why?"

"I just…want to take it off…"

"Is that all you can think about now that you're out of jail?"

He grinned at her.

"Well, I purposely wore a turtleneck because I'm *not* in the mood!"

"Is that so?" He appeared up for a challenge.

"Yes, that's *so*."

"You're killing me. I just want to kiss you, that's all." He tilted his head to negotiate.

"Really? Well, maybe I'll let you…if you give Bradley his job back!"

"Maggie, I can't! You have to trust my decision. I know what's best, okay?

"People make mistakes! Why can't you just forgive him?"

"I wish it were that simple."

"So now you hate him?"

"No, I would never hate him, but you should have never dragged him into your adventures!"

"So it's all my fault?" Maggie pouted.

"I wouldn't say *all* your fault. But you do have a way of finding trouble."

"You might want to quit while you're ahead! And just for the record, I could still check into a different hotel. This has been a day from raging hell."

"I would check into the room next to you." He gave her a wink.

"You would?"

"Yeah. Would you let me in?"

"Maybe."

"A toast to that." Antonio held up his glass.

"We aren't done talking. Why did Nicolette come by today, asking for money? If her father is so rich, then why does she need your money?"

"Like I said, it's complicated."

"Wrong answer…try again."

"Okay…well, her father has pretty much disowned her after the whole drug problem. She had nearly half a million dollars just given to her—she blew it, mindlessly. Her father refuses to share any more with her."

"So now *you* take care of her like some charity project?"

"Yes…but I feel somewhat responsible."

"How is *that*?"

Antonio turned away, afraid to speak.

"What, Antonio? What can be so bad?"

"Oh, it's terrible. You have no idea."

"Just tell me."

"I was there that night. It's my fault she got pregnant. If I hadn't left to go get food for her that night, then none of this would have happened. She was passed out on her bed…from her 'concoction,' and that's when the guy raped her."

"Oh my gosh… Seriously?"

"Yes…and that is the night she got pregnant! But she doesn't remember a thing. She thinks we…you know…and she doesn't want to let go of the possibilities, but I always tell her there is no 'us.' She even did an interview saying we were together and expecting, and I thought, 'What does it matter?' I thought if I countered her accusations, she would go off the deep end."

"That is one crazy mess…."

"This is just between us, Maggie. Don't tell anyone. Her life and battles with addiction are very real and she has suffered enough. I don't want that ending up in the press. Luckily, they were too busy focusing on us as a couple. One time she ended up in the hospital and almost died. I was by her side, but the reason she was admitted was never made public."

"So she's not on drugs anymore? She seems like she is; she asked how many women you had in our room. Why would she talk like that to me when she knows I'm your wife?"

"She's messed up from the drugs—no doubt about that. But strangely, I think she's a decent mom."

"I highly doubt that. She's a lunatic."

"Trust me! She was just messing with you."

"*Messing* with me? She broke the photo of us dancing! I had to call maintenance to clean up the glass from the picture frame! It was shattered all over our floor!"

"I'm sorry about that, but you have to realize that she still thinks that Mickey is mine, so she's very jealous."

"She should know the truth."

"Don't you see? That is why she loves him so much! She thinks he's mine, and I can't tell her the truth. But I could not let her win the court case. She wanted millions. The test came back negative—thankfully—but she's fully convinced that I paid someone off to tamper with the evidence."

"This is just so lovely. Now she's going to follow us for the rest of our lives?" Maggie's face was bleak.

"Probably not. I took away her key to the fourth floor today. She won't be walking the halls anymore, and despite your confrontation today, I don't think she's a threat to you."

Maggie's eyes got wide. "You don't know that for sure!"

"She's been paid to stay away. If she comes to visit, I cut off the funds, see?"

"How can you give her money, Antonio?"

"Charity…I write it off—or rather, Stanley does. It's not such a big deal, because I have a surplus anyway. Now, you know everything…so you feel better now?"

"No…the whole thing's just disturbing…"

"Okay, well, welcome to my world." Antonio finally started on his wine.

Maggie set down her empty glass, staring back at him.

"Why do you have to give her money? Isn't that just inviting her to ask for more? Aren't there programs to take care of her?"

"Look… there probably are, but her father owns this hotel, and she can stay here for free. She used to stay here; I pay money so that she doesn't…get it? We can't both be here, you know?"

"Why didn't you tell me about her?" Maggie asked.

"Why would I want to talk about this? It's not fun to talk about. And I would rather not have my crew knowing any of this. People talk and want to know stuff that just isn't their business. If I tell you, that means it stays between us! You tell one person, and then everyone knows! And no one respects my privacy! That's how my life is, and I have to be so careful. Pretty soon, the truth becomes distorted and then…you never know how it ends up… Just better left unsaid."

"I won't say anything."

"I know, and I trust you. You should know that when I'm with you I just want to escape and be in that world with you that is just us…understand? Who wants to talk about all the garbage? Only you…"

He raised an eyebrow at her.

"I guess I feel better knowing," Maggie said.

"Yeah, but not much, right?" Antonio studied her. "See, I hate dragging you through the mud, Maggie, and my life has a *lot* of mud puddles. It's just part of the *game* of fame: so idolized from the outside, but inside you wish you could escape the ball of corruption." He looked downcast. "You know, it's so true what they say: money talks. What they don't tell you is that it talks trouble. Some days I wish I were broke. It would be so much simpler. The more you have, the more people expect from you, and honestly, I can't just turn my back and not care, but I also can't save the world. Nicolette is special in a way to me, but not like you…it's like I was meant to be her guardian angel. And she's a prime example of how money destroys people. I take care of her because I feel sorry for her, not because there's something between us."

"Well, who am I to stand in the way of your good deeds..." Maggie mustered a small smile.

The chef came up and set down a big platter with two plates. "A little bit of everything," he said. "Bon appetit!"

"Is it French?" Maggie wanted to know.

"No, but enjoy anyway..." The chef walked away.

"It's Italian food, silly," Antonio teased her. "We have a little bit of everything, and while we eat, we are not talking about Nicolette anymore. You can tell me what you did while I was away."

"I just...missed you. That's all..." Maggie wondered what Bradley had told him.

"Hmm...that doesn't sound very exciting," he said, picking up a crostino.

"It was miserable... What else do you need to know?"

"So, there is nothing *else* you want to tell me?" He eyed her suspiciously.

She wondered what he knew.

"No...I just really missed you..." Maggie stared into his eyes, which darted back at her. He looked debonair in his plaid dress shirt and tie...*so adorable and so deliciously refined...better than orange, which just wasn't his color...*

Maggie thought about kissing him.

"And now I'm back..." Antonio smiled. "Just like magic!"

Maggie felt relieved to know more about Mickey, but now she

recalled she had an unfinished agenda.

"I just remembered something else I want to know." She stared at Antonio.

"What's that?"

"How did you get out? I mean, how much did it cost? I'm just confused, and I hate to be confused."

"Let's just say I had to fight fire with fire. Don't like to play that game, but sometimes I have no choice," Antonio said vaguely.

"That's it? So…I stay confused. Figures."

"I can't talk about it just yet…until things are finished…" Antonio gave her a wink.

"Antonio! There you go again! Why can't you let me in? I have the right to know; I am your wife!"

"Yes, but there are some things you can't know, Maggie. I mean it for the best…to protect you…"

"Protect me from who? Francis?"

"If people have information, other people want it…but if you don't know, then you are useless to them…get it? Francis is…I'm not going to spend our evening together talking about him either, okay? Case closed!"

"Case opened! I am working for him again!" Maggie spilled her secret, hoping he would share his.

"Son of a…*no*, Maggie! Have you lost your mind? Please tell me you're not!" Antonio looked at her in disbelief. "Tell him you quit. If you don't, I will!"

"Why do you even care that I work for him? You can't prove that he put anything in my drink! I think you just don't want me to work because…I don't know…it hurts your ego!" Maggie considered how to extract the truth. "When, in fact…I take pride in my work and want to have something to do that I love! Why can't you just be happy for me, Antonio?"

"Then work for Gia!"

"I could, but she walked by me all snooty."

"She did?"

"Yeah, after I did my speech, she gave me a pitiful look as if she had regrets for nominating me!"

"She was probably just embarrassed."

"Thanks for *that* reminder. She did tell me to send a file, but of *fifty* new dress designs—that will take forever! I haven't had time to make *that* many! And she just does not seem that friendly to me, for some reason. Francis is right here in New York and at least he *wants* to work together. It's just way more convenient."

"Convenient? There is nothing about that man that is convenient, and you should know that by now! When does he return to London? Soon, I hope."

"He's here for a while. I have no idea why."

"Because he's up to no good. He's a troublemaker and he lives to bring it my way! Why do you even want to work for the guy, Maggie?"

"Because he's a ticket to success, Antonio. And you know it's true."

"Gia's there too, trust me. She will get you where you want to be. I promise!"

"Fine, I'll email her tomorrow and let her know I am still working on the file," Maggie said, realizing the gap between Antonio and Francis would never come to a close. "I just don't know what to think. Is Francis the monster that you make him out to be or not?" Maggie made one last attempt.

Antonio gave her an irritated look. "Just…tell me you are quitting!"

"I'll think about it, but you won't give me a good reason to quit. Or tell me how you got out of jail! Francis said he assisted in your release."

"He did?"

She nodded.

"Interesting."

"So, what about that?"

"I don't know."

"Who did you pay?"

"That's not up for discussion. For legal reasons I can't say." He shook his head and sighed in frustration.

I have no choice…I'm meeting Francis for lunch… Maggie stared back at Antonio, despising his secrecy. *At Blue Hill…tomorrow. Perhaps he will tell me what I want to know.*

Chapter 14

"I'm meeting with Francis," Maggie told Julia. "Just so you know where I'll be."

"Okay, just be careful." Julia shook her head.

"I'm not really afraid of him. But I *am* afraid of what Antonio refuses to tell me. Who even knows if Francis tainted my drink? I don't like mysteries," Maggie grumbled.

"I love your disguise." Julia admired the blonde wig.

"Yeah, well, I can hardly sit next to Francis as I am. The press will be all over that. And I'm getting too smart for that. Antonio wants me to quit working for Francis—figures, because it's the only way to stay informed! I want to know the details and I am about to find out *everything*." Maggie adjusted her wig. "So, what do you think? Am I good blonde?"

"Just…marvelous…" But Julia still looked concerned.

"I know what you're thinking, and I know it's a bad idea to meet with him, but we're meeting in public. I need to do this because Antonio is all secretive with me, and there are things I want to know! Francis may have his list of flaws, but the one thing he is—is upfront—nearly to a fault. After this, I will try not to ever see him again."

"Can I get that in writing?"

"Ha, ha…we'll see."

"I think you're making a mistake, but I know better than to tell you not to go. You will do as you wish, but don't say I didn't warn you."

An hour later, Maggie stepped out of a cab and walked into Blue Hill.

Francis was patiently awaiting her arrival. He did a double take when she walked up to his table, then laughed.

"Incognito. I like it!" he said. "And you're even on time. Would that be a first?"

"Maybe…but you still arrived ahead of me," Maggie said.

"Got the champagne waiting for you," Francis told her. "It's an expensive one, and it's on me."

"Uh…thanks. I probably need some."

"So let me guess…we're not here on business?" Francis sounded amused.

"Depends what you mean by business." Maggie took a seat.

"Well, I assume that since you have such a wonderful opportunity to work for Gia Tellies that your decision to work for me was just a front for a whole new agenda." Francis wore a wicked frown. "Am I right? And here I go and order champagne. So tell me: exactly *what* are we celebrating?"

"Okay, here's what I want to know, Francis. I want to know why Stanley was unable to post bond and how then all of a sudden Antonio was free. Also, I want to know how the drug test came up clean. I know something was put in my drink and I want the truth. Why don't you start with the drug test. How did you pull that one off?"

"Maggie, I am so surprised that you couldn't figure this out on your own, but since you can't, I will move past the humor and tell you how it is. But, after I do, you will regret meeting with me. Sometimes the less you know the better."

"Now you sound like Antonio. But I'm not afraid of you."

"You're a smart woman not to be afraid of me…but you *should* be afraid of what I'm about to tell you, because I have information that could pretty much destroy your marriage." He paused. "I assume you aren't ready for that." He took a sip of his champagne.

"Francis…that's ridiculous. You and I both know that Antonio's a great guy. And we love each other. What I need to know is who paid who. Sorry, but I already know that you have a history of blackmail and fraud and Antonio said he had to 'fight fire with fire.' Of course, he had to stoop to your level and pay someone off to get out of jail, but you said that's not true and that *you* pulled strings to get him out! That doesn't even make any sense! Why you would do that when he pushed you off a boat?"

"Maggie…it never ceases to amaze me how innocent your mind is and how Antonio has managed to pull the wool over your eyes. Do you have *any* idea who the jail guard is?"

"Your friend, relative…acquaintance…I don't know, but I assume you know him somehow, and—what? Just tell me."

"I know that you and Bradley were following me, and it was so…cute, by the way. But, I have nothing to hide. The guard is simply a friend I have known for years. And it may surprise you to know that Bradley—Antonio's paid security officer— is also friends with him, as is Nicolette's father! You see, we all have things in common, and a few friends as well. Perhaps Antonio would want you to *think* that he would never keep company with people in my circle, but the truth is that they own a large share of stock in his corporation. How do you think he got where he is? His brother's death? Ha! Now *that* is funny! Perhaps he would like you to think it happened innocently enough, but there is something else you should know! A lot of people have their fingers in Antonio's pile of money. And you would not approve of the majority of them. Maybe that is shocking to you, but there's something even more shocking. I may as well go ahead and drop the bomb: Nicolette and he share a son! He will never admit it, even after the press had that topic exhausted several years ago. And if you want to know the truth, you'll have to pay someone off to see Mickey's biological records. Antonio was the perfect match! Problem is, Antonio did not want to marry her because of her drug addiction. So, he claims that she was raped by her supplier. It works, doesn't it? He is busy paying people off *all* the time, but the press always uncovers the truth!"

"How do you know all of this?" Maggie asked. "Why would Antonio lie about it?"

"Oh, he plays the 'clean' card! He entertains children, right? He can't be caught up in a drug affair." Francis leaned back in his chair. "I would say he is an excellent magician. But his best magic trick ever?" Francis leaned over the table and whispered: "Making the truth disappear!"

"No way." Maggie tapped her nails on the base of her champagne glass. "Antonio is the best guy I have ever met, Francis. Why would you say such a thing? Besides, he told me those rumors were lies! I just wanted to know about the jail ordeal. It was strange—whatever went down did not make any sense!"

"Maggie, I think you're in over your head. But hopefully the past year of your life will make up for the lie you have been living."

Maggie gave him a blank stare. "Look, Francis, how am I supposed to believe any of this? I was looking for the truth, but obviously you are not cooperating."

"Fine, you don't believe me. Then I will tell you who got Antonio out of jail. That's really what you want to know, right?"

"Who?" Maggie rolled her eyes in disbelief.

"Nicolette's father," Francis said. "Yeah, as long as Antonio's around, making money, he takes care of Nicolette… Get it?" He paused to locate his cell phone. "He doesn't want anything to do with her. I called him to let him know that her precious Antonio was being detained and—"

"He paid more than you?"

"Hey, I had to save my skin. I'm fighting false accusations, just like your husband."

"What are you talking about? So you admit it? You paid money to taint the test results after you drugged my champagne?"

"Now *why* would I taint your champagne, Maggie? You know you don't believe that for a second or you wouldn't be sitting here drinking it with me!"

Maggie shifted her eyes between him and her untouched glass.

"Do you know who the bartender at the event was?" He waited until he had her full attention. "Take a guess…"

Maggie remained silent, uncomfortable in her own skin.

"I know you dropped a little surprise in my glass, Francis. You were jealous of my first award—too soon."

"The bartender is a friend of Nicolette's father, and…*he* poured your drink. His plan backfired, I would say…"

"That is such a lie, Francis! You wanted Gia Tellies to notice you, and instead she noticed my designs!"

"Ah, I'm glad you mentioned her. She's just another one of your beloved Antonio's friends! How do you think you won? Sorry, but I know Gia quite well, and she told me that your husband paid her a large sum. She's quite fond of that husband of yours. And he's been a good customer. He used to buy her designs for the women he paraded around with before he met you. She is quick to do him any favor. And I mean *any* favor. Those two have an interesting past."

"They dated? Wait, I thought you wanted me to introduce you to Gia. You already know her?"

"Had to play along. Already knew she was giving you an award. And who am I to stand in the way of such a huge payout. "

"Antonio paid Gia?"

"You're getting smarter."

"This is so…awful." Maggie's heart sank as she absorbed Francis' plate of information.

"Come on…weren't you just a little startled that you won?"

"Well, yeah, but…why? Why did Antonio do this to me?"

"Is it a secret that he does not want you working for me? Simply because he knows I know everything about him!"

"I feel sick…"

"See, Maggie, you need me. I can tell you anything you want to know."

"I'm done. This is enough for one day." She paused. "How do I know you aren't confusing me with more lies?"

"If only the truth could be what you wanted to hear," Francis said, amused.

"You can never prove any of it, so…I need to leave."

"I can prove it—if you need proof that you are wise to listen to me," Francis challenged her. "I'm sure Antonio thinks he knows all about me, but *I* know all about *him.* See, long before you two met, he contacted me to do business with him. He wanted me to make his costumes. He existed in my circle of friends, and so he knows all about us—maybe more than he should. But I should never worry! I have more than enough information on him, and that is why he wants to dissolve our working relationship. Problem is, you never asked me until now."

"I can't even listen to this anymore." Maggie stood, feeling shaky.

"Sit down, Maggie," Francis said. "You need to think back to when you first met Antonio…"

Maggie sat back down. "Yeah…I was in Biagio's. I told him I was here on business, for a fashion show, and that I worked for you."

"And?"

"Antonio said, 'You work for Francis?' And then asked if I was from the UK," she recalled.

"See! He knew I was in the UK. Now, how did he know that?"

"I don't know."

"Gia's on my voicemail. You wanna listen?" He held up his phone. "Got the proof right here that Antonio gave Gia money to take you under her wing. Sorry Maggie, you are talented, but Antonio is funding your success. And so…it's only a matter of time before you are at the top with me. Money buys almost anything!"

"No, no…don't say that, please…" Maggie faltered. *Antonio would not do that.* She tried to dismiss the crazy thoughts racing about in her head. *Would he?*

"Simplicity…" Francis said smugly. "*That* is always the key to logical thinking. Things are always simple. You already know that Antonio despises your desire to work for me, right? Gia's a simple solution. She runs at his command, but he pays her anyway." Francis handed Maggie his phone. "Go ahead, listen…"

Reluctantly, she took the phone and held it to her ear. It was Gia's voice: "Next year, Francis, I will vote for you—I promise. Antonio's so sweet trying to protect his precious Maggie from you, but how long can he keep his own secrets, right?"

Maggie slowly handed the phone back to Francis, her stomach tying a new knot.

"I have to go." Maggie got up as the waitress approached to take their order. "And, for the record, I no longer work for you or Gia! You both make me ill."

"Don't ruin my day, Maggie, just because I ruined yours! You really should learn to play nice. I always do." He let go of a grin. "No more for us," he told the waitress. "Just the bill for the champagne."

Maggie felt tense as she reached for her bag.

"You could at least finish your champagne." Francis chuckled.

"There's nothing to celebrate," Maggie said, turning to leave.

"I'd say there is! You've learned so much. Now, why leave? So you can celebrate his infidelity, alone?" Francis called out.

Maggie stopped in her tracks and turned around to look at him, one last time.

Why won't he shut up?

Francis wore a wicked smile.

She rushed back to the table and grabbed her glass of champagne. "Maybe I do need this…" She took a sip. "And I forgot to thank you," she said. She dumped the remaining champagne into the crotch of his pants. "Have a nice day!"

"Maggie!" Francis shouted at her on her way out.

"Revenge is sweet," she whispered as she made her exit.

Maggie sat in the cab, her head spinning. She couldn't even properly organize all the information Francis had openly shared. Was any of it true? Gia's voicemail was definitely disturbing. Was she one of Francis' allies, yet friends with Antonio as well? It was hard to imagine someone walking that fence, but surely it was a possibility.

Now she tried to sort out the bits and pieces of information, hoping to determine what—if any of it—made sense. She was staring out the cab window when she heard the driver ask, "Isn't it a little dark for those?"

"Huh?" Maggie was jolted out of her murky thoughts.

"The sunglasses," the driver said. "It's overcast, looks like a storm is brewing. I just heard the sirens go off a minute ago. They supposedly spotted a tornado west of us."

"Great," Maggie muttered. She took off her sunglasses and looked out the window. "Wow… It is pretty dark," she agreed.

"Hey…don't tell me…you're Mrs. DeLuca…Antonio's woman…what a crazy day for me! What are you doing in a cab?"

"Hiding out…" Maggie said. "Paparazzi like to follow me in the limo, you know. This way I'm undercover!"

"Ah…you're not really a blonde, are you?"

"No, and you're a bit too smart to be a cab driver, aren't you?"

"Maybe so, and—sorry, Mrs. D., but I was told to drop you off at this here US Bank building."

"What! I'm not getting out here! My hotel is three miles away!"

"Sorry, but I was told to just drop you off here."

"You can't just drop me off wherever—I'm not paying you if you let me out here."

"No worries, someone has already paid me double the fare, so you don't owe me a thing."

"Look! I don't have time for this bullshit! I will pay you twice that to take me—"

"Just following orders!" The driver came to an abrupt halt at the side of the road. Maggie fell forward, catching herself on the back of the driver's seat. The contents of her purse spilled out onto the cab floor. She quickly gathered the items and put them into her purse, but as she grabbed onto her phone, she noticed that the back had popped off. *What the heck is that?*

Maggie reached for the cover to her phone.

"Got everything?" the cab driver asked.

"Just about…" Maggie stared in disbelief. *Who would bug my phone?* "Can you *please* take me to Manhattan's Pavilion? I really do not want to get out here," Maggie insisted.

"Sorry, ma'am. I got strict orders. And value my life."

"Orders from who?" Maggie asked.

"You should know."

"I need to call another cab."

"Whatever you need to do." He waited patiently for her to get out.

Maggie stepped outside, into a downpour.

Shit is my luck... She scurried into a hotel lobby adjacent to the US Bank. She headed for the ladies' room and closed herself into a stall.

Her wig was saturated and her eyes were burning from the mascara that had run into them.

WHO would bug my phone? And why? This is getting scary. Why did he drop me off here of all places?

Then she received a text: LIMO IS OUT FRONT!

Antonio? How does he know?

Julia? No way...

Maggie sheepishly exited the bathroom, and was instantly accosted by a reporter.

"Maggie! Maggie DeLuca! Can you tell us the details of Antonio's imprisonment? How did this get settled out of court so quickly?"

Maggie walked past the reporter, but the woman relentlessly chased her.

"Maggie! Is it true that Shagan paid to get Antonio out of jail?"

They know? Great... so much for incognito.

Such a disaster... and there's the limo! Yippee!

Maggie quickly ducked into the limo as Salvador held the door open for her.

"*There* you are!" Antonio said. "What do I have to do, Maggie? I told you to stay away from Francis and now you just ate lunch with the guy? I left practice to come get you!"

"You bugged my phone," she said harshly. "This is ridiculous!"

"Damn right I bugged your phone! Why would you even think of meeting with him?"

"Why do you care? Mr. Mysterious, can't tell my wife my business because it's too—what? Too dark? Too strange? Too much for me to handle? Well, I'm sick of it. I am your wife, and you had better start treating me like one!"

"I take good care of you! What are you talking about?"

"I want in, Antonio! I want to know what makes your world tick! The whole shit and caboodle! You say Francis is bad news! Well, I am starting to think, so are you! If you were so 'clean' then what would the hush-hush, can't tell you this and that be about?"

"Maggie, listen to you, talking nonsense!" He shook his head. "Julia wouldn't say where you went. And you should know your whereabouts are my business! I can't take any chances!" His voice rose. "Finally, she told me."

"What are you talking about?"

"You are in so much trouble when we get back to the hotel. You are so grounded!"

"Ha, ha, ha…let me guess. You're going to ground me—after I check into a different hotel? That's so funny!" She paused to consider. "Are you kidding? You must be, because I am not your child, Antonio! And speaking of children, it will be a cold day down south before I *ever* feel ready for that! So you'd better hope that none of those sperm of yours have impregnated me just yet! Now that you're out of jail, I'll be eating the birth-control candies again!"

"I'm going to have to tie you up to keep you away from Francis," Antonio said, ignoring the other issues. "You give me no choice!"

"You are not going to tie me up!" Maggie slapped his arm.

"Yes, I think I might!" Antonio told her. "After three months of marriage, you are sneaking around and causing trouble, all because you do not trust me! Why? I have no idea! You lie to me about being on the pill and then keep questioning me about Nicolette! What is *with* you?"

"Francis says that you two share friends! Yeah, that's right…pretty interesting! He came right out and told me that Nicolette's father told the bartender to taint my drink! Do you know how wonderful that makes me feel? She's not only a crazy psycho herself; it runs in the family! And you just keep giving her money! Now what am I supposed to do with that information, Antonio? And thanks for bugging my phone by the way—you are such a jerk!"

"You leave me no choice! I have no problem being married to an independent woman, but you give that a whole new meaning! You are riding around with Bradley trying to bring down Francis! My God, Maggie, if someone was capable of that, it would have been done a long time ago, all right? Why would you even think you could pull that off! The guy is dangerous, okay? I might as well turn myself into a psycho ward, with you, Francis, and Nicolette!"

"Oh, really? Well, I'm ready for the psycho ward myself!" Maggie glared at him. "You need a recap? I have been in two tabloids already—both presenting me in the worst way after I parachute from a plane, live two days in the forest, then get drugged, watch you get hauled off to jail… and just about the time things return to 'normal'—if that word even exists in my vocabulary anymore—Nicolette shows up, breaks the photo of us, and I find out you pay her large sums of money! So, I finally meet with Francis, hoping he can shed some light on the situation because you leave me in the dark." She continued to glare at him. "And now I find out that instead of sharing with me, you bug my phone, have me followed, and then some crap-shooter cab driver arrives to drop me off in the middle of nowhere so that you can pick me up in the limo! And one more thing: I just had my photo taken *again* in this stupid blonde wig! Thanks a lot, Antonio! I was doing just fine without your help! And Francis doesn't frighten me, okay? You know what does frighten me? The thought of whether or not Mickey is yours! You had better not even *think* of lying to me about that!"

"I ought to wash your mouth out with soap! I have given you everything and I have never done anything to give you reason to doubt me, and this is what you dish out! I may as well be the dishonest son of a bitch that you think I am! Go ahead, call up Francis and eat dinner with the guy. Listen to all the lies you want! It all comes down to who you trust, Maggie, and obviously you will never trust me."

"You should be me! I am sick of all this shit! Every day, a new piece of 'news' going down, and when you keep secrets from me, it just irritates the hell out of me! Why can't you tell me what happened? Did you pay to get out of jail? Francis said Shagan paid to get you out! Is it true?"

Antonio looked out the window, refusing to speak.

"Seems strange that the next day *she* shows up..." Maggie continued. "Now it all makes sense! And I am all of a sudden supposed to share you with her! She has your undivided attention, doesn't she, Antonio? There lies another mystery! Why? You seriously think I am supposed to believe that you take care of her like some charity project? Give me a break, Antonio—I don't believe any of it."

"Fine! Mickey is mine! There! I said it. That's what you want to hear, isn't it?" Antonio shouted at her. "So go ahead, now tell me what I am waiting to hear… We're done, right?"

Maggie just stared at him, wondering what to do with his latest confession.

"You knew Francis before we met, didn't you?"

"Yes," he admitted.

"And his circle of friends endorse your show?"

"Yes, Maggie, but that is also complicated. It's not my choice…it is the nature of the beast." Antonio exhaled. "Just…I live my life in a circus of chaos…I told you that people are dirty in my world….You were the one piece of innocence that came into my world and you have to believe me! I seriously…love you…"

"You lied to me."

"You lied to me as well." Antonio stared back at her. "We are even."

"I don't even want to talk to you right now! Just…don't even look at me."

"I'm sorry, Maggie. My life was a bit of a mess before I met you, and you can't say that yours was all that grand before you met me, right? Phillip? What a jerk! Well, life with Nicolette was no better, believe me. She was high all the time, and I—you know I don't use drugs. I'm clean, and it did not take long to realize that I could never have a decent relationship with someone like that. It was just messed up."

"*This* is just messed up, Antonio! You have a child with her! What now? She's just a sudden addition to our lives? This sucks! Now you want me to have your child? Why? You already have one! And he looks just like you, doesn't he? I can't take this anymore! I was an idiot to marry you!"

"Please, don't say that, Maggie. I would *never* cheat on you. But Nicolette and I were only together that one night—we were just friends at the time."

"You slept with her and you were just friends!?"

"It's not like you think. We both had too much to drink."

"I don't know who's worse…you or Phillip…"

"Maggie, don't say that."

"You're such a liar!"

"It's the only thing I have ever lied to you about, and I was just afraid that—"

"That what? I would be pissed? Well, I am!" Maggie paused. "So you lied about her rape?"

"No…that actually happened. That's part of the reason she was using drugs. I didn't see the signs or even realize until she showed up one day, totally wasted, and since then it was never the same between us. But she wanted to be with me, and I thought it would help her heal. She wanted to let go of her bad memory, and I was helping her get clean, but then she got pregnant."

"You are so loyal it makes me ill."

"Sorry." Antonio looked mysteriously at her. "Now you heard

what you want to hear, so we are better?"

"No, we are not better, Antonio! This is a disaster."

"But you should trust me now, because I told you the truth, right?"

"No…yes…no… I can't even think straight anymore."

"Maggie!"

"What?"

"What do you want from me? We are wrong either way, don't you see?"

"I don't know what I see anymore, Antonio. Just a nightmare. All I see now is just a nightmare."

"We love each other…that's all that matters. You don't miss Philip and I don't miss Nicki."

"I guess…" Maggie stared out the dark window of the limo, which obstructed her view. A tear trickled down her cheek as she remembered the first time she had sat in the limo with him. *Idiot!* She could not help but feel like she had been on the ride of her life.

Chapter 15

Maggie lay in bed, the tears rolling down her cheeks. She turned to Antonio, who was facing away from her.

"Antonio?" Her whisper fell on the still air of the night.

"What?" His voice was uneasy.

"Did you pay Gia to give me an award?"

Antonio did not respond.

"You did!" Maggie sniffled, overcome by tears, completely distraught. "Why? You don't think I can make it on my own? Why would you do that?" She sat up in bed. "*Antonio!* I hate that you did that!" she screamed. "You think you can just buy whatever you want with money? I hate the world you live in."

"Just stop, Maggie. It is…just how things work."

"No, Antonio, that's not true. I don't want it to work like that."

"Well, sorry, welcome to reality. Life is all about who you know, and money moves everything in the game of life."

"I seriously hate you right now."

"Sorry, I meant it for the best. And *I* seriously hate that you want to work for Francis, and I would pay my last dime to keep you away from him. Don't you know my intentions by now, Maggie? I love you. The guy is scum! What am I supposed to do?"

"I thought I won because I had talent."

"You do! Believe me, you do! But I cannot wait for that to get you where you want to go! I can cut corners for you. Why won't you let me?"

"Francis said you and Gia had a thing."

"He's a lying sack of crap! Gia and I are friends. I love her designs, though, and bought quite a few as gifts for my mamma and some friends in Italy. I'm not the Casanova he claims I am. I thought you and Gia would work well together. Better than you and Francis, but of course that's not saying much. And if she's gonna fly back and forth from LA to New York, I feel it's only fair to pay for that!"

"I heard her on his voicemail! She said something about how you can't hide the truth from me forever. What was she talking about?"

"Probably that I told her to nominate you… So what?"

"I'm just numb to everything right now…I can't believe you would do that!"

"Maybe it wasn't right, Maggie, but I am out of ideas when it comes to keeping you from working for Francis! Don't you see? This is how my world operates! It spins on the dollar bill! Nothing is free—ever! You can't just rise to the top without sacrifice. You have either a long, hard road ahead of you or I clip corners for you and get you where you want to go sooner, but without Francis. Gia will work with you. I said I would compensate her to show you the ropes, get you where you want to be. Like I said, this is my world."

"I hate your world, Antonio…I seriously *hate* it."

"Then…I'm sorry that I made you marry me."

"Me too."

Maggie hid under the sheets, feeling like she was in bed with a complete stranger. What else was he up to? She could not digest his way of thinking. Paying your way to the top? It was just corrupt.

She wished she could crawl in a hole and die. She had pushed for the truth until she found it, but it had left her miserable. She wondered where they would go from here. Obviously, he had lived in his delusional world for so long now that she would never convince him he had done wrong. He was last to admit his failures, and his ego and temper were never far away. He simply did what he wanted and justified the means by the end. It sent red flags flashing before her closed eyelids, until she knew what she had to do.

She needed to get away from him for a few days and think everything through.

Tomorrow she would fly back to England and visit Dana. Hopefully, time away would help clear her head. Right now, she was not sure what love was worth.

Was love even enough?

Maggie crawled quietly out of bed. Gathering a few belongings, she threw them into a bag. She tiptoed into the bathroom that was lit with a nightlight, where she grabbed her toothbrush and a few makeup items and a small box.

This is all I need.

Maggie walked quietly over to the bed. "Goodbye, Antonio," she whispered. He continued to lie still. She leaned over and grabbed the Kleenex box off the nightstand and stuck it in her duffle bag. She saw the photo of them dancing at the benefit, which now sat in a frame without the glass. She tried to recall the good memories of them together, but they were quickly subsumed beneath thoughts of him with Nicolette.

She headed for the door to make her exit quietly.

Three, four months…just as Francis predicted.

“Maggie?” Antonio sat up in bed. “Where are you going?”

“Back to London, Antonio.” She stared at his silhouette, facing her in the dark.

“My show is tomorrow night. You won’t be my lady in the ring of fire?” he said softly.

“I have to go.” She swallowed, realizing there were no words to heal the moment.

“Okay, do what you have to do…” He suddenly sounded fine with it.

“We are such a joke, Antonio,” Maggie shouted at him.

“No, Maggie, we’re not! Sometimes love just gets complicated.”

“*Too* complicated,” she said, staring back at him.

Silence followed. Finally he spoke:

“When will you return?”

“I don’t know if I ever will….” Her heart pounded at her own words.

Antonio got out of bed. He started to approach her, but then stopped and said, “Can I kiss you goodbye?”

“No, Antonio, I should have never taken that risk.” Maggie felt the tears roll down her cheek.

“I am sorry…so sorry. I love you, Maggie…hopefully, that’s enough.”

“I wish it were.” She felt her heart, heavy and aching at the reality.

She quickly opened the door and headed to Julia’s room.

Her hand in a weak fist, she knocked on the door.

“What’s wrong? You seem so sad,” Julia said as soon as she

opened the door. "What happened?"

"I'm leaving…to go back to London for a while."

"What? No…" Julia looked at her in disbelief.

"It's a long story. I just have…too much…it's been really bad ever since we got back. I had high hopes, you know, returning to where we met, and now ever since we got back it has been one disaster after the next and…" Maggie held her breath, trying to keep the sobs in, then released them. "Nicolette and Antonio have a son—Mickey!" she cried in despair. "It's been in the papers and he denied it, and now finally told me that it's true! Talk about a brick landing in the middle of the fire! I just can't deal with it right now. And he gives her money, and now I just found out from Francis that Antonio gave Gia money to help me with my fashion ambitions. That's just wrong! I thought I'd earned her respect and it turns out he knows her and that's why I got my award! I am just so miserable, I can't even think straight anymore." Maggie suddenly noticed the suitcase on Julia's bed was packed. "Where…what are you doing? Are you leaving too?"

"Yes, it's time for me to go. I feel I've done more harm than good. And even at my age, there are lessons to be learned. Antonio came looking for you and I said I did not know where you went, but then he stared me down until I told him and…Maggie, I feel like a traitor! But he was so sure he had to protect you…so I told him. Sorry to disappoint you."

"No, Julia, it's not your fault. Antonio would have figured it out anyway. He bugged my phone to keep track of me! I just cannot exist in his crazy world anymore! He lives in this constant paranoia over

Francis! He tells me how he's so dangerous, when all the guy ever did was kiss me once!" Maggie's eyes started to fill with more tears. "Francis said that Nicolette's father was the one who told the bartender to taint my drink simply because I am standing in the way of his daughter's happily ever after with Antonio and he doesn't want to spend another dollar on her! So he leaves that to Antonio! And he helped get Antonio out of jail when his plan backfired! See, the truth is that Francis had nothing to do with any of it! Then there's Nicolette, who Antonio calls 'Nicki,' and that already makes my stomach churn! But it gets even better! He claims he helped her get clean and in the process got her pregnant! It just makes me sick! Oh, sorry, I forgot to mention that she's an addict!"

Julia closed her suitcase. "Sounds like it's time for both of us to move on."

"So you think I am doing the right thing?"

"Only you can decide that…but just remember there are no glass houses. Every relationship has difficulties and running away won't solve a thing. If you can't forgive Antonio, then you will have no other choice but to move on."

"Everything I thought we had has just been shattered." Maggie took a deep breath, and then explained: "Misery…it just wants to find me, so here I am! You found me!" Maggie shouted. "Congratulations!"

"Time heals…hopefully it can for you," Julia said.

"I don't think so. I will always love him. I just hope…never mind."

"What?" Julia asked.

Maggie frowned. "I just hope I'm not pregnant. I never went back on the pill because he was in jail…He already has a child. I don't need to add another. He wants a large family—it's not going to be with me."

"Sometimes even the worst of times work out, Maggie. Love always finds a way."

"Love…it's my greatest enemy! And I am going to do everything I can to just—try to forget him."

"Forgiveness works once in a while…"

"That list is way too long," Maggie said.

"You took off your rings?"

"I did," Maggie said. "I left them next to our picture. You know, it was strange. Antonio seemed relieved that I was leaving…like he expected it. And—I just don't get him—then he asked if he could kiss me goodbye." She paused to consider. "I said 'no.'"

"Keep in touch." Julia reached out for a hug.

"I will." Maggie hugged her. "Thanks for everything… You are a really good friend. I'm just sorry this all ended like this."

"Me too…more than you know," Julia said as she watched Maggie leave.

"Salvador," Maggie said into her phone, "I need to go to the airport, ASAP!"

"I'm parked out front. Just come down."

"Be right there." She hurried toward the exit sign.

Maggie rode the elevator to the first floor. With a baseball cap covering her head, she could only hope no one would spot her on her way out.

Maybe my luck is on the mend, she thought as she got into the limo, face lowered.

“Maggie,” Salvador asked, “what are you up to in the middle of the night?”

“I am going back to London. You can drive me to La Guardia.”

“To London?” Salvador questioned. “Tired of New York already?”

“Pretty much.”

“I bet Antonio is sad you are leaving.”

“No, he’s fine.” Maggie suddenly snapped. “Look, Salvador, I don’t mean to be rude, but everything with us is over! Done! I can’t take it anymore.”

“Oh no! Really? I had no idea. I thought everything was great between you.”

“I’d rather not talk about it.”

“Maybe I should turn around and take you back?”

“No, Salvador, keep driving to the airport. I’m going back.”

“Yes, ma’am.” He glowered at her through the rearview mirror.

Maggie stared at the liquor shelf.

I really need something...anything would be fine...it all looks good. Never mind...what’s the point...? Sober...drunk...it’s all the same. It’s not like there’s a genie in any of those bottles...unfortunately...

How did things end up like this? Why didn’t Nicolette ever come up in past discussions? That was simple...Antonio always focused on the fun...playful adventures...and in the end...he was mysterious...his true colors hidden. It wasn't fair. How deceitful. If I would have known, then what?

Could she love Mickey? Of course she could, but she had never even met him. It was a bit odd. Did Antonio not care about his own son? Never once had he mentioned him. And if he had, would she have run? Children always complicate matters, but she loved children. She wanted a family, someday. But he had deliberately kept her in the dark! First, he adamantly denied the charges…then he confessed after Francis spilled the truth. And he admitted to paying Gia! That she could maybe live with…but forgetting to mention that he had a child? That's a bit hard to excuse. Why would he? It didn't pay to think about it. She could easily drive herself insane over the "what ifs" and "how comes." But as things stood, she was not sure where she would go from here.

After a six-hour wait at the airport, Maggie finally held a boarding pass for first class on the next British Airways flight. She was exhausted, and hoping that soon she could sleep on the plane…but that would only happen if she could remove her thoughts of Antonio.

Finally she crawled into her window seat. She grabbed a pillow and leaned against the glass, staring out into the sunrise. In New York it was the beginning of a new day, but when she landed in London, the sun would be setting.

THE FOLLOWING DAY…

"Maggie! Come in! I made up the spare bedroom for you; I thought you wouldn't be visiting until autumn, but here you are already!"

"Yeah, here I am. Hi Shane," Maggie said, managing a grin.

"Hey! It's not so bad! What are friends for, right? A couple days here, and soon it will be just like old times, right?" Shane said.

"Yeah…right." Maggie suddenly felt sick. "I think I'm going to go lie down. I…it must be the flight…just tired and… It has been… Sorry, I will try to be good company while I am here." Maggie tried to set aside her personal tragedy. She stared at Dana. "You look so pregnant, finally!"

"This little monkey is taking over! And I seriously love eating for two! It might be the only nine months I have ever lived without having to count calories!"

"That is funny! And so true, right?" Maggie's face glowed, thinking that Dana would be a mum soon.

"You're staying for a while, I assume?"

"Uh, yeah. Thanks for not making me check into a hostel! All the hotels are booked. That's the last thing I need…appearing in the tabloids! My first night without Antonio spent in one of those! Lord have mercy!"

"I owe you a day of privacy after our photo… See, I framed it and put it outside the loo!" Dana led the way to show off her picture.

"Seriously, Dana? That belongs right above the toilet, so you can barf when you look at it."

"Why's that? I look great, don't you think? And so do you! And Kin looks like he's having fun…"

"Like I said, above the toilet! That is the last time I flag down the paparazzi to take my picture!"

"Come on, we had fun, don't you think?"

"One of the better days in New York, actually. After you left, it was all downhill! Anything beats finding out that Antonio already has a son!"

"What…you aren't serious?"

"Yes…for once they were right."

"Are you sure?"

"Francis is the one who told me! Can you believe it? And that's when I finally got Antonio to admit it!" Maggie paused. "So absurd—and so infuriating! I even got to meet Nicolette—she's 'Nicki' to Antonio—how sweet—and just when you think meeting her is appalling enough, she has the audacity to break the photo of us dancing at the benefit. I ended up despising her in a matter of minutes. She is so unlikable. I never met Mickey, and although it seems a bit creepy that he is their son, I have to say I could never hate a child. It's not his fault, you know. But why didn't Antonio just tell me about him? He feeds me some line of bull about how I stepped into his world, all innocent, and he just loves that about me…so delusional." Maggie paused as exhaustion washed over her. "I have to go to bed. We can talk more tomorrow."

"Okay. I will have tea made when you get up, and some porridge?"

"Crumpets?"

"Fine, crumpets!"

A DAY LATER…

"I feel bad…I should be taking care of you; you're the pregnant one!" Maggie told Dana as she placed the tea and crumpets on the table.

"It's okay, Maggie. What are friends for? I really don't feel that different. The morning sickness has passed, and now I'm just excited! I have to show you the clothes that I bought!"

"You bought clothes already? You don't even know if it's a boy or girl!"

"Actually I do! We're having a girl!"

"No kidding!" Maggie was excited. "Can I make her a dress?"

"Absolutely! I would love it. I don't have a sewing machine here, but Shane's mum has one. She never uses it… We could go get it!"

"That would be great! I may as well make myself useful while I'm here!"

"So…" Dana's eyes shifted. "Are you leaving Antonio permanently?"

"I don't know…I'd rather not talk about it."

"I understand…hey! I couldn't handle that one myself! That is a *huge* cover-up! I can't believe he never told you!"

"Yeah, I just need to get my mind on something else. I've decided that I'm going to start an online clothing business. And I'll make that dress for your baby girl!"

"I'm so excited, and just so you know, you are welcome to stay with us as long as you like."

"Thanks, but I don't want to intrude," Maggie said. "I'll call a hotel, stay there for a while…" She considered her options.

"I have a friend in Oxford. You could stay with her. She has a shop that sells baby clothes—isn't that funny? And she could probably use some help in the shop. You should go visit for a day and take a look! She would probably give you a job…that is, if you want one."

Maggie nodded. "I definitely need a job."

"I figured you would," Dana said. "And don't be angry, but I already checked with her and she is excited…I told her who you were, but she swears not to tell a soul…"

"What…oh no, Dana… Well—I guess it's okay…who cares?"

"You still love him, don't you?"

Maggie gave her a blank look. "Love is not always enough, Dana. His life is crazy. I'm not used to that. If I stay with him, I might have a heart attack!"

"Aww." Dana curled her bottom lip. "You were so cute together."

"Cute?" Maggie questioned. "Right now I am just numb to everything, recovering from shock. If I spend time away, I will hopefully be able to think straight!" She paused, reaching for clarity. "Maybe I will try to forget him. It seems the right thing." Maggie cringed at her own words. "I never thought I'd say that."

"Me neither, Maggie. I know it is strange that he did not tell you he has a child, but you still love him, right?"

"Well, yeah, but he lied about it, and how can I ever forgive him for *that?* It changes…everything!"

"Everyone makes mistakes." Dana wore puppy-dog eyes. "Try to forgive him?"

"Easier said than done! And I already know that I'm going to be miserable without him, but I have no other choice. I am seriously done with men…completely done! What was I thinking, getting married to a celebrity? I must have been crazy."

Three weeks later, Maggie was living with Maia in Oxford, and it felt like she was back home in a weird kind of way.

www.lovetheillusion.com/2221.htm

Today was a work day and Dana was visiting Maggie at Maia's shop.

"I love it in here. I could shop for hours!" Dana admired all the tiny clothing.

"So do you want to see the dress I made for Patrina?"

"Yes! Where is it?"

Maggie led Dana to the back of the shop.

www.lovetheillusion.com/2264.htm

"I absolutely *love* it! It looks just like the picture you sent. Thanks! You and your designs…they're genius! Can you make some more? You could make her whole wardrobe!"

"I could...and you know, Dana, I really like it here. I meet mums, just like you, all excited to have their babies, and it just makes me glow inside—their excitement is so contagious."

"It's great that Maia's letting you work here until you get your clothing line going. How's that coming along?"

"This might come as a surprise, but after seeing how excited you were about the dress I made for you, I duplicated the pattern in an assortment of colors and have already sold two dozen online. I know it's a small start, but I'm getting labels and business cards, and Maia said that I could put a few designs in the window here at her shop. I made that little sailor outfit!" She pointed to it.

"Really? So you aren't making dresses for women?"

"This is really fun! The clothes are so small and cute; I can't help myself!"

"I think it's great, Maggie! I'm so excited for you. So..." Dana perked up. "Have you talked to Antonio lately?"

"No, he's never called me, so why would I call him? He must not care that I left."

"Maggie, that's just strange. I don't even know what to say. You should call him! That's what I think."

"I will *not* call him." Maggie retorted. "He wanted to kiss me goodbye; I said no. I knew if he kissed me, I would have stayed, but after I refused, I think he assumed it was over. I just try not to think about it."

"Come on, Maggie! You can't just completely forget him!"

"I'm trying." Maggie held up another outfit. "What do you think?

I'm putting this in the storefront. Do you like it?"

"Now I want a boy, too!" Dana laughed. "Maybe our next child will be a boy."

"You want more than one?"

"Eventually, but not for a while." Dana smiled, and then said, "I should probably get going. But maybe we can get together again soon? Let me know."

"I will," Maggie said. "Thanks for stopping in!"

Maggie held the tiny sailor outfit that she had made. Maia was out for the day, and had put Maggie in charge of the shop. She stood amid all the tiny clothes, and could not forget her own discussion with Antonio to have a child. She was not ready. He was. It felt strange being surrounded by baby clothes and every day she met women who were more than ready to bring that special someone into their lives that would someday call them "mum."

That evening, Maggie turned on the TV. She frowned as she listened to the latest hype:

"And now the latest in the buzz…Antonio DeLuca and his new bride, Maggie, call it quits after only four months of marriage! Antonio spills the beans that Mickey belongs to him and up until this point, Maggie supposedly had no idea! And that's the latest in the buzz."

"Just shut up!" Maggie shouted at the TV as she sipped her favorite tea, nestled under a blanket on her sofa. Maia was working late, unpacking the new arrivals.

She looked down at Lucy, Maia's longhaired Persian cat. It had white hair that seemed to attach to everything. Lucy purred loudly as she cuddled next to her. She had to admit that after only a few weeks, Lucy felt like her best friend. She followed her around, and Maggie had even bought treats for her. She slept in Maia's bed at night, but was quick to assume Maggie was part of the family.

Maia was busy living the single life, and Maggie found it hard to believe she functioned on so little sleep. She would come back at late hours of the night, and one night she did not return at all. But Maggie was grateful for Lucy; she was always around. And although the white hair attached to pretty much everything she wore, she could not deny it was a small price to pay for a friend. When Maggie had shown up for work the other day with a rather generous amount of white cat hair on her backside, Maia was quick to find the humor and located her pet roller right away, removing the unsightly mess.

Yesterday, a woman came in who was expecting twins. She looked very uncomfortable—eight months along—but it did not slow her down a bit. She was grabbing various pieces of clothing off the shelf, and matching different outfits with the tiny little shoes. Maggie noticed that she had chosen all neutrals, indicating that the sex of the twins was still in question. Two babies? All at once? Maggie couldn't help but think she was one brave woman. But what choice did she have, right? Pregnancy was maybe a choice, but having twins was not! Before Maggie could feel any sympathy, she realized the woman had left the store a complete mess after rummaging through the various tables of clothing.

Shortly after that, another woman had come in with her newborn baby boy. She had come in specifically to purchase the outfit in the window—the one Maggie had designed. During her visit, Maggie could not keep her eyes off the woman's little baby boy. He had a full head of dark hair. His skin was flawless and his eyes were closed as he lay against his mother's chest in a carrier pouch designed specifically to keep one's hands free to shop, but it was obvious he had no idea that his mother was even shopping for him. His cheeks were plump and his dark hair reminded her of Antonio's. What would their child have looked like? She couldn't help but wonder. She felt sad, wondering now if she would ever have that opportunity.

Once again, Maggie sat on the couch with Lucy.

Lucy did not seem to have any problems at all, other than wanting her belly scratched. She would roll over and stretch as if she knew Maggie would respond, and Maggie was starting to enjoy her company more and more.

Maia was not home very often, and Maggie was getting used to being home by herself. Maia liked to go out, and once again she was out late. And it seemed she had quite a few friends in the area. She had invited Maggie to come along, but Maggie knew better than to hang out with her. The last thing she needed was to end up wasted, with her photo plastered on the front pages, looking as if she could not handle life without Antonio.

Things were improving, slowly but surely. Maggie was helping out at the store, in exchange for rent. Maia paid the other bills, and even bought food, which left Maggie feeling like she was in debt.

But last week Maggie noticed that the online business she had started was bringing sales, and she had even sold a couple outfits she had placed in the front window. She had always thought she would design dresses for women, for formal events, but this had become a gift in the making. She loved it! And it was starting to show signs of success. It was strange how things were turning out, but clothes for little people was a fascinating world of fashion all its own.

It seemed that in a short time, she was finding a new life, without Antonio. But she could not help but wonder what he was doing. *Does he still think about me? Does he even miss me?* Some nights she really missed him…almost every night, if she was truthful. But she tried to keep her mind focused on work. Certainly, if he had any regrets, he would call her.

Once, when they were in the Vegas desert, he had told her: "If you want to be with me, it will be like that…crazy…and that's the honest truth." His words seemed to echo endlessly in her brain, as she tried to make sense of their relationship. *Were things really over?* She never thought she would leave him. But when she left that night, she never thought she would leave for good, even though she said she was not sure she was coming back. She wondered why he never begged her to stay. Perhaps he realized he was better off without her standing in the way of his career. Now he did not have to worry about her anymore. It was hard to believe that he had made no effort to keep in contact.

He was stubborn, but so was she.

She thought about the weeks in New York City and soon, despite their turbulent adventures, she felt the pains of missing him. In fact, she really missed him. Her career seemed to be moving in a rewarding direction, and it gave her great satisfaction. But she felt so incomplete. Was it because she still had high hopes where her career was concerned? She thought not; she felt very happy with simplicity—that she was just a hermit in a small town, living with Dana's friend who already had a full life without her company. And she loved the privacy she now had.

Maggie went into her room and rummaged through her pile of fabrics. Maia's absence left her feeling lonely at times. Perhaps she could sew a few more little dresses. She had a yard of pink cotton fabric, another yard of yellow printed fabric with smocking, and a white fabric with red roses. It looked like the special rose-printed fabric she and her mother had used to make the dress she wore the first day of school. A vintage print never dated: it would always feel as though it belonged to the past. And now she could not help but recall more memories of her childhood.

"I want a big white quilt with lots of flowers in pots!" Maggie had told her mother. "And the flowers have to all be pink!"

"Okay," her mother agreed, "but if we make a white quilt, you will have to be very careful not to get it dirty." Maggie remembered having it for less than a week and spilling purple Kool-Aid on it. That same day, her quilt hung on the clothesline outside, after her mother had scrubbed out the stain. She could still vividly remember the quilt.

www.lovetheillusion.com/2197.htm

Suddenly, she remembered being at the Night Owl when the beer was spilt on her dress. She remembered looking into Antonio's dark eyes, and feeling her heart racing at the thought of kissing him. She closed her eyes, wishing he was with her.

Should I have let him kiss me goodbye?

Maybe we would still be together.

Maggie set down the fabric. She was starting to wonder why he had not called. *Does he miss me?* Despite the circumstances, she had to admit she missed his company. Some days were better than others, but most every day, he was her first thought in the morning and the last when she finally closed her eyes at night. Maggie sat still, going back over the events. Had she acted in haste? Everything was calm now. Things in her world had returned to normal, except that she was without Antonio. And that was huge.

She wondered if he had told Mamma and Papa. Surely, they would be disappointed. Maggie felt sad, wondering if she would ever see them again. This whole situation was out of hand. But as the weeks had gone by, Maggie was left more confused than ever. Though her heart ached from the separation, she felt strange calling him. And as she spent time away, her resolution became clear as day: she should have stayed. But only because she knew she still loved him—despite everything. She had never had feelings for anyone as she had for him. But why he never bothered to call her after she left raised additional concerns. All she could do was find her way with her career. That was a safe investment, and it at least made her feel as though she had landed back in London with a purpose: She would make it on her own, and without Gia Tellies or Francis. She wanted nothing to do with either of them anymore.

While she mildly appreciated Antonio's efforts—aside from his delusional thinking— she was quite certain that she would never feel fulfillment in being a charity case for success. Perhaps Antonio had good intentions, but she could not accept those terms. She had too much pride. Her mother would roll over in her grave if she made it to the top after a "payout." That couldn't be called genuine success. Antonio claimed his brother's death was instrumental in leading to his fame, but that was sheer coincidence! It was not the same. Maggie had a choice, and she would rather be a happy nobody, doing what she loved, creating her own designs, than being at the top, forcefully driven at someone else's command.

Francis had pretty much stifled her creativity from the moment she started working for him. "Maggie," he would say, "I think it needs to have a little more zing! Try adding a ruffle or perhaps a brooch—and make sure, whatever you do, it does not look like anything you have already seen! There are enough of those out there and we do not need to make duplicates of what someone else has already made! If you do not look twice at the dress, then it should never make it onto a hanger!" Maggie could still hear his tinny, whiny voice. She did not miss him. The money was good when she worked for him, but she often wondered if it was worth tossing aside her own creative efforts. She only recalled one dress that she had made that met his approval without changes. Now she was living the dream. Maybe not financially, but creatively. She had never had so much fun, watching people come into the boutique and buy for their precious child the very dress that she had designed herself. It was so rewarding. So far, she had made twenty dresses for the store and sold ten. And each dress was so special; it was truly her own.

Despite the fact that she was missing Antonio, London was feeling like home again, rather quickly. She had bought a wig and was sporting a new look, hoping to keep her identity undercover. And she had made herself a new jacket.

www.lovetheillusion.com/2222.htm

Chapter 16

On a lunch break, Maggie sat staring out of a McDonald's window, with her Americano coffee and fish sandwich. She checked her phone, wondering if she should just break down and make the first move.

I can't believe he still has not called me.

He is so stubborn.

With every day that went by, she grew more and more anxious. Five weeks had passed now, and she was growing weary. *Were they over? Completely over?* It was hard to imagine so much time had passed, neither one of them making any effort. He had always taken the initiative to win her heart and her trust, but now what? Had he thrown in the towel? From the beginning, he had been the one to chase her. Perhaps she assumed he still would. But since he was not trying to keep in contact, it left her even more convinced that things would never work out. It was out of his character not to chase what he wanted, so she thought he maybe had his own regrets.

The one thing that kept her sane was her work. Though her relationship with Antonio was on hold, everything else was moving forward, at least where her clothing line for infants was concerned. In fact, one of the vendors in the US had contacted her via email, requesting her to meet with their buyers in New York. If they placed a substantial order, she would have to locate a factory to produce her designs in large quantities. And if she came to New York on business, she would undoubtedly see Antonio. It would be too strange to go there without at least stopping in to say hi.

She felt the tension mounting inside her. *Was he spending time with Nicolette and Mickey while she was away?* She could not help but wonder. And a part of her was still aching, wishing that she had never left him. She had vivid memories of his silhouette, facing her in the dark. That was her last memory of him, just sitting on the bed. The image left a burning sensation in her heart. She longed to be with him again, and she could not deny there was no job out there or amount of success that would fill the empty space of his absence. She knew she still loved him. She always would.

Should I just forgive him? He said he loved me. And I love him...

If she had to fly back to New York, it would provide another opportunity; she could at least gauge his reaction to their separation. He, too, was busier with work than ever. She felt sad, suddenly, thinking about how she was supposed to be on stage in the ring of fire. Had he found a replacement? She couldn't help but wonder. And if she had to be completely honest, she missed him more than she thought she would. And there it was again…the lingering question… Did he miss her? She hoped so, but she had left him. Perhaps he was angry. And perhaps he was weary at the thought of chasing her down again, only for her to run from him. He also had his pride, and he surely could find plenty of women to spend time with him. Now she wondered, even more, what he had been up to.

The thought of him with someone else made her feel ill. Maggie got up, but as she stood, she felt suddenly lightheaded. She braced herself on the counter and watched as people scurried by. That's when she realized where she needed to go, and quick! She headed for the restroom. A moment later she was leaning over the toilet, losing her lunch.

I just hate throwing up... Maggie recalled the last time—and she was much younger, but old enough to remember: "You must have the flu," her mother had told her, "but there is always a little good news with the bad news! You're staying home from school!"

Maggie stared into the toilet where she had let go of her lunch.

Why did I eat at McDonald's? Oh yeah...it's cheap.

Maggie washed her face, then leaned against the sink and rummaged through her purse. She got her phone and waited to hear Maia's voice.

"Hey! What's up?"

"Uuh...my lunch...I just got sick...must have the flu...I'm at McDonald's right now and...it can't be food poisoning already... I doubt it would hit me this fast, but I think I am going to just go home and get some sleep... Is that okay?"

"It's fine, but...are you coming back for your bike? Or should I bring it into the back office?"

"Oh, yeah, the bike...uh...I think I'll just walk. It's less than a mile from here."

"Are you sure? Should I come get you? I can put a sign on the door."

"No, I'm fine," Maggie said. "Thanks for the offer, though."

She had been riding Maia's bike to work. The shop was a short ride away from their flat, and Maggie had been struggling to keep her finances under control. She had only a small savings account that she had set aside—before she married Antonio, and since then, he had paid for everything. Although she still had his credit card in her wallet, she was only holding on to it for emergencies. So far, she had not had to use it, and she had not taken a dime of his money with her when she left. That was the last thing she wanted.

When Maggie returned, someone she had never met before was sitting in the kitchen. His hair was dishwater blond and she guessed he was her own age. "Hi," Maggie said, a bit alarmed. "Who are *you?*"

"Sorry, I didn't mean to scare you. I'm waiting for Maia. She should be off work soon, right?"

"Uh, no…I think she's there till five."

"I'm Gabriel, by the way."

"Nice to meet you; I'm Maggie." She headed for the sofa to lie down. "I got sick at lunch…must have the flu. Luckily I wasn't in the baby shop. Everything looks so sterile in there." She positioned a pillow behind her head.

"Yeah, it's a cute shop she has." Gabriel followed into the lounge and sat down across from her in a chair. "I just got back from my tutorial at All Souls."

"What are you studying?"

"I'm getting my DPhil in economics." He held up a book. "I come here once in a while, just to study or catch up on my sleep during the day. My housemates are a bit loud at times."

"Oh, yeah, college life…I remember those days…living on a few hours of sleep, and then trying to catch up in class!" Maggie smiled. "It's pretty quiet here. But Lucy has been keeping me company."

She looked down at the cat, who had curled up in a ball next to her feet.

"So you got the flu? That sucks."

"Yeah, either that or food poisoning."

"There's a bad case of the flu going around, but I seem to be immune."

"Lucky you," Maggie said as she took off her wig and dropped it on the floor. It stank. Obviously, it needed washing after her trip to the toilet.

"So…why do you wear a wig? You don't like fixing your hair?" Gabriel stared at the mop of hair on the floor.

"Something like that," Maggie said happily; he had no clue who she was.

So far, Oxford seemed to be a private oasis, away from the paparazzi, and people did not seem to recognize her. But she still proceeded cautiously, wearing her disguise—at least when she worked in the shop.

She also knew that maybe it was just a matter of time before things would unravel, but she was moving quickly to get her online business going so that she could work out of her home. She hated being the subject of attention, and since she had returned to London, it seemed a breath of fresh air to have "escaped" *that*, at least for a while.

Gabriel kept staring in disbelief at the wig.

"From short and reddish blonde to long and…brownish…it looks better like that—your natural color," he said.

"Thanks, but I didn't ask for your opinion." Maggie stared at him. "Don't you have to study?"

"No, just here for my afternoon catnap with the cat!" He managed a grin. "But now you are in my bed with my favorite cat!"

"Sorry, I can move."

"That's okay, I can leave…there's always tomorrow."

"I'll just go to my room," Maggie sat up slowly. "I still feel dizzy, lightheaded. I haven't had the flu in years. I guess it's about time." She moved slowly across the room.

"Aren't you forgetting something?" He grabbed her wig and placed it on his head.

Maggie started laughing. "You can wear that if you want."

"Uh, maybe not…it reeks!" He quickly flung it across the room. "See you later," she heard him call out as she left the room.

"Yeah…later."

Three hours later, Maia returned from work.

Maggie opened her eyes and saw her standing over her bed.

"Hey, Maggie! Gabriel and I are going to the pub to get a bite to eat. Should we get some takeaway for you?"

"Oh, no, I'm fine."

"Are you okay? You look flushed."

"I feel much better after I got some sleep. But I'll just make some oatmeal."

"Are you sure?"

"Yeah, but thanks for asking." Maggie pulled the covers up to break her chills. "I met Gabriel, by the way. He seems nice."

"Oh, I know! He's a saint!" Maia told her. "I'm lucky to have him!"

Another week passed. Maggie was staring at a small calendar she kept in her wallet. With a pen in hand, she was counting out the days, trying to recall when she'd had her last period.

That can only mean one thing, right?

Her cycle was a perfect biological clock. And she had been too busy to notice until now. Her flu-like symptoms had subsided, but now returned, and as she sat on the edge of the tub in the bathroom, she wondered if she would make it into work.

Maia had already left, and Maggie thought about eating some crackers to see if she would feel better. Her morning diet for the past week had consisted of saltines and white soda, and the coffee that she used to drink in the mornings was now giving her nausea.

I hope it's not true. Maggie sat in the bathroom, alone. She could hear Lucy scratching at the bathroom door, wishing to curl up and keep her company. She would take a shower; then maybe she would feel better. She stepped into the shower stall, remembering when she and Antonio would shower together. It was part of their morning routine. They would get ready together. *I'd better not be pregnant.* Maggie feared the worst. She was in no position to take care of a child. She could barely take care of herself. Antonio had already one child to take care of—one whom he spent no time with, leaving all the parenting duties to Nicolette. Surely he would have no interest in adding to his plate of responsibilities. She could get financial support from him, she was sure, but she did not want any child of hers influenced by his sick, twisted world.

Maggie stepped out of the shower, reaching onto the shelf where there was a stack of fresh towels. She grabbed hold of one, and then her eyes fell on a stash of pregnancy tests, located in a plastic basket that hosted a variety of other remedies....

Preparation H, Antifungal cream, Pepto-Bismol...

If only I had hemorrhoids or ringworm or simply an upset stomach! Any of those sounds wonderful...just please not pregnancy...

Maggie reached for what she knew she needed. She stared at the package while her stomach continued to churn. She felt sicker than ever. Was she pregnant? Or just lovesick? Maybe the stress was just getting to her. Too much energy, bottled up, and she hadn't been jogging as regularly because she was so busy trying to make a living.

There was a trail that she loved to jog on. It ran along a river canal, and often there were ducks swimming in the water, and occasionally she even saw a swan. It was a perfect getaway from the realities of life, and maybe that is where she needed to go today.

www.lovetheillusion.com/2200.htm

She opened up the package and read the instructions: Place the indicator under a full stream of urine. She then read: Quick and easy results within a day after your missed period.

Easy result? They forgot to add "with a nightmare of

possibilities!"

I hope I do this right.

An hour later, Maggie sat under a tree, absorbing the "bad news." She stared into the canal where a grouping of swans swam together. They seemed to represent a happy family. Was there such a thing? Maybe only in the animal kingdom.

www.lovetheillusion.com/2225.htm

www.lovetheillusion.com/2201.htm

Julia had said there was no such thing as glass houses. But she could not imagine life with a child. She was barely making ends meet. She was too proud to ask Antonio for money. What was he doing, anyway? It seemed he had become callous, perhaps desensitized to their breakup. Did he think eventually she would return on her own? *What was he waiting for?*

"Maggie, what are you doing here?"

It was Gabriel. He stared down at her.

"I should ask you the same…" Maggie stared up at Gabriel.

"I like to walk here," he said.

"Oh, well, I was going jogging, but changed my mind." Maggie slowly stood up, attempting to dust the dirt off of her backside. "Too weak from the flu…"

"You're feeling better now?"

"Yes, I think I am over it." Maggie tried to smile.

"That's good." Gabriel reached over and patted her shoulder. "Why aren't you at the shop?"

"Just taking a mental day."

He gave her a strange look. "Everyone needs one of those once in a while," he agreed.

"Sometimes more than one…" Maggie said.

"Did you ever go punting?" He nodded at a group of kids who were poling down the river.

www.lovetheillusion.com/2224.htm

"No." Maggie stared into the mucky waters.

"It's a lot of fun—I could show you how. I know where the boats are!"

Maggie pondered his suggestion.

"I shouldn't…I could fall in…and I was just sick." She shook her head.

"But now you're better," he said as he walked alongside her. "I think we should! Come on!"

"It does look fun, but then I will feel even guiltier that I'm not at work."

"Guilt is easier to manage than the flu," he teased.

Maggie sat in a boat, while Gabriel stood with the pole, pushing the boat along the river. As they floated down the river, Maggie felt her worries slipping away. She enjoyed the scenery and was soon pleased that she had tried a new adventure.

"So you like Oxford?" he asked.

"It's wonderful. I used to live in London…for six years, and in Italy recently, but I grew up in the States. Boston."

"Great city; I was there for the marathon."

"Really?"

"Yes, I'm into jogging—just like you—but I have a bad knee right now. Fell out of the boat last time I was punting."

"Oh no!"

"I'm joking!" He laughed. "Actually, I was in a car accident."

"That sounds worse."

"I was lucky. Could have been worse. I'm taking it easy now…just walking, but it's good…seems when you walk, you see a lot more."

"It's beautiful here. I am finding a new trail every day. Every college has its own trail, and each one is a new adventure."

"I know what you mean."

Maggie was certain he had no idea who she was. It was so nice of him to be treating her so kindly. She suddenly felt strange in his company, and a bit guilty, thinking that perhaps Maia would not want her spending so much time with him.

"This is so nice and relaxing." Maggie stared at the calm waters.

"The queen owns all of the swans, did you know?"

"Yes…I know they are protected."

"Otherwise I would have a couple—as pets."

"You would?"

"Now what would I do with a swan?" He chuckled. "But they are quite a sight, aren't they?"

"They are…and they look so happy swimming with their young. Makes you want a family, doesn't it?"

"Oh…don't know about that. They look far more obedient than any child I've ever seen."

"Ha! That's true." Maggie smiled in agreement.

"Do you want to get tea?" he asked as they dragged the boat back onto the shore.

"Tea?" Maggie wondered if Maia would mind. Gabriel seemed so friendly.

Perhaps they both could use a friend. "Sure, why not."

"Follow me. I know a place we can go."

Maggie followed him off the trail until they got to a quaint teashop, located on the main street. "In here," he said, a step ahead of her.

"You don't have class today?" she asked, as they sat down at a table after choosing their tea.

"Not on Friday. So, what do you usually do on the weekends?"

"Not much. I usually just hang out with Lucy," Maggie confessed. "Maia is always out, but I'm happy just sitting home and relaxing. You would never imagine how crazy life can—" Maggie paused, realizing she was beginning to mention her life with Antonio.

"That's a drag." He gave her an odd look. "Just sitting home, alone? No wonder Lucy likes you so much."

"I have a lot I should be doing. Weekends have become workdays, too, until I get my feet on the ground. But I think I have a lead…a vendor in New York is interested in my baby clothes. And if that's the case, I need to hurry up and find someone to mass-produce my tiny little clothes ASAP…and I need a label."

"A label?"

"Yeah, I have to print designer tags, and I have to name my clothing line…I was thinking of 'Cutie Pies,' or maybe 'Chubby Cheeks!'" Maggie started laughing, but then realized she would soon need to clothe her own child. Her face grew sour.

"What's wrong? You look like you're having second thoughts…" Gabriel said. "I think you can do better than that…How 'bout 'Little Angels'…or maybe 'Little Dickens'?" He gave a laugh. "Either way, I am sure people notice the clothes before the label."

"You think?" Maggie was enjoying his company. "You are probably right. It should be the least of my concerns." For a moment her mind had wandered from her latest disaster. "I do have a habit of stressing over those small details."

"Small details are important. It's always those small details that people overlook—like when viewing the economy. Will it ever recover? People look at the grand scheme of things, but it is not that simple. Progress takes time, and so does recovery. People get impatient and try to Band-Aid the economy, but it only makes it worse!" He smiled and said, "One wonders…will the pound always be more valuable than the euro? And the US dollar…what a joke! They need to quit leveraging themselves out to China! Make George proud again and quit mass-producing his face, right?" He gave a smile.

"I have no time to worry about world economics. I just look in my own wallet every day, realizing that it sits in a huge deficit."

"It takes time to make a profit. You have to be patient."

"I'm operating my business online. It saves a lot of money. I will not have to pay for a storefront, and Maia has been so kind to let me put a few things in the store."

"She's a sweetheart," Gabriel told her. "I'm lucky."

"I like staying with her."

Gabriel laughed. "I was going to move in, but I got a full scholarship, free housing, and I can always bother her whenever I want." He grinned.

"You have a scholarship to Oxford? Are you genius?"

"'Man is an intellect served by organs'…Ralph Waldo Emerson."

Maggie sipped her tea, somewhat fascinated by him. "You study American philosophers?"

"We study everything here." He smiled. "You want to go to the cinema tonight? Maia and I want to see *Dashing Extravagance*."

"What's that about?"

"Living the life of the rich and famous, starring Pete Hampton."

"Oh, I don't know," Maggie said. The subject was too close to home. "I'll think about it."

After they finished their tea, Gabriel offered: "We can walk back together. I wonder if Maia's back yet."

Maggie checked her watch. "She should be."

"I brought some baguettes for dinner…" Gabriel said, "…with tuna and cucumbers…"

Maggie suddenly felt sick again. "Sounds…good…" She placed her hand over her stomach.

Tuna?

That sounds…so nauseating.

I used to love tuna.

Maggie lay on her bed, staring up at the ceiling. Maia and Gabriel had gone to the film. She did not want to intrude on Maia's time with Gabriel. Besides, she needed alone time now more than ever—she was going to be a mother. It was too soon. And yet, it seemed to direct her thoughts to a new purpose—one that would be very fulfilling.

She stared at the small box—the one she could not leave behind in Italy. She had not left it behind in New York, either.

Maggie finally got out of bed and went over to the box. She sat down next to it, removed the lid, and took out the small bunny quilt. She studied the pattern, designed by her mother.

www.lovetheillusion.com/2263.htm

This quilt was the only item she'd had in her baby hope chest. She held it up. And as she did, she remembered her mother's words: "Someday, Maggie, you will know how much I love you when you have your own child."

Maggie had treasured this quilt since her mother had gotten sick. Perhaps she knew that she would never hold a grandchild in her arms, but that this tiny quilt would envelop that child in something that was made with love.

Maggie brought the quilt up to her face and breathed in a heavenly, familiar scent. It reminded her of the house where she grew up. And as she closed her eyes, the fragrance took her back in time, to her own childhood.

"Whatever you do in life, no matter what… There is no greater joy than being a mother," a voice seemed to whisper a reminder, as if her mother were sitting right there in the room with her. Perhaps, her mother was aware, in her own way, wherever she was, sharing in that "piece of heaven."

"I still love you, Mom," she whispered as she clung to the quilt. She could not believe that now she would also be a mom. As much as she had dreaded the possibility, she felt a certain calming effect, embracing her, telling her everything would be okay. Tears filled her eyes as she felt overcome with joy and tremendous responsibility, all at once.

What would Antonio say? She wanted to tell him, but it was not a good time. His dream had finally come true, but it seemed that all of their other dreams were shattered. The irony of life was catching up to her. Just about the time she took a few steps forward, it seemed she took a few more steps backward.

Everything would work out, right? It always did…at least that's what her mother would always say.

Maggie got out her phone. It was time to call a friend.

"Maggie!" Julia answered.

"Yes, it's me…" She paused. "I'm calling with news."

"Are you back together with Antonio? I knew you would be!"

"No…I'm not, but I'm pregnant," Maggie said.

"Congratulations!"

"I don't know if that is the right response, Julia. Things are a mess; I'm still in London."

"Well then, you had better get your butt back to New York! Don't you think that your child will want a father?"

"It's not that simple. Antonio has not tried once to contact me! Who knows if he even wants to see me again? He is *very* busy being famous. And he seems to have no interest in Mickey. That bothers me, too. But I have started my own clothing line, here in Oxford. You won't believe it; I'm making baby clothes. It's almost funny now, isn't it?"

"I bet they're just adorable."

"They are way cuter than anything we could ever wear!" Maggie giggled.

"Now you will have to send me photos."

"Absolutely… Of course I will. You can check out my website. I'll email you the address," Maggie promised, delighted that Julia was so interested.

"I would love to see it," Julia assured her. "So how are you coping?"

"I'm doing all right, I suppose," Maggie said. "Somehow I'll make it on my own. I need to raise this child on my own…away from all the craziness."

"Listen to you talking stupid now…" Julia said. "You know you belong with Antonio. And the only craziness is thinking that he does not have an interest in his own child."

"I don't know, Julia. He's not who I thought he was."

"Don't be so sure about that. I happen to like that young man of yours. Famous or not, he has a good head on his shoulders. And I have the information to prove it."

"Let me guess—he called you to ask about me."

"No, but listen! I was thinking about you again today, and I was going to call you. I heard back, finally—and I know it has been over a month—but Felicia sent an email to me that they are uncovering some interesting facts about Francis—and I can finally tell you. Just promise me you will call Antonio and tell him that you are okay."

"He called you?" Maggie sat on the edge of her bed.

"No, Maggie, he didn't, but you need to turn on your telly! There is supposedly drug trafficking between New York and London that takes place behind the scenes—at the fashion shows. They think Francis is involved. Now he has disappeared."

"No way! How did you find all this out?"

"It's going to be on the news any minute now! They think they have located Francis in a hotel in Belize. They have sequestered the area and are just waiting for him to surrender."

"No way…"

"You really should turn on the news. The helicopters are hovering over the area where they think he is staying and—"

"How did they figure this out?"

"They've been on his tail ever since Felicia got a list of his contacts. I just got the email an hour ago."

"This is so…strange." Maggie tried to imagine Francis in jail.

"Perhaps you owe Antonio an apology. You know he was just worried about you."

"Oh, no, well, if that's true—do you know what this means? Julia!" Maggie felt a chill run through her as she made a conclusion. "Antonio let me leave to keep me safe! He still loves me!"

"You need to call him and tell him the news that he will be a father!" Julia told her.

"Maybe I do, but don't forget he still has a child with that Nicolette, and he lied to me about that, Julia."

"I know. That's not right, but…I just really like him, anyway," Julia confessed. "Sorry, I can't help it. Every time I speak with him, I think he is one of the most genuine people I have ever met."

"Well, he told a huge lie, Julia. That would disqualify him from being genuine, don't you think? I don't know what my problem is, but

I just need to stay out of relationships. Each ends up worse than the last. And I will never understand men. Did I tell you that I am staying with Maia, and her boyfriend seems so sweet, but yesterday, he said that I should come with him to the pub next week! At first I thought, how nice, he's so friendly, but now I can't help but wonder why he keeps trying to spend time with me. Maia would hate me if she found out, and I am *not* going to do that to a friend."

"And you are married, right?"

"He doesn't know…he hasn't even recognized me. Strange fate, huh? But, I have to admit, I seem to have regained my privacy now. Perhaps the media only cares about me if I'm attached to their dearly beloved Antonio who everyone wants to read about. I try not to read the latest papers. I don't even want to know about the new woman that they have assigned to him. I completely avoid that paper aisle every time I go into Tesco!"

"Sounds like you have a mission, but I haven't read a thing…other than that Antonio was out for vengeance after Francis had him put in jail."

"It just seems so…unbelievable…Francis, tied to all that?"

"Now you know why Antonio did not like you keeping company with Francis, much less working for him."

"I feel bad…" Maggie thought for a moment. "Maybe I will call him."

"I think you should," Julia said.

Maggie picked up her phone.

She put it down again.

I will call him, but I'm not telling him he is a father…yet.

Was he glad I left?

He should have been worried that I was leaving for London! Francis was returning, eventually. Although it was strange that he was in New York for so long…

Julia must be right… She hesitated, but then picked up her phone and finally made the call.

"Maggie…" Antonio's voice sounded distant.

There was a long pause. She wondered what he was thinking.

"I heard about Francis," she finally said.

"Yep." He was not only short, he was cold.

"I guess…I'm sorry…"

"You *guess* you're sorry?" Antonio said. "That's pathetic, Maggie!"

"What do you want from me? Why haven't you called?"

"What do you want from *me*?" he asked. "You disappear like there is nothing between us, after you refuse to listen to me to stay away from Francis. And you left me!" He paused for a second. "I have to go."

"No! Antonio!" Maggie screamed into the phone. "You can't just hang up on me. You are the one who lied to me about Mickey. And now what…you have found someone else already?"

"Don't call me back!" he warned before the phone went dead.

What have I done? Maggie felt her heart ache. *He's so angry.* She tried to make sense of everything. Maybe she could call Dana. She had to talk to someone after that sour conversation. She was starting to feel guilty for having left in the first place. Her anger over Mickey seemed to have subsided—she felt ready to forgive. It did not matter that he had Mickey, because she loved him, regardless. And she would forgive the lie. Certainly, it was understandable. And she had been guilty as well—hiding the fact that she was on the pill. Was it a wash? He was hiding his child; she was hiding her plans to wait. Which was more deceitful?

She dialed Dana's number, but then quickly changed her mind. Who was Dana to give advice? She lived in fantasy land. Shane was no celebrity, and there were no paparazzi following her when she used the loo. Now, they would easily add a child. No big deal, and nothing ever was to Dana. Maggie could only wish that things could be simple for her and Antonio. They never would be. But, regardless, she knew she still loved him.

I will call him—again—to find out why HE is so mad. I'm the one who should be mad.

Were they ruined in such a short time? She hoped not. She had only meant to get away for a while, but now she feared her decision to leave was a mistake. She assumed he would call, and they would talk things out, but he never did. He was at fault, but he did not care. And had she stayed, she feared getting pregnant, and she was not able to take that risk after finding out that he already had Mickey and had lied about it. Now becoming pregnant was no longer a fear, but rather reality. Of course she would love her child, and she even hoped that it looked just like Antonio. And she feared that someday, that would be the only remainder of their love.

"Are you chasing me?" Antonio sounded amused.

"I love you." Maggie spoke the words to keep his attention.

"You…think so?"

"I know so." Maggie explained. "I shouldn't have left."

"Right, but you did—for six weeks, Maggie!"

"About Mickey…I can forgive you, I promise." Then she spoke softly, "I miss you…a lot. Do you miss me?"

"What do you think?" Antonio kept her attention, "You left your rings, the ones I gave you."

"Nicolette broke our photo. Did you forget?"

"No, but why are you so threatened? I can duplicate that photo and put it in a hundred new frames. I already replaced it—it's better than the last. Don't you see? When things get broken, you fix them, and then it's better than before."

"Is…that what you think about us? That we can be better than before?"

"I have my doubts." Antonio's voice was firm.

"You do?"

"Yes."

"Why?" She couldn't help but draw the worst conclusion. "You don't love me anymore?"

"Of course I love you, but you jeopardize your own safety by following Francis, when I told you to stay away. And there is a *huge* problem with us, Maggie. You *still* do not trust me, after everything I have done for you. And you don't listen to anything I say!"

"But now you lied to me, Antonio! How am I supposed to trust you?"

"Do me a favor," he asked.

"What?"

“Don’t come back until you do.”

“What is that supposed to mean, Antonio? You should be me! Do you ever once think about how I feel?”

“Are you kidding me, Maggie? That is all I think about!”

“You still want to be with me?”

“I do, but, you are messing up our love. You keep messing everything up! And I am just sick of it. Love should be natural…free…not restricting… You suffocate it until it no longer can exist! And you kill the fire!”

“I kill the fire?”

“Yes, you kill the fire, until we are standing inside a broken circle with no flame!”

“Are you saying you no longer love me?”

“I can’t have a relationship with you if you don’t trust me.”

“I am trying, Antonio! What do you want from me? I said I love you! And now you said I killed the fire! What are you talking about?”

“If you love me, you will trust me, and if you trust me, we will be standing in a circle that cannot be broken, and our love will burn like a hot flame, surrounding us and protecting us from the outside elements, whatever they may be. But you chose to trust Francis instead of me. You broke our circle, don’t you get it? You let him in to destroy us. It can’t work like that, Maggie.”

“I said, I will try.”

Maggie heard silence.

“Antonio?” Maggie spoke his name cautiously.

“What?” His voice was edgy.

“I will try to trust you,” she said sweetly.

"I am not Phillip, Maggie. I would never cheat on you, but love cannot survive without trust. I do not want you to have to try, don't you get it? Why can't you get that?" He let out a huff. "Just…don't come back."

Maggie realized he had hung up.

Yep! Just like Antonio! He was done talking, and so he hung up. *Great.* He has not matured one bit, and now he is going to be a father—again. I can't believe I called back.

Absolutely nothing accomplished.

Chapter 17

Seven weeks since I last saw him... One hundred and twenty-six hours since I last talked to him. Maggie sat on her bed again in the evening, alone. *Maybe I shouldn't have listened to Francis, but why couldn't Antonio just tell me what was going on?*

And what is up with Maia and Gabriel? Are they just friends? They seem so casual. I can't ask or she will think I like Gabriel! But lately, it seems he's my best friend. And when I'm with him, it feels so refreshing...so relaxing...

Antonio's world is so demanding. Twenty-four-seven alert at all times—to the invasion of the paparazzi that decides on any given day that it's your turn for attention. So painful. Antonio's well-adjusted; he's so carefree; couldn't care less what ends up in print... I always care...can't help it...we are just two different people with two different agendas! He's happy being famous. Who am I to stand in his way? I hate attention. Maybe things are better this way...and he's figured that out. But there's only one problem: I still love him.

Maggie reached under the bed, where she had hidden a book from Maia's baby shop. She was reading all about what was taking place in her body, and had started taking vitamins. Julia was the only one who knew; she could not risk telling anyone else.

She set the book down as she contemplated her next move. He had said, "Don't come back." Those were his final words to her. But in only two weeks, she would be in New York meeting with a buyer for Tiny Matteo's; a meeting she had earned without the help of

Francis or Gia. Maggie suddenly wore a smile, proud of her accomplishment, but it disappeared as she contemplated how she would see Antonio.

"Hey!" Gabriel stood in the doorway.

"What's up?" She quickly slid her book under her pillow.

"I thought maybe you could help me with something."

"What's that?"

"There's a baby duck that's stranded from its mother and the others. It somehow got trapped."

"Oh no…where is it?"

"By the meadows."

"You want to go *now*?"

"The sooner the better. I have a ten-page paper due tomorrow…didn't start yet."

"Bummer," Maggie said, getting up to follow him. "How far is it?"

"Not too far…maybe a mile or so, and we'll have to get a boat to rescue it."

"Another boat ride…okay…sounds fun." Maggie smiled.

There was a slight chill to the evening air as they approached the canal.

"This way." Gabriel took the lead.

Maggie tagged behind him. "Does Maia ever come out on the river with you?" she asked.

"No." Gabriel gave her a strange look. "She doesn't like it so much."

"Really? Why not?"

"She likes to stay indoors—I think she's a workaholic."

"We just got a new shipment; she's unpacking tonight."

"See…just what I said. She needs to hire more help."

Maggie suddenly felt guilty, realizing Maia's generosity.

Silence followed, during which Maggie wondered how long they had been dating.

"So are you going to stay in Oxford?" he asked.

"I don't know. Probably not." She instantly thought of Antonio and wondered what he was doing.

"So what brought you here? Fashion in Oxford?" He chuckled slightly. "Gonna compete with Barbour?"

"Just…time for a change." Maggie walked alongside him.

"Change is good."

"Sometimes," she said, still thinking of Antonio. "So your family lives around here?"

"Yep…a few in Wales, but mostly in the London area. After I graduate who knows where I'll be."

"You graduate this year, right?"

"Yes, and I already have a couple leads—" He changed the subject. "This way's the shortcut."

Maggie tagged behind him.

"Look! There it is!" Gabriel stopped in his tracks and pointed to the duck that was sandwiched between a log and a pile of rocks.

"Oh no!" Maggie watched as it paddled aimlessly through the brush.

"The boats are down this way. We can borrow one, and then

paddle over and get him loose."

"Sounds like a plan."

They found a boat tied to a small pier. It was old but it would do.

"This boat sits here all the time. I have no idea who it belongs to, but hopefully they don't mind."

"We could get in trouble."

"We'll have it back before they realize it's gone."

Maggie watched as Gabriel quickly untied it and motioned for her to get in. She followed him down the pier, and he reached for her hand, helping her in.

Maggie positioned herself in the stern as Gabriel seized the pole and started to move them away from the pier.

"Let me guess. I'm the weight at the other end, for balance?" She tried to keep things light.

"Yes, but we could still tip!" He maneuvered the stick, and soon managed to move the boat away from the pier.

"Just remember, I'm still recovering from the flu." She smiled.

"You look good to me." He smiled back. "To the rescue!" he called out.

"Baby Donald, here we come!" she joined in with a giggle.

They approached the duckling, who was flopping around, attempting to free himself. "Here, you hold on to the pole," he told Maggie, passing it to her, as she watched him bend over in the boat. He reached down and grabbed the duckling. It suddenly fluttered out of his hands, landing in the water next to the rest of the duck family. "There!" He turned and grinned at Maggie.

But the boat took a turn, and she felt it begin to tip. "Oh no!" he called out, before making a splash. The next thing Maggie knew, she was joining him in the mucky waters, next to the ducks—all which took off in a hurry, showing no gratitude.

"What now?" Maggie asked. She could feel her jeans absorbing enough water to add an extra ten pounds to her body weight.

"Just swim…swim to the edge," he said, his head just above the water. "Maybe we should get the boat." He started moving in its direction. "Help me," he called out, waiting for Maggie to assist.

Maggie swam ahead of him and grabbed the edge of the boat. "I got it, hurry up, get over here," she said, hanging on as tightly as she could.

He swam up next to the boat and took hold of it, attempting to hoist himself back into the cavity. "Wow! You're fast in the water!"

"I was on the swim team…"

"I can tell." He managed to somehow maneuver his body back into the boat and motioned for her to join him.

"Never thought it would pay off quite like this…and I'm freezing!"

"Here! Grab my hand," he offered as the water trickled down his face.

"So much for animal rescue," Maggie said, pulling herself to safety. "They're so ungrateful!"

"Yeah, well, what did you expect, a standing ovation?"

"Hardly, but I did *not* expect to be joining them for a swim, either." She started to shiver, her cold wet clothing stuck to her skin.

"We have to hurry, it'll be dark soon."

"No flashlight, I assume."

"No, but we can take a shortcut through the meadows, and we can stop and see the horses. You'll love it."

They approached the field of bright green grass and yellow flowers and began to tramp through the uneven mud. Cattle and horses appeared in large numbers as they carefully picked their way across the uneven ground.

"This is so beautiful out here. If I weren't so freezing cold, I would enjoy this way more," Maggie said as her heavy, wet clothing clung to her cold skin.

"Look, there's Buckwheat." Gabriel pointed.

"Buckwheat?"

"Yeah, he's my favorite," Gabriel said as he stood by his favorite horse. It seemed to recognize him as if they had a special connection. "Whenever I come out here, I look for him."

www.lovetheillusion.com/2248.htm

"He's beautiful." Maggie reached out to touch his mane. "Do you like to ride?"

"Yes, I do, but these horses are wild… Who knows where you'd end up…" Gabriel held his gaze, looking in her eyes. "We should get back," he redirected his thoughts, "before you get sick again. We can stop by my flat and—it's closer."

Maggie stood, shivering, breaking their eye contact. He was charming, yet simple—unlike Antonio. For a moment, she wondered… No, it wasn't possible; he was not interested in her. And she felt nothing for him—other than friendship.

"Sorry we ended up all wet," he said.

"It's okay…it was an adventure I won't forget; and we saved a duckling…good deed for the day, right?"

"Yep. Good deed for the day is done."

They walked alongside each other, anxious to get into dry clothing.

"Hopefully Maia will be home when you get back," Gabriel said.

"I should have left a note so she knows where I was. I left my phone—good thing now or it would be wet, right?"

"Yeah, that was a wise decision."

"So…" Maggie grew suddenly curious. "How long have you and Maia been dating?"

"Whoa…where did that come from?" He burst out laughing. "She's my cousin."

"She's your…cousin?"

"Yeah, why would you think we were dating—'cause she's gorgeous?" He laughed again.

"I don't know. She seems like your type."

"And what type is that?"

"Kinda brainy."

"Hmm…well, we *are* related."

"Yeah, well she talks about you like she's so fond of you and—

my mistake, I guess."

"I'll forgive you."

"Thanks. Sometimes I can ignore the obvious."

"Me too," he said.

"So…no girlfriends?" she said lightly. "Surely those college girls are claiming you by the dozens."

"No way."

She was beginning to wonder if maybe he had another preference when he explained, "Everyone I like is taken and…it's not easy finding someone who just enjoys the simple things, like I do." He paused. "Other than that silly wig you wear to the shop, you seem to be a simple person."

Yikes. Where did that come from…?

Maggie picked up the pace, walking a bit faster now, realizing they had ended up in some strange relationship together.

DON'T TELL HIM…

A huge mess! All at once…

They walked on in silence as Maggie tried to find the right words to say.

"We're almost there," Gabriel said. "Wait till you see my flat. You can see a castle from the bathroom window."

"Nice." Maggie's feet were nearly numb, frozen inside her shoes, although she had been wise enough to skip the socks.

They arrived at his dormitory. It was charming—old, yet well-preserved. His living quarters appeared quite messy: simple yet accommodating.

"We can put our clothes in the dryer," he said.

"You mean the washer and *then* the dryer."

"Yeah, probably. I'll find something you can wear."

"Okay, but I really need to get back," Maggie said, feeling uncomfortable with him for the first time:

Problem number one: I can't even tell him who I am! Problem number two: I certainly can't tell him that I'm pregnant. Problem number three: he's very sweet—perhaps in another lifetime it could have worked out. And problem number four: I'm SO in love with Antonio and I have no feelings for Gabriel whatsoever. He's nice, he's cute, he's smart, he's considerate, he's fun, he's simple like me, and he has an interest in me, but I am in love with Antonio…rings or no rings… Even miles away…my heart is locked to his and I don't have the key to free myself.

"I have to go." Maggie stood, wearing the flannel shirt. "Thanks for everything." She held the wet clothes in hand, while standing in her wet shoes.

"Sorry," he finally admitted. "I didn't mean for us to end up all wet and…let me at least find a bag that you can carry that in."

"Sure, that would be nice…" Maggie waited.

He disappeared for a while, leaving her to her thoughts.

I miss Antonio so much…it's killing me.

"Here you go," Gabriel came back with a plastic bag. "Don't worry about the shirt—I have plenty. Now, hurry back so no one sees you dressed like that." He gave a quick laugh.

"It's a bit embarrassing, but I'll manage. Only a few blocks away, and hey—just a new fashion statement that hasn't hit London yet, right?"

"You're funny!" he told her, his eyes smiling. "But the wig is worse, believe me. You should just wear your hair like that—natural."

"Well, that's your opinion. Maybe that's your clue: I'm not so simple after all."

"I think I'm right…we would get along great." He took a step closer to her. Maggie felt her eyes widen, realizing she was in over her head. He reached out and grabbed her hand and stood with his face inches from hers. And a second later, he kissed her.

Maggie stepped back, shaking her head. "Gabriel! This isn't what you think."

"Why? You have no interest in me?"

"No, I…this is…I thought we were just friends! You were supposed to be dating Maia!"

"This *is* funny, you know… "

"I guess," Maggie said, allowing a quick laugh to escape.

"And now?" He looked at her as if she had his heart.

Maggie swallowed, as her face grew serious. "Gabriel, I appreciate how sweet you are, but I'm not the person you think I am."

"Yes, you are…you are just the sort of girl I could like…for a really long time…" He looked confused. "So you're just not into me? Fine…that's what always happens… What's the reason? You don't feel connected or attracted to me like that, right? Just friends…I can take the truth, just tell me."

"No, you can't take the truth and I can't tell you or…" Maggie let out a breath, exhausted by his efforts. "Just trust me!"

Now I sound just like Antonio, whom I can't seem to trust!

"Whatever…" Gabriel gave her an unpleasant grunt. "A girl with a past…how bad can it be?"

Maggie smiled at him, suddenly feeling bad—she thought he was extremely sweet. "I wish I could say, and you should know that I value our friendship."

"So you don't feel *any* attraction?" He gave her a sharp look.

"I didn't say that." Maggie wished he would drop the subject.

"I'll walk you back," he suddenly decided.

"Okay," she agreed, wondering if her secrets would be safe with him.

They walked in silence, each a bit confused.

And when they finally arrived at the door, Maggie turned to say goodbye.

"So, are we friends?" he asked, suddenly amused.

"Sure," Maggie agreed, thinking that perhaps if Antonio and his child weren't in the picture, she and Gabriel could possibly have a chance.

"I think we are more than that," he said, wearing a grin.

"Why?"

His coy behavior seemed to vanish.

"There's only one way to find out." He leaned into her and started kissing her again.

Maggie pushed him back and, with alarm in her voice, exclaimed, "I'm married!"

He backed off, surprised at her confession.

"And…pregnant…" she revealed. "I just found out."

"Shit!"

Gabriel stood in shock, letting her proclamation sink in.

"So, you know the father?" he finally asked.

"Of course I know the father; I'm married to him!"

"Then where is he?" He paused briefly. "Oh!" His eyes grew wide. "Abuse…the wig…you're hiding out and… You're running from him and—am I right?" He waited for her response, puzzled, as she stood silent. "So that's it?" he finally assumed.

"No…it's just complicated." Maggie paused and then said, "I think I've told you all I can."

"There's more?"

"We are just spending time away from each other…hoping to sort things out."

"He's an idiot to let you go!" He told her.

"*I'm* the one who left, Gabriel," Maggie explained, and then confessed: "And I'm an idiot. I still really love him. Problem is, I don't know what he feels for me anymore. I haven't told him I'm pregnant because he told me not to come back. I'm not going to make him reunite with me out of guilt."

"Why did you leave?"

"He has a child already, with someone else, and I found out *after* we were married. He'd said nothing of it before and—"

"Wow…that's ridiculous." Gabriel shook his head. "The secrets people keep, huh?"

Maggie couldn't help but wonder how long he could remain clueless as to her identity. Would it completely freak him out? She decided she would hang on to that information—he could never know. She had already shared more than enough, and perhaps now he would accept her as just a friend.

Chapter 18

"So what's the matter with you and Gabriel?" Maia handed Maggie a cup of tea. Their conversations normally consisted primarily of shop talk, so this was a bit of a departure.

"I didn't realize he was your cousin." Maggie held the cup of tea, warming her hands on the heated porcelain. "I thought you two were, you know, dating or something."

"He's only twenty-four," Maia explained. "Why would I be going out with him? I'm nearly thirty."

"You look young..." Maggie said, hoping to keep things moving in a positive direction.

"You are his age—problem is, you are married—but I told him I thought it was over." She rolled her eyes.

"What?" Maggie stared blankly into the open air. "He knew?"

"He's good at that." Maia shrugged as she sipped her tea. "He doesn't have any trouble getting the attention of women, you know. And he never seems to stick with anyone in particular, but he seems different around you. I think he really likes you."

"So...he's a player after his own heart."

"No, just not easily impressed."

"Then he is impressed with my marital status?" Maggie burst out laughing, but then her face suddenly grew serious. "You never told anyone, right? Or did Gabriel fake that too?"

"Don't worry." Maia assured her. "I didn't give out your identity—or tell anyone about your steamy affairs with that Antonio.

But what is happening with the two of you, anyway? Are you still together? Or was your marriage just another event to make the news?"

Maggie's face turned bleak and she looked out the window.

"Sorry, I know it's none of my business," Maia continued, "and believe it or not, I don't get into the latest gossip in the papers, like your friend Dana. I can't believe she made it into one herself, just hanging out with you! What does that feel like, being stalked just for a photo and never knowing what caption they will paste over the top?"

"It's pretty devastating. I'm taking a break from it all…" Maggie let out a sigh.

"You miss Antonio, don't you?"

"Well, yeah, but he told me not to come back."

"Oh, that's not good. Do you think he's going out with someone else?"

"No," Maggie said. "I doubt it, but he has a child with that Nicolette and forgot to tell me about it!"

"So they say…" Maia seemed sweet, sincere. "That must be rough; I can't imagine…"

"It was *not* a pleasant surprise, believe me." Maggie sipped her tea.

"So celebrity love affairs come and go—like the weather, right?"

"Money and fame complicate things—that's for sure," Maggie said, "but regardless, I love him. I guess I'm aware of that more than ever now." She felt hopeless. "It's such torture being away, but I'm *not* crawling back on my hands and knees, preg—" Maggie stopped suddenly and put her hand to her mouth.

"Pregnant?" Maia filled in the blanks. "You're pregnant?"

Maggie sat motionless.

Crap...

"Does he know?" Maia asked.

"No—and please promise me—you can't say a thing. But I did tell Gabriel."

"When are you due?" Maia looked concerned.

"In maybe seven months, but I don't really know my due date."

"Let me guess, you haven't been to the doctor?" she asked in disbelief.

"No…not yet; I can't afford to have that hitting the press when Antonio still does not know."

"You should tell him, don't you think? And you need to get to a doctor—they are sworn to secrecy."

"It's not that simple."

"I might know someone who could see you…at least a nurse. Maggie, you need to make sure the baby has proper care."

"I do *not* want Antonio finding out in the news! Things have a way of 'leaking.'"

"What difference does it make if he finds out—he should know, don't you think?"

"Because then he will feel obligated. I'm not about that."

There was a knock on the door.

"It's probably Gabriel," Maggie said. "I told him I washed his shirt…" Maggie opened up the door, and faced the surprise of her life.

"Bradley! What are you doing here?"

"I need to talk to you." He wore a stern look on his face.

Maggie stepped outside, speechless.

"You wanna go to that pub down there?" he asked.

"Uh…sure, let me grab my purse."

The chill of the air was refreshing. They walked in silence to the nearby pub. Maggie could not help but feel a sudden connection to Antonio while in the company of Bradley. *Why had he come?*

"Fish and chips?" Bradley asked her as they walked into the pub.

"Sure," Maggie agreed.

She instantly felt her stomach flinch, as if it had ignited into flames, quenching her appetite. It was terrifyingly apparent that her feelings for Antonio were stronger than ever. And now, in the company of Bradley, his very presence seemed a razor-sharp reminder—a portfolio of memories, revealing her helplessly deep connection to Antonio. And in a simple moment of truth, she was well aware that she could never get over him.

"You want a beer or wine or something?" he called out.

"No…just tea is fine." Maggie sat down, watching as Bradley patiently waited to place their order with the bartender. Moments later, he made his way back to their table.

"So, what are you doing here, Bradley?" she asked after he took a seat and took a swallow of Nicholson's Ale.

"I should ask you the same, Maggie. Antonio is still so upset that you just took off like that."

"You two are still talking? I thought he fired you."

"Are you kidding? He didn't fire me! He sent me on the vacation of my life with Rainelle. We're staying in Scotland, by the way—but then Antonio sent me to find you. He's busy performing."

"He sent you to talk to me? That is just so *lame!*" Maggie folded her arms, disgusted.

"Not quite…" Bradley explained. "I'm here to get you. Francis is being detained at Otisville, but supposedly his partner in crime just landed in London and Antonio is worried about you and not taking any chances. We leave tomorrow." He handed her the printed itinerary.

"What?" Maggie stared at the flight information. "I'm not flying out to Scotland! What am I going to do there? I have to fly to New York in a few days to meet with a buyer, and I was hoping to see Antonio, finally—that is, if he even wants to see me!"

"He's pretty mad at you right now."

"You know what? That's just his stupid ego taking over! He told me not to come back, because I don't trust him, but how am I supposed to manage that when he suddenly admits that he has a child with Nicolette?"

Bradley grinned. "Is that right? I never knew."

"I'm just disgusted by the whole thing, and then he ends up mad at me! Figure that out!"

"I just did!" Bradley frowned at her. "Maybe I don't have the right to say this to you, Maggie, but you need to wake up and smell the coffee!"

"They drink tea, here, Bradley, in case you don't know…milk instead of cream in Americano coffee? It's just not the same…I might as well just drink tea."

"Okay…well, as you drink your tea, I want you to remember

being at Night Owls, when I threw you into Antonio's arms. I know you were pretty freaked out back then when you first learned who he was, and yet that night was pretty memorable, wasn't it?"

"Right, so now what? You're going to tell me that you're sorry for bringing me into a crazy world with a guy I am madly in love with, only to discover that we can never be normal?"

"Listen, girl, I don't know what went down between the two of you, but I am not going to apologize for bringing the two of you together. The only thing I *am* sorry for is that you both are very *stubborn* individuals!"

"Me? I called him, twice! He told me not to call back and to stay away!" Maggie complained. "Oh, and I am supposed to trust him, by the way!"

"And what's the problem?"

"He's all secretive with me, acting like he can't tell me this or that, and when I finally can't take it anymore he finally admits that he has a child with that repulsive Nicolette! She comes into our suite, unannounced, with no invitation, to find Antonio. Then, when he's not there, she breaks our photo, claiming that Antonio won't own up to his responsibilities as a father! He then arrives, has a private conversation with her—behind my back—and it turns out that he gives her money!"

"Okay, slow down now. I know for a *fact* that Mickey's not his! He's not romantically involved with Nicki—he feels sorry for her. It's hardly a love affair, Maggie."

"No, Bradley, he finally told me. It's true!"

"No…I think he was just telling you what you wanted to

hear…that's what he told me… You kept accusing him, and then finally told you what you wanted to hear!"

"You *must* be kidding! Why would he mess with me like that?"

"Why would you mess with *him* like that? He said you kept asking, like you thought the rumors were true. Problem is, you just don't understand Antonio. He was just dishing it back to you."

Maggie sat in shock, absorbing what Bradley had said.

"He wants your trust and loyalty," Bradley explained. "What is love worth, if you don't have trust?"

"So Mickey's not his?"

"No, Maggie! He told you that three times and when you asked again, he just blew a fuse and made up some confession. And then you were quick to believe him. He couldn't believe it!"

What? You must be joking.

"That's…terrible… Now I feel bad." Maggie stared at her plate of fish, which had just arrived. "Why would he do that?"

"I don't know why he does what he does, but I think you should tell him that you're sorry."

"He told me not to come back."

"He wants your trust."

"Fine, he can have it," Maggie confessed as her eyes flooded with tears. "I hope it's not too late for us."

"Look, everyone makes mistakes, and sometimes you have to suck it up and forgive and forget, but Antonio does not have some mysterious past that you have to chisel away at to uncover the truth. He is a decent guy, living in a crazy world. And he wants you to be that stable 'piece of normal' in his life."

"I really messed things up. I mean, he has never done anything before that I should have doubted, but everything that took place that week just finally sent me into paranoia—Francis and Nicolette, all in a week—it was just too much to take."

Bradley nodded. "As for Francis, Antonio was having him investigated, and everything was undercover, Maggie. Try to understand…he doesn't want you involved in that. You have to support Antonio. He has a hard enough time dealing with all the craziness, and you need to be that anchor—that stability for him, understand?"

"I can try," Maggie felt a surge of relief, realizing that she was the mother of Antonio's only child. "I really do love him. I think that's why all of this happened. I can't stand to think of him caring for another woman, and everything was getting stranger by the minute!"

"Whatever Antonio tells you, you need to believe that, okay? You need to exist in his world *with* him, not against him."

"Is he open to second chances?"

Bradley grinned. "Absolutely…I know he still cares, or he wouldn't have sent me after you. He said you are to stay in Scotland with me, until they find Bedeck—he's supposedly in charge of everything. He's arrived here in London now, and Antonio is worried that they may try to take you hostage, but don't worry, I won't let anything happen to you."

Did he say "hostage"?

"This is such a nightmare. I just wish it was over."

"I know, me too." Bradley finished his beer. "And when it is, I promise that you can be with Antonio again. Now, there's just one more thing I have to tell you."

"What?"

"Antonio told me to tell you that he still loves you." Bradley gave her a smile.

Maggie smiled back.

"That's good…really good…."

"We need to head back, though," Bradley said. "So you can pack up your stuff. And then we need to take a taxi to Stansted."

"So I'm leaving Oxford, for good?"

"Yes, and I have to tell you, when you left New York, Antonio was so upset. But he said, 'If she loves me, she'll come back. At least for now, she'll be away from Francis.' Strange the guy was hanging out for so long just for a fashion show, don't you think? Now they have stepped up the security around the building after I left—you never know what those drug lords will do."

"Does Francis know who turned him in?"

"I think your friend Julia got the ball rolling on that, but Antonio already had people working undercover, keeping an eye out for the right opportunity to bring him down."

"They know each other, don't they?" Maggie wondered if Bradley would explain.

"Francis and Antonio? That's an interesting one…how about we wait until the plane ride…" Bradley suggested.

"You're going to tell me?"

"Sure, why not."

"You don't think he'll fire you?" Maggie teased.

"Are you kidding me? He owes me big time; I got his wife to go to Scotland!"

Maggie laughed. "You are pretty cool, Bradley, just so you know."

"That's what they say." He grinned. "Now, after we pack your stuff—which had better fit into a *small* suitcase—we have to head back to the hotel and get Rainelle. She's excited to see you."

"Oh! I can't wait to see her too!" Maggie wore a big smile.

Things were finally looking up. Just knowing that Antonio still cared was enough to give her tremendous relief. And it seemed for the first time in a long time, she felt complete. Soon they would be together. And she could not wait to tell him, in person, that he would be a father.

Chapter 19

"Excuse me. Maggie…Maggie DeLuca?" she heard someone yelling from behind them as they left the pub. *I should have washed the wig.* She turned and faced a man who was undoubtedly working for the papers. "Look! I'm not really into blackmail," he said, "and it may seem a bit harsh, but I got hold of this photo and am wondering if you want to pay money to keep it from making the front page. Either that or I pay *you* to do an interview."

"You want to do *what?*" Maggie asked, irritated. Bradley stood by her side as she was given a quick glance at a photo of her standing in a flannel shirt that belonged to Gabriel who had her in his arms, enjoying a kiss.

www.lovetheillusion.com/2219.htm

Time to leave Oxford! "That's not me…" Maggie defended herself. "You're wasting your time!" she explained, standing next to Bradley.

"So you say, but I can tell you that we're getting ready to do a three-page article on why you left Antonio! So, you can either cooperate with me or let us print our assumptions!"

Maggie looked up at Bradley, who wore a frown. "Knock it off, you circus clown," he said. "No one wants to read that garbage you print, so I suggest you go in that pub there and drink down a six-pack or two if you need something to do." He looked at Maggie. "Let's go."

"Bradley—wait! Maybe I should just interview with him, so that they can print the truth! I cannot even imagine what will come of that, with that photo they have. How did they find me? Just when I thought I was hiding out and—" Maggie paused. "I can't wait to get to Scotland." She kept in step with Bradley as they walked away from the reporter.

"Just keep walking. Don't worry about that guy. You do an interview, and it will still be their interpretation. And it's useless giving them money! They make enough on the garbage they print."

"But what if Antonio sees it?"

"You have to just tell him, Maggie; be honest with him. That's all he wants from you."

"How's *that* going to work?" Maggie contemplated her apology to Antonio. "'Oh, hi Antonio. I just found out I was pregnant with your child and then I kissed Gabriel and I'm *so* sorry that I didn't trust you!'" She contemplated the outcome, mindlessly sharing her concerns with Bradley. "This is never-ending…he's never going to forgive me!"

"Did you just say that you're pregnant?" Bradley chuckled. "Antonio's having a baby? He should like that surprise!"

"Yes, if he still even wants to see me," Maggie said.

"So that's you in the photo…but it's Antonio's baby?" Bradley suddenly seemed confused.

"Yes, it's me…and of course it's Antonio's…I am just a fortress of disaster!" Maggie started to explain: "Gabriel and I…we're just friends. I thought he was dating Maia, but it turns out they're cousins! The same day I found that out, he kissed me after we fell out of a boat rescuing ducks and…what I *should* be trying to rescue is my relationship with Antonio!"

"Well sounds like you're keeping busy in London."

"Not funny, but the time away wasn't all bad. I started a clothing line for infants," Maggie said. "And now I can't wait to make a few clothes for our own."

Bradley chuckled again. "I can't *wait* for you to tell Antonio. He's gonna be one happy dude."

"I hope so. Perhaps it will mend everything…promise me you won't tell him? *I* want to be the one to tell him."

"I promise," he agreed. "Your secret's safe with me." He nodded.

"Yes, and now that I have told you *that*…maybe you can tell me what's up with Antonio and Francis."

"Like I said, on the plane…" He nodded.

Yes! Maggie felt overjoyed. *I am finally going to know everything!*

They arrived back at Maia's and, to Maggie's surprise, Gabriel was there.

She stood by Bradley as he made an introduction. "I'm Bradley—Maggie's bodyguard. I'll just be waiting here while she packs." He walked over to the couch and took a seat. "She's leaving tonight."

"*Body*guard?" Gabriel looked confused.

I should just tell him, Maggie thought.

"I'll go help Maggie pack," Maia said.

"Wait. I think Gabriel and I need to talk," Maggie said, still absorbing his look of confusion. She motioned for him to follow her into her room.

"Please don't hate me when I tell you this," Maggie started to explain. "I came here—to Oxford—to escape, but not from abuse."

"But you have a bodyguard… Are you in danger?"

"No! Gabriel! How can you not recognize me? And I need you to do me a favor…" She then explained: "I am Maggie DeLuca…married to Antonio…you know…the magician."

"What?" he said in disbelief. Then his eyes grew wide. "Seriously?" He opened his mouth to speak again, but no words came out.

"I know, I should have said. Maia knew, but it's just a big risk for me. The paparazzi are everywhere, and now they finally located me and want to interview me. They have a photo of you and me kissing outside the door to your place."

"A photo of us…" Gabriel was confused. "How did they…?"

"You have to promise me not to talk to any reporters. When Bradley and I leave, they will find you and want to talk to you. They threatened to do an article on my breakup with Antonio, attached with the photo, unless I did an interview. Bradley said no, and now I need to warn you."

Gabriel just stood dumbfounded.

"Sorry. Now you know why we can only be friends," Maggie

explained. "And I want to thank you for being that friend. I needed one, and it was great to get away from everything, but I have to go back. Antonio and I aren't over. We never will be."

"Okay, so that's it. Well, it was nice knowing you. The wig…I guess it worked for a while," he said, finding a thread of humor.

"Yeah, until I damaged it…how could I ever put that on my head again, right?" Maggie laughed.

"Keep in touch by email," he said. "Still friends?"

"Sure," she smiled back at him. "Did you want your shirt?" She handed it to him.

"Oh, yeah, now that it will make the news," he said, taking it from her. "I will think of you in it every time I wear it."

"I hope the papers show a little mercy." Maggie imagined the possibilities.

"I doubt that, but either way, I had fun getting to know you."

Maggie packed her things, thinking about the time she spent in London. It was a bittersweet memory. But nothing compared to the memories she had of being with Antonio. How could she have doubted him? Now she could not wait to stand in his arms again.

The plane took off, headed to Scotland.

Maggie sat next to Rainelle, who sat next to Bradley. Maggie couldn't help but wonder if Bradley was stalling to tell her all about how Francis and Antonio first met. Now she was specifically recalling the 'tone of alarm' in Antonio's voice when she had first spoken to Antonio at Biagio's, after her flight in from London. He had said, "You work for Francis? That's interesting."

She should have known they had a past. Instead, she assumed that

Antonio was too cheap to employ Francis to make his costumes. And Francis had told her it was "too petty" to mess with. They had both managed, in their own ways, to pull the wool over her eyes. But now she hoped she was within seconds of learning the truth.

Maggie leaned over Rainelle. "Bradley!" she whispered. "Don't think that I have forgotten. It's only an hour flight to Edinburgh, so let's not waste any time!"

"Okay, Maggie, I'll tell you what you want to know," he explained in front of Rainelle.

"Rainelle knows?" Maggie asked.

"She's my honey buns. She knows everything…almost."

"I'd better know everything," Rainelle said, turning to Maggie. "But let me tell you… We women are way better at telling the stories than men are…so let me do the tellin' and I promise not to leave out *any* details."

Maggie gave her a curious look.

"Now, before I start," Rainelle said, "you have to promise to wait until I am done to ask questions and you might not like everything you hear, but it's the truth." Maggie agreed, and Rainelle sat back and told the story: "Shortly after Matteo died, Antonio had made it big time…his sales for his shows were at record highs and he contacted Francis to make costumes. We wanted a new look, and Francis was always in New York, doing business as a fashion designer—or so we thought. Now, the man definitely designs clothing, that is true, but he is designing a whole new way of dealing as well—behind the fashion scenes! But Antonio met with Francis to do business—that would be fashion, not the other…and Francis acted like Antonio couldn't afford him, and gave some ridiculous quote that was at least twice what the other designers were charging. Well, Antonio was like, 'No way am I paying his crazy wages,' but little did Antonio know, Francis was making quite a bit of money on the side when he was in New York, and he did not have the *time* to deal with something so big. Remember when you met Antonio in New York? But then Antonio flew you both to Chicago to finalize a contract. Not only was Antonio performing there, but he did not want Francis to have another excuse to be at Shagan's hotel, dealing! And while you were there, Francis offered some ridiculous proposal, and Antonio ends up accepting, anyway… He wanted to see you again; he cared about you and was concerned that you worked for the guy. As for Francis, he was designing dresses, and that did not take as much of his time since the patterns were cut out already, and somewhat duplicated in various colors. But costumes for a huge production like Antonio's? That was a *whole new* venue. And Francis was busy! They were in the process of passing shipments between Mexico and the US and London, and Francis was not about to get sidetracked with Antonio's proposal."

"How did you find this out?" Maggie asked.

"It was shortly after he met Nicolette…maybe four years ago. Her father owns the hotel that Antonio stays in and also contributes large sums of money to support AD Magic. He is invested in the company…and this is where things get sticky. His daughter takes a huge liking to Antonio, and Antonio likes her as well. Little does he know, Daddy's girl is caught up in drugs, and her own father is a dealer and knows Francis. How do you think he got so filthy rich? Now, it's not Antonio's fault. He and Stanley had no idea when they bought their shares of stock in Antonio's company, and Antonio's hands are tied. Shagan is somewhat fond of Antonio because he was dating his daughter. Then, after she used up her half a million dollars that was just given to her, her father cut her off and said, 'That's enough, let Antonio deal with her.' I think they must have dated for about three months when Antonio started to see the light of day. So you have to wonder…Francis stays in Shagan's hotel on business, right? And so did *you* when you came along with Francis. Shagan has made accommodations for Antonio to stay there and has spent some of his own money to renovate a place for Cheetos. And the fourth floor belongs to AD Enterprises. Shagan wants them there! It's a *huge* profit for him, but his daughter, Nicolette, was also staying there. Finally, Antonio said that's enough of that, and he started paying to house her elsewhere. He figured it was easier to get rid of her than find a new place to house the entire staff and renovate a new place. Antonio could live anywhere, but it felt like home and he liked the people there and when it comes to Antonio he is all about his crew and we are just like family. He didn't want to leave." Rainelle paused for a moment to make sure she still had Maggie's attention.

"Now, about Nicolette…" Rainelle continued. "She got pregnant one night, in her room. Her own dealer got her pregnant. Antonio was with her that night, and went to get them something to eat, and that's when it happened. He wanted to take care of her after he learned of her addiction, but I don't think he was ever in love with her; he was very attracted to her in the beginning, but her life was a mess and it did not take long for Antonio to figure that out. If it weren't for Antonio, she would probably be dead by now. He got her to come clean, after she got pregnant. Now, she is so in love with him and wants to believe they have a child together. Antonio doesn't have the heart to tell her, because it's all about why she loves Mickey so much—and he does, strangely, look just like Antonio, with his dark eyes and hair. But did you see Weston? That's the father! He is also dark. Most of Antonio's crew know nothing about any of this, but Bradley works security and noticed there were some strange things going on. He and Antonio have been working ever since to try to bring down the house, but problem is even the NYPD has a few involved, so it's hard to know who to trust. Antonio has a few people working inside their circle of friends, but he can never prove anything. And Antonio's been waiting it out, patiently, hoping to put Francis away for good, along with everyone else involved. But at the same time, he has to be careful and remain on friendly terms so that no one suspects anything."

"Wow!" Maggie said. "It's more complicated than I'd thought."

Bradley leaned over. "You should also know that Felicia, the woman Julia knows, was able to send the ball rolling into the hands of the right people...with the information that she gathered from Francis' list of connections, and now Francis is behind bars. But there are still others. As for Shagan, he has his loyalties where Antonio is concerned because of the huge profits his show brings in. Antonio and his crew are safe. They will never harm them. I'm a different story, though. Antonio was concerned and sent me to Scotland, just to make sure. But I'm pretty convinced that if something happened to anyone in Antonio's circle of friends, suspicions would escalate and they do *not* want to stir up any trouble. But you must see now why Antonio didn't want you to work for Francis and why he takes care of Nicolette."

"Yes, it's all starting to make sense now."

"And that's why Antonio paid Gia to help you get your feet off the ground. He did not mean to insult you, but he didn't know what to do. You wouldn't listen to him and he couldn't risk you keeping company with Francis!"

"So how did Antonio get out of jail so suddenly?" Maggie asked.

"Well, obviously, Antonio pushed Francis off the boat," Bradley said. "Not a wise decision on his part, but Shagan pulled strings to get Antonio out of jail when Francis told him that they weren't going to release him, due to Antonio's confession that he wanted to kill him! Antonio needs to mind his temper, but that's not possible when it comes to protecting the people he loves. And he didn't know what to do anymore to keep you away from Francis."

"Why couldn't he just tell me?"

"It's not that simple, Maggie. You need to realize that all this has to stay undercover if it's going to be effective. One small leak, then they take off, go into hiding. They could disappear for years. You worked for the guy—a totally bad move, yet it kept them vulnerable. They have to think you have no clue. But Antonio's way smarter than they think he is."

"So is Shagan in jail?"

"No. "

"So that's it…he goes free?"

"Well, not exactly. Two of them are locked up now…Francis and the head of the organization are done. That has crippled them immensely. It should put a stop to things because someone has to move it all. No one is left to do the dirty work. Shagan is involved, but only because he got sucked in. It was easy money for him. And basically, he is involved because it goes on at his hotel but he doesn't do the dealing. He gets paid to shut up. Once Francis is out of the picture, and Weston—I think he's been detained—Antonio wanted to get him on rape charges, but he was protecting Nicolette from the media. That would have been a mess if it ended up in the press. And it would have sent her off the deep end."

"It's sad that Mickey will grow up thinking his dad never spends time with him."

"It's simple. Antonio has his career. But he used to hang out with them on occasion before he met you. And he always gives Mickey gifts."

"It's really sad…the whole story. And Francis…I still find that hard to believe."

"It's one crazy, messed-up world, but you gotta believe me when I tell you that Antonio's a great guy, Maggie. We were all rooting for you to fall in love with him."

"That was easy to do," she said, recalling when she first saw him. "There always seemed to be that layer of mystery about him, like he knows more than he says. I wish things weren't like that."

"Antonio wants you to live in his world, but sheltered from everything, if that makes any sense. But, the media will still chase you down—there's nothing he can do about that. Just one of those things you gotta live with."

"I wish, just once, we could write our own story."

"Don't hold your breath." Bradley looked out the window. The plane was swiftly approaching the tarmac.

Chapter 20

Being in Scotland was not enough of a distraction to keep Maggie's mind off of Antonio. She could not wait to see him. She wanted desperately to call him, but his words—"Don't come back"—kept echoing in her mind, leaving her to wonder what she would say if she did manage to get the courage to call him.

Bradley seemed convinced that everything would be okay. Hopefully, it was true—that Antonio still loved her. Otherwise, it was only a futile attempt on Bradley's behalf to patch things up between the two of them.

Should I call him? She felt as if time was against her. She hoped she could see him before that picture ended up in the press. Antonio never cared about press coverage, or so he claimed, but she was certain he would care about that—another man kissing her? It was enough to destroy them before they even got back on track. She wondered if she should have explained it to the reporter as an honest mistake; a simple, but huge, misunderstanding.

A mistake?

How will I ever explain this to Antonio?

She remembered how angry Antonio was after Francis kissed her. If only Antonio could understand how much she loved him, it would be so much easier. Everything that had left her with doubts had now been completely explained, but now she had to somehow get into his good graces once again, and she longed to be in his arms. *Was it even possible?*

Maggie stood in front of the mirror, tying up her hair, wishing Bradley would let her know when they would return to New York. They were waiting for the final word that there were no more "loose ends" where Francis and his friends were concerned.

They were all staying in the same room, for security reasons. Antonio had told Bradley not to let Maggie out of his sight. The room had two queen beds and she had her own bed now, larger than what she had back in Oxford, but the circumstances were a bit alarming. Bradley was hoping that the press would not leak information on their whereabouts. Luckily, they left the London area where those involved were lurking around. Bradley had a gun with him, which made Maggie feel both protected and alarmed.

As they sat in the room, waiting for Stanley to give instructions, the ringtone of Bradley's phone destroyed the silence.

"Yeah, Davis here." Maggie and Rainelle sat quietly, listening to Bradley's phone conversation. "You're kidding. He's shot? What? When did this happen?"

Maggie froze. "No," she whispered.

Rainelle placed her hand on Maggie's knee. "No…*nooo*…" Maggie cried out. "Not Antonio…please…no."

"It's Shagan," Bradley announced. "He's been shot. He has a bullet wound to the back of his neck and it does not sound good. He's been taken—flight for life."

"Shh, Maggie," Rainelle whispered, "Antonio's going to be fine."

Maggie's heart was still pounding. "I'm so afraid for him—he's at that hotel."

"Yeah, along with the rest of his staff. They'll be fine." Bradley told her. “Shagan is aware of the drug ring. But they aren’t about to harm the hotel guests.”

“You don’t know that for sure!” Maggie shouted at him. “Tell Antonio to get out of that hotel!”

“He’s not going to cancel his show, Maggie,” Bradley said, “and— just a minute—” He reached for his phone to take another call. “Really…is that right?” After a lengthy conversation, Bradley finally ended the call: “Okay…sounds good…we’ll catch the next flight.”

“Now what?” Rainelle asked.

“They got the guy that shot Shagan—he works for the NYPD—how’s that for crazy? He offered Shagan immunity but that went sour as soon as he started to give out information, hoping to save his neck—instead, he was shot in the neck. Now the two guys that were involved are in custody, including the jail guard that Francis paid a visit to that day.” Bradley shook his head. “So far, they’ve made half a dozen arrests. But this one just went down in the middle of the night. They think everything is over now—they’ve taken down the entire mob. We can catch the next flight back to the States tomorrow.”

“Are you *sure* Antonio will be okay?” Maggie asked.

“It’s over, Maggie. Get ready for normal…everything normal. Sounds good, doesn’t it?” Bradley told her.

THE NEXT DAY…

“Ladies and gentlemen, you will notice that the seatbelt light has come on. Please make sure your seatbelts are secure as we prepare to make our landing at Kennedy Airport in about twenty minutes."

Maggie looked at her watch, feeling very tired from the flight, yet awake from an adrenaline rush of anticipation. It was six p.m. already, and Antonio's show started at eight. She took a deep breath as she mentally rehearsed her first words to him: "I'm sorry, Antonio. I hope you can forgive me because we are having a baby and the press has this photo of me and..." *I can't tell him that yet. That is like pouring salt into a wound before it can heal...*

"Bradley, I need your help." She turned to him. "Can you *please* tell Antonio that we ran into that crazy reporter who happened to have a photo that...well, you know the story, and I think you could explain it better than me... Please?"

"Maggie, I could, but Antonio needs to hear it from you. I can't be the mentor for the two of you. It doesn't work like that."

Why does he have to be right? Maggie slouched in her seat while the plane came in to land.

An hour later, Maggie opened up the room to their hotel suite, but Antonio was not there.

Does he know I'm back? Maggie set down her luggage. *Of course he does.*

Everything was just as she remembered, only Antonio was missing.

He must have left for the show already.

She stepped into the shower. And as soon as she closed her eyes under the pour of water, all she could think was how Antonio would look at her.

I should go to his show. Tonight I'll be one of his fans. I will speak to him afterward. Hopefully he will be glad to see me.

Soon she stood at her closet, searching for something to wear. Thumbing through the various articles, she came to the white dress. She ran her fingertips across its fine satiny fabric—it was the dress she wore as the lady in the ring of fire.

Was it appropriate?

Maybe she could get there in time and talk to him before the show, but it started in less than a half hour.

She tried the best she could to apply her own makeup and then slipped into the white dress. She stood in front of the mirror, hoping that, after tonight, they would be together again. But amid her high hopes of reconciliation, his harsh words still rang in her ears: "Don't come back." Fear took over, and she soon landed on the edge of the bed.

I'm so afraid to see him. If he didn't care, he wouldn't have sent Bradley looking for me.

Bradley said he still loved me. I hope so.

But it has been two months, and...

She stood up.

I just need to put an end to this.

She went over to the nightstand next to the bed, and suddenly saw the photo of the two of them—the one Nicolette had broken. It was in a new frame. She picked it up, admiring the silver stainless steel, with its swirling design. As she held it, she remembered that night they had danced together.

As she set it down, she noticed her two rings sitting on the nightstand. They had been hidden behind the frame. She picked them up and slipped them back on her fingers. She brought the DeLuca ring to her lips, remembering when they had danced at the Night Owls. That night would be framed in her memory forever:

www.lovetheillusion.com/2281.htm

A half hour later, Maggie stepped out of a cab, her eyes glued to Radio City.

www.lovetheillusion.com/2286.htm

She took off, nearly running into the building to find Antonio. But when she arrived at the base of a stairwell leading to the back stage, the security guard let her know: "The show starts in less than five. You gotta wait till afterwards to talk to him."

"That's okay." Maggie suddenly felt out of place.

She left, making her way down a side aisle, hoping to find a place to sit. She leaned against the wall, looking around. Just when she thought she had drawn the attention of the crowd, the lights went out. The crowd started screaming in anticipation.

Maggie ran to the back of the theater, where she saw an usher.

"Maggie!" The woman recognized her. "You're back?" she whispered. "You want me to find you a seat?"

"Sure…" Maggie's voice was weak.

"Wait here," the woman told her as Maggie scanned the audience. The theater was filled to capacity. It seemed every seat was taken. Perhaps she did not belong. She suddenly felt a foreigner, in a place that had once brought them together.

Moments later, she exited the auditorium, feeling like a stranger, unwelcomed.

He probably doesn't even care that I'm here.

Her eyes turned watery, wondering where their relationship now stood. It had been an exhausting day—the long flight, the news Rainelle and Bradley had shared, as well as her hormones—it all added to the complexity of feeling thrown back into Antonio's world.

I'll just go back and wait in the room, she decided, feeling overwhelmed.

Showing up like this is irrational. She headed for the ladies' room, where she finally broke down in tears.

Twenty minutes passed before she finally dried her eyes and made her way back to the empty main lobby. She paced, debating her next move. Then she stopped in her tracks, reaching a decision: *I really need to see him now!*

www.lovetheillusion.com/2244.htm

She headed to the main doors where she could hear the music, energizing, causing her to stop in her tracks and reconsider. Turning, she headed to the exit, wondering if Salvador still parked the limo out back. Maybe she could just wait there.

I really want to see him, even if it's only on stage.

"I found a seat," a familiar voice said.

Maggie turned to see the usher. "Okay."

"Center aisle…row three, seat A," the woman told her. "On your right through those doors. Sorry, it took me so long—I didn't know where you went."

"I can find it," Maggie said, feeling suddenly squeamish. She waited until the lady disappeared behind closed doors, and then made her entrance.

Now she could see Antonio on stage.

She walked slowly down the aisle, and as she did it seemed as though the crowd assumed she was participating in the show. She felt a rush of embarrassment—as people were turning to watch her—leaving her to feel like a bride walking down a wedding aisle only to find no groom.

She glued her eyes on Antonio as she continued to walk to her seat. He was standing on a platform with Cheetos. A rainbow of colors danced in the air while he held the ring of fire. Now she was sure that he saw her. And it seemed, despite the flickering lights, that they held eye contact.

She picked up the pace, until she stood next to the third row. She watched as a crewmember led Cheetos off the stage, while Antonio stood facing the audience. Now she was certain his eyes were on her.

Then the music stopped, and the lights went out. And a second later, she saw a security guard making his way toward her. *What now?*

"You, miss, come with me," he said, grabbing her arm.

"No—I'll just have a seat right here," Maggie said, trying to wrest her arm away.

"I don't think so." He held her arm in a tight grip. "Follow me."

He led her over to the steps leading up to the stage. *This is so awkward.* She hesitated, knowing she would soon be face to face with Antonio.

She carefully walked up the steps, her nervous stomach repeatedly sending the message of how much time had passed since she had last seen him.

The crowd started cheering as soon as she stepped on stage.

Maggie stood still at the edge of the stage, frozen in fear, as Antonio made his way over to her.

"You're back," he whispered, as she peered into his eyes.

"I am." She stared up at him.

He turned to the crowd, not wanting to keep them waiting. "This is my wife, Maggie. She's my lady in the ring of fire." He grabbed her hand in his, holding it in the air.

That's it?

What is he thinking?

The crowd was screaming, and to her surprise, he then took her in his arms and started kissing her. The discomfort of being on stage was a small side effect as Maggie felt her heart melt, relieved to be in his arms again, even if it had to be on stage. Now she could hear the crowd screaming even louder, but she was deaf to the noise as she leaned against him, in the shelter of his arms.

www.lovetheillusion.com/2218.htm

Antonio grabbed hold of her hand, leading her to the table. "You aren't mad at me?" Maggie asked in a loud whisper as the music started up again.

"I am," he whispered, "but you'll always be my lady in the ring of fire." He took her shoulders and looked into her eyes.

After the show ended, Maggie was back in their suite, sitting on the end of the bed, waiting for Antonio to return. She had left shortly after the show, not wishing to stand around and answer the many questions that the crew undoubtedly would have for her. Today was not the day for that; she needed to talk to Antonio first.

She felt a bit of relief. He had kissed her. Surely, it was a sign that everything would be okay. But his kiss had felt cold—not sweet and passionate like the kisses she recalled.

Moments later, the noise of the door opening caused her to look up. Antonio entered the hotel suite. He stared at her, silent, hands on his hips, waiting for her to speak. She sensed he was still angry.

"You…kissed me…on stage." She stared up at him.

"What was I supposed to do? It's been months, Maggie. People think it's over between us. So I told my fans it's not." But his eyes were cold.

"I think I'm one of your fans…in need of that information…"

"I'm glad you're back…safe…" Antonio kept a stern look.

"So what happened on stage was…just a performance?" she asked, still feeling distant from him.

"You trust me not to burn you on stage, but in real life you still fear getting burned by me?"

"I shouldn't have left."

"Really?" he said, and shook his head, lost for words.

"Yes, Antonio." Maggie spoke quietly as she sat on the bed, facing him. "I am a fool to have doubted you. And I'm sorry I didn't listen to you about Francis."

"It's about time you listened to me. You know I just care about you." He came and stood in front of her.

"I know, but the secrets were killing me." She stared into his eyes, melting at the sight of him, realizing how much she loved him. "I think I live haunted by my past with Phillip, and…and I want to believe we are different, but it's hard for me..." She paused. "*Why* couldn't you call me and tell me?"

"Tell you what?"

"That it's not true about Mickey being your son! You let me sit in London for weeks, believing that you'd finally confessed!"

"I told you the truth—three times! I finally just told you what you wanted to hear. Just trying to make you happy. Either way you don't trust me, right? And I have no idea why...I tell you to stay away from Francis—you eat lunch with him anyway. I tell you Mickey's not mine, but you keep on asking about it! I had no choice!"

"So you *lied* to me? That was your solution?"

"I had to teach you a lesson on trust. Without it, you have nothing, don't you see?"

"How sweet," she said sarcastically.

"What else could I do to get through to you? Honestly, I could not believe that you bought that whole story. It just goes to show where your head is at—doubting my love for you and the sincerity of our relationship... That's just frustrating to me, Maggie! What can I do?"

"I let Phillip ruin us," she said softly.

"Yeah, well, I am *not* him!"

"I'm sorry; I didn't mean to hurt you," Maggie confessed. "I just...love you."

She waited for his reply as her tears reinforced her words.

"Trust and love go together, Maggie." Antonio's voice was firm. "Why can't you understand that?"

"I promise to trust you, if you can just forgive me."

"It's not about forgiveness; it's about trust, Maggie. I can forgive, but then what? Our relationship will never go anywhere without trust, especially in the world I live in."

"I know. I really missed you."

"That's good. I missed you too." His expression softened.

"I have a surprise for you."

"I know—" he surprised her instead—"there's a photo of you and some guy that might end up on some front cover…" He gave her a tired look as he let out a sigh.

Maggie sat still, wondering how he knew. "How do you…?" *Bradley? No, he promised not to…* "Did someone from the press contact you?"

"What do you think? They wanted me to pay them to keep your 'affair' undercover. Tell me what to do, Maggie. I gave them money. But now you can tell me what you were doing in London with him. Should be entertaining…" He sounded irritated. "Now I *should* be really mad at you—how does a picture lie? But you know what; I will wait for your explanation…hoping that it's some strange occurrence with some stranger explanation."

"He's Maia's cousin. That's Dana's friend; I was staying with her. He kissed me—I told him I was married—end of story. Please don't be mad at me." Maggie paused for a moment, then went on: "The shirt was his, after I ended up in the river, trying to save a duck! The whole thing…just a huge misunderstanding. The photo is not what it looks like…"

"Fine." Antonio stared up at the ceiling, his arms folded. "Hopefully, that's the end of it—my attorney is going to sue the press if they print that. They only print to make money…I paid them well, and they made their sinful dollar."

"I thought you didn't care about the tabloids!"

"Well, I care about that one—it makes me sick—I don't want my wife looking like that…"

"So you care about my reputation, but not yours?"

"I used to find it somewhat entertaining…what they'd print about me and all the women…so funny…but now that we're married it has to stop, right?"

"Yeah, but how?"

"I kissed you on stage so that my fans know the truth…that we're together no matter what they see in print."

"Really?"

"Yeah…" He pulled her into a tight hug. "I knew you would come back eventually." Maggie melted in his arms as he explained: "I will try to stay on top of all the scandals. Now that we are together, it matters more, for the both of us. And from now on, I will talk to you about everything."

"Promise?"

"Yes."

"I'm sorry you had to see that photo," Maggie said.

"Yeah, well, I'm sorry you had to see the one with Nicki."

"So, we're still friends?"

"No, we're just lovers." Antonio winked at her.

"I'll take that." Maggie smiled up at him.

He started laughing, his face brightly melting into hers as she stared up at him, glad to be back in his arms.

"I still have a surprise for you," she told him.

"You mean, that wasn't it?"

"No…" She rolled her eyes.

"What is it? I can hardly wait." He grinned.

"Well…I was very busy while I was away…" She went over to her suitcase and rummaged through it until she found a small corduroy vest with plaid pants and a matching bowtie. "I made something for you. I hope you like it."

He took it in his hands and studied it, a bit confused. "What is this…it can't be for me…it's way too small." He held it against himself.

"I started my own clothing line for infants… Go ahead, look at the label."

She watched as Antonio searched for the label. "Tiny Matteo's…Nice…sixty-five dollars…you listened to me for a change…I like that."

"You can take the tag off. I'm not selling it."

"Why not? It's pretty cute!" Antonio stared down at the little outfit. "Sorry, but I'm quite sure it doesn't fit me, so you might as well sell it."

"You think?"

"Somebody's going to look really cute in it, but it's not me." He gave a quick laugh.

"I think we should keep it—" her eyes twinkled—"because…I think it would look really great…on our son." Maggie watched his face.

"So, you want children someday, I know, but we could have a girl and if she takes after her mother, she will not want to wear this."

"I think it's a boy, Antonio. I had a dream," Maggie told him. "And Bradley made me go to a doctor in Scotland. The ultrasound revealed that I'm about twelve weeks along."

Antonio raised his eyebrows and gaped. "Seriously?"

"Yes, we're gonna have a baby!" She smiled at him.

"So, we're a family now, already?"

"We are…" Maggie saw him afresh, picturing him as a father.

"Come here. I need to hug you and….my son."

"It feels good, Antonio. Better than I thought it would," Maggie said, feeling really happy for the first time in a while.

"Too bad we can't celebrate with a champagne toast."

"I know."

"I'll have to drink the champagne for the both of us!"

"Pregnant or not…I may not be in the mood for champagne ever again!" She giggled, aware that champagne now reminded her of Francis.

"I know how we can celebrate." He smiled down at her until he started kissing her. Now his kiss felt just as she remembered, and then she heard him whisper in her ear: "Last one in the shower's a rotten egg!"

Chapter 21

Antonio was away, practicing some new tricks for an upcoming show, while Maggie was on her computer checking for incoming orders. She had just met with the New York buyer and things had gone well. They had placed an order for several boxes of infant clothing for fall—all from the exclusive Tiny Matteo collection. She had even located a company in Italy that was able to sew the designs. The tags would say "Made in Italy," which she thought was special, since Antonio was a native.

It had been a great week. She was elated that they were finally back together and her morning sickness seemed to be improving as she approached the benchmark of three months. Antonio had ordered steaks—room service—to celebrate and they spent the evening contemplating what it would be like to be parents.

And she had called Dana, along with her family, to tell them the news. Antonio had also called Mamma and Papa and they were overjoyed. Papa was now busy making a crib.

Maggie was on her way to Central Park, where she usually went to get her morning exercise. It was always nice to get some fresh air and it was one of the few places she never worried about running into reporters. Surely they visited there also, but since she moved in a fast jog with her sunglasses, cap, and iPod, she always felt pretty inconspicuous, and a step ahead of them.

"You heard the news?" Salvador asked, shortly after she got into the steel-gray Mercedes—it was a little less obvious than the Hummer limo.

"What news?" Maggie asked, adjusting her sunglasses.

"Shagan died last night. A week in a coma in ICU and I guess he took a turn for the worse."

"No…Really? No…" Maggie sat in disbelief. "Antonio never said anything about it."

"Should get interesting," Salvador predicted. "Now his daughter has inherited his fortune, and it was on the news this morning that she is going to take over the hotel chain that he owns."

"You mean…Nicolette?" Maggie felt her stomach churn.

"Yeah, who else? He only has one daughter, no sons."

Maggie shook her head.

"Word is she's moving back to the hotel so that she can keep an eye on everything, and she wants to be on Antonio's floor. How's that for trouble in paradise?"

"You must be joking!"

"No, and she now owns the place…what can anyone do about it? I bet she knows nothing about hotel management."

"Does Antonio know all of this?"

"Depends if he's been watching the news…"

"There is no *way* I want her on our floor! She's nothing but trouble! She broke the picture of Antonio and me dancing together!"

"No worries…I doubt she's your competition," Salvador let her know. "Just wear a smile and pretend she's not there."

"Wear a smile? Pretend she's not there? This is never going to work! Antonio said he took away her entry card, and now what? She could have keys to our room for all I know!"

"Don't be so upset just yet. How soon can she move in? The renovation will take time…She won't stay in one small room…they will have to convert many…into…a palace—" He managed a chuckle.

"Stop…Just stop!" Maggie said, completely annoyed. "Just—I don't mean talking, sorry—I mean the car! Turn around and take me back! I need to see Antonio, right now!"

"You might as well go ahead to Central Park and release your energy; he's at practice now anyway."

"Not once I arrive, he won't be! Just drive me back, now!" Maggie ordered, feeling her emotions and hormones crashing together like ocean waves.

Maggie hurried into the practice room, which was in the lower level of the hotel, not too far from where they housed Cheetos. She stood just inside the entrance, and seconds later she knew she had Antonio's attention.

"Can I talk to you for a second?" she shouted over the music, her hands cupped at her mouth.

"Sure!" Antonio sounded happy, compliant.

She stood with her arms folded, waiting as he approached.

"What's up? You miss me already?" He grinned.

"No—I was on my way, and—just tell me it's not true that…that…that Nicolette is moving onto our floor!" She frowned, trying to picture the catastrophe. "There is *no way* I'm having her next to us—for all I know, she'll have a key to our room!"

"Hey, hey, calm down, baby." He put his arms around her.

"What's going on? Who told you all this?"

"Salvador!" Maggie explained. "I was on my way to Central Park—to exercise and unwind! And now I'm so tightly wound up that I don't think there's enough booze in the lounge to calm my nerves and even if there was I can't drink—I'm pregnant with the child that you can't wait to have!"

"Okay, well, I promise everything's okay. Try to relax."

"Re*lax?* Don't tell me to relax! Did you forget the five minutes that I spent with that woman? She couldn't possibly have gone through personality rehab since then!"

Antonio looked away and nodded.

"Did you know?" she asked.

"I knew Shagan died, but…"

"She has everything now, Antonio, don't you see?"

"I promise she won't bother us; I'll see to it."

"She wants to be on our floor! That bothers me already! I don't want to see her ever again, much less walking our hotel hallway!"

"Who said she's gonna be on our floor?"

"Salvador just told me! So I told him to take me back to the hotel and that's when I saw them—four contractors parked outside the hotel already. I just saw them!"

"I *promise* I'll take care of it. She will not bother you. You have my word. Meanwhile, try not to be upset. It's not good for the baby."

"Ugh!" Maggie turned around and marched off. *This is just unbelievable... a total NIGHTMARE...* starring Nicolette!

SUNRISE, THE NEXT DAY…

"The pounding kept me up all night, Antonio! Didn't you hear it? Oh, no you didn't…you were snoring. Well, bang, bang, bang…and then there was the drill sound. Why can't they be done at five o'clock so that we can get some peace and quiet?" She rested her elbows on her pillow. "I don't think I slept more than three hours! And just as I was getting to sleep, I heard them again! Why is she in such a hurry? Can't you pay for her to live anywhere but here? Send her to Tahiti!" Maggie groaned in frustration. "Oh! And I forgot to mention that she said 'hi' to me yesterday, but it wasn't 'Hi Maggie,' it was '*Hiiiii* Maggie,' as if she was annoyed by me, when I should be the one annoyed by her! And Mickey is spoiled rotten! You should have seen him! He was running up and down the hallway screaming: 'There's a ghost in the house, there's a ghost in the house!' while he threw his open bag of cheese popcorn into the air! Housekeeping's going to be just thrilled they've arrived."

"I'll talk with her," Antonio said, stretching.

"Where's that going to take place…in some cocktail bar with the paparazzi snapping photos of the two of you? Honestly, I just wish she would disappear! Now she's going to make our life hell. She already hates me, and when she finds out I'm having your son it will be even worse!"

"Maggie." Antonio leaned over, his dark eyes settling into hers as his hair stuck out in various directions. "Just stop talking and kiss me."

"Kiss you?" she questioned. "When will you learn that kissing doesn't make our problems go away—unless I can kiss Nicolette goodbye."

"Trust me. She won't cause *any* trouble for us."

"She's going to be *living* several doors down! How can you even say that? She's keeping me up every night already and she hasn't even moved in!"

"I'll talk to the crew and tell them they are done at five...Does that work? Or do you prefer them done at a different hour?" He sounded amused. "Say two...or should we give them an even shorter workday? You decide..."

"This is *not* funny, Antonio! Why can't you understand that she is my *worst* nightmare?"

"She's no competition for you Maggie. You're the love of my life. I love you—only you. But I can't keep her from moving in—she owns the whole chain now, so what you need to focus on is this: We are having our own child. I already told you, Mickey's not mine. And Nicki? She's got a tough life as a single mom, so try to have a little mercy."

"Mercy?" Maggie jumped out of bed. "How merciful am I expected to be? She lives to cause trouble. And she's still in love with you!"

"So...you wouldn't be up for an outing with Mickey and Nicki?" He grinned wildly at her.

"How can you be funny at a time like this?"

"Because you're so sexy when you're mad."

"I have every right to be mad."

"Just think...you could practice your parenting skills with Mickey...see what works and what doesn't. Then you'll have a little experience when ours comes along," he teased.

"You're just sooo funny, aren't you?" She glared at him until she finally started to laugh. "Since you made the suggestion, perhaps I will try…" Maggie spoke facetiously. "We could be best friends, me and Nicki—imagine! And you can play daddy for the both of us!"

"Come here, Maggie! Why ruin our time in New York worrying about Nicki? Why can't you just let it go?"

"How can you…just let it go? There's nothing you can do about this?" Maggie pouted, unable to separate her hormones from reality.

"If she bothers us…or you…I will have words with her. I promise, okay?" He sat up in bed. "I have lived here the past five years…My crew and I like it here; it's home. And you make it even better, understand? No one's going to take that away. I will see to it." He climbed out of bed and came to her.

"You are so wrong, Antonio…." Maggie said, still pouting as he pulled her into a hug. Now, standing in his arms, she leaned against his bare chest, closing her eyes, trying to let go of her fears. "We are so perfect," she finally said, "but everything around us…always a disaster."

"We love each other…it's all that matters, Maggie. Everything else comes and goes, but love will always be ours."

As she stood in his arms, all her worries seemed to vanish into the clouds.

THREE DAYS LATER…

"You want to get that?" Antonio called out from the bathroom, a white towel wrapped around his waist. "I think our breakfast is here."

"Sure." Maggie grabbed her robe and threw it over her nightshirt.

She opened the door, and saw two brown eyes staring up at her under a mop of dark brown hair.

www.lovetheillusion.com/2288.htm

"Is Daddy here?"

"Uh…" Maggie tried to erase her frown. "Yeah…come on in. You must be Mickey." She tried to sound polite.

"Mickey!" Antonio said as he came around the corner to greet him. "Are you moved in already?"

"We moving today…I visit you." He spoke well for a child that just turned three.

"Sorry about Grampy," Antonio said. "Now you will have to take care of your mamma."

"She says he bub-by…up dere." He pointed to the ceiling.

Maggie suddenly felt sorry for him. "You know…the people we love are always in our hearts." She placed her hand over his, thinking about Matteo and her mother.

"I wanna see big kitty," he announced out of the blue.

"I'm going to Cheetos in a bit," Antonio told him. "You want to feed him?" Antonio winked at Maggie.

"Yes!" He jumped up and down and spun around. "Yes, yes, yes, I love him!"

"Okay, we can go, the three of us—" Antonio carefully glanced at Maggie—"after we eat. Did you eat yet?"

"I had jellybeans!" he shouted, as he raced over to the bed, which was still not made. He crawled on top and started jumping up and down. "Now I'm a jellybean!"

"You had jellybeans for breakfast?" Maggie asked with concern.

"Yes! I eat them every day!" He jumped a bit higher.

Antonio came over and grabbed him off the bed. "You shouldn't jump on beds! You can fall off and land on your head!"

"Mommy lets me jump on *her* bed!" he said, struggling and kicking as Antonio held on to him.

"You can stay, but no jumping," Antonio told him. "Take a seat over by the table. You can watch the cars go by and tell me how many you see."

Maggie watched as Mickey went and stood next to the window, looking out.

"Lots and lots and lots of cars…one, two," Mickey tried to count them. "One, two…three…three and three and lots of cars!" He watched, amused.

They heard another knock on the door. "I'll get it," Maggie offered.

"Mickey, there you are!" Nicolette stood in a yellow satin robe, with her hair in a loosely defined cloud atop her head. "You can't leave when Mommy's in the shower now, okay?"

"I go see kitty!" Mickey said.

"No, we have to go shopping today. We are getting you your own bed!"

"I don't want a bed! I want to play with kitty!"

"Well, maybe after we get your bed, we can get a kitty," Nicolette said with a smile, reaching out to grab his hand.

"No!" he shouted as he pushed her away. "I want to see *big* kitty!" He stomped his foot.

Just then the room service arrived.

Maggie took the tray. "Thanks…" She handed the caterer a fifty-dollar tip, motioning him away from the fiasco.

"Yummy!" Mickey said, standing on his tippy toes to see the arrangement of fruit and bagels.

Without thinking, Maggie took charge. "He can stay with us for a couple hours, then I'll bring him back," she offered, her eyes skimming over Nicolette.

She looks like she peeled herself out of a Victoria's Secret catalogue. So annoying.

Nicolette reached for her hair while eyeing Antonio, who still had a towel around his waist.

www.lovetheillusion.com/2258.htm

"Does that work for you?" Maggie asked.

"Yes, it does. And thank you, I'll see you all later then," she said on her way out. "I could use some peace and quiet."

The door closed.

Great, I know the feeling...

Maggie sat down at the table with Antonio and Mickey. "So, Mickey, are you excited to feed Cheetos?" she asked.

"I feed him and pet him and love him!" Mickey explained, grabbing a handful of grapes from the platter and shoving them into his mouth.

"Hey, buddy, there's a thing called a fork." Antonio took the silverware from the white linen napkin and handed him a fork. Mickey used it to stab a bagel, holding it up it the air.

"Like this!" He waved it around.

Maggie started laughing and Antonio shook his head, smiling, happy that Maggie was living in the moment—although it was a strange one.

"Maggie, can I talk to you for a second…" Antonio stood.

"Sure." She set down her coffee cup.

"In the bathroom?"

"Uh…okay." She stood to follow him.

"Mickey, if you want to go see Cheetos, you have to be really good for the next few minutes, okay?" Antonio explained. "You sit and eat quietly, while I talk to Maggie."

"Okay, I will be…good boy!" Mickey said with his mouth full as Maggie followed Antonio into the bathroom.

"Sorry about this, Maggie. I know this is probably the last thing you expected when you crawled out of bed this morning, but—"

"Shh…it's okay," she whispered. "I understand more than you think. This is just…really tough."

"I know. Now you see how I am sucked into this 'daddy role' thing. What can I do? He's a child. He needs love and attention, and he thinks…." Antonio fell silent.

"…he thinks you're his dad," she finished for him. "I see that. And I hate to say it, but he's kind of cute. I almost feel bad for him."

"Me too, Maggie. Me too. And believe me, I know this isn't fair to you, so if you want to move…just let me know what you want me to do."

"It's fine, Antonio. We can take him to see Cheetos. I don't have a problem with that, okay?"

"Okay, well, thanks for being so understanding. And if she keeps this up, I will have a word with her, because she has to respect our privacy."

"It's fine…really…"

"No, it's not fine…I love you and our baby…I don't need you stressed out."

"My bagel is yummy!" Mickey called out. "It's yummy!"

"It's not him—it's her." Maggie rolled her eyes. "He's an innocent child—well, maybe not innocent, but helpless, and she…well, she is as far from innocent and helpless as they come. Showing up here in her lingerie while I'm pregnant and feeling fat…"

"Stop. Just stop, Maggie…"

"Did you not see her? She's drop-dead gorgeous."

"And I'm not interested, okay?"

"What you doing?" Mickey stood outside the bathroom door.

"We're just talking," Maggie said, waiting for Antonio to take charge.

"Yep. We're almost ready to see big kitty, okay?"

"Should I eat more bagel?" Mickey asked.

"Sure." Antonio smiled and then turned to Maggie. "Promise this will be quick; promise I love you; promise she won't keep this up."

"Okay."

"You sure?"

"Yeah, I'm sure. I love you," she said with a smile.

"Mmm…that's what I like to hear." He kissed her cheek. "I love you too."

That morning the three of them went to visit Cheetos, and Mickey seemed to enjoy every minute. Antonio indicated his constant concern, hoping Maggie was not upset by the situation, but she surprised him and enjoyed the adventure of having Mickey along. The two hours passed quickly, and soon it was time to take him back.

"I can take him," Antonio offered.

"No…I'll take him," Maggie said.

"You sure?"

"Yeah…I said I would so I will."

She took Mickey's hand and a moment later knocked on the door to Nicolette's room.

Nicolette was wearing designer clothes, just as Amber had predicted. She was also smoking.

"There you are, my little prince. Did you get to see your daddy?"

"I saw big kitty. And I pet him."

"Yeah? Well, I got my shopping done," Nicolette said. "It's going to take *months* to finish this place."

Maggie listened, hoping they could be on friendly terms.

"My decorator says gray on that wall over there, but that sounds drab."

"Looks like it's coming together." Maggie smiled, a bit surprised by how extravagant her taste was. "It's very posh."

"Decorating can be so exhausting. I change my mind ten times before I finally decide. But eventually I get it right." She smiled at Maggie for the first time.

Days passed, and Maggie was growing convinced that perhaps Antonio was right: it would not be a big deal—other than their occasional inconsideration. Perhaps the worst was just the thought of his ex living a few doors down. But in the end, it was not a threat to their relationship. Even if Nicolette was still fond of Antonio, he was not interested, and the attention he gave to Mickey was hard to refuse—perhaps on a rare occasion would be all—and it was the right thing to do: allow him to feel as if he had a father, even if it was for short stretches of time here and there. Antonio did not mind throwing kindness his way, and Maggie was starting to feel confident in the fact that she was carrying his "real" child.

But the following night became a disaster. Maggie and Antonio were snuggling under the sheets when they heard a loud knock on their door.

"Shh, we don't have to get that," Antonio whispered.

But then they heard Amber shouting, disrupting the silence. "Hey,

Antonio! I need to talk to you, *now*!"

Antonio quickly got out of bed, stepped into his boxer shorts and threw his T-shirt back on, while Maggie ran into the bathroom and closed the door.

"Antonio!" Amber exclaimed, the second the door opened. "Did you see the hallway? There are toys everywhere! And I am right across from them! That Mickey is wild! He makes noise twenty-four-seven and I have asked Nicolette politely three times to keep him quiet. I can't even hear my TV over the racket. And yesterday morning when I left to practice with the dance team, there was a huge stain on the carpet outside my door. I thought, 'What could that be?' So I was down on all fours, trying to smell it—it was gooey and dark—and I think someone dumped an entire bottle of Hershey's syrup by my door. So maintenance came and—did I forget to mention that Nicolette told me 'Get lost!' the last time I asked her to not let Mickey play in the halls? You must have been gone, but he was riding his tricycle up and down the halls as he yells out: 'The police are coming, the police are coming!'"

www.lovetheillusion.com/2287.htm

"All right, I will talk to her…" Antonio shook his head, baffled. "I hope she isn't leaving him alone…" He paused. "He stops by here on occasion and when I ask 'where's your mamma?' he shrugs and says he doesn't know."

"Well, I can't take this anymore. He's a brat and she's a total witch! You are the only one she will listen to, so I suggest you do something! Because since she's arrived, we all hate it here!"

"Okay," Antonio agreed, realizing he had his hands full.

"Sorry," Amber said, "but I was appointed to let you know, so I am speaking for the entire hallway! And I should probably also mention that this hall is supposed to be blocked for security reasons, but the other day there were three guys—no one knew who they were—walking the halls, and we saw them go into her place. For all I know, they could be living here too, now!"

"Are you serious?" Antonio sighed. "I'll get right on this."

"Thanks. I know it's late, but she is still up, and so is that son of hers! I can hear music blaring from their room!"

Antonio closed the door as Maggie came out, dressed in his bathrobe, which had been hanging on the bathroom door. "What's going on?" she asked.

"That was Amber. Apparently everyone's completely annoyed by Mickey and Nicolette could care less. I'm going to have a word with her now," Antonio told Maggie.

"Well, I'm doing all I can to stay peaceful with that woman. Did you know the other day she came over wondering if I had a scarf that would match her outfit? I couldn't believe it! She came right into my walk-in closet and took off with several items of clothing and I thought, 'Whatever it takes to keep peace, right? It's only clothing…'"

"That's ridiculous!" Antonio frowned. "Why didn't you say something?"

"Well, if I did, I would have destroyed all your dreams—that she is no problem at all, when in fact she is one huge problem, don't you see? I am trying to keep peace but it's getting out of control!"

"I'll be right back," Antonio said. "I'm not putting up with this!"

Antonio banged on Nicolette's door; seconds later it opened.

"Daddy! What you doing?"

"Where's Mamma?"

"I don't know. She left."

"She left? With who?"

"Mean Dexter…he hits me."

"What?" Antonio knelt down next to him, holding his arms. "Who's Dexter? When did she leave?"

"Dinner…" Mickey shrugged.

Antonio looked around the main living quarters.

The cushions were off the couch, beer cans stood on the coffee table next to an ashtray with cigars, and powdered donuts, with bites out of each one, were stranded on an end table.

"Were you eating those?" Antonio asked, looking at the donuts.

Mickey laughed. "I try each one."

"I see." Antonio stared at the beer cans. "And who was drinking that?"

"Mommy and Jared…"

"Okay…well…" Antonio reviewed the situation. "You need to come with me. You're way too young to be left alone." He found the stereo and unplugged it.

"Do I get to see Maggie again?"

"Uh, yeah. She's there…" Antonio grabbed his hand and walked back to his room.

Maggie frowned as they entered the suite, waiting for Antonio to give an explanation.

"I know," Antonio whispered. "This is not what you were expecting. He was all alone and I just couldn't leave him unsupervised."

"Antonio! It's the middle of the night! Where is she?"

"Derek came and got her!" Mickey said, wide-eyed and alert.

"Who's that?" Maggie asked, watching as Mickey charged over to the bed and crawled on top.

"Who knows?" Antonio looked disgusted. "I hate that we are involved with this, Maggie, and I know you're probably thinking 'I told you so,' but—" Antonio shook his head. "I have to call her." He picked up his phone.

Mickey had managed to crawl under the covers and Maggie noticed he still had his shoes on. She walked over to the edge of the bed, and took off his shoes, dropping them onto the floor one by one, and then brushed his hair out of his eyes. "You must be tired out from a long day by now," she said sweetly, suddenly feeling sorry for him. It wasn't his fault that he was caught up in Nicolette's irresponsible ways. "Just close your eyes and get some rest, okay?"

His eyelids immediately started to droop, and finally he blinked for the last time and fell sound asleep.

"Nicki! Where are you?" Maggie heard Antonio shouting into his phone. "You left Mickey alone? How stupid are you? You can't leave a three-year-old alone while you go off and party with your pimps!"

Maggie pressed her lips together, trying not to show her amusement as Antonio let Nicolette have it. It seemed as though she was now informing him, as he silently held the phone to his ear. Finally he spoke again. "All right, he can stay here till tomorrow, but in the future, you need to find someone more responsible to watch him! Or I will call social services and they will take him into foster care! And by the way, your place is a filthy mess! One look at that, and they will question his living conditions!" Antonio put his phone away. "Sorry, he's going to have to stay the night." He looked at Maggie.

"He's already sleeping," Maggie said. "Poor guy…how can she not care about her own child?"

"Oh, she left Dexter in charge, and Mickey was sleeping—or so she says. Now Dexter left…who knows where he went." Antonio paused. "This is so ridiculous…I seriously can't believe it!"

"Well, she's definitely strange….He's probably not even safe living with her." Maggie considered the circumstances.

"Of course he's not safe…he said that Dexter guy hits him." Antonio looked upset.

"Oh *no*!" Maggie looked down at the little boy. "That's so terrible!"

"I had no idea," Antonio said. "She always has him dressed so well. But now I think I need to call social services. It's the right thing to do. You know what Mickey asked me on the way here? He asked if you were going to be here…"

"He did?" Maggie was surprised. "He likes me?"

"Of course he likes you, Maggie. What child wouldn't? That Nicolette is not fit as a human being, much less a mother…and I am going to report her tomorrow."

"That's just going to set off more trouble, Antonio. There must be something else we can do, because how can we prove anything? It's our word against hers!"

"You see what she does now? She uses Mickey to get to me and expects me to provide for them when he isn't even my son! Now she has money again, of her own, but who knows how long that will last?"

"I'm worried for him," Maggie said sadly. "Do you think *she* is abusing him?"

"Who knows?" Antonio said. "She always seems to spoil him rotten but I have no idea who she leaves him with…"

"For now, I will move him to the couch, so we can have our bed back," Antonio decided, before crawling back in.

"No," Maggie said. "Just let him stay."

Chapter 22

"I'm afraid of toilet. I peed in bathtub."

Maggie woke up to Mickey's voice echoing from the bathroom. She sat up slowly, realizing she had the bed to herself, right next to a wet spot.

"That's impolite, Mickey," she heard Antonio tell him. "When you are a visitor, you have to mind your manners. What you did is just not acceptable! It's inappropriate!"

"I *sorry!* Are you going to tell Mommy?"

"No, but you need to come with me. I just got a message that she's back."

"No, I want to stay with *you*, Daddy! Can't we go to park today? I want to go down slide!"

"You need to get back."

"Why?"

"I have to get ready for the show tonight."

"Why?"

"Because that's my work."

"I want to come! I want to come!"

"No, you can't come this time, okay? Maybe next time."

Maggie pulled the covers over her head, wondering when the last time was that she had a full eight hours of sleep. Her pregnancy was the last thing on her mind as she played "second mother" to Mickey, who had no idea that Antonio was not his real father. She scooted away from the damp, soiled area.

"Bye, Maggie…" Mickey's voice trailed off as Antonio led him back to his suite.

"Bye," Maggie muttered, feeling frustrated, yet sorry for him. She wondered where Nicolette had gone and who the man in charge of watching Mickey was. *Why had he left?* None of it made any sense. And hopefully, Antonio would be back soon with all the answers. But would the answers bring more questions? Maggie was soon lost in a daydream, pondering the possibilities.

What am I doing! She quickly got out of bed and pulled the sheets off the bed, rolling them into a wad. She placed the damp sheets under the bathroom vanity, out of sight.

It's just SO gross…so disgusting!

She crawled back into bed, wrapping herself in the zebra-print comforter.

She waited patiently, realizing Antonio had now been gone for a half hour.

Should I go down the hall and find him?

And her?

Maggie closed her eyes, trying to go back to sleep, but it was impossible to sleep. That's when she heard the door open.

"Do you want to come?" Maggie heard Antonio question her as soon as he returned.

"Where?"

"To file a complaint."

"Maybe you should just call," Maggie suggested.

"No…I am dragging them over here, if it's the last thing I accomplish today. We are not waiting for them to make a call at their convenience."

"What did Nicolette say?"

"Honestly, Maggie, I think she's using again! She claims she was out with Derek Winsor—her financial advisor. But who has business meetings in the middle of the night? Mickey was left with Dexter, who is a friend. I'm not sure where she found him, but he is obviously irresponsible. I told her to let me know next time she needed someone to watch him; perhaps someone from the crew could help out...."

"They aren't going to want to watch him.... Amber can't stand him, and Angie calls him 'the little devil!' Just the other day she says, 'The little devil was out of his cage again running up and down the halls!' And by the way, he peed in our bed...I just removed the sheets. They're under the vanity, for now."

"Uh...sorry...I'll call maid service...." Antonio shook his head. "Yeah, he's quite a handful, isn't he? I noticed he drew a 'mural' on the wallpaper outside the door to their suite—which is completely trashed by the way...I mean, jeez...if you don't want to clean, then pay someone else to do it! I can't believe she lives like that."

"Living conditions...maybe that's her own business, but she can't let Mickey play in the halls as if it's an extension of their living parameters! I've heard complaints that he likes to bang on doors and then play hide-and-seek."

"Like I said, we have to report her."

"That is just going to make matters worse," she told him.

"Are you coming or not?" He stood at the door.

"I don't know...I think I'll stay and work on some designs. Gia called me yesterday when I wasn't returning her emails and insisted that I send a few. Maybe I will, after all. What do you think?"

"I told you she's nice. You two would get along great. I called her out on her snobbish attitude and she apologized and said it was a misinterpretation…she had just been shocked by the entire evening."

"Well it was shocking, to say the least. But you know she and Francis are friends now." Maggie recalled her meeting with Francis. "Did you know I heard her on his voicemail?"

"Maggie! Gia plays along with him but she wants nothing to do with him, trust me! I'm so glad he's finally in jail!" Antonio appeared angered by just the thought of Francis. "Perhaps Nicolette and Francis can share a cell!" he said, letting the door slam on his way out.

Maggie felt bad that she had brought up Francis. Now she could not help but wonder how he was doing. Hopefully, he would be there for a while. If not, they would have even more to worry about.

Ten minutes after Antonio left, Nicolette showed up at the door.

"You want to tell me what happened to Mickey?" she asked, staring at Maggie.

"Why…what do you mean?" Maggie felt intimidated, facing Nicolette.

"The bruises on his back, Maggie!"

"I have no idea…he just fell asleep here and…"

"Cut the crap! What did you do to him? He said you hit him because he peed in the tub!"

"*What?* I didn't hit him! I would never hit him.… He said that?"

"Yeah, he did! Now I need to speak to Antonio because they need to have that father-son time, but not when you're around!"

"That's insane! I would never hit a child!" Maggie defended herself.

"What are you saying then? Antonio?" Nicolette started laughing. "Antonio would never hurt a child, especially Mickey, and Mickey adores him! But he's afraid of you, and why *is* that? You don't want to *share* Antonio?" She put her face inches from Maggie's. "You'd better not even think of getting in the way or I will make your life living hell!"

"Nicolette! There must be some misunderstanding. Mickey said Dexter hit him. Maybe you should check and see what Dexter has to say about that."

"You think I'm a fool to leave my child with someone like that? Dexter has watched him before, but this is the first time he's been around you and everyone knows you don't want children! It's all over the press: 'Selfish Maggie wants Antonio all to herself but he can't wait to start a family.' I can read, Maggie."

"They print lies!"

"I wouldn't be so sure about that!" Nicolette said. "The question they need to answer is how you got Antonio to marry you! He could have any woman he wanted and he picks you! What makes you so special? You aren't even pretty! And you barely have enough to wear a bra!" She stared Maggie up and down, hurling her insults.

"Get out!" Maggie pushed her toward the door. "I didn't invite you, and you are no longer welcome to step foot in here!"

"I am not leaving! I need to speak to Antonio!"

"Well, he's not here, so get out!"

"Actually, I think I'll stay and have a drink while I wait." Nicolette walked over to the small cabinet and found a bottle of vodka—it was evident she knew her way around. She opened it and took a drink.

"Go ahead…help yourself!" Maggie just stared at her, feeling a bit frightened. "Where's Mickey?"

"Mickey is sleeping! It was a long night for him. Antonio used to spend time with him, until you came along!"

"None of this is my fault, Nicolette! Believe me, I did not hit him! I let him sleep in our bed!"

"Oh, you think you're going to play mommy to him? Well, you're not!" Nicolette shouted. "Next time Mickey spends time with his father, you need to find something else to do with yourself, you hear?"

Maggie stood silent, realizing her attempts to keep peace with Nicolette were a lost cause.

"Don't get too accustomed to the finer things, dear," Nicolette said, taking another drink of vodka. "Antonio never keeps a woman around for too long, you know." She paused. "But I was a different story! I used to stay at his place before you came along and we had a lot of fun together. I used to get all dressed up and go to his shows, and then I'd wait for him, right here on this bed. I knew just how to drive him crazy."

"Get out! Just get out! *Now!*" Maggie went to the door and motioned for her to leave, "Or I'll call Bradley and have him remove you!"

"Aw…you're threatening me now.… Well, two can play that game!" She headed for the door, still holding the bottle of vodka. "You mess my life up…I'll mess up yours!"

Maggie shut the door and leaned against it.

What am I going to do with her?

She gives the word 'bitch' a whole new meaning....

Maggie lay down on the bed. *How could Antonio let Nicolette believe that he was Mickey's father?* Perhaps she simply chose to believe it, but it was time for the truth. Though she did not want to hurt Mickey, she could not put up with any of this much longer. The whole situation was insane. Nicolette was taking advantage of Antonio's kindness and he needed to step up to the plate and put an end to it.

But then what would become of Mickey? He was a small child in a bad situation. If it was true that his mother was using drugs, it was no environment for him to survive in. And if anything happened to him, Maggie would feel terrible. None of it was his fault. His wild ways could probably be tamed with a little attention and positive discipline. But as it was, it was obvious Nicolette did not spend time teaching him manners and proper etiquette.

She hates me...figures...I never did anything to her. I am just in the way of her so-called relationship with Antonio. He wants nothing to do with her, but that doesn't matter; she assumes otherwise. Great! Wait until she finds out I'm pregnant. It will only make matters worse!

Why me?

I knew we should have waited to have a child!

She told me I have no boobs!

I hate her!

I really, really, really hate her!

Maggie was lying on the bed, staring up at the ceiling, when Antonio finally returned.

"That ought to put an end to it. Social services is at her place now!" Antonio called, then realized that Maggie was still in bed. "What's wrong? Too tired to work today? You know you don't have to work if you don't want to. It's more important you take care of the baby. You have your whole life to—"

"Antonio!" Maggie interrupted him, realizing he had no clue.

"What? Are you okay?" Antonio suddenly looked concerned.

Maggie shook her head, still in a fog from the morning's events. "I'm so glad you're back. I can't take this anymore. That Nicolette woman is a lunatic! She came right after you left, accusing me of hitting Mickey, telling me I was not going to play mommy to him. I can't just…can't…. I tried to be nice, but it's not working!"

"She came *here?*" Antonio asked. "And harassed you?"

"She did more than harass me, Antonio! She said she is going to make my life hell…*and* she said I have no boobs!" Maggie sulked.

"What!" He looked furious. "No one talks to my woman like that!" He headed for the door.

"No, Antonio! Don't! I'm afraid of her!" Maggie cried from her pillow.

"Well *I'm* not!" he told her on his way out. "She's done!"

The door slammed again and Maggie buried her head in her pillow, wishing they were back in Italy. For three short months, everything had been perfect. Now, it was one disaster after the next.

She lay silently, waiting for him to return.

But when he did, he had company.

"This is my wife, Maggie," Antonio explained to the woman in charge for social services. "Nicolette was verbally abusive to her after Maggie was kind enough to let Mickey spend the night here. I want a full investigation done on that Dexter guy who was put in charge of watching Mickey and then took off! Why would she leave Mickey with him? And regardless of who the bag of pot belongs to, she's an unfit mother!" Antonio fumed. "Now, I've spent half my day resolving matters that are not mine to resolve. So you need to see to it that Mickey gets good foster care—and Nicolette needs to move out of here because I'm filing a restraining order as soon as the police arrive!"

"Okay, Antonio," the woman agreed. "We will take care of things, immediately."

Maggie watched in shock as the issue was resolved in under a minute.

The woman made a hasty exit as Antonio called after her: "And let Nicki know, if she steps foot in this hotel again, I'll have her arrested!"

Maggie stared up at Antonio. "I hope we're doing the right thing," she said.

"Of course it's the right thing, Maggie. I'm not putting up with that!" He wore a sour look. "The last thing you need is to be stressed out while you're pregnant." His dark eyes stared into hers. "And you can be sure that I will see to it that she doesn't bother you again!"

The next few days things seemed to be going well. Calm returned to the floor now that Nicolette and Mickey were gone. The word was that she flew out to Cancun while she awaited the charges of neglect, which her attorney assured her would be dropped, since she had no idea that Dexter was a pothead who would leave his responsibilities, or so she claimed. And Mickey would be returned to her, eventually. For now, he was in custody of the state while they found a family to watch him temporarily.

Rainelle was standing behind Maggie as she styled her hair and makeup. Maggie wore a smile, happy to be getting ready for another show. Things were looking up. And it was about time. She would be the lady in the ring of fire again.

"We're so glad you're back!" Maggie told Rainelle as she lined up the bobby pins around the hair that was stacked on top of Maggie's head.

"Yeah, me too…and we are *all* glad that *you* are back! Antonio was so upset when you left, but he knew you would come back. He just wasn't sure when."

"I won't leave again. So much has happened in the last month…our relationship seems to be in fast forward. Maybe it will always be that way, but we have come a long way since a year ago."

"And now you are going to be a family." Rainelle sounded excited. "I bet Antonio will have that baby on stage the day it is born."

"Oh, I hope not," Maggie said. "It's funny—Antonio loves the spotlight, but I hate it. I'm such a private person and living in his world is very challenging. But I really love him, and I'm trying to adjust to everything."

"I know he loves you too." Rainelle picked up a tube of lipstick and finished off her makeup. "You are going to be so beautiful as the lady in the ring of fire."

An hour later, Maggie sat backstage, watching Antonio's performance and waiting until it was time for her entrance. It seemed strange: she was no longer nervous to be on stage, but five minutes of being in the spotlight was still plenty. Now she smiled, recalling when she wore the gold heels on stage after being in the limo with Shane and Dana. She wondered if the fans were anticipating another "surprise" when she appeared, but she knew better—that was best left to Antonio.

Soon she heard the music signaling her cue. She stood and gracefully made her way across the stage until she stood in front of Antonio. *Where's the ring of fire?* Maggie wondered but then saw it floating in the air above her. *How did he do that?* Her eyes grew wide, wondering why he had not mentioned a change of plans. Usually, he held the ring with a heat-protected fireproof glove. She waited for Antonio to take her hand, but instead he held both his hands in the air, signaling the music to stop.

Then he spoke into the audience: "This is my favorite part of the show."

The fans started screaming. He waited until the noise subsided.

Maggie glanced at him out of the corner of her eye, wondering what he was up to.

"You like surprises?" he asked.

They started screaming again.

"Ok. Watch this." He reached his hands out to the audience.

Music started up again as paper magician hats in assorted colors flew into their midst. Then he turned to the ring of fire and redirected his aim. The crowd was going crazy trying to collect what had landed, but then the lights went out. When they came back on, the hats were flying into the ring of fire, but as they hit the ring they disintegrated instantly from the heat. Suddenly the music stopped. "That fire is hot!" He turned to Maggie. "Are you sure you trust me?"

"I do." She smiled at him.

"That's good." He smiled back and then took her hand in his, bringing it to his lips. "Now, stand still and don't move," he told her.

Maggie obeyed, watching as the ring of fire floated towards her in the air, pausing above her head. She closed her eyes as it lowered around her until it rested on the stage. Antonio clapped his hands to extinguish the flame and then reached out to Maggie. She stepped out of the metal ring.

Two stuntmen flipped across the stage as the twins in the red dresses wheeled in the table for the next stunt. Antonio helped Maggie onto the table until she lay horizontally. She held the sides as the table floated into the air. Antonio clapped his hand to the music until the ring burst into flames once again. The audience screamed as they watched the ring of fire float into the air and encircle the table where Maggie lay.

Antonio turned to the audience. "It's all about trust," he said. "You can't always believe what you read, but you can believe what you see." Antonio helped Maggie off the table.

The music intensified, and the audience watched in awe as the ring of fire floated up into the air until it was no longer visible.

Chapter 23

The hotel phone rang continuously, until Maggie got out of bed to answer it. *It was already noon?* Antonio had already left, but his coffee cup and newspaper were still sitting on the table by their fourth-story window.

"Hello?"

"This is the front desk. An envelope was just dropped off for Antonio this morning. Can you let him know?"

"Sure…no problem."

"Thanks, Maggie."

Maggie wondered about the envelope.

What was in it? Who was it from?

Should I go get it?

She couldn't help but be curious. Was his business hers? She still thought it was. *I could just do him the favor of picking it up…I won't open it,* she promised.

But an hour later, she stood in the bathroom with a hairdryer, trying to steam off the glue.

Finally it peeled loose.

She felt a little guilty as she removed the documents, but then she started reading.

…A name…an address…it was the foster-care placement information for Mickey. Although the court case had been quickly resolved, she knew Antonio was still legally considered partial guardian.

So strange.... Maggie scanned the documents, over and over, finally staring at the lines declaring the family's name and exact address where he would be staying. Surely Mickey would want a visit, and what would Antonio do? She could only guess. He would undoubtedly visit. Would he include her? Or make a visit all on his own?

Maggie sealed the envelope back up. She was just about ready to set it on top of the newspaper when Antonio walked into the room.

"Antonio!" Maggie swallowed, feeling shaken by her latest discovery. "I just went to the front desk and got this—" She passed the envelope to him. "They called and..."

She watched as he grabbed it, but then set it down on a pile of books. She studied him closely, wondering if perhaps he already knew what it contained.

"Aren't you going to open it?" she asked.

"No, I know what it is." He gave her a strange look. "What?" he asked.

"Nothing..." She lowered her brows. "You're *sure* you know?"

"Yeah, why?" His dark eyes studied hers.

Maggie wore a look of frustration, wishing he would say what it was so that they could discuss it. "So that's it? More secrets?" Maggie challenged him.

"You want to go with me?" he said bluntly.

Maggie's eyes widened as she bit her bottom lip.

He knows I peeked?

"I...sure..." Maggie agreed, puzzled. *How does he do that?*

"The seal…It's broken, Maggie," Antonio explained, staring back at her.

"Sorry…" She confessed.

"Right…" He spoke stiffly. Then he explained: "I used to visit him once a month. I know you don't want to be bothered by any of this and… Now he's there—" Antonio nodded at the envelope—"and I really should—" He stopped, realizing his words were upsetting her. "What?" he finally asked.

"It's just terrible!" Maggie told him. "Don't you see? Mickey probably thinks that you're neglecting him!"

"Yeah…it's complicated, that's for sure," Antonio agreed. "There really are no simple solutions. It's the best I can do."

"No, Antonio, it's not…I think we should go together."

"You *want* to come?" Antonio sounded surprised. "You don't have to. The last thing you need is to feel overwhelmed with additional responsibilities."

"It's not like that." Maggie stood looking at Antonio.

"Okay," he said, then paused. "Well, I was thinking about taking him to the zoo tomorrow, to see Tigger. I know…next thing, the press will make its assumptions that I am indeed his father, but you have to know this: I have been a part of Mickey's life since he was born. And I just can't break the news to him. It seems a terrible lie that just keeps sucking me in, but his real father never shows up. He's just a loser."

"It's sweet of you, Antonio. Believe me…I understand more than you know."

"So you're sure you want to come?"

"Of course I do." Maggie smiled at him.

The following day, the three of them headed to the zoo. It would be a short visit early in the morning, two hours before it opened to the public. Antonio's prediction was now a reality, as a cameraman hovered in the background, hoping to get a grand photo of the three of them. But fortunately, Mickey was completely unaware that he existed in any kind of spotlight, other than what Maggie and Antonio were providing for him. They had glanced at each other a few times, wishing that they could escape the attention, but soon Mickey kept them focused on the real issues. He was well behaved for once, and delighted as held hands with both of them and walked from enclosure to enclosure.

Just before ten, Antonio told him it was time to leave, but Mickey started throwing a tantrum and said he did not want to go back to the family that was watching him. "Come on! They probably miss you by now!" Antonio winked at Maggie. She grinned back at Antonio, thinking he had surely exhausted his creative efforts to convince Mickey that their time together had come to an end.

Finally, Mickey said, "They don't like me!"

"They don't like you?" Maggie asked him. "Why do you think that?"

"I in my room…*all* day!" He stomped his foot. "And can't come out."

"Do you want to come back with us?" Maggie offered.

"He can't," Antonio explained to Maggie. "I have a full day…"

"Then I'll watch him. He can stay with me for a few hours."

Maggie smiled at Mickey.

"Do you want to hang out with Maggie?" Antonio asked.

"Yes!" Mickey smiled up at her, grabbing onto her arm.

"Are you sure?" Antonio asked her, giving her a chance to change her mind.

"It's fine…" Maggie smiled.

When they got back, Maggie stopped in the gift shop with him, wondering how to keep a boy his age entertained. She decided to pick up a couple of books so that she could read to him. He seemed pleased, and she even bought him a stuffed tiger, which Mickey dubbed "Tigger" at first sight.

There was no doubt that Mickey was part of Antonio's life. Perhaps to a lesser extent, now that they were married. But Maggie could not help but understand his loyalty to the situation.

"What is in here?" Mickey asked as soon as they got back to the room. Maggie watched as he raced into the new addition.

"That's my sewing room," Maggie told him.

"Why?" Mickey said as he went inside to look at all the clothing she had made. "What you do in here?"

"I sew little clothes," Maggie explained, handing him a tiny outfit. "See?"

"I don't wear this…" He held the outfit in his hands.

"Oh, no, it's way too small for you." Maggie grinned. "Maybe a long time ago you could have worn that."

"A long, *long* time ago," Mickey said as he picked up a dress with a ruffle trim. "I can't wear this!" He started to laugh.

"No, you'd look really strange in a dress!" Maggie laughed too.

"Can you make socks?"

Maggie laughed again. "No, you can't sew socks. Only shorts and shirts…maybe a tie," she said.

"Make me a tie!" He sounded excited.

"That's not so easy…I don't have a pattern."

Mickey suddenly wore a pout.

"It's okay, Mickey. You don't need a tie. Where would you wear a tie?" Maggie said.

"I want gold tie, like Daddy."

Maggie cringed at his use of the word, then nodded. "Okay…maybe I can make you one…but I have to get some gold fabric first," she said, hoping he would forget.

But then he had a new idea.

"Make a shirt!"

Maggie paused to consider.

"That would take a while… and what would you do while I sewed?"

"Sit here."

She watched as he sat down cross-legged, resting his chin in his hand.

"Well, maybe we could start one, and…finish next time," she finally decided.

"Okay!" Mickey jumped up and down.

"But you have to be good!" she warned. "You may not touch the pincushion or the scissors…you could cut yourself!"

Maggie suddenly paused, recalling her mother's words of warning to her when she held the scissors for the first time.

"I just watch!" Mickey sat quietly.

Yeah, right...

Maggie went over to the storage bin and took out a piece of fabric that had a fish design on it. And as Maggie held the fabric in her hands, she remembered the first dress that she and her mother had made.

"You will have to take that one off, so I have a pattern." Maggie pointed to the shirt Mickey was wearing.

"No! I can't!" He crossed his arms and held them tightly against his chest.

Maggie looked at him, wondering why he would not cooperate.

"Well! Then I guess I will have to put the fabric away, because unless I am a magician, like...your father—" Maggie paused, questioning her own sanity—"I can't make it just appear!"

Maggie watched as he slowly stood, letting his hands fall to his sides. "Fine, you can take it."

She suddenly realized he was probably unable to undress himself. He spoke so well for his age; she almost forgot he had just turned three.

"Do you need help with that?" Maggie finally asked.

"I can't do buttons...only zipper..."

"Okay..." Maggie came over to him, and started helping him unbutton his shirt. "Should we make your new shirt with a zipper?"

He looked as if he was thinking about it, but then he surprised her.

"You're pretty," Mickey said gazing at Maggie. "My mommy said you were ugly, but you're pretty."

Maggie was taken back. "You're cute too," Maggie told him. "And I bet you miss your mommy."

"No…she mean to me."

Maggie got the last button undone, but as she took off his shirt, her jaw dropped. She knelt in front of him speechless for a moment, until she could no longer be silent. "What happened to you?" Maggie stared at the bruises on his torso.

"She grabs me!" Mickey said. "Like this!" He took his hand and grabbed Maggie's arm, making a mean face while displaying all of his teeth.

"Does she hurt you?" Maggie finally asked.

"She does like this!" He grabbed her arm again, pinching it. She watched as Mickey went over to the chair and sat down, and as he did she noticed three more bruises on his back. Maggie held her breath, wondering if Antonio knew.

"You making my shirt?" Mickey asked, as Maggie just sat there staring at him.

"Uh…yeah…" Maggie got up, holding his shirt in her hands. She placed it over the fish fabric and started to mark the fabric with chalk.

She wondered how she would manage to concentrate on sewing a shirt after her discovery, but then she noticed that Mickey had located her button jar. He picked it up, without asking.

"Do you want to see those?" Maggie asked, thinking she was going to have trouble keeping him entertained while sewing. "Here," she said, "we can dump them out and you can play in a pile of buttons, but don't put them in your mouth."

"I no eat buttons!" Mickey started laughing.

"Okay, just making sure," Maggie said, turning around to continue her project. She glanced at him, and then once more, until she was certain he was lost in a new adventure.

Maggie cut the fabric, trying to work as quickly as possible. And as she kept an eye on Mickey, he seemed to be having the time of his life, studying each and every button. She could not believe he was being so good, without even having any of his toys to play with.

A half hour later, Maggie had the shirt sewn together—enough to try it on.

"Mickey! Come here! You can try your shirt on!"

"I still playing with buttons."

"Okay," Maggie smiled, "but let's just see if it fits. It still needs a zipper and—" Maggie noticed he had made a big smiley face out of the buttons—"after you try it on, then you can play with the buttons some more."

"Okay!" He popped up and came to stand by her side. She placed the shirt over his arms and then held the front closed.

"It works!" Maggie said proudly.

Mickey seemed more fascinated by her than by his shirt. He wore a big smile and Maggie couldn't help but smile back. "You know, you aren't the monster you pretend to be," she told him.

He stood quietly, as if he was keeping his thoughts to himself.

"I'm almost done," Maggie told him, as she tried to find a matching zipper.

The door opened. Antonio was back.

"What are you two up to?" He came into the room to find the carpet covered with buttons.

"Maggie sewing me fishy shirt," Mickey told Antonio. "Want to see?"

"Is that right?" Antonio looked surprised that she had him under control.

"Yep…it's almost done!" Maggie said, holding it up. "Just have to sew in the zipper. It'll be done in just a few minutes."

"Where's mine?" Antonio asked.

"Not today, Antonio," Maggie said, smiling at him, realizing he loved to cause trouble.

"You got a tiger and some books?" Antonio noticed the tiger was sitting inside a circle of buttons.

"I put him inside ring…like in your show!" Mickey explained with a big smile.

"Sweet…" Antonio seemed amazed.

"Okay, come here. It's all done!" Maggie motioned for Mickey to try on his shirt. "I bet you're going to look really great in this."

She placed the shirt over his shoulders and zipped it up.

"Yep! He does!" Antonio agreed, eyeing him up in his new shirt.

www.lovetheillusion.com/2268.htm

Mickey picked the books off the floor, holding them up to Antonio, wanting him to read them.

"First I think you need to clean up that." Antonio pointed to the collage of buttons. "Here, I can help," he offered as he bent down.

Together they gathered the loose buttons.

A minute later they were all back in the jar. Maggie got up from her sewing table and joined them on the couch, where Antonio had started reading the two books that Maggie had bought. But in a matter of minutes, Mickey, in his new shirt, was falling asleep against Antonio's arm.

"He's all tired out watching you sew?" Antonio asked with a smile.

"He was actually pretty good," Maggie told him.

"That was nice of you…you didn't have to go to all that trouble."

"It was no trouble," Maggie said. "I think I had more fun than he did."

"You are going to be a good mamma," Antonio said. "Now you know…it's not so hard; you are good with him."

"I feel bad for him," Maggie admitted.

"I know. Me too."

"Where is his father?"

"I have no idea, but it doesn't seem like he likes where he is staying."

"Mickey says his mother hurts him…she pinches him…and he has bruises. I saw them when I was sewing his shirt," Maggie told Antonio.

Maggie waited for Antonio to respond, but instead he just took in a deep breath, slowly letting it out, remaining silent, and closing his eyes as if it was his way of blocking the disturbing news.

Finally, she spoke again. “Did you know?”

“No.”

“Well, I wish there was something we could do.”

“Ah…she won’t be around him for a while…She’s back in rehab.”

“Oh, no…how did you find out?”

“My attorney. Funny thing is, she’s got money again, but now a whole new set of problems!”

“Maybe he should stay with us.”

“I don’t know…how would that work?”

“It’s simple, Antonio. He needs us.”

Antonio started laughing. “You didn’t even want one child…now you want two?”

“He already thinks you’re his father. Think about it. If you let him stay in foster care, he will think you don’t care about him.”

“You understand what will happen, don’t you? If we take him in, the press will have no problem convincing the public that he is my son. Won’t that bother you?”

“Maybe…” Maggie thought about it. “But there are more important things than what people think.”

“It’s strange you would say that,” Antonio told her. Then his face lit up. “I have to show you something.”

“No surprises, Antonio. There have been too many of those lately.”

“But this is a good one, I promise.” He went over to a drawer and took out a file. “Check this place out! It’s in a secluded area on a river, very peaceful and private and…I looked at the property twice and love it. And I met with the real estate agent and they are willing to negotiate. It wasn't for sale, but…for the right amount of money people are willing to consider." He handed the photos to Maggie. "So, now the question is…do you like it?"

www.lovetheillusion.com/2290.htm

"It's nice…really nice…" she said. She looked up at him. "So, you don't want to stay here anymore?"

"Not once we have a baby! We need a yard…maybe a dog or cat, and…this is no environment for a child to grow up in. We can have a playground and—"

"It looks wonderful…I love it." Maggie continued to study the photos.

He stood behind her as she thumbed through the color photos of all the rooms, each with a breathtaking view, as he explained: "We would stay here…all year. But we'll keep the house in Italy for vacation."

"Five bedrooms?" Maggie questioned, staring down at the information sheet.

"Well, you never know." He wore a grin.

"I would love to move here!" Maggie returned his grin. "But…I have to ask you a favor."

"What's that? You need more space for your shoes?"

"No…I think Mickey should stay with us. We have plenty of room."

"Are you serious?"

She smiled at him. "I am."

"Okay…if you want, I will call social services and tell them we'll take him. I hope we aren't making a mistake."

"It's the right thing Antonio, and right choices are never a mistake."

Antonio pulled Maggie into his arms. "I really love you," he said as he looked down at her. He kissed her gently, as if each kiss had a meaning all of its own. Now she remembered the first time she had kissed him. She had been so afraid of that kiss. But she had taken that risk, and now she had to face the truth: She lived with no regret.

Perhaps motherhood would not be such a scary adventure after all. It seemed that they had been through so many obstacles since they had returned to New York that something as simple as sharing your life with someone was really no obstacle at all. Now, in a strange way, she felt well equipped for motherhood. It would certainly come with many challenges, but in the end, she knew she could provide what a child needed…just a little bit of love.

THREE WEEKS LATER…

Antonio rested his hands on Maggie's shoulders, as she stared at the calendar that hung above the desk in their suite. They would be moving to their new home in only a few weeks. Mickey sat at their table with a coloring book and an assortment of crayons, each with the paper already peeled off. He had just about colored the entire book in only ten minutes.

"Just think," Maggie said, leaning her head back against Antonio's chest, "in only five months, we will be parents!" She paused. "Isn't that scary?"

"No, Maggie," Antonio whispered, as they watched Mickey. "I love children, and I think you do too."

"I know.... I don't know what I was so afraid of."

"You have such a glow; motherhood becomes you already." He admired her. "You're so beautiful, and this dress you're wearing is just gorgeous on you…with those leggings…I love it."

"You really like it?"

"It looks great on you. Where did you get it?"

"I made it." Maggie closed her eyes as they quickly filled with tears.

"What's wrong, dear? I'm sorry—what did I say?"

"Nothing…it's not you, it's…"

Maggie left to go into her sewing studio and then returned holding a dress tag. "I am the first one to wear my new label. Tomorrow I am adding five new designs to my website. Now I'll have Tiny Matteo's and…this…"

She handed the label to Antonio.

"Katie White…" He smiled. "Imagine that…" He reached out and pulled her into a hug. "Your mother would be so proud."

www.lovetheillusion.com/2271.htm

POSTSCRIPT

Dear Diary,

I am on my way to visit Maggie today. Several weeks after they moved into their new home, I got a call from Antonio that they just returned from the hospital after Maggie suffered from preterm labor contractions, at only twenty-five weeks. Now she is on bed rest until term, but they did find out that it is indeed a boy.

Antonio cancelled his last show in NYC, and was going to cancel his upcoming six-week Euro Tour, but Maggie insisted that he go. She was going to come along with Mickey, but due to the circumstances, they stayed behind. Needless to say, Antonio hired help to take care of them both, and I plan to soon be an addition to that, although I have already decided I will leave the responsibilities of watching Mickey to one of the young nurses.

Antonio was going to put Mickey back in foster care, but Maggie said, "No! Let him stay. He is my inspiration to wait this out, patiently, in hopes that soon I will be a mom."

My best guess is that Maggie has fallen in love with him. And Mickey needs what every other child needs—parents to love him.

At my age very few things surprise me. And so when Maggie told me that she and Antonio wanted to adopt him, it did not come as a surprise. But what did surprise me was how long *I* kept smiling after I heard the news.

Julia

www.lovetheillusion.com/2199.htm

Find out in…

Final Flame

www.lovetheillusion.com/2291.htm

Made in the USA
Columbia, SC
27 August 2018